DREAMS
UNDERFOOT

Tor books by
Charles de Lint

★forthcoming

DREAMS UNDERFOOT

THE NEWFORD COLLECTION

Charles de Lint

A Tom Doherty Associates Book
New York

The city, characters and events to be found in these pages are fictitious. Any resemblance to actual persons living or dead is purely coincidental.

DREAMS UNDERFOOT

This book is printed on acid-free paper.

A Tor Book
Published by Tom Doherty Associates, Inc.
175 Fifth Avenue
New York, N.Y. 10010

Edited by Terri Windling.

Tor® is a registered trademark of Tom Doherty Associates, Inc.

Library of Congress Cataloging-in-Publication Data
de Lint, Charles
        Dreams underfoot / Charles de Lint.
                p. cm.
        "A Tom Doherty Associates book."
        ISBN 0-312-85205-3
        I. Title.
    PR9199.3.D357D74   1993
    813'.54—dc20   92-40376
                                                        CIP

First edition: April 1993

Printed in the United States of America

0 9 8 7 6 5 4 3 2 1

❧ COPYRIGHT ❧ ACKNOWLEDGMENTS

✳ ACKNOWLEDGMENTS ✳

Creative endeavors require inspiration and nurturing, and these stories are no exception. I'd like to take this opportunity to thank a few people who were important to the existence of this collection:

First and foremost, my wife MaryAnn, not only for her indefatigable work as first reader and editor, but also for her part in the genesis of many of the individual stories;

Terri Windling, for her ongoing support, both professionally and personally, especially with this cycle of stories, and for providing the collection's title, which was also the title of her 1992 one-woman art show at the Book Arts Gallery in Tucson, Arizona;

Kris Rusch and Dean Smith of Axolotl Press/Pulphouse Publishing, who were always asking for more stories and provided the first home for many of these;

And for all those other editors who gave me the opportunity to take a holiday from longer work to explore Newford's streets: Bruce Barber, Ellen Datlow, Gardner Dozois, Robert T. Garcia, Ed Gorman, Martin H. Greenberg, Cara Inks, Paul F. Olson, Jan and George O'Nale, Byron Preiss and David B. Silva.

≍ CONTENTS ≍

TREAD SOFTLY BECAUSE YOU TREAD ON MY DREAMS.
—W. B. YEATS, FROM ''HE WISHES
FOR THE CLOTHS OF HEAVEN''

~ INTRODUCTION ~

The book you hold is neither a novel nor a simple gathering of short stories. Rather, it is a cycle of urban myths and dreams, of passions and sorrows, romance and farce woven together to create a tapestry of interconnected dramas, interconnected lives—the kind of magic to be found at the heart of any city, among any tightly knit community of friends. If the imaginary city of Newford is more mythic, more mysterious than the cities you have known, that may be only because you've not seen them through Charles de Lint's eyes, through the twilight dreams he weaves out of language and music. Here he spreads these dreams before us and bids us, in the words of Yeats's poem, to *tread softly,* for urban magic is fleeting and shy . . . and its touch is a transformation.

Joseph Campbell, Carl Jung, James Hillman, Louise-Marie von Franz and others have written eloquently and extensively about the importance of myth in our modern society, the need for tales rich in archetypal images to give coherence to fragmented modern lives. "Using archetypes and symbolic language," writes folklore scholar and author Jane Yolen, "[fantasy tales] externalize for the listener conflicts and situations that cannot be spoken of or explained or as yet analyzed. They give substance to dreams . . . [and] lead us to the understanding of the deepest longings and most daring visions of humankind. The images from the ancients speak to us in modern tongue though we may not always grasp the 'meanings' consciously. Like dreams, the meanings slip away, leaving us shaken into new awarenesses. We are moved by them, even when—or perhaps *because*—we do not understand them on a conscious level. They are penumbral, partially lit, and it is the dark side that has the most power. So when the modern mythmaker, the writer of literary fairy tales, dares to touch the old magic and try to make it work in new ways, it must be done with the surest of touches."

De Lint is one of those writers who mine this vein with a deft, sure touch. Readers new to his distinctive brand of "urban fantasy" might find his mix of ancient folklore motifs and contemporary urban characters somewhat startling—for ours is a society that loves to separate and classify, putting "fantasy" fiction on a shelf far away from books of "realistic" or "mainstream" fiction (despite the fact that the mainstream shelves include works of modern fantasy by foreign authors such as Calvino, Allende and Garcia Marquez). While American book distributors and critics continue to build up genre walls, writers like de Lint are quietly laboring to take them down again, brick by brick, story by story. Forget the labels. Forget the assumptions you make when you think of *fantasy,* or even *short story collections*. And then you will be able to fully enter the enchanted streets de Lint has created.

We enter Newford via the more familiar streets of Los Angeles, via the tales of Newford author Christy Riddell; and then de Lint leads us on to Newford itself, a North American city that might exist anywhere or nowhere, thousands of miles away or just past the next exit on the Interstate. Like any city, Newford has its posh districts, its slums, its day-life and night-life and the twilight between; but most of all it's the street people, the downtown people, that de Lint wants us to meet: the buskers and artists, punkers and gypsies, street walkers and wizards and runaway kids, people for whom magic is not just a supernatural visitation but a manifestation of the soul's deepest longings and a bright spark of hope lodged within a desperate heart. The greatest magic on the streets of Newford is the magic of community, of friendship and love, support and compassion—for these are the larger themes de Lint uses the bright symbols of folklore to address.

In Newford, *creation* is the supreme act of magic, whether that creation be a painting, a fiddle tune or a poem, an AIDS clinic or battered children's shelter, or one's own family and a harmonious way of life. By these acts we create magic in our own lives; by these acts, large and small, we reinvent the world. For de Lint, these acts are transformed into stories to nurture the growth of his Tree of Tales, which contains the collective stories of the world:

"The Tree of Tales," says de Lint's Conjure Man, "is an act of magic, an act of faith. Its existence becomes an affirmation of the power that the human spirit can have over its own destiny. The stories are just stories—they entertain, they make one laugh or cry—but if they have any worth they carry with them a deeper resonance that remains long after the final page is turned. . . ."

The interconnected stories of the Newford cycle are a particularly lovely new limb on that ancient tree, and one that shall grow and flower beyond the pages of this single book as de Lint continues to explore Newford's myriad streets.

In his own city of Ottawa, in Canada, Charles de Lint is a novelist, a poet, a fiddler, a flute-player, a painter, a critic and folklore scholar; but most of all he is a magician: the kind who makes magic with his multi-disciplined creativity, with the tools of myth, folklore and fantasy. "I think those of us who write fantasy," said fellow author Susan Cooper in her Newbery Award acceptance speech, "are dedicated to making impossible things seem likely, making dreams seem real. We are somewhere between the Abstract and Impressionist painters. Our writing is haunted by those parts of our experience which we do not understand, or even consciously remember. And if you, child or adult, are drawn to our work, your response comes from that same shadowy land. . . . I have been attempting definitions, but I am never really comfortable when writing about 'fantasy.' The label is so limiting. It seems to me that every work of art is a fantasy, every book or play, painting or piece of music, everything that is made, by craft and talent, out of somebody's imagination. We have all dreamed, and recorded our dreams as best we could."

In these pages, de Lint has recorded dreams: Jilly Coppercorn's and Geordie's, Sophie's and Christy's, Tallulah's and the dreams of Newford itself. There are dreams underfoot here, some fragile as spiders' webs, others solid as asphalt and brick-cobbled streets. As you walk into the heart of the city of Newford, remember: tread warily. Tread softly.

—Terri Windling
(Co-editor of "The Year's Best Fantasy" annual collection)
Weaver's Cottage, Devon, 1992

⋙ UNCLE DOBBIN'S ⋙
PARROT FAIR

1

She would see them in the twilight when the wind was right, roly-poly shapes propelled by ocean breezes, turning end-over-end along the beach or down the alley behind her house like errant beach balls granted a moment's freedom. Sometimes they would get caught up against a building or stuck on a curb and then spindly little arms and legs would unfold from their fat bodies until they could push themselves free and go rolling with the wind again. Like flotsam in a river, like tumbleweeds, only brightly colored in primary reds and yellows and blues.

They seemed very solid until the wind died down. Then she would watch them come apart the way morning mist will when the sun burns it away, the bright colors turning to ragged ribbons that tattered smoke-like until they were completely gone.

Those were special nights, the evenings that the Balloon Men came.

In the late sixties in Haight-Ashbury, she talked about them once. Incense lay thick in the air—two cones of jasmine burning on a battered windowsill. There was an old iron bed in the room, up on the third floor of a house that no one lived in except for runaways and street people. The mattress had rust-colored stains on it. The incense covered the room's musty smell. She'd lived in a form of self-imposed poverty back then, but it was all a part of the Summer of Love.

"I know what you mean, man," Greg Longman told her. "I've seen them."

He was wearing a dirty white T-shirt with a simple peace symbol on it and scuffed plastic thongs. Sticking up from the waist of his bell-bottomed jeans at a forty-five degree angle was a descant recorder. His long blonde hair was tied back with an elastic. His features were thin—an ascetic-looking face, thin and drawn-out from too much time on the streets with too little to eat, or from too much dope.

"They're like . . ." His hands moved as he spoke, trying to convey what he didn't feel words alone could say—a whole other language, she often thought, watching the long slender fingers weave through the air between them. ". . . they're just too much."

"You've really seen them?" she asked.

"Oh, yeah. Except not on the streets. They're floating high up in the air, y'know, like fat little kites."

It was such a relief to know that they were real.

" 'Course," Greg added, "I gotta do a lot of dope to clue in on 'em, man."

Ellen Brady laid her book aside. Leaning back, she flicked off the light behind her and stared out into the night. The memory had come back to her, so clear, so sharp, she could almost smell the incense, see Greg's hands move between them, little colored after-image traces following each movement until he had more arms than Kali.

She wondered what had ever happened to the Balloon Men.

Long light-brown hair hung like a cape to her waist. Her parents were Irish—Munster O'Healys on her mother's side, and Bradys from Derry on her father's. There was a touch of Spanish blood in her mother's side of the family, which gave her skin its warm dark cast. The Bradys were pure Irish and it was from them that she got her big-boned frame. And something else. Her eyes were a clear grey—twilight eyes, her father had liked to tease her, eyes that could see beyond the here and now into somewhere else.

She hadn't needed drugs to see the Balloon Men.

Shifting in her wicker chair, she looked up and down the beach, but it was late and the wind wasn't coming in from the ocean. The book on her lap was a comforting weight and had, considering her present state of mind, an even more appropriate title. *How to Make the Wind Blow*. If only it *was* a tutor, she thought, instead of just a collection of odd stories.

The author's name was Christy Riddell, a reed-thin Scot with a head full of sudden fancies. His hair was like an unruly hedgerow nest and he was half a head shorter than she, but she could recall dancing with him in a garden one night and she hadn't had a more suitable partner since. She'd met him while visiting friends in a house out east that was as odd as any flight of his imagination. Long rambling halls connected a bewildering series of rooms, each more fascinating than the next. And the libraries. She'd lived in its libraries.

"When the wind is right," began the title story, the first story in the book, "the wise man isn't half so trusted as the fool."

Ellen could remember when it was still a story that was told without the benefit of pen and paper. A story that changed each time the words traveled from mouth to ear:

There was a gnome, or a gnomish sort of a man, named Long who lived under the pier at the end of Main Street. He had skin brown as dirt, eyes blue as a clear summer sky. He was thin, with a fat tummy and a long crooked nose, and he wore raggedy clothes that he found discarded on the beach and wore until they were thread-bare. Sometimes he bundled his tangled hair up under a bright yellow cap. Other times he wove it into many braids festooned with colored beads and the discarded tabs from beer cans that he polished on his sleeve until they were bright and shiny.

Though he'd seem more odd than magical to anyone who happened to spy him out wandering the streets or along the beach, he did have two enchantments.

One was a pig that could see the wind and follow it anywhere. She was pink and fastidiously clean, big enough to ride to market—which Long sometimes did—and she could talk. Not pig-talk, or even pig-Latin, but plain English that anyone could understand if they took the time to listen. Her name changed from telling to telling, but by the time Long's story appeared in the book either she or Christy had settled on Brigwin.

Long's other enchantment was a piece of plain string with four complicated elf-knots tied in it—one to call up a wind from each of the four quarters. North and south. East and west. When he untied a knot, that wind would rise up and he'd ride Brigwin in its wake, sifting through the debris and pickings left behind for treasures or charms, though what Long considered a treasure, another might throw out, and what he might consider a charm, another might see as only an old button or a bit of tangled wool. He had a good business trading his findings to woodwives and witches and the like that he met at the market when midnight was past and gone, ordinary folk were in bed, and the beach towns belonged to those who hid by day, but walked the streets by night.

Ellen carried a piece of string in her pocket, with four complicated knots tied into it, but no matter how often she undid one, she still had to wait for her winds like anyone else. She knew that strings to catch and call up the wind were only real in stories, but she liked thinking that maybe, just once, a bit of magic could tiptoe out of a tale and step into the real world. Until that happened, she had to be content with what writers like Christy put to paper.

He called them mythistories, those odd little tales of his. They were the ghosts of fancies that he would track down from time to time and trap on paper. Oddities. Some charming, some grotesque. All of them enchanting. Foolishness, he liked to say, offered from one fool to others.

Ellen smiled. Oh, yes. But when the wind is right . . .

She'd never talked to Christy about the Balloon Men, but she didn't doubt that he knew them.

Leaning over the rail of the balcony, two stories above the walkway that ran the length of the beach, Christy's book held tight in one hand, she wished very hard to see those roly-poly figures one more time. The ocean beat its rhythm against the sand. A light breeze caught at her hair and twisted it into her face.

When the wind is right.

Something fluttered inside her, like wings unfolding, readying for flight. Rising from her chair, she set the book down on its wicker arm and went inside. Down the stairs and out the front door. She could feel a thrumming between her ears that had to be excitement moving blood more quickly through her veins, though it could have been the echo of a half-lost memory—a singing of small deep voices, rising up from diaphragms nestled in fat little bellies.

Perhaps the wind *was* right, she thought as she stepped out onto the walkway. A quarter moon peeked at her from above the oil rigs far out from the shore. She put her hand in the pocket of her cotton pants and wound the knotted string she found there around one finger. It was late, late for the Balloon Men to be rolling, but she didn't doubt that there was something waiting to greet her out on the street. Perhaps only memories. Perhaps a fancy that Christy hadn't trapped on a page yet.

There was only one way to find out.

2

Peregrin Laurie was as sharp-faced as a weasel—a narrow-shouldered thin whip of a teenager in jeans and a torn T-shirt. He sat in a doorway, knees up by his chin, a mane of spiked multi-colored hair standing straight up from his head in a two-inch Mohawk swath that ran down to the nape of his neck like a lizard's crest fringes. Wrapping his arms around bruised ribs, he held back tears as each breath he took made his chest burn.

Goddamn beach bums. The bastards had just about killed him and he had no one to blame but himself. Scuffing through a parking lot, he should have taken off when the car pulled up. But no. He had to be the poseur and hold his ground, giving them a long cool look as they came piling drunkenly out of the car. By the time he realized just how many of them there were and what they had planned for him, it was too late to run. He'd had to stand there then, heart hammering in his chest, and hope bravado'd see him through, because there was no way he could handle them all.

They didn't stop to chat. They just laid into him. He got a few licks in, but he knew it was hopeless. By the time he hit the pavement, all he could do was curl up into a tight ball and take their drunken kicks, cursing them with each fiery gasp of air he dragged into his lungs.

The booger waited until he was down and hurting before making its appearance. It came out from under the pier that ran by the parking lot, black and greasy, with hot eyes and a mouthful of barracuda teeth. If it hadn't hurt so much just to breathe, he would have laughed at the way his attackers backed away from the creature, eyes bulging as they rushed to their car. They took off, tires squealing, but not before the booger took a chunk of metal out of the rear fender with one swipe of a paw.

It came back to look at him—black nightmare head snuffling at him as he lifted his head and wiped the blood from his face, then moving away as he reached out a hand towards it. It smelled like a sewer and looked worse, a squat creature that had to have been scraped out of some monstrous nose, with eyes like hot coals in a smear of a face and a slick wet look to its skin. A booger, plain and simple. Only it was alive, clawed and toothed. Following him around ever since he'd run away. . . .

His parents were both burnouts from the sixties. They lived in West Hollywood and got more embarrassing the older he became. Take his name. Laurie was bad enough, but Peregrin . . . Lifted straight out of that *Lord of the Rings* book. An okay read, sure, but you don't use it to name your kid. Maybe he should just be thankful he didn't get stuck with Frodo or Bilbo. By the time he was old enough to start thinking for himself, he'd picked out his own name and wouldn't answer to anything but Reece. He'd gotten it out of some book, too, but at least it sounded cool. You needed all the cool you could get with parents like his.

His old man still had hair down to his ass. He wore wire-framed glasses and listened to shit on the stereo that sounded as burned-out as he looked. The old lady wasn't much better. Putting on weight like a whale, hair a frizzy brown, as long as the old man's, but usually hanging in a braid. Coming home late some nights, the whole house'd have the sweet smell of weed mixed with incense and they'd give him these goofy looks and talk about getting in touch with the cosmos and other spacey shit. When anybody came down on him for the way he looked, or for dropping out of school, all they said was let him do his own thing.

His own thing. Jesus. Give me a break. With that kind of crap to look forward to at home, who wouldn't take off first chance they got? Though wouldn't you know it, no sooner did he get free of them than the booger latched onto him, following him around, skulking in the shadows.

At first, Reece never got much of a look at the thing—just glimpses out of the corner of his eyes—and that was more than enough. But sleeping on the beaches and in parks, some nights he'd wake with that sewer smell in his nostrils and catch something slipping out of sight, a dark wet shadow moving close to the ground. After a few weeks, it started to get bolder, sitting on its haunches a half-dozen yards from wherever he was bedding down, the hot coal eyes fixed on him.

Reece didn't know what it was or what it wanted. Was it looking out for him, or saving him up for its supper? Sometimes he thought, what with all the drugs his parents had done back in the sixties— good times for them, shit for him because he'd been born and that was when his troubles had started—he was sure that all those chemicals had fucked up his genes. Twisted something in his head so that he imagined he had this two-foot high, walking, grunting booger following him around.

Like the old man'd say. Bummer.

Sucker sure seemed real, though.

Reece held his hurt to himself, ignoring Ellen as she approached. When she stopped in front of him, he gave her a scowl.

"Are you okay?" she asked, leaning closer to look at him.

He gave her a withering glance. The long hair and jeans, flowered blouse. Just what he needed. Another sixties burnout.

"Why don't you just fuck off and die?" he said.

But Ellen looked past the tough pose to see the blood on his shirt, the bruising on his face that the shadows half-hid, the hurt he was trying so hard to pretend wasn't there.

"Where do you live?" she asked.

"What's it to you?"

Ignoring his scowl, she bent down and started to help him to his feet.

"Aw, fuck—" Reece began, but it was easier on his ribs to stand up than to fight her.

"Let's get you cleaned up," she said.

"Florence fucking Nightingale," he muttered, but she merely led him back the way she'd come.

From under the pier a wet shadow stirred at their departure. Reece's booger drew back lips that had the rubbery texture of an octopus' skin. Row on row of pointed teeth reflected back the light from the streetlights. Hate-hot eyes glimmered red. On silent leathery paws, the creature followed the slow-moving pair, grunting softly to itself, claws clicking on the pavement.

3

Bramley Dapple was the wizard in "A Week of Saturdays," the third story in Christy Riddell's *How to Make the Wind Blow*. He was a small wizened old man, spry as a kitten, thin as a reed, with features lined and brown as a dried fig. He wore a pair of wire-rimmed spectacles without prescription lenses that he polished incessantly, and he loved to talk.

"It doesn't matter what they believe," he was saying to his guest, "so much as what *you* believe."

He paused as the brown-skinned goblin who looked after his house came in with a tray of biscuits and tea. His name was Goon, a tallish creature at three-foot-four who wore the garb of an organ-grinder's monkey: striped black and yellow trousers, a red jacket with yellow trim, small black slippers, and a little green and yellow cap that pushed down an unruly mop of thin dark curly hair. Gangly limbs with a protruding tummy, puffed cheeks, a wide nose, and tiny black eyes added to his monkey-like appearance.

The wizard's guest observed Goon's entrance with a startled look, which pleased Bramley to no end.

"There," he said. "Goon proves my point."

"I beg your pardon?"

"We live in a consensual reality where things exist because we want them to exist. I believe in Goon, Goon believes in Goon, and you, presented with his undeniable presence, tea tray in hand, believe in Goon as well. Yet, if you were to listen to the world at large, Goon is nothing more than a figment of some fevered writer's imagination—a literary construct, an artistic representation of something that can't possibly exist in the world as we know it."

Goon gave Bramley a sour look, but the wizard's guest leaned forward, hand outstretched, and brushed the goblin's shoulder with a feather-light touch. Slowly she leaned back into the big armchair, cushions so comfortable they seemed to embrace her as she settled against them.

"So . . . anything we can imagine can exist?" she asked finally.

Goon turned his sour look on her now.

She was a student at the university where the wizard taught; third year, majoring in fine arts, and she had the look of an artist about her. There were old paint stains on her jeans and under her fingernails. Her hair was a thick tangle of brown hair, more unruly than Goon's curls. She had a smudge of a nose and thin puckering lips, workman's boots that stood by the door with a history of scuffs and stains written into their leather, thick woolen socks with a hole in the left heel, and one shirttail that had escaped the waist of her jeans. But her eyes were a pale, pale blue, clear and alert, for all the casualness of her attire.

Her name was Jilly Coppercorn.

Bramley shook his head. "It's not imagining. It's knowing that it exists—without one smidgen of doubt."

"Yes, but someone had to think him up for him to . . ." She hesitated as Goon's scowl deepened. "That is . . ."

Bramley continued to shake his head. "There is some semblance of order to things," he admitted, "for if the world was simply everyone's different conceptual universe mixed up together, we'd have nothing but chaos. It all relies on will, you see—to observe the changes, at any rate. Or the differences. The anomalies. Like Goon—oh, do stop scowling," he added to the goblin.

"The world as we have it," he went on to Jilly, "is here mostly because of habit. We've all agreed that certain things exist—we're taught as impressionable infants that this is a table and this is what it looks like, that's a tree out the window there, a dog looks and sounds just so. At the same time we're informed that Goon and his like don't exist, so we don't—or can't—see them."

"They're not made up?" Jilly asked.

This was too much for Goon. He set the tray down and gave her leg a pinch. Jilly jumped away from him, trying to back deeper into the chair as the goblin grinned, revealing two rows of decidedly nasty-looking teeth.

"Rather impolite," Bramley said, "but I suppose you do get the point?"

Jilly nodded quickly. Still grinning, Goon set about pouring their teas.

"So," Jilly asked, "how can someone . . . how can I see things as they really are?"

"Well, it's not that simple," the wizard told her. "First you have to know what it is that you're looking for—before you can find it, you see."

Ellen closed the book and leaned back in her own chair, thinking about that, about Balloon Men, about the young man lying in her bed. To know what you were looking for. Was that why when she went out hoping to find Balloon Men, she'd come home with Reece?

She got up and went to the bedroom door to look in at him. After much protesting, he'd finally let her clean his hurts and put him to bed. Claiming to be not the least bit hungry, he'd polished off a whole tin of soup and the better part of the loaf of sourdough bread that she had just bought that afternoon. Then, of course, he wasn't tired at all and promptly fell asleep the moment his head touched the pillow.

She shook her head, looking at him now. His rainbow Mohawk made it look as though she'd brought some hybrid creature into her home—part rooster, part boy, it lay in her bed snoring softly, hardly real. But definitely not a Balloon Man, she thought, looking at his thin torso under the sheets.

About to turn away, something at the window caught her eye. Frozen in place, she saw a dog-like face peering back at her from the other side of the pane—which was patently impossible since the bedroom was on the second floor and there was nothing to stand on outside that window. But impossible or not, that dog-like face with its coal-red eyes and a fierce grin of glimmering teeth was there all the same.

She stared at it, feeling sick as the moments ticked by. Hunger burned in those eyes. Anger. Unbridled hate. She couldn't move, not until it finally disappeared—sliding from sight, physically escaping rather than vanishing the way a hallucination should.

She leaned weakly against the doorjamb, a faint buzzing in her head. Not until she'd caught her breath did she go to the window, but of course there was nothing there. Consensual reality, Christy's wizard had called it. Things that exist because we want them to exist. But she knew that not even in a nightmare would she consider giving life to that monstrous head she'd seen staring back in at her from the night beyond her window.

Her gaze went to the sleeping boy in her bed. All that anger burning up inside him. Had she caught a glimpse of something that *he'd* given life to?

Ellen, she told herself as she backed out of the room, you're making entirely too much out of nothing. Except something had certainly seemed to be there. There was absolutely no question in her mind that *something* had been out there.

In the living room she looked down at Christy's book. Bramley Dapple's words skittered through her mind, chased by a feeling of . . . of strangeness that she couldn't shake. The wind, the night, finding Reece in that doorway. And now that thing in the window.

She went and poured herself a brandy before making her bed on the sofa, studiously avoiding looking at the windows. She knew she was being silly—she had to have imagined it—but there was a feeling in the air tonight, a sense of being on the edge of something vast and grey. One false step, and she'd plunge down into it. A void. A nightmare.

It took a second brandy before she fell asleep.

Outside, Reece's booger snuffled around the walls of the house, crawling up the side of the building from time to time to peer into this or that window. Something kept it from entering—some disturbance in the air that was like a wind, but not a wind at the same time. When it finally retreated, it was with the knowledge in what passed for its mind that time itself was the key. Hours and minutes would unlock whatever kept it presently at bay.

Barracuda teeth gleamed as the creature grinned. It could wait. Not long, but it could wait.

4

Ellen woke the next morning, stiff from a night spent on the sofa, and wondered what in God's name had possessed her to bring Reece home. Though on reflection, she realized, the whole night had proceeded with a certain surreal quality of which Reece had only been a small part. Rereading Christy's book. That horrific face at the window. And the Balloon Men—she hadn't thought of them in years.

Swinging her feet to the floor, she went out onto her balcony. There was a light fog hazing the air. Boogie-boarders were riding the waves close by the pier—only a handful of them now, but in an hour or so their numbers would have multiplied beyond count. Raking machines were cleaning the beach, their dull roar vying with the pounding of the tide. Men with metal detectors were patiently sifting through the debris the machines left behind before the trucks came to haul it away. Near the tide's edge a man was jogging backwards across the sand, sharply silhouetted against the ocean.

Nothing out of the ordinary. But returning inside she couldn't shake the feeling that there was someone in her head, something flying dark-winged across her inner terrain like a crow. When she went to wash up, she found its crow eyes staring back at her from the mirror. Wild eyes.

Shivering, she finished up quickly. By the time Reece woke she was sitting outside on the balcony in a sweatshirt and shorts, nursing a mug of coffee. The odd feeling of being possessed had mostly gone away and the night just past took on the fading quality of half-remembered dreams.

She looked up at his appearance, smiling at the way a night's sleep had rearranged the lizard crest fringes of his Mohawk. Some of it was pressed flat against his skull. Elsewhere, multi-colored tufts stood up at bizarre angles. His mouth was a sullen slash in a field of short beard stubble, but his eyes still had a sleepy look to them, softening his features.

"You do this a lot?" he asked, slouching into the other wicker chair on the balcony.

"What? Drink coffee in the morning?"

"Pick up strays."

"You looked like you needed help."

Reece nodded. "Right. We're all brothers and sisters on starship earth. I kinda figured you for a bleeding heart."

His harsh tone soured Ellen's humour. She felt the something that had watched her from the bathroom mirror flutter inside her and her thoughts returned to the previous night. Christy's wizard talking. *Things exist because we want them to exist.*

"After you fell asleep," she said, "I thought I saw something peering in through the bedroom window. . . ."

Her voice trailed off when she realized that she didn't quite know where she was going with that line of thought. But Reece sat up from his slouch, suddenly alert.

"What kind of something?" he asked.

Ellen tried to laugh it off. "A monster," she said with a smile. "Red-eyed and all teeth." She shrugged. "I was just having one of those nights."

"You *saw* it?" Reece demanded sharply enough to make Ellen sit up straighter as well.

"Well, I thought I saw something, but it was patently impossible so . . ." Again her voice trailed off. Reece had sunk back into his chair and was staring off towards the ocean. "What . . . what was it?" Ellen asked.

"I call it a booger," he replied. "I don't know what the hell it is, but it's been following me ever since I took off from my parents' place. . . ."

The stories in Christy's book weren't all charming. There was one near the end called "Raw Eggs" about a man who had a *Ghostbusters*-like creature living in his fridge that fed on raw eggs. It pierced the shells with a needle-fine tooth, then sucked out the contents, leaving rows of empty eggshells behind. When the man got tired of replacing his eggs, the creature crawled out of the fridge one night, driven forth by hunger, and fed on the eyes of the man's family.

The man had always had a fear of going blind. He died at the end of the story, and the creature moved on to another household, more hungry than ever. . . .

★　　★　　★

Reece laid aside Christy Riddell's book and went looking for Ellen. He found her sitting on the beach, a big, loose T-shirt covering her bikini, her bare legs tucked under her. She was staring out to sea, past the waves breaking on the shore, past the swimmers, body-surfers and kids riding their boogie-boards, past the oil rigs to the horizon hidden in a haze in the far-off distance. He got a lot of weird stares as he scuffed his way across the sand to finally sit down beside her.

"They're just stories in that book, right?" he said finally.

"You tell me."

"Look. The booger it's—Christ, I don't know what it is. But it can't be real."

Ellen shrugged. "I was up getting some milk at John's earlier," she said, "and I overheard a couple of kids talking about some friends of theirs. Seems they were having some fun in the parking lot last night with a punker when something came at them from under the pier and tore off part of their bumper."

"Yeah, but—"

Ellen turned from the distant view to look at him. Her eyes held endless vistas in them and she felt the flutter of wings in her mind.

"I want to know how you did it," she said. "How you brought it to life."

"Look, lady. I don't—"

"It doesn't have to be a horror," she said fiercely. "It can be something good, too." She thought of the gnome that lived under the pier in Christy's story and her own Balloon Men. "I want to be able to see them again."

Their gazes locked. Reece saw a darkness behind Ellen's clear grey eyes, some wildness that reminded him of his booger in its intensity.

"I'd tell you if I knew," he said finally.

Ellen continued to study him, then slowly turned to look back across the waves. "Will it come to you tonight?" she asked.

"I don't kn—" Reece began, but Ellen turned to him again. At the look in her eyes, he nodded. "Yeah," he said then. "I guess it will."

"I want to be there when it does," she said.

Because if it was real, then it could all be real. If she could see the booger, if she could understand what animated it, if she could learn to really *see* and, as Christy's wizard had taught Jilly Coppercorn, *know* what she was looking for herself, then she could bring her own touch of wonder into the world. Her own magic.

She gripped Reece's arm. "Promise me you won't take off until I've had a chance to see it."

She had to be weirded-out, Reece thought. She didn't have the same kind of screws loose that his parents did, but she was gone all the same. Only, that book she'd had him read . . . it made a weird kind of sense. If you were going to accept that kind of shit as being possible, it might just work the way that book said it did. Weird, yeah. But when he thought of the booger itself . . .

"Promise me," she repeated.

He disengaged her fingers from his arm. "Sure," he said. "I got nowhere to go anyway."

5

They ate at The Green Pepper that night, a Mexican restaurant on Main Street. Reece studied his companion across the table, re-evaluating his earlier impressions of her. Her hair was up in a loose bun now and she wore a silky cream-colored blouse above a slim dark skirt. Mentally she was definitely a bit weird, but not a burnout like his parents. She looked like the kind of customer who shopped in the trendy galleries and boutiques on Melrose Avenue where his old lady worked, back home in West Hollywood. Half the people in the restaurant were probably wondering what the hell she was doing sitting here with a scuzz like him.

Ellen looked up and caught his gaze. A smile touched her lips. "The cook must be in a good mood," she said.

"What do you mean?"

"Well, I've heard that the worse mood he's in, the hotter he makes his sauces."

Reece tried to give her back a smile, but his heart wasn't in it. He wanted a beer, but they wouldn't serve him here because he was underage. He found himself wishing Ellen wasn't so much older than him, that he didn't look like such a freak sitting here with her. For the first time since he'd done his hair, he was embarrassed about the way he looked. He wanted to enjoy just sitting here with her instead of knowing that everyone was looking at him like he was some kind of geek.

"You okay?" Ellen asked.

"Yeah. Sure. Great food."

He pushed the remainder of his rice around on the plate with his fork. Yeah, he had no problems. Just no place to go, no place to fit in. Body aching from last night's beating. Woman sitting there across from him, looking tasty, but she was too old for him and there was something in her eyes that scared him a little. Not to mention a nightmare booger dogging his footsteps. Sure. Things were just rocking, mama.

He stole another glance at her, but she was looking away, out to the darkening street, wine glass raised to her mouth.

"That book your friend wrote," he said.

Her gaze shifted to his face and she put her glass down.

"It doesn't have anything like my booger in it," Reece continued. "I mean it's got some ugly stuff, but nothing just like the booger."

"No," Ellen replied. "But it's got to work the same way. We can see it because we believe it's there."

"So was it always there and we're just aware of it now? Or does it exist *because* we believe in it? Is it something that came out of us—out of me?"

"Like Uncle Dobbin's birds, you mean?"

Reece nodded, unaware of the flutter of dark wings that Ellen felt stir inside her.

"I don't know," she said softly.

"Uncle Dobbin's Parrot Fair" was the last story in Christy Riddell's book, the title coming from the name of the pet shop that Timothy James Dobbin owned in Santa Ana. It was a gathering place for every kind of bird, tame as well as wild. There were finches in cages and parrots with the run of the shop, not to mention everything from sparrows to crows and gulls crowding around outside.

In the story, T. J. Dobbin was a retired sailor with an interest in

nineteenth-century poets, an old bearded tar with grizzled red hair
and beetling brows who wore baggy blue cotton trousers and a
white T-shirt as he worked in his store, cleaning the bird cages,
feeding the parakeets, teaching the parrots words. Everybody called
him Uncle Dobbin.

He had a sixteen-year-old assistant named Nori Wert who helped
out on weekends. She had short blonde hair and a deep tan that she
started working on as soon as school was out. To set it off she
invariably wore white shorts and a tanktop. The only thing she liked
better than the beach was the birds in Uncle Dobbin's shop, and that
was because she knew their secret.

She didn't find out about them right away. It took a year or so of
coming in and hanging around the shop and then another three
weekends of working there before she finally approached Uncle
Dobbin with what had been bothering her.

"I've been wondering," she said as she sat down on the edge of
his cluttered desk at the back of the store. She fingered the world
globe beside the blotter and gave it a desultory spin.

Uncle Dobbin raised his brow questioningly and continued to fill
his pipe.

"It's the birds," she said. "We never sell any—at least not since
I've started working here. People come in and they look around, but
no one asks the price of anything, no one ever buys anything. I guess
you could do most of your business during the week, but then why
did you hire me?"

Uncle Dobbin looked down into the bowl of his pipe to make
sure the tobacco was tamped properly. "Because you like birds," he
said before he lit a match. Smoke wreathed up towards the ceiling.
A bright green parrot gave a squawk from where it was roosting
nearby and turned its back on them.

"But you don't sell any of them, do you?" Being curious, she'd
poked through his file cabinet to look at invoices and sales receipts
to find that all he ever bought was birdfood and cages and the like,
and he never sold a thing. At least no sales were recorded.

"Can't sell them."

"Why not?"

"They're not mine to sell."

Nori sighed. "Then whose are they?"

"Better you should ask what are they."

"Okay," Nori said, giving him an odd look. "I'll bite. What are they?"

"Magic."

Nori studied him for a moment and he returned her gaze steadily, giving no indication that he was teasing her. He puffed on his pipe, a serious look in his eyes, then took the pipe stem from his mouth. Setting the pipe carefully on the desk so that it wouldn't tip over, he leaned forward in his chair.

"People have magic," he said, "but most of them don't want it, or don't believe in it, or did once, but then forgot. So I take that magic and make it into birds until they want it back, or someone else can use it."

"Magic."

"That's right."

"Not birds."

Uncle Dobbin nodded.

"That's crazy," Nori said.

"Is it?"

He got up stiffly from his chair and stood in front of her with his hands outstretched towards her chest. Nori shrank back from him, figuring he'd flaked out and was going to cop a quick feel, but his hands paused just a few inches from her breasts. She felt a sudden pain inside—like a stitch in her side from running too hard, only it was deep in her chest. Right in her lungs. She looked down, eyes widening as a beak appeared poking out of her chest, followed by a parrot's head, its body and wings.

It was like one of the holograms at the Haunted House in Disneyland, for she could see right through it, then it grew solid once it was fully emerged. The pain stopped as the bird fluttered free, but she felt an empty aching inside. Uncle Dobbin caught the bird, and soothed it with a practiced touch, before letting it fly free. Numbly, Nori watched it wing across the store and settle down near the front window where it began to preen its feathers. The sense of loss inside grew stronger.

"That . . . it was in me . . . I . . ."

Uncle Dobbin made his way back to his chair and sat down, picking up his pipe once more.

"Magic," he said before he lit it.

"My . . . my magic . . . ?"

Uncle Dobbin nodded. "But not anymore. You didn't believe."

"But I didn't know!" she wailed.

"You got to earn it back now," Uncle Dobbin told her. "The side cages need cleaning."

Nori pressed her hands against her chest, then wrapped her arms around herself in a tight hug as though that would somehow ease the empty feeling inside her.

"E-earn it?" she said in a small voice, her gaze going from his face to the parrot that had come out of her chest and was now sitting by the front window. "By . . . by working here?"

Uncle Dobbin shook his head. "You already work here and I pay you for that, don't I?"

"But then how . . . ?"

"You've got to earn its trust. You've got to learn to believe in it again."

Ellen shook her head softly. Learn to believe, she thought. I've always believed. But maybe never hard enough. She glanced at her companion, then out to the street. It was almost completely dark now.

"Let's go walk on the beach," she said.

Reece nodded, following her outside after she'd paid the bill. The lemony smell of eucalyptus trees was strong in the air for a moment, then the stronger scent of the ocean winds stole it away.

6

They had the beach to themselves, though the pier was busy with strollers and people fishing. At the beach end of the long wooden structure, kids were hanging out, fooling around with bikes and skateboards. The soft boom of the tide drowned out the music of their ghetto blasters. The wind was cool with a salt tang as it came in from over the waves. In the distance, the oil rigs were lit up like Christmas trees.

Ellen took off her shoes. Carrying them in her tote bag, she walked in the wet sand by the water's edge. A raised lip of the beach hid the shorefront houses from their view as they walked south to the rocky spit that marked the beginning of the Naval Weapons Station.

"It's nice out here," Reece said finally. They hadn't spoken since leaving the restaurant.

Ellen nodded. "A lot different from L.A."

"Two different worlds."

Ellen gave him a considering glance. Ever since this afternoon, the sullen tone had left his voice. She listened now as he spoke of his parents and how he couldn't find a place for himself either in their world, nor that of his peers.

"You're pretty down on the sixties," she said when he was done.

Reece shrugged. He was barefoot now, too, the waves coming up to lick the bottom of his jeans where the two of them stood at the water's edge.

"They had some good ideas—people like my parents," he said, "but the way they want things to go . . . that only works if everyone agrees to live that way."

"That doesn't invalidate the things they believe in."

"No. But what we've got to deal with is the real world and you've got to take what you need if you want to survive in it."

Ellen sighed. "I suppose."

She looked back across the beach, but they were still alone. No one else out for a late walk across the sand. No booger. No Balloon Men. But something fluttered inside her, dark-winged. A longing as plain as what she heard in Reece's voice, though she was looking for magic and he was just looking for a way to fit in.

Hefting her tote bag, she tossed it onto the sand, out of the waves' reach. Reece gave her a curious look, then averted his gaze as she stepped out of her skirt.

"It's okay," she said, amused at his sudden sense of propriety. "I'm wearing my swimsuit."

By the time he turned back, her blouse and skirt had joined her tote bag on the beach and she was shaking loose her hair.

"Coming in?" she asked.

Reece simply stood and watched the sway of her hips as she headed for the water. Her swimsuit was white. In the poor light it was as though she wasn't wearing anything—the swimsuit looked like untanned skin. She dove cleanly into a wave, head bobbing up pale in the dark water when she surfaced.

"C'mon!" she called to him. "The water's fine, once you get in."

Reece hesitated. He'd wanted to go in this afternoon, but hadn't had the nerve to bare his white skinny limbs in front of a beach full of serious tanners. Well, there was no one to see him now, he thought as he stripped down to his underwear.

The water hit him like a cold fist when he dove in after her and he came up gasping with shock. His body tingled, every pore stung alert. Ellen drifted further out, riding the waves easily. As he waded out to join her, a swell rose up and tumbled him back to shore in a spill of floundering arms and legs that scraped him against the sand.

"Either go under or over them," Ellen advised him as he started back out.

He wasn't much of a swimmer, but the water wasn't too deep except when a big wave came. He went under the next one and came up spluttering, but pleased with himself for not getting thrown up against the beach again.

"I love swimming at night," Ellen said as they drifted together.

Reece nodded. The water was surprisingly warm, too, once you were in it. You could lose all sense of time out here, just floating with the swells.

"You do this a lot?" he asked.

Ellen shook her head. "It's not that good an idea to do this alone. If the undertow got you, it'd pull you right out and no one would know."

Reece laid his head back in the water and looked up at the sky. Though they were less than an hour by the freeway out of downtown L.A., the sky was completely different here. It didn't have that glow from God-knows-how-many millions of lights. The stars seemed closer, too, or maybe it was that the sky seemed deeper.

He glanced over at Ellen. Their reason for being out here was forgotten. He wished he had the nerve to just sort of sidle up to her and put his arms around her, hold her close. She'd feel all slippery, but she'd feel good.

He paddled a little bit towards her, riding a swell up and then down again. The wave turned him slightly away from her. When he glanced back, he saw her staring wide-eyed at the shore. His gaze followed hers and then that cold he'd felt when he first entered the water returned in a numbing rush.

The booger was here.

It came snuffling over a rise in the beach, a squat dark shadow in the sand, greasy and slick as it beelined for their clothing. When it reached Ellen's tote bag, it buried its face in her skirt and blouse, then proceeded to rip them to shreds. Ellen's fingers caught his arm in a frightened grip. A wave came up, lifting his feet from the bottom. He kicked out frantically, afraid he was going to drown with her holding on to him like that, but the wave tossed them both in towards the shore.

The booger looked up, baring its barracuda teeth. The red coals of its eyes burned right into them both, pinning them there on the wet sand where the wave had left them. Leaving the ruin of Ellen's belongings in torn shreds, it moved slowly towards them.

"Re-Reece," Ellen said. She was pressed close to him, shivering.

Reece didn't have the time to appreciate the contact of her skin against his. He wanted to say, this is what you were looking for, lady, but things weren't so cut and dried now. Ellen wasn't some nameless cipher anymore—just a part of a crowd that he could sneer at—and she wasn't just something he had the hots for either. She was a person, just like him. An individual. Someone he could actually relate to.

"Can—can't you stop it?" Ellen cried.

The booger was getting close now. Its sewer reek was strong enough to drown out the salty tang of the ocean. It was like something had died there on the beach and was now getting up and coming for them.

Stop it? Reece thought. Maybe the thing had been created out of his frustrated anger, the way Ellen's friend made out it could happen in that book of his, but Reece knew as sure as shit that he didn't control the booger.

Another wave came down upon them and Reece pushed at the sand so that it pulled them partway out from the shore on its way back out. Getting to his knees in the rimy water, he got in front of Ellen so that he was between her and the booger. Could the sucker swim?

The booger hesitated at the water's edge. It lifted its paws fastidiously from the wet sand like a cat crossing a damp lawn and relief went through Reece. When another wave came in, the booger backstepped quickly out of its reach.

Ellen was leaning against him, face near his as she peered over his shoulder.

"It can't handle the water," Reece said. He turned his face to hers when she didn't say anything. Her clear eyes were open wide, gaze fixed on the booger. "Ellen . . . ?" he began.

"I can't believe that it's really there," she said finally in a small voice.

"But you're the one—you said . . ." He drew a little away from her so that he could see her better.

"I know what I said," Ellen replied. She hugged herself, trembling at the stir of dark wings inside her. "It's just . . . I *wanted* to believe, but . . . wanting to and having it be real . . ." There was a pressure in the center of her chest now, like something inside pushing to get out. "I . . ."

The pain lanced sharp and sudden. She heard Reece gasp. Looking down, she saw what he had seen, a bird's head poking gossamer from between her breasts. It was a dark smudge against the white of her swimsuit, not one of Uncle Dobbin's parrots, but a crow's head, with eyes like the pair she'd seen looking back at her from the mirror. Her own magic, leaving her because she didn't believe. Because she couldn't believe, but—

It didn't make sense. She'd always believed. And now, with Reece's booger standing there on the shore, how could she help *but* believe?

The booger howled then, as though to underscore her thoughts. She looked to the shore and saw it stepping into the waves, crying out at the pain of the salt water on its flesh, but determined to get at them. To get at her. Reece's magic, given life. While her own magic . . . She pressed at the half-formed crow coming from her chest, trying to force it back in.

"I believe, I believe," she muttered through clenched teeth. But just like Uncle Dobbin's assistant in Christy's story, she could feel that swelling ache of loss rise up in her. She turned despairing eyes to Reece.

She didn't need a light to see the horror in his eyes—horror at the booger's approach, at the crow's head sticking out of her chest. But he didn't draw away from her. Instead, he reached out and caught hold of her shoulders.

"Stop fighting it!" he cried.

"But—"

He shot a glance shoreward. They were bracing themselves against the waves, but a large swell had just caught the booger and sent it howling back to shore in a tumble of limbs.

"It was your needing proof," he said. "Your needing to see the booger, to know that it's real—that's what's making you lose it. Stop trying so hard."

"I . . ."

But she knew he was right. She pulled free of him and looked towards the shore where the booger was struggling to its feet. The creature made rattling sounds deep in its throat as it started out for them again. It was hard, hard to do, but she let her hands fall free. The pain in her chest was a fire, the aching loss building to a crescendo. But she closed herself to it, closed her eyes, willed herself to stand relaxed.

Instead of fighting, she remembered. Balloon Men spinning down the beach. Christy's gnome, riding his pig along the pier. Bramley Dapple's advice. Goon pinching Jilly Coppercorn's leg. The thing that fed on eggs and eyeballs and, yes, Reece's booger too. Uncle Dobbin and his parrots and Nori Wert watching her magic fly free. And always the Balloon Men, tumbling end-over-end, across the beach, or down the alleyway behind her house. . . .

And the pain eased. The ache loosened, faded.

"Jesus," she heard Reece say softly.

She opened her eyes and looked to where he was looking. The booger had turned from the sea and was fleeing as a crowd of Balloon Men came bouncing down the shore, great round roly-poly shapes, turning end-over-end, laughing and giggling, a chorus of small deep voices. There was salt in her eyes and it wasn't from the ocean's brine. Her tears ran down her cheeks and she felt herself grinning like a fool.

The Balloon Men chased Reece's booger up one end of the beach and then back the other way until the creature finally made a stand.

Howling, it waited for them to come, but before the first bouncing round shape reached it, the booger began to fade away.

Ellen turned to Reece and knew he had tears in his own eyes, but the good feeling was too strong for him to do anything but grin right back at her. The booger had died with the last of his anger. She reached out a hand to him and he took it in one of his own. Joined so, they made their way to the shore where they were surrounded by riotous Balloon Men until the bouncing shapes finally faded and then there were just the two of them standing there.

Ellen's heart beat fast. When Reece let go her hand, she touched her chest and felt a stir of dark wings inside her, only they were settling in now, no longer striving to fly free. The wind came in from the ocean still, but it wasn't the same wind that the Balloon Men rode.

"I guess it's not all bullshit," Reece said softly.

Ellen glanced at him.

He smiled as he explained. "Helping each other—getting along instead of fighting. Feels kind of good, you know?"

Ellen nodded. Her hand fell from her chest as the dark wings finally stilled.

"Your friend's story didn't say anything about crows," Reece said.

"Maybe we've all got different birds inside—different magics." She looked out across the waves to where the oil rigs lit the horizon.

"There's a flock of wild parrots up around Santa Ana," Reece said.

"I've heard there's one up around San Pedro, too."

"Do you think . . . ?" Reece began, but he let his words trail off. The waves came in and wet their feet.

"I don't know," Ellen said. She looked over at her shredded clothes. "Come on. Let's get back to my place and warm up."

Reece laid his jacket over her shoulders. He put on his T-shirt and jeans, then helped her gather up what was left of her belongings.

"I didn't mean for this to happen," he said, bundling up the torn blouse and skirt. He looked up to where she was standing over him. "But I couldn't control the booger."

"Maybe we're not supposed to."

"But something like the booger . . ."

She gave his Mohawk a friendly ruffle. "I think it just means that we've got to be careful about what kind of vibes we put out."

Reece grimaced at her use of the word, but he nodded.

"It's either that," Ellen added, "or we let the magic fly free."

The same feathery stirring of wings that she felt moved in Reece. They both knew that that was something neither of them was likely to give up.

In Uncle Dobbin's Parrot Fair, Nori Wert turned away from the pair of cages that she'd been making ready.

"I guess we won't be needing these," she said.

Uncle Dobbin looked up from a slim collection of Victorian poetry and nodded. "You're learning fast," he said. He stuck the stem of his pipe in his mouth and fished about in his pocket for a match. "Maybe there's hope for you yet."

Nori felt her own magic stir inside her, back where it should be, but she didn't say anything to him in case she had to go away, now that the lesson was learned. She was too happy here. Next to catching some rays, there wasn't anywhere she'd rather be.

≈ THE STONE DRUM ≈

THERE IS NO QUESTION THAT THERE IS AN UNSEEN WORLD. THE PROBLEM IS HOW FAR IS IT FROM MID-TOWN AND HOW LATE IS IT OPEN?
                    —ATTRIBUTED TO WOODY ALLEN

It was Jilly Coppercorn who found the stone drum, late one afternoon.

She brought it around to Professor Dapple's rambling Tudor-styled house in the old quarter of Lower Crowsea that same evening, wrapped up in folds of brown paper and tied with twine. She rapped sharply on the Professor's door with the little brass lion's head knocker that always seemed to stare too intently at her, then stepped back as Olaf Goonasekara, Dapple's odd little housekeeper, flung the door open and glowered out at where she stood on the rickety porch.

"You," he grumbled.

"Me," she agreed, amicably. "Is Bramley in?"

"I'll see," he replied and shut the door.

Jilly sighed and sat down on one of the two worn rattan chairs that stood to the left of the door, her package bundled on her knee. A black and orange cat regarded her incuriously from the seat of the other chair, then turned to watch the progress of a woman walking her dachshund down the street.

Professor Dapple still taught a few classes at Butler U., but he wasn't nearly as involved with the curriculum as he had been when Jilly attended the university. There'd been some kind of a scandal—something about a Bishop, some old coins and the daughter of a Tarot reader—but Jilly had never quite got the story straight. The Professor was a jolly fellow—wizened like an old apple, but more active than many who were only half his apparent sixty years of age. He could talk and joke all night, incessantly polishing his wire-rimmed spectacles.

What he was doing with someone like Olaf Goonasekara as a housekeeper Jilly didn't know. It was true that Goon looked comical enough, what with his protruding stomach and puffed cheeks, the halo of unruly hair and his thin little arms and legs, reminding her of nothing so much as a pumpkin with twig limbs, or a monkey. His usual striped trousers, organ grinder's jacket and the little green and yellow cap he liked to wear, didn't help. Nor did the fact that he was barely four feet tall and that the Professor claimed he was a goblin and just called him Goon.

It didn't seem to allow Goon much dignity and Jilly would have understood his grumpiness, if she didn't know that he himself insisted on being called Goon and his wardrobe was entirely of his own choosing. Bramley hated Goon's sense of fashion—or rather, his lack thereof.

The door was flung open again and Jilly stood up to find Goon glowering at her once more.

"He's in," he said.

Jilly smiled. As if he'd actually had to go in and check.

They both stood there, Jilly on the porch and he in the doorway, until Jilly finally asked, "Can he see me?"

Giving an exaggerated sigh, Goon stepped aside to let her in.

"I suppose you'll want something to drink?" he asked as he followed her to the door of the Professor's study.

"Tea would be lovely."

"Hrumph."

Jilly watched him stalk off, then tapped a knuckle on the study's door and stepped into the room. Bramley lifted his gaze from a desk littered with tottering stacks of books and papers and grinned at her from between a gap in the towers of paper.

"I've been doing some research since you called," he said. He poked a finger at a book that Jilly couldn't see, then began to clean his glasses. "Fascinating stuff."

"And hello to you, too," Jilly said.

"Yes, of course. Did you know that the Kickaha had legends of a little people long before the Europeans ever settled this area?"

Jilly could never quite get used to Bramley's habit of starting conversations in the middle. She removed some magazines from a club chair and perched on the edge of its seat, her package clutched to her chest.

"What's that got to do with anything?" she asked.

Bramley looked surprised. "Why everything. We *are* still looking into the origins of this artifact of yours, aren't we?"

Jilly nodded. From her new position of vantage she could make out the book he'd been reading. *Underhill and Deeper Still,* a short story collection by Christy Riddell. Riddell made a living of retelling the odd stories that lie just under the skin of any large city. This particular one was a collection of urban legends of Old City and other subterranean fancies—not exactly the factual reference source she'd been hoping for.

Old City was real enough; that was where she'd found the drum this afternoon. But as for the rest of it—albino crocodile subway conductors, schools of dog-sized intelligent goldfish in the sewers, mutant rat debating societies and the like . . .

Old City was the original heart of Newford. It lay deep underneath the subway tunnels—dropped there in the late eighteen hundreds during the Great Quake. The present city, including its sewers and underground transportation tunnels, had been built above the ruins of the old one. There'd been talk in the early seventies of renovating the ruins as a tourist attraction—as had been done in Seattle—but Old City lay too far underground for easy access. After numerous studies on the project, the city council had decided that it simply wouldn't be cost efficient.

With that decision, Old City had rapidly gone from a potential tourist attraction to a home for skells—winos, bag ladies and the other homeless. Not to mention, if one was to believe Bramley and Riddell, bands of ill-mannered goblin-like creatures that Riddell called skookin—a word he'd stolen from old Scots which meant, variously, ugly, furtive and sullen.

Which, Jilly realized once when she thought about it, made it entirely appropriate that Bramley should claim Goon was related to them.

"You're not going to tell me it's a skookin artifact, are you?" she asked Bramley now.

"Too soon to say," he replied. He nodded at her parcel. "Can I see it?"

Jilly got up and brought it over to the desk, where Bramley made a great show of cutting the twine and unwrapping the paper. Jilly couldn't decide if he was pretending it was the unveiling of a new piece at the museum or his birthday. But then the drum was sitting on the desk, the mica and quartz veins in its stone catching the light from Bramley's desk lamp in a magical glitter, and she was swallowed up in the wonder of it again.

It was tube-shaped, standing about a foot high, with a seven-inch diameter at the top and five inches at the bottom. The top was smooth as the skin head of a drum. On the sides were what appeared to be the remnants of a bewildering flurry of designs. But what was most marvelous about it was that the stone was hollow. It weighed about the same as a fat hardcover book.

"Listen," Jilly said and gave the top of the drum a rap-a-tap-tap.

The stone responded with a quiet rhythm that resonated eerily in the study. Unfortunately, Goon chose that moment to arrive in the doorway with a tray laden with tea mugs, tea pot and a platter of his homemade biscuits. At the sound of the drum, the tray fell from his hands. It hit the floor with a crash, spraying tea, milk, sugar, biscuits and bits of crockery every which way.

Jilly turned, her heartbeat double-timing in her chest, just in time to see an indescribable look cross over Goon's features. It might have been surprise, it might have been laughter, but it was gone too quickly for her to properly note. He merely stood in the doorway now, his usual glowering look on his face, and all Jilly was left with was a feeling of unaccountable guilt.

"I didn't mean . . ." Jilly began, but her voice trailed off.

"Bit of a mess," Bramley said.

"I'll get right to it," Goon said.

His small dark eyes centered their gaze on Jilly for too long a moment, then he turned away to fetch a broom and dustpan. When Jilly turned back to the desk, she found Bramley rubbing his hands together, face pressed close to the stone drum. He looked up at her over his glasses, grinning.

"Did you see?" he said. "Goon recognized it for what it is, straight off. It has to be a skookin artifact. Didn't like you meddling around with it either."

That was hardly the conclusion that Jilly would have come to on her own. It was the sudden and unexpected sound that had more than likely startled Goon—as it might have startled anyone who wasn't expecting it. That was the reasonable explanation, but she knew well enough that reasonable didn't necessarily always mean right. When she thought of that look that had passed over Goon's features, like a trough of surprise or mocking humor between two cresting glowers, she didn't know what to think, so she let herself get taken away by the Professor's enthusiasm, because . . . well, just what if . . . ?

By all of Christy Riddell's accounts, there wasn't a better candidate for skookin-dom than Bramley's housekeeper.

"What does it mean?" she asked.

Bramley shrugged and began to polish his glasses. Jilly was about to nudge him into making at least the pretense of a theory, but then she realized that the Professor had simply fallen silent because Goon was back to clean up the mess. She waited until Goon had made his retreat with the promise of putting on another pot of tea, before she leaned over Bramley's desk.

"Well?" she asked.

"Found it in Old City, did you?" he replied.

Jilly nodded.

"You know what they say about skookin treasure . . . ?"

They meaning he and Christy, Jilly thought, but she obligingly tried to remember that particular story from *Underhill and Deeper Still*. She had it after a moment. It was the one called "The Man with the Monkey" and had something to do with a stolen apple that was withered and moldy in Old City but became solid gold when it was brought above ground. At the end of the story, the man who'd stolen it from the skookin was found in little pieces scattered all over Fitzhenry Park. . . .

Jilly shivered.

"Now I remember why I don't like to read Christy's stuff," she said. "He can be so sweet on one page, and then on the next he's taking you on a tour through an abattoir."

"Just like life," Bramley said.

"Wonderful. So what are you saying?"

"They'll be wanting it back," Bramley said.

Jilly woke some time after midnight with the Professor's words ringing in her ears.

They'll be wanting it back.

She glanced at the stone drum where it sat on a crate by the window of her Yoors Street loft in Foxville. From where she lay on

her Murphy bed, the streetlights coming in the window wove a
haloing effect around the stone artifact. The drum glimmered with
magic—or at least with a potential for magic. And there was something else in the air. A humming sound, like barely audible strains
of music. The notes seemed disconnected, drifting randomly
through the melody like dust motes dancing in a beam of sunlight,
but there was still a melody present.

She sat up slowly. Pushing the quilt aside, she padded barefoot
across the room. When she reached the drum, the change in perspective made the streetlight halo slide away; the drum's magic fled.
It was just an odd stone artifact once more. She ran her finger along
the smoothed indentations that covered the sides of the artifact, but
didn't touch the top. It was still marvelous enough—a hollow stone,
a mystery, a puzzle. But . . .

She remembered the odd almost-but-not-quite music she'd heard
when she first woke, and cocked her ear, listening for it.

Nothing.

Outside, a light drizzle had wet the pavement, making Yoors
Street glisten and sparkle with its sheen. She knelt down by the
windowsill and leaned forward, looking out, feeling lonely. It'd be
nice if Geordie were here, even if his brother did write those books
that had the Professor so enamoured, but Geordie was out of town
this week. Maybe she should get a cat or a dog—just something to
keep her company when she got into one of these odd funks—but
the problem with pets was that they tied you down. No more
gallivanting about whenever and wherever you pleased. Not when
the cat needed to be fed. Or the dog had to be walked.

Sighing, she started to turn from the window, then paused. A
flicker of uneasiness stole up her spine as she looked more closely
at what had caught her attention—there, across the street. Time
dissolved into a pattern as random as that faint music she'd heard
when she woke earlier. Minutes and seconds marched sideways; the
hands of the old Coors clock on her wall stood still.

A figure leaned against the wall, there, just to one side of the
display window of the Chinese groceteria across the street, a figure
as much a patchwork as the disarray in the shop's window. Pumpkin
head under a wide-brimmed hat. A larger pumpkin for the body
with what looked like straw spilling out from between the buttons

of its too-small jacket. Arms and legs as thin as broom handles. A wide slit for a mouth; eyes like the sharp yellow slits of a jack-o'-lantern with a candle burning inside.

A Halloween creature. And not alone.

There was another, there, in the mouth of that alleyway. A third clinging to the wall of the brownstone beside the groceteria. Four more on the rooftop directly across the street—pumpkinheads lined up along the parapet, all in a row.

Skookin, Jilly thought and she shivered with fear, remembering Christy Riddell's story.

Damn Christy for tracking the story down, and damn the Professor for reminding her of it. And damn the job that had sent her down into Old City in the first place to take photos for the background of the painting she was currently working on.

Because there shouldn't be any such thing as skookin. Because . . .

She blinked, then rubbed her eyes. Her gaze darted left and right, up and down, raking the street and the faces of buildings across the way.

Nothing.

No pumpkin goblins watching her loft.

The sound of her clock ticking the seconds away was suddenly loud in her ears. A taxi went by on the street below, spraying a fine sheet of water from its wheels. She waited for it to pass, then studied the street again.

There were no skookin.

Of course there wouldn't be, she told herself, trying to laugh at how she'd let her imagination run away with itself, but she couldn't muster up even the first hint of a smile. She looked at the drum, reached a hand towards it, then let her hand fall to her lap, the drum untouched. She turned her attention back to the street, watching it for long moments before she finally had to accept that there was nothing out there, that she had only peopled it with her own night fears.

Pushing herself up from the sill, she returned to bed and lay down again. The palm of her right hand itched a little, right where she'd managed to poke herself on a small nail or wood sliver while she was down in Old City. She scratched her hand and stared up at the ceiling, trying to go to sleep, but not expecting to have much luck. Surprisingly, she drifted off in moments.

And dreamed.

Of Bramley's study. Except the Professor wasn't ensconced behind his desk as usual. Instead, he was setting out a serving of tea for her and Goon, who had taken the Professor's place behind the tottering stacks of papers and books on the desk.

"Skookin," Goon said, when the Professor had finished serving them their tea and left the room. "They've never existed, of course."

Jilly nodded in agreement.

"Though in some ways," Goon went on, "they've always existed. In here—" He tapped his temple with a gnarly, very skookin-like finger. "In our imaginations."

"But—" Jilly began, wanting to tell him how she'd *seen* skookin, right out there on her very own street tonight, but Goon wasn't finished.

"And that's what makes them real," he said.

His head suddenly looked very much like a pumpkin. He leaned forward, eyes glittering as though a candle was burning there inside his head, flickering in the wind.

"And if they're real," he said.

His voice wound down alarmingly, as though it came from the spiraling groove of a spoken-word album that someone had slowed by dragging their finger along on the vinyl.

"Then. You're. In. A. Lot. Of—"

Jilly awoke with a start to find herself backed up against the frame of the head of her bed, her hands worrying and tangling her quilt into knots.

Just a dream. Cast off thoughts, tossed up by her subconscious. Nothing to worry about. Except . . .

She could finish the dream-Goon's statement.

If they were real . . .

Never mind being in trouble. If they were real, then she was doomed.

She didn't get any more sleep that night, and first thing the next morning, she went looking for help.

"Skookin," Meran said, trying hard not to laugh.

"Oh, I know what it sounds like," Jilly said, "but what can you do? Christy's books are Bramley's pet blind spot and if you listen to him long enough, he'll have you believing anything."

"But skookin," Meran repeated and this time she did giggle.

Jilly couldn't help but laugh with her.

Everything felt very different in the morning light—especially when she had someone to talk it over with whose head wasn't filled with Christy's stories.

They were sitting in Kathryn's Cafe—an hour or so after Jilly had found Meran Kelledy down by the Lake, sitting on the Pier and watching the early morning joggers run across the sand: yuppies from downtown, health-conscious gentry from the Beaches.

It was a short walk up Battersfield Road to where Kathryn's was nestled in the heart of Lower Crowsea. Like the area itself, with its narrow streets and old stone buildings, the cafe had an old world feel about it—from the dark wood paneling and hand-carved chair backs to the small round tables, with checkered tablecloths, fat glass condiment containers and straw-wrapped wine bottles used as candle-holders. The music piped in over the house sound system was mostly along the lines of Telemann and Vivaldi, Kitaro and old Bob James albums. The waitresses wore cream-colored pinafores over flower-print dresses.

But if the atmosphere was old world, the clientele were definitely contemporary. Situated so close to Butler U., Kathryn's had been a favorite haunt of the university's students since it first opened its doors in the mid-sixties as a coffee house. Though much had changed from those early days, there was still music played on its small stage on Friday and Saturday nights, as well as poetry recitations on Wednesdays and Sunday morning storytelling sessions.

Jilly and Meran sat by a window, coffee and homemade banana muffins set out on the table in front of them.

"Whatever were you *doing* down there anyway?" Meran asked. "It's not exactly the safest place to be wandering about."

Jilly nodded. The skells in Old City weren't all thin and wasted. Some were big and mean-looking, capable of anything—not really the sort of people Jilly should be around, because if something went wrong . . . well, she was the kind of woman for whom the word petite had been coined. She was small and slender—her tiny size only accentuated by the oversized clothing she tended to wear. Her brown hair was a thick tangle, her eyes the electric blue of sapphires.

She was too pretty and too small to be wandering about in places like Old City on her own.

"You know the band, No Nuns Here?" Jilly asked.

Meran nodded.

"I'm doing the cover painting for their first album," Jilly explained. "They wanted something moody for the background—sort of like the Tombs, but darker and grimmer—and I thought Old City would be the perfect place to get some reference shots."

"But to go there on your own . . ."

Jilly just shrugged. She was known to wander anywhere and everywhere, at any time of the night or day, camera or sketchbook in hand, often both.

Meran shook her head. Like most of Jilly's friends, she'd long since given up trying to point out the dangers of carrying on the way Jilly did.

"So you found this drum," she said.

Jilly nodded. She looked down at the little scab on the palm of her hand. It itched like crazy, but she was determined not to open it again by scratching it.

"And now you want to . . . ?"

Jilly looked up. "Take it back. Only I'm scared to go there on my own. I thought maybe Cerin would come with me—for moral support, you know?"

"He's out of town," Meran said.

Meran and her husband made up the two halves of the Kelledys, a local traditional music duo that played coffee houses, festivals and colleges from one coast to the other. For years now, however, Newford had been their home base.

"He's teaching another of those harp workshops," Meran added.

Jilly did her best to hide her disappointment.

What she'd told Meran about "moral support" was only partly the reason she'd wanted their help because, more so than either Riddell's stories or Bramley's askew theories, the Kelledys were the closest thing to real magic that she could think of in Newford. There was an otherworldly air about the two of them that went beyond the glamour that seemed to always gather around people who became successful in their creative endeavors.

It wasn't something Jilly could put her finger on. It wasn't as though they went on and on about this sort of thing at the drop of a hat the way that Bramley did. Nor that they were responsible for anything more mysterious than the enchantment they awoke on stage when they were playing their instruments. It was just there. Something that gave the impression that they were aware of what lay beyond the here and now. That they could see things others couldn't; knew things that remained secret to anyone else.

Nobody even knew where they had come from; they'd just arrived in Newford a few years ago, speaking with accents that had rapidly vanished, and here they'd pretty well stayed ever since. Jilly had always privately supposed that if there was a place called Faerie, then that was from where they'd come, so when she woke up this morning, deciding she needed magical help, she'd gone looking for one or the other and found Meran. But now . . .

"Oh," she said.

Meran smiled.

"But that doesn't mean I can't try to help," she said.

Jilly sighed. Help with what? she had to ask herself. The more she thought about it, the sillier it all seemed. Skookin. Right. Maybe they held debating contests with Riddell's mutant rats.

"I think maybe I'm nuts," she said finally. "I mean, goblins living under the city . . . ?"

"I believe in the little people," Meran said. "We called them bodachs where I come from."

Jilly just looked at her.

"But you laughed when I talked about them," she said finally.

"I know—and I shouldn't have. It's just that whenever I hear that name that Christy's given them, I can't help myself. It's so silly."

"What I saw last night didn't feel silly," Jilly said.

If she'd actually seen anything. By this point—even with Meran's apparent belief—she wasn't sure what to think anymore.

"No," Meran said. "I suppose not. But—you're taking the drum back, so why are you so nervous?"

"The man in Christy's story returned the apple he stole," Jilly said, "and you know what happened to him. . . ."

"That's true," Meran said, frowning.

"I thought maybe Cerin could . . ." Jilly's voice trailed off.

A small smile touched Meran's lips. "Could do what?"

"Well, this is going to sound even sillier," Jilly admitted, "but I've always pictured him as sort of a wizard type."

Meran laughed. "He'd love to hear that. And what about me? Have I acquired wizardly status as well?"

"Not exactly. You always struck me as being an earth spirit—like you stepped out of an oak tree or something." Jilly blushed, feeling as though she was making even more of a fool of herself than ever, but now that she'd started, she felt she had to finish. "It's sort of like he learned magic, while you just are magic."

She glanced at her companion, looking for laughter, but Meran was regarding her gravely. And she did look like a dryad, Jilly thought, what with the green streaks in the long, nut-brown ringlets of her hair and her fey sort of Pre-Raphaelite beauty. Her eyes seemed to provide their own light, rather than take it in.

"Maybe I did step out of a tree one day," Meran said.

Jilly could feel her mouth forming a surprised "O," but then Meran laughed again.

"But probably I didn't," she said. Before Jilly could ask her about that "probably," Meran went on: "We'll need some sort of protection against them."

Jilly made her mind shift gears, from Meran's origins to the problem at hand.

"Like holy water or a cross?" she asked.

Her head filled with the plots of a hundred bad horror films, each of them clamoring for attention.

"No," Meran said. "Religious artifacts and trappings require faith—a belief in their potency that the skookin undoubtedly don't have. The only thing I know for certain that they can't abide is the truth."

"The truth?"

Meran nodded. "Tell them the truth—even it's only historical facts and trivia—and they'll shun you as though you were carrying a plague."

"But what about after?" Jilly said. "After we've delivered the drum and they come looking for me? Do I have to walk around carrying a cassette machine spouting dates and facts for the rest of my life?"

"I hope not."

"But—"

"Patience," Meran replied. "Let me think about it for awhile."

Jilly sighed. She regarded her companion curiously as Meran took a sip of her coffee.

"You really believe in this stuff, don't you?" she said finally.

"Don't you?"

Jilly had to think about that for a moment.

"Last night I was scared," she said, "and I'm returning the drum because I'd rather be safe than sorry, but I'm still not sure."

Meran nodded understandingly, but, "Your coffee's getting cold," was all she had to say.

Meran let Jilly stay with her that night in the rambling old house where she and Cerin lived. Straddling the border between Lower Crowsea and Chinatown, it was a tall, gabled building surrounded by giant oak trees. There was a rounded tower in the front to the right of a long screen-enclosed porch, stables around the back, and a garden along the west side of the house that seemed to have been plucked straight from a postcard of the English countryside.

Jilly loved this area. The Kelledys' house was the easternmost of the stately estates that stood, row on row, along McKennitt Street, between Lee and Yoors. Whenever Jilly walked along this part of McKennitt, late at night when the streetcars were tucked away in their downtown station and there was next to no other traffic, she found it easy to imagine that the years had wound back to a bygone age when time moved at a different pace, when Newford's streets were cobblestoned and the vehicles that traversed them were horse-drawn, rather than horse-powered.

"You'll wear a hole in the glass if you keep staring through it so intently."

Jilly started. She turned long enough to acknowledge her hostess's presence, then her gaze was dragged back to the window, to the shadows cast by the oaks as twilight stretched them across the lawn, to the long low wall that bordered the lawn, to the street beyond.

Still no skookin. Did that mean they didn't exist, or that they hadn't come out yet? Or maybe they just hadn't tracked her here to the Kelledys' house.

She started again as Meran laid a hand on her shoulder and gently turned her from the window.

"Who knows what you'll call to us, staring so," Meran said.

Her voice held the same light tone as it had when she'd made her earlier comment, but this time a certain sense of caution lay behind the words.

"If they come, I want to see them," Jilly said.

Meran nodded. "I understand. But remember this: the night's a magical time. The moon rules her hours, not the sun."

"What does that mean?"

"The moon likes secrets," Meran said. "And secret things. She lets mysteries bleed into her shadows and leaves us to ask whether they originated from otherworlds, or from our own imaginations."

"You're beginning to sound like Bramley," Jilly said. "Or Christy."

"Remember your Shakespeare," Meran said. " 'This fellow's wise enough to play the fool.' Did you ever think that perhaps their studied eccentricity protects them from sharper ridicule?"

"You mean all those things Christy writes about are *true*?"

"I didn't say that."

Jilly shook her head. "No. But you're talking in riddles just like a wizard out of some fairy tale. I never understood why they couldn't talk plainly."

"That's because some things can only be approached from the side. Secretively. Peripherally."

Whatever Jilly was about to say next, died stillborn. She pointed out the window to where the lawn was almost swallowed by shadows.

"Do . . ." She swallowed thickly, then tried again. "Do you see them?"

They were out there, flitting between the wall that bordered the Kelledys' property and those tall oaks that stood closer to the house. Shadow shapes. Fat, pumpkin-bodied and twig-limbed. There were more of them than there'd been last night. And they were bolder. Creeping right up towards the house. Threats burning in their candle-flicker eyes. Wide mouths open in jack-o'-lantern grins, revealing rows of pointed teeth.

One came sidling right up to the window, its face monstrous at such close proximity. Jilly couldn't move, couldn't even breathe. She remembered what Meran had said earlier—

they can't abide the truth

—but she couldn't frame a sentence, never mind a word, and her mind was filled with only a wild unreasoning panic. The creature reached out a hand towards the glass, clawed fingers extended. Jilly could feel a scream building up, deep inside her. In a moment that hand would come crashing through the window, shattering glass, clawing at her throat. And she couldn't move. All she could do was stare, stare as the claws reached for the glass, stare as it drew back to—

Something fell between the creature and the house—a swooping, shapeless thing. The creature danced back, saw that it was only the bough of one of the oak trees and was about to begin its approach once more, but the cries of its companions distracted it. Not until it turned its horrible gaze from her, did Jilly feel able to lift her own head.

She stared at the oaks. A sudden wind had sprung up, lashing the boughs about so that the tall trees appeared to be giants, flailing about their many-limbed arms like monstrous, agitated octopi. The creatures in the yard scattered and in moments they were gone— each and every one of them. The wind died down; the animated giants became just oak trees once more.

Jilly turned slowly from the window to find Meran pressed close beside her.

"Ugly, furtive and sullen," Meran said. "Perhaps Christy wasn't so far off in naming them."

"They . . . they're real, aren't they?" Jilly asked in a small voice.

Meran nodded. "And not at all like the bodachs of my homeland. Bodachs are mischievous and prone to trouble, but not like this. Those creatures were weaned on malevolence."

Jilly leaned weakly against the windowsill.

"What are we going to *do*?" she asked.

She scratched at her palm—the itch was worse than ever. Meran caught her hand, pulled it away. There was an unhappy look in her eyes when she lifted her gaze from the mark on Jilly's palm.

"Where did you get that?" she asked.

Jilly looked down at her palm. The scab was gone, but the skin was all dark around the puncture wound now—an ugly black discoloration that was twice the size of the original scab.

"I scratched myself," she said. "Down in Old City."

Meran shook her head. "No," she said. "They've marked you."

Jilly suddenly felt weak. Skookin were real. Mysterious winds rose to animate trees. And now she was marked?

She wasn't even sure what that meant, but she didn't like the sound of it. Not for a moment.

Her gaze went to the stone drum where it stood on Meran's mantel. She didn't think she'd ever hated an inanimate object so much before.

"Marked . . . me . . . ?" she asked.

"I've heard of this before," Meran said, her voice apologetic. She touched the mark on Jilly's palm. "This is like a . . . bounty."

"They really want to kill me, don't they?"

Jilly was surprised that her voice sounded as calm as it did. Inside she felt as though she was crumbling to little bits all over the place.

"Skookin are real," she went on, "and they're going to tear me up into little pieces—just like they did to the man in Christy's stupid story."

Meran gave her a sympathetic look.

"We have to go now," she said. "We have to go and confront them now, before . . ."

"Before what?"

Jilly's control over her voice was slipping. Her last word went shrieking up in pitch.

"Before they send something worse," Meran said.

Oh great, Jilly thought as waited for Meran to change into clothing more suitable for the underground trek to Old City. Not only were skookin real, but there were worse things than those pumpkinhead creatures living down there under the city.

She slouched in one of the chairs by the mantelpiece, her back to the stone drum, and pretended that her nerves weren't all scraped raw, that she was just over visiting a friend for the evening and everything was just peachy, thank you. Surprisingly, by the time Meran returned, wearing jeans, sturdy walking shoes and a thick woolen shirt under a denim jacket, she did feel better.

"The bit with the trees," she asked as she rose from her chair. "Did you do that?"

Meran shook her head.

"But the wind likes me," she said. "Maybe it's because I play the flute."

And maybe it's because you're a dryad, Jilly thought, and the wind's got a thing about oak trees, but she let the thought go unspoken.

Meran fetched the long, narrow bag that held her flute and slung it over her shoulder.

"Ready?" she asked.

"No," Jilly said.

But she went and took the drum from the mantelpiece and joined Meran by the front door. Meran stuck a flashlight in the pocket of her jacket and handed another to Jilly, who thrust it into the pocket of the coat Meran was lending her. It was at least two sizes too big for her, which suited Jilly just fine.

Naturally, just to make the night complete, it started to rain before they got halfway down the walkway to McKennitt Street.

For safety's sake, city work crews had sealed up all the entrances to Old City in the mid-seventies—all the entrances of which the city was aware, at any rate. The street people of Newford's back lanes and allies knew of anywhere from a half-dozen to twenty others that could still be used, the number depending only on who was doing the bragging. The entrance to which Jilly led Meran was the most commonly known and used—a steel maintenance door that was situated two hundred yards or so down the east tracks of the Grasso Street subway station.

The door led into the city's sewer maintenance tunnels, but had long since been abandoned. Skells had broken the locking mechanism and the door stood continually ajar. Inside, time and weathering had worn down a connecting wall between the maintenance tunnels and what had once been the top floor of one of Old City's proud skyscrapers—an office complex that had towered some four stories above the city's streets before the quake dropped it into its present subterranean setting.

It was a good fifteen minute walk from the Kelledys' house to the

Grasso Street station and Jilly plodded miserably through the rain at Meran's side for every block of it. Her sneakers were soaked and her hair plastered against her scalp. She carried the stone drum tucked under one arm and was very tempted to simply pitch it in front of a bus.

"This is crazy," Jilly said. "We're just giving ourselves up to them."

Meran shook her head. "No. We're confronting them of our own free will—there's a difference."

"That's just semantics. There won't be a difference in the results."

"That's where you're wrong."

They both turned at the sound of a new voice to find Goon standing in the doorway of a closed antique shop. His eyes glittered oddly in the poor light, reminding Jilly all too much of the skookin, and he didn't seem to be the least bit wet.

"What are *you* doing here?" Jilly demanded.

"You must always confront your fears," Goon said as though she hadn't spoke. "Then skulking monsters become merely unfamiliar shadows, thrown by a tree bough. Whispering voices are just the wind. The wild flare of panic is merely a burst of emotion, not a terror spell cast by some evil witch."

Meran nodded. "That's what Cerin would say. And that's what I mean to do. Confront them with a truth so bright that they won't dare come near us again."

Jilly held up her hand. The discoloration was spreading. It had grown from its pinprick inception, first to the size of a dime, now to that of a silver dollar.

"What about this?" she asked.

"There's always a price for meddling," Goon agreed. "Sometimes it's the simple curse of knowledge."

"There's always a price," Meran agreed.

Everybody always seemed to know more than she did these days, Jilly thought unhappily.

"You still haven't told me what you're doing here," she told Goon. "Skulking about and following us."

Goon smiled. "It seems to me, that you came upon me."

"You know what I mean."

"I have my own business in Old City tonight," he said. "And since we all have the same destination in mind, I thought perhaps you would appreciate the company."

Everything was wrong about this, Jilly thought. Goon was never nice to her. Goon was never nice to anyone.

"Yeah, well, you can just—" she began.

Meran laid a hand on Jilly's arm. "It's bad luck to turn away help when it's freely offered."

"But you don't know what he's like," Jilly said.

"Olaf and I have met before," Meran said.

Jilly caught the grimace on Goon's face at the use of his given name. It made him seem more himself, which, while not exactly comforting, was at least familiar. Then she looked at Meran. She thought of the wind outside the musician's house, driving away the skookin, the mystery that cloaked her which ran even deeper, perhaps, than that which Goon wore so easily. . . .

"Sometimes you just have to trust in people," Meran said, as though reading Jilly's mind.

Jilly sighed. She rubbed her itchy palm against her thigh, shifted the drum into a more comfortable position.

"Okay," she said. "So what're we waiting for?"

The few times Jilly had come down to Old City, she'd been cautious, perhaps even a little nervous, but never frightened. Tonight was different. It was always dark in Old City, but the darkness had never seemed so . . . so watchful before. There were always odd little sounds, but they had never seemed so furtive. Even with her companions—maybe because of them, she thought, thinking mostly of Goon—she felt very much alone in the eerie darkness.

Goon didn't appear to need the wobbly light of their flashlights to see his way and though he seemed content enough to simply follow them, Jilly couldn't shake the feeling that he was actually leading the way. They were soon in a part of the subterranean city that she'd never seen before.

There was less dust and dirt here. No litter, nor the remains of the skells' fires. No broken bottles, nor the piles of newspapers and ratty blanketing that served the skells as bedding. The buildings seemed in better repair. The air had a clean, dry smell to it, rather than the close, musty reek of refuse and human wastes that it carried closer to the entrance.

And there were no people.

From when they'd first stepped through the steel door in Grasso Street Station's east tunnel, she hadn't seen a bag lady or wino or any kind of skell, and that in itself was odd because they were always down here. But there was something sharing the darkness with them. Something watched them, marked their progress, followed with a barely discernible pad of sly footsteps in their wake and on either side.

The drum seemed warm against the skin of her hand. The blemish on her other palm prickled with itchiness. Her shoulder muscles were stiff with tension.

"Not far now," Goon said softly and Jilly suddenly understood what it meant to jump out of one's skin.

The beam of her flashlight made a wild arc across the faces of the buildings on either side of her as she started. Her heartbeat jumped into second gear.

"What do you see?" Meran asked, her voice calm.

The beam of her flashlight turned towards Goon and he pointed ahead.

"Turn off your flashlights," he said.

Oh sure, Jilly thought. Easy for you to say.

But she did so a moment after Meran had. The sudden darkness was so abrupt that Jilly thought she'd gone blind. But then she realized that it wasn't as black as it should be. Looking ahead to where Goon had pointed, she could see a faint glow seeping onto the street ahead of them. It was a little less than a half block away, the source of the light hidden behind the squatting bulk of a half-tumbled-down building.

"What could it . . . ?" Jilly started to say, but then the sounds began, and the rest of her words dried up in her throat.

It was supposed to be music, she realized after a few moments, but there was no discernible rhythm and while the sounds were blown or rasped or plucked from instruments, they searched in vain for a melody.

"It begins," Goon said.

He took the lead, hurrying them up to the corner of the street.

"What does?" Jilly wanted to know.

"The king appears—as he must once a moon. It's that or lose his throne."

Jilly wanted to know what he was talking about—better yet, *how* he knew what he was talking about—but she didn't have a chance. The discordant not-music scraped and squealed to a kind of crescendo. Suddenly they were surrounded by the capering forms of dozens of skookin that bumped them, thin long fingers tugging at their clothing. Jilly shrieked at the first touch. One of them tried to snatch the drum from her grip. She regained control of her nerves at the same time as she pulled the artifact free from the grasping fingers.

"1789," she said. "That's when the Bastille was stormed and the French Revolution began. Uh, 1807, slave trade was abolished in the British Empire. 1776, the Declaration of Independence was signed."

The skookin backed away from her, as did the others, hissing and spitting. The not-music continued, but its tones were softened.

"Let me see," Jilly went on. "Uh, 1981, the Argentines invade—I can't keep this up, Meran—the Falklands. 1715 . . . that was the year of the first Jacobite uprising."

She'd always been good with historical trivia—having a head for dates—but the more she concentrated on them right now, the further they seemed to slip away. The skookin were regarding her with malevolence, just waiting for her to falter.

"1978," she said. "Sandy Denny died, falling down some stairs. . . ."

She'd got that one from Geordie. The skookin took another step back and she stepped towards them, into the light, her eyes widening with shock. There was a small park there, vegetation dead, trees leafless and skeletal, shadows dancing from the light cast by a fire at either end of the open space. And it was teeming with skookin.

There seemed to be hundreds of the creatures. She could see some of the musicians who were making that awful din—holding their instruments as though they'd never played them before. They were gathered in a semi-circle around a dais made from slabs of pavement and building rubble. Standing on it was the weirdest looking skookin she'd seen yet. He was kind of withered and stood stiffly. His eyes flashed with a kind of dead, cold light. He had the grimmest look about him that she'd seen on any of them yet.

There was no way her little bits of history were going to be enough to keep back this crew. She turned to look at her companions. She couldn't see Goon, but Meran was tugging her flute free from its carrying bag.

What good was that going to do? Jilly wondered.

"It's another kind of truth," Meran said as she brought the instrument up to her lips.

The flute's clear tones echoed breathily along the street, cutting through the jangle of not-music like a glass knife through muddy water. Jilly held her breath. The music was so beautiful. The skookin cowered where they stood. Their cacophonic noise-making faltered, then fell silent.

No one moved.

For long moments, there was just the clear sound of Meran's flute, breathing a slow plaintive air that echoed and sang down the street, winding from one end of the park to the other.

Another kind of truth, Jilly remembered Meran saying just before she began to play. That's exactly what this music was, she realized. A kind of truth.

The flute-playing finally came to an achingly sweet finale and a hush fell in Old City. And then there was movement. Goon stepped from behind Jilly and walked through the still crowd of skookin to the dais where their king stood. He clambered up over the rubble until he was beside the king. He pulled a large clasp knife from the pocket of his coat. As he opened the blade, the skookin king made a jerky motion to get away, but Goon's knife hand moved too quickly.

He slashed and cut.

Now he's bloody done it, Jilly thought as the skookin king tumbled to the stones. But then she realized that Goon hadn't cut the king. He'd cut the air above the king. He'd cut the—her sudden realization only confused her more—strings holding him?

"What . . . ?" she said.

"Come," Meran said.

She tucked her flute under her arm and led Jilly towards the dais.

"This is your king," Goon was saying.

He reached down and pulled the limp form up by the fine-webbed strings that were attached to the king's arms and shoulders. The king dangled loosely under his strong grip—a broken marionette. A murmur rose from the crowd of skookin—part ugly, part wondering.

"The king is dead," Goon said. "He's been dead for moons. I wondered why Old City was closed to me this past half year, and now I know."

There was movement at the far end of the park—a fleeing figure. It had been the king's councilor, Goon told Jilly and Meran later. Some of the skookin made to chase him, but Goon called them back.

"Let him go," he said. "He won't return. We have other business at hand."

Meran had drawn Jilly right up to the foot of the dais and was gently pushing her forward.

"Go on," she said.

"Is he the king now?" Jilly asked.

Meran smiled and gave her another gentle push.

Jilly looked up. Goon seemed just like he always did when she saw him at Bramley's—grumpy and out of sorts. Maybe it's just his face, she told herself, trying to give herself courage. There were people who look grumpy no matter how happy they are. But the thought didn't help contain her shaking much as she slowly made her way up to where Goon stood.

"You have something of ours," Goon said.

His voice was grim. Christy's story lay all too clearly in Jilly's head. She swallowed dryly.

"Uh, I never meant . . ." she began, then simply handed over the drum.

Goon took it reverently, then snatched her other hand before she could draw away. Her palm flared with sharp pain—all the skin, from the base of her hand to the ends of her fingers was black.

The curse, she thought. It's going to make my hand fall right off. I'm never going to paint again. . . .

Goon spat on her palm and the pain died as though it had never been. With wondering eyes, Jilly watched the blackness dry up and begin to flake away. Goon gave her hand a shake and the blemish scattered to fall to the ground. Her hand was completely unmarked.

"But . . . the curse," she said. "The bounty on my head. What about Christy's story . . . ?"

"Your curse is knowledge," Goon said.

"But . . . ?"

He turned away to face the crowd, drum in hand. As Jilly made her careful descent back to where Meran was waiting for her, Goon tapped his fingers against the head of the drum. An eerie rhythm started up—a real rhythm. When the skookin musicians began to play, they held their instruments properly and called up a sweet stately music to march across the back of the rhythm. It was a rich tapestry of sound, as different from Meran's solo flute as sunlight is from twilight, but it held its own power. Its own magic.

Goon led the playing with the rhythm he called up from the stone drum, led the music as though he'd always led it.

"He's really the king, isn't he?" Jilly whispered to her companion. Meran nodded.

"So then what was he doing working for Bramley?"

"I don't know," Meran replied. "I suppose a king—or a king's son—can do pretty well what he wants just so long as he comes back here once a moon to fulfill his obligation as ruler."

"Do you think he'll go back to work for Bramley?"

"I know he will," Meran replied.

Jilly looked out at the crowd of skookin. They didn't seem at all threatening anymore. They just looked like little men—comical, with their tubby bodies and round heads and their little broomstick limbs—but men all the same. She listened to the music, felt its trueness and had to ask Meran why it didn't hurt them.

"Because it's their truth," Meran replied.

"But truth's just truth," Jilly protested. "Something's either true or it's not."

Meran just put her arm around Jilly's shoulder. A touch of a smile came to the corners of her mouth.

"It's time we went home," she said.

"I got off pretty lightly, didn't I?" Jilly said as they started back the way they'd come. "I mean, with the curse and all."

"Knowledge can be a terrible burden," Meran replied. "It's what some believe cast Adam and Eve from Eden."

"But that was a good thing, wasn't it?"

Meran nodded. "I think so. But it brought pain with it—pain we still feel to this day."

"I suppose."

"Come on," Meran said, as Jilly lagged a little to look back at the park.

Jilly quickened her step, but she carried the scene away with her. Goon and the stone drum. The crowd of skookin. The flickering light of their fires as it cast shadows over the Old City buildings.

And the music played on.

Professor Dapple had listened patiently to the story he'd been told, managing to keep from interrupting through at least half of the telling. Leaning back in his chair when it was done, he took off his glasses and began to needlessly polish them.

"It's going to be very good," he said finally.

Christy Riddell grinned from the club chair where he was sitting.

"But Jilly's not going to like it," Bramley went on. "You know how she feels about your stories."

"But she's the one who told me this one," Christy said.

Bramley rearranged his features to give the impression that he'd known this all along.

"Doesn't seem like much of a curse," he said, changing tack.

Christy raised his eyebrows. "What? To know that it's all real? To have to seriously consider every time she hears about some seemingly preposterous thing, that it might very well be true? To have to keep on guard with what she says so that people won't think she's gone off the deep end?"

"Is that how people look at us?" Bramley asked.

"What do you think?" Christy replied with a laugh.

Bramley humphed. He fidgeted with the papers on his desk, making more of a mess of them, rather than less.

"But Goon," he said, finally coming to the heart of what bothered him with what he'd been told. "It's like some retelling of 'The King of the Cats,' isn't it? Are you really going to put that bit in?"

Christy nodded. "It's part of the story."

"I can't see Goon as a king of anything," Bramley said. "And if he *is* a king, then what's he doing still working for me?"

"Which do you think would be better," Christy asked. "To be a king below, or a man above?"

Bramley didn't have an answer for that.

≫≡ TIMESKIP ≡≪

Every time it rains a ghost comes walking.

He goes up by the stately old houses that line Stanton Street, down Henratty Lane to where it leads into the narrow streets and crowded backalleys of Crowsea, and then back up Stanton again in an unvarying routine.

He wears a worn tweed suit—mostly browns and greys with a faint rosy touch of heather. A shapeless cap presses down his brown curls. His features give no true indication of his age, while his eyes are both innocent and wise. His face gleams in the rain, slick and wet as that of a living person. When he reaches the streetlamp in front of the old Hamill estate, he wipes his eyes with a brown hand. Then he fades away.

Samantha Rey knew it was true because she'd seen him.

More than once.

She saw him every time it rained.

"So, have you asked her out yet?" Jilly wanted to know.

We were sitting on a park bench, feeding pigeons the leftover crusts from our lunches. Jilly had worked with me at the post office, that Christmas they hired outside staff instead of letting the regular employees work the overtime, and we'd been friends ever since. These days she worked three nights a week as a waitress, while I made what I could busking on the Market with my father's old Czech fiddle.

Jilly was slender, with a thick tangle of brown hair and pale blue eyes, electric as sapphires. She had a penchant for loose clothing and fingerless gloves when she wasn't waitressing. There were times, when I met her on the streets in the evening, that I mistook her for a bag lady: skulking in an alleyway, gaze alternating between the sketchbook held in one hand and the faces of the people on the streets as they walked by. She had more sketches of me playing my fiddle than had any right to exist.

"She's never going to know how you feel until you talk to her about it," Jilly went on when I didn't answer.

"I know."

I'll make no bones about it: I was putting the make on Sam Rey and had been ever since she'd started to work at Gypsy Records half a year ago. I never much went in for the blonde California beach girl type, but Sam had a look all her own. She had some indefinable quality that went beyond her basic cheerleader appearance. Right. I can hear you already. Rationalizations of the North American libido. But it was true. I didn't just want Sam in my bed; I wanted to know we were going to have a future together. I wanted to grow old with her. I wanted to build up a lifetime of shared memories.

About the most Sam knew about all this was that I hung around and talked to her a lot at the record store.

"Look," Jilly said. "Just because she's pretty, doesn't mean she's having a perfect life or anything. Most guys look at someone like her and they won't even approach her because they're sure she's got men coming out of her ears. Well, it doesn't always work that way. For instance—" she touched her breastbone with a narrow hand and smiled "—consider yours truly."

I looked at her long fingers. Paint had dried under her nails.

"You've started a new canvas," I said.

"And you're changing the subject," she replied. "Come on, Geordie. What's the big deal? The most she can say is no."

"Well, yeah. But . . ."

"She intimidates you, doesn't she?"

I shook my head. "I talk to her all the time."

"Right. And that's why I've got to listen to your constant mooning over her." She gave me a sudden considering look, then grinned. "I'll tell you what, Geordie, me lad. Here's the bottom line: I'll give you twenty-four hours to ask her out. If you haven't got it together by then, I'll talk to her myself."

"Don't even joke about it."

"Twenty-four hours," Jilly said firmly. She looked at the chocolate-chip cookie in my hand. "Are you eating that?" she added in that certain tone of voice of hers that plainly said, all previous topics of conversation have been dealt with and completed. We are now changing topics.

So we did. But all the while we talked, I thought about going into the record store and asking Sam out, because if I didn't, Jilly would do it for me. Whatever else she might be, Jilly wasn't shy. Having her go in to plead my case would be as bad as having my mother do it for me. I'd never been able to show my face in there again.

Gypsy Records is on Williamson Street, one of the city's main arteries. It begins as Highway 14 outside the city, lined with a sprawl of fast food outlets, malls and warehouses. On its way downtown, it begins to replace the commercial properties with ever-increasing handfuls of residential blocks until it reaches the downtown core where shops and low-rise apartments mingle in gossiping crowds.

The store gets its name from John Butler, a short round-bellied man without a smidgen of Romany blood, who began his business out of the back of a hand-drawn cart that gypsied its way through the city's streets for years, always keeping just one step ahead of the municipal licensing board's agents. While it carries the usual best-sellers, the lifeblood of its sales are more obscure titles—imports and albums published by independent record labels. Albums, singles and compact discs of punk, traditional folk, jazz, heavy metal and alternative music line its shelves. Barring Sam, most of those who work there would look just as at home in the fashion pages of the most current British alternative fashion magazines.

Sam was wearing a blue cotton dress today, embroidered with silver threads. Her blonde hair was cut in a short shag on the top, hanging down past her shoulders at the back and sides. She was dealing with a defect when I came in. I don't know if the record in question worked or not, but the man returning it was definitely defective.

"It sounds like there's a radio broadcast right in the middle of the song," he was saying as he tapped the cover of the Pink Floyd album on the counter between them.

"It's supposed to be there," Sam explained. "It's *part* of the song." The tone of her voice told me that this conversation was going into its twelfth round or so.

"Well, I don't like it," the man told her. "When I buy an album of music, I expect to get just music on it."

"You still can't return it."

I worked in a record shop one Christmas—two years before the post office job. The best defect I got was from someone returning an in-concert album by Marcel Marceau. Each side had thirty minutes of silence, with applause at the end—I kid you not.

I browsed through the Celtic records while I waited for Sam to finish with her customer. I couldn't afford any of them, but I liked to see what was new. Blasting out of the store's speakers was the new Beastie Boys album. It sounded like a cross between heavy metal and bad rap and was about as appealing as being hit by a car. You couldn't deny its energy, though.

By the time Sam was free I'd located five records I would have bought in more flush times. Leaving them in the bin, I drifted over to the front cash just as the Beastie Boys' last cut ended. Sam replaced them with a tape of New Age piano music.

"What's the new Oyster Band like?" I asked.

Sam smiled. "It's terrific. My favorite cut's 'The Old Dance.' It's sort of an allegory based on Adam and Eve and the serpent that's got a great hook in the chorus. Telfer's fiddling just sort of skips ahead, pulling the rest of the song along."

That's what I like about alternative record stores like Gypsy's— the people working in them actually know something about what they're selling.

"Have you got an open copy?" I asked.

She nodded and turned to the bin of opened records behind her to find it. With her back to me, I couldn't get lost in those deep blue eyes of hers. I seized my opportunity and plunged ahead.

"Areyouworkingtonight — wouldyouliketogooutwithmesome-where?"

I'd meant to be cool about it, except the words all blurred together as they left my throat. I could feel the flush start up the back of my neck as she turned and looked back at me with those baby blues.

"Say what?" she asked.

Before my throat closed up on me completely, I tried again, keeping it short. "Do you want to go out with me tonight?"

Standing there with the Oyster Band album in her hand, I thought she'd never looked better. Especially when she said, "I thought you'd never ask."

* * *

I put in a couple of hours of busking that afternoon, down in Crowsea's Market, the fiddle humming under my chin to the jingling rhythm of the coins that passersby threw into the case lying open in front of me. I came away with twenty-six dollars and change—not the best of days, but enough to buy a halfway decent dinner and a few beers.

I picked up Sam after she finished work and we ate at The Monkey Woman's Nest, a Mexican restaurant on Williamson just a couple of blocks down from Gypsy's. I still don't know how the place got its name. Ernestina Verdad, the Mexican woman who owns the place, looks like a showgirl and not one of her waitresses is even vaguely simian in appearance.

It started to rain as we were finishing our second beer, turning Williamson Street slick with neon reflections. Sam got a funny look on her face as she watched the rain through the window. Then she turned to me.

"Do you believe in ghosts?" she asked.

The serious look in her eyes stopped the half-assed joke that two beers brewed in the carbonated swirl of my mind. I never could hold my alcohol. I wasn't drunk, but I had a buzz on.

"I don't think so," I said carefully. "At least I've never seriously stopped to think about it."

"Come on," she said, getting up from the table. "I want to show you something."

I let her lead me out into the rain, though I didn't let her pay anything towards the meal. Tonight was my treat. Next time I'd be happy to let her do the honors.

"Every time it rains," she said, "a ghost comes walking down my street. . . ."

She told me the story as we walked down into Crowsea. The rain was light and I was enjoying it, swinging my fiddle case in my right hand, Sam hanging onto my left as though she'd always walked there. I felt like I was on top of the world, listening to her talk, feeling the pressure of her arm, the bump of her hip against mine.

She had an apartment on the third floor of an old brick and frame building on Stanton Street. It had a front porch that ran the length of the house, dormer windows—two in the front and back, one on each side—and a sloped mansard roof. We stood on the porch, out of the rain, which was coming down harder now. An orange and white tom was sleeping on the cushion of a white wicker chair by the door. He twitched a torn ear as we shared his shelter, but didn't bother to open his eyes. I could smell the mint that was growing up alongside the porch steps, sharp in the wet air.

Sam pointed down the street to where the yellow glare of a streetlamp glistened on the rain-slicked cobblestone walk that led to the Hamill estate. The Hamill house itself was separated from the street by a low wall and a dark expanse of lawn, bordered by the spreading boughs of huge oak trees.

"Watch the street," she said. "Just under the streetlight."

I looked, but I didn't see anything. The wind gusted suddenly, driving the rain in hard sheets along Stanton Street, and for a moment we lost all visibility. When it cleared, he was standing there, Sam's ghost, just like she'd told me. As he started down the street, Sam gave my arm a tug. I stowed my fiddle case under the tom's wicker chair, and we followed the ghost down Henratty Lane.

By the time he returned to the streetlight in front of the Hamill estate, I was ready to argue that Sam was mistaken. There was nothing in the least bit ghostly about the man we were following. When he returned up Henratty Lane, we had to duck into a doorway to let him pass. He never looked at us, but I could see the rain hitting him. I could hear the sound of his shoes on the pavement. He had to have come out of the walk that led up to the estate's house, at the same time as that sudden gust of wind-driven rain. It had been a simple coincidence, nothing more. But when he returned to the streetlight, he lifted a hand to wipe his face, and then he was gone. He just winked out of existence. There was no wind. No gust of rain. No place he could have gone. A ghost.

"Jesus," I said softly as I walked over to the pool of light cast by the streetlamp. There was nothing to see. But there had been a man there. I was sure of that much.

"We're soaked," Sam said. "Come on up to my place and I'll make us some coffee."

The coffee was great and the company was better. Sam had a small clothes drier in her kitchen. I sat in the living room in an oversized housecoat while my clothes tumbled and turned, the machine creating a vibration in the floorboards that I'm sure Sam's downstairs neighbors must have just loved. Sam had changed into a dark blue sweatsuit—she looked best in blue, I decided—and dried her hair while she was making the coffee. I'd prowled around her living room while she did, admiring her books, her huge record collection, her sound system, and the mantel above a working fireplace that was crammed with knickknacks.

All her furniture was the kind made for comfort—they crouched like sleeping animals about the room. Fat sofa in front of the fireplace, an old pair of matching easy chairs by the window. The bookcases, record cabinet, side tables and trim were all natural wood, polished to a shine with furniture oil.

We talked about a lot of things, sitting on the sofa, drinking our coffees, but mostly we talked about the ghost.

"Have you ever approached him?" I asked at one point.

Sam shook her head. "No. I just watch him walk. I've never even talked about him to anybody else." That made me feel good. "You know, I can't help but feel that he's waiting for something, or someone. Isn't that the way it usually works in ghost stories?"

"This isn't a ghost story," I said.

"But we didn't imagine it, did we? Not both of us at the same time?"

"I don't know."

But I knew someone who probably did. Jilly. She was into every sort of strange happening, taking all kinds of odd things seriously. I could remember her telling me that Bramley Dapple—one of her professors at Butler U. and a friend of my brother's—was really a wizard who had a brown-skinned goblin for a valet, but the best thing I remembered about her was her talking about that scene in Disney's *101 Dalmatians,* where the dogs are all howling to send a message across town, one dog sending it out, another picking it up and passing it along, all the way across town and out into the country.

"That's how they do it," she'd said. "Just like that."

And if you walked with her at night and a dog started to howl—if no other dog picked it up, then she'd pass it on. She could mimic any dog's bark or howl so perfectly it was uncanny. It could also be embarrassing, because she didn't care who was around or what kinds of looks she got. It was the message that had to be passed on that was important.

When I told Sam about Jilly, she smiled, but there wasn't any mockery in her smile. Emboldened, I related the ultimatum that Jilly had given me this afternoon.

Sam laughed aloud. "Jilly sounds like my kind of person," she said. "I'd like to meet her."

When it started to get late, I collected my clothes and changed in the bathroom. I didn't want to start anything, not yet, not this soon, and I knew that Sam felt the same way, though neither of us had spoken of it. She kissed me at the door, a long warm kiss that had me buzzing again.

"Come see me tomorrow?" she asked. "At the store?"

"Just try and keep me away," I replied.

I gave the old tom on the porch a pat and whistled all the way home to my own place on the other side of Crowsea.

Jilly's studio was its usual organized mess. It was an open loft-like affair that occupied half of the second floor of a four-story brown brick building on Yoors Street where Foxville's low rentals mingle with Crowsea's shops and older houses. One half of the studio was taken up with a Murphy bed that was never folded back into the wall, a pair of battered sofas, a small kitchenette, storage cabinets and a tiny box-like bathroom obviously designed with dwarves in mind.

Her easel stood in the other half of the studio, by the window where it could catch the morning sun. All around it were stacks of sketchbooks, newspapers, unused canvases and art books. Finished canvases leaned face front, five to ten deep, against the back wall. Tubes of paint covered the tops of old wooden orange crates—the new ones lying in neat piles like logs by a fireplace, the used ones in a haphazard scatter, closer to hand. Brushes sat waiting to be used in mason jars. Others were in liquid waiting to be cleaned. Still more, their brushes stiff with dried paint, lay here and there on the floor like discarded pick-up-sticks.

The room smelled of oil paint and turpentine. In the corner furthest from the window was a life-sized fabric mâché sculpture of an artist at work that bore an uncanny likeness to Jilly herself, complete with Walkman, one paintbrush in hand, another sticking out of its mouth. When I got there that morning, Jilly was at her new canvas, face scrunched up as she concentrated. There was already paint in her hair. On the windowsill behind her a small ghetto blaster was playing a Bach fugue, the piano notes spilling across the room like a light rain. Jilly looked up as I came in, a frown changing liquidly into a smile as she took in the foolish look on my face.

"I should have thought of this weeks ago," she said. "You look like the cat who finally caught the mouse. Did you have a good time?"

"The best."

Leaving my fiddle by the door, I moved around behind her so that I could see what she was working on. Sketched out on the white canvas was a Crowsea street scene. I recognized the corner—McKennitt and Lee. I'd played there from time to time, mostly in the spring. Lately a rockabilly band called the Broken Hearts had taken over the spot.

"Well?" Jilly prompted.

"Well what?"

"Aren't you going to give me all the lovely sordid details?"

I nodded at the painting. She'd already started to work in the background with oils.

"Are you putting in the Hearts?" I asked.

Jilly jabbed at me with her paint brush, leaving a smudge the color of a Crowsea red brick tenement on my jean jacket.

"I'll thump you if you don't spill it all, Geordie, me lad. Just watch if I don't."

She was liable to do just that, so I sat down on the ledge behind her and talked while she painted. We shared a pot of her cowboy coffee, which was what Jilly called the foul brew she made from used coffee grounds. I took two spoons of sugar to my usual one, just to cut back on the bitter taste it left in my throat. Still, beggars couldn't be choosers. That morning I didn't even have used coffee grounds at my own place.

"I like ghost stories," she said when I was finished telling her about my evening. She'd finished roughing out the buildings by now and bent closer to the canvas to start working on some of the finer details before she lost the last of the morning light.

"Was it real?" I asked.

"That depends. Bramley says—"

"I know, I know," I said, breaking in.

If it wasn't Jilly telling me some weird story about him, it was my brother. What Jilly liked best about him was his theory of consensual reality, the idea that things exist *because* we agree that they exist.

"But think about it," Jilly went on. "Sam sees a ghost—maybe because she expects to see one—and you see the same ghost because you care about her, so you're willing to agree that there's one there where she says it will be."

"Say it's not that, then what could it be?"

"Any number of things. A timeslip—a bit of the past slipping into the present. It could be a restless spirit with unfinished business. From what you say Sam's told you, though, I'd guess that it's a case of a timeskip."

She turned to grin at me, which let me know that the word was one of her own coining. I gave her a dutifully admiring look, then asked, "A what?"

"A timeskip. It's like a broken record, you know? It just keeps playing the same bit over and over again, only unlike the record it needs something specific to cue it in."

"Like rain."

"Exactly." She gave me a sudden sharp look. "This isn't for one of your brother's stories, is it?"

My brother Christy collects odd tales just like Jilly does, only he writes them down. I've heard some grand arguments between the two of them comparing the superior qualities of the oral versus written traditions.

"I haven't seen Christy in weeks," I said.

"All right, then."

"So how do you go about handling this sort of thing?" I asked. "Sam thinks he's waiting for something."

Jilly nodded. "For someone to lift the tone arm of time." At the pained look on my face, she added, "Well, have you got a better analogy?"

I admitted that I didn't. "But how do you do that? Do you just go over and talk to him, or grab him, or what?"

"Any and all might work. But you have to be careful about that kind of thing."

"How so?"

"Well," Jilly said, turning from the canvas to give me a serious look, "sometimes a ghost like that can drag you back to whenever it is that he's from and you'll be trapped in his time. Or you might end up taking his place in the timeskip."

"Lovely."

"Isn't it?" She went back to the painting. "What color's that sign Duffy has over his shop on McKennitt?" she asked.

I closed my eyes, trying to picture it, but all I could see was the face of last night's ghost, wet with rain.

It didn't rain again for a couple of weeks. They were good weeks. Sam and I spent the evenings and weekends together. We went out a few times, twice with Jilly, once with a couple of Sam's friends. Jilly and Sam got along just as well as I'd thought they would—and why shouldn't they? They were both special people. I should know.

The morning it did rain it was Sam's day off from Gypsy's. The previous night was the first I'd stayed over all night. The first we made love. Waking up in the morning with her warm beside me was everything I thought it would be. She was sleepy-eyed and smiling, more than willing to nestle deep under the comforter while I saw about getting some coffee together.

When the rain started, we took our mugs into the living room and watched the street in front of the Hamill estate. A woman came by walking one of those fat white bull terriers that look like they're more pig than dog. The terrier didn't seem to mind the rain but the woman at the other end of the leash was less than pleased. She alternated between frowning at the clouds and tugging him along. About five minutes after the pair had rounded the corner, our ghost showed up, just winking into existence out of nowhere. Or out of a slip in time. One of Jilly's timeskips.

We watched him go through his routine. When he reached the streetlight and vanished again, Sam leaned her head against my shoulder. We were cozied up together in one of the big comfy chairs, feet on the windowsill.

"We should do something for him," she said.

"Remember what Jilly said," I reminded her.

Sam nodded. "But I don't think that he's out to hurt anybody. It's not like he's calling out to us or anything. He's just there, going through the same moves, time after time. The next time it rains . . ."

"What're we going to do?"

Sam shrugged. "Talk to him, maybe?"

I didn't see how that could cause any harm. Truth to tell, I was feeling sorry for the poor bugger myself.

"Why not?" I said.

About then Sam's hands got busy and I quickly lost interest in the ghost. I started to get up, but Sam held me down in the chair.

"Where are you going?" she asked.

"Well, I thought the bed would be more . . ."

"We've never done it in a chair before."

"There's a lot of places we haven't done it yet," I said.

Those deep blue eyes of hers, about five inches from my own, just about swallowed me.

"We've got all the time in the world," she said.

It's funny how you remember things like that later.

The next time it rained, Jilly was with us. The three of us were walking home from Your Second Home, a sleazy bar on the other side of Foxville where the band of a friend of Sam's was playing. None of us looked quite right for the bar when we walked in. Sam was still the perennial California beach girl, all blonde and curves in a pair of tight jeans and a white T-shirt, with a faded jean-jacket overtop. Jilly and I looked like the scruffs we were.

The bar was a place for serious drinking during the day, serving mostly unemployed blue-collar workers spending their welfare checks on a few hours of forgetfulness. By the time the band started around nine, though, the clientele underwent a drastic transformation. Scattered here and there through the crowd was the odd individual who still dressed for volume—all the colors turned up loud—but mostly we were outnumbered thirty-to-one by spike-haired punks in their black leathers and blue jeans. It was like being on the inside of a bruise.

The band was called the Wang Boys and ended up being pretty good—especially on their original numbers—if a bit loud. My ears were ringing when we finally left the place sometime after midnight. We were having a good time on the walk home. Jilly was in rare form, half-dancing on the street around us, singing the band's closing number, making up the words, turning the piece into a punk gospel number. She kept bouncing around in front of us, skipping backwards as she tried to get us to sing along.

The rain started as a thin drizzle as were making our way through Crowsea's narrow streets. Sam's fingers tightened on my arm and Jilly stopped fooling around as we stepped into Henratty Lane, the rain coming down in earnest now. The ghost was just turning in the far end of the lane.

"Geordie," Sam said, her fingers tightening more.

I nodded. We brushed by Jilly and stepped up our pace, aiming to connect with the ghost before he made his turn and started back towards Stanton Street.

"This is not a good idea," Jilly warned us, hurrying to catch up. But by then it was too late.

We were right in front of the ghost. I could tell he didn't see Sam or me and I wanted to get out of his way before he walked right through us—I didn't relish the thought of having a ghost or a timeskip or whatever he was going through me. But Sam wouldn't move. She put out her hand, and as her fingers brushed the wet tweed of his jacket, everything changed.

The sense of vertigo was strong. Henratty Lane blurred. I had the feeling of time flipping by like the pages of a calendar in an old movie, except each page was a year, not a day. The sounds of the city around us—sounds we weren't normally aware of—were noticeable by their sudden absence. The ghost jumped at Sam's touch. There was a bewildered look in his eyes and he backed away. That sensation of vertigo and blurring returned until Sam caught him by the arm and everything settled down again. Quiet, except for the rain and a far-off voice that seemed to be calling my name.

"Don't be frightened," Sam said, keeping her grip on the ghost's arm. "We want to help you."

"You should not be here," he replied. His voice was stiff and a little formal. "You were only a dream—nothing more. Dreams are to be savoured and remembered, not walking the streets."

Underlying their voices I could still hear the faint sound of my own name being called. I tried to ignore it, concentrating on the ghost and our surroundings. The lane was clearer than I remembered it—no trash littered against the walls, no graffiti scrawled across the bricks. It seemed darker, too. It was almost possible to believe that we'd been pulled back into the past by the touch of the ghost.

I started to get nervous then, remembering what Jilly had told us. Into the past. What if we *were* in the past and we couldn't get out again? What if we got trapped in the same timeskip as the ghost and were doomed to follow his routine each time it rained?

Sam and the ghost were still talking but I could hardly hear what they were saying. I was thinking of Jilly. We'd brushed by her to reach the ghost, but she'd been right behind us. Yet when I looked back, there was no one there. I remembered that sound of my name, calling faintly across some great distance. I listened now, but heard only a vague unrecognizable sound. It took me long moments to realize that it was a dog barking.

I turned to Sam, tried to concentrate on what she was saying to the ghost. She was starting to pull away from him, but now it was his hand that held her arm. As I reached forward to pull her loose, the barking suddenly grew in volume—not one dog's voice, but those of hundreds, echoing across the years that separated us from our own time. Each year caught and sent on its own dog's voice, the sound building into a cacophonous chorus of yelps and barks and howls.

The ghost gave Sam's arm a sharp tug and I lost my grip on her, stumbling as the vertigo hit me again. I fell through the sound of all those barking dogs, through the blurring years, until I dropped to my knees on the wet cobblestones, my hands reaching for Sam. But Sam wasn't there.

"Geordie?"

It was Jilly, kneeling by my side, hand on my shoulder. She took my chin and turned my face to hers, but I pulled free.

"Sam!" I cried.

A gust of wind drove rain into my face, blinding me, but not before I saw that the lane was truly empty except for Jilly and me. Jilly, who'd mimicked the barking of dogs to draw us back through time. But only I'd returned. Sam and the ghost were both gone.

"Oh, Geordie," Jilly murmured as she held me close. "I'm so sorry."

★   ★   ★

I don't know if the ghost was ever seen again, but I saw Sam one more time after that night. I was with Jilly in Moore's Antiques in Lower Crowsea, flipping through a stack of old sepia-toned photographs, when a group shot of a family on their front porch stopped me cold. There, among the somber faces, was Sam. She looked different. Her hair was drawn back in a tight bun and she wore a plain unbecoming dark dress, but it was Sam all right. I turned the photograph over and read the photographer's date on the back. 1912.

Something of what I was feeling must have shown on my face, for Jilly came over from a basket of old earrings that she was looking through.

"What's the matter, Geordie, me lad?" she asked.

Then she saw the photograph in my hand. She had no trouble recognizing Sam either. I didn't have any money that day, but Jilly bought the picture and gave it to me. I keep it in my fiddle case.

I grow older each year, building up a lifetime of memories, only I've no Sam to share them with. But often when it rains, I go down to Stanton Street and stand under the streetlight in front of the old Hamill estate. One day I know she'll be waiting there for me.

⋟ FREEWHEELING ⋟

1

He stood on the rain-slick street, a pale fire burning behind his eyes. Nerve ends tingling, he watched them go—a slow parade of riderless bicycles.

Ten-speeds and mountain bikes. Domesticated, urban. So inbred that all they were was spoked wheels and emaciated frames, mere skeletons of what their genetic ancestors had been. They had never known freedom, never known joy; only the weight of serious riders in slick, leather-seated shorts, pedaling determinedly with their cycling shoes strapped to the pedals, heads encased in crash helmets, fingerless gloves on the hands gripping the handles tightly.

He smiled and watched them go. Down the wet street, wheels throwing up arcs of fine spray, metal frames glistening in the streetlights, reflector lights winking red.

The rain had plastered his hair slick against his head, his clothes were sodden, but he paid no attention to personal discomfort. He thought instead of that fat-wheeled aboriginal one-speed that led them now. The maverick who'd come from who knows where to pilot his domesticated brothers and sisters away.

For a night's freedom. Perhaps for always.

The last of them were rounding the corner now. He lifted his right hand to wave goodbye. His left hand hung down by his leg, still holding the heavy-duty wire cutters by one handle, the black rubber grip making a ribbed pattern on the palm of his hand. By fences and on porches, up and down the street, locks had been cut, chains lay discarded, bicycles ran free.

He heard a siren approaching. Lifting his head, he licked the rain drops from his lips. Water got in his eyes, gathering in their corners. He squinted, enamored by the kaleidoscoping spray of lights this caused to appear behind his eyelids. There were omens in lights, he knew. And in the night sky, with its scattershot sweep of stars. So many lights . . . There were secrets waiting to unfold there, mysteries that required a voice to be freed.

Like the bicycles were freed by their maverick brother.

He could be that voice, if he only knew what to sing.

He was still watching the sky for signs when the police finally arrived.

"Let me go, boys, let me go. . . ."

The new Pogues album *If I Should Fall From Grace With God* was on the turntable. The title cut leaked from the sound system's speakers, one of which sat on a crate crowded with half-used paint tubes and tins of turpentine, the other perched on the windowsill, commanding a view of rainswept Yoors Street one floor below. The song was jauntier than one might expect from its subject matter while Shane MacGowan's voice was as rough as ever, chewing the words and spitting them out, rather than singing them.

It was an angry voice, Jilly decided as she hummed softly along with the chorus. Even when it sang a tender song. But what could you expect from a group that had originally named itself Pogue Mahone—Irish Gaelic for "Kiss my ass"?

Angry and brash and vulgar. The band was all of that. But they were honest, too—painfully so, at times—and that was what brought Jilly back to their music, time and again. Because sometimes things just had to be said.

"I don't get this stuff," Sue remarked.

She'd been frowning over the lyrics that were printed on the album's inner sleeve. Leaning her head against the patched backrest of one of Jilly's two old sofas, she set the sleeve aside.

"I mean, music's supposed to make you feel good, isn't it?" she went on.

Jilly shook her head. "It's supposed to make you feel *something*—happy, sad, angry, whatever—just so long as it doesn't leave you brain-dead the way most Top Forty does. For me, music needs meaning to be worth my time—preferably something more than 'I want your body, babe,' if you know what I mean."

"You're beginning to develop a snooty attitude, Jilly."

"*Me?* To laugh, dahling."

Susan Ashworth was Jilly's uptown friend, as urbane as Jilly was scruffy. Sue's blonde hair was straight, hanging to just below her shoulders, where Jilly's was a riot of brown curls, made manageable tonight only by a clip that drew it all up to the top of her head before letting it fall free in the shape of something that resembled nothing so much as a disenchanted Mohawk. They were both in their twenties, slender and blue-eyed—the latter expected in a blonde; the electric blue of Jilly's eyes gave her, with her darker skin, a look of continual startlement. Where Sue wore just the right amount of makeup, Jilly could usually be counted on having a smudge of charcoal somewhere on her face and dried oil paint under her nails.

Sue worked for the city as an architect; she lived uptown and her parents were from the Beaches, where it seemed you needed a permit just to be out on the sidewalks after eight in the evening—or at least that was the impression that the police patrols left when they stopped strangers to check their ID. She always had that upscale look of one who was just about to step out to a restaurant for cocktails and dinner.

Jilly's first love was art of a freer style than designing municipal necessities, but she usually paid her rent by waitressing and other odd jobs. She tended to wear baggy clothes—like the oversized white T-shirt and blue poplin lace-front pants she had on tonight—and always had a sketchbook close at hand.

Tonight it was on her lap as she sat propped up on her Murphy bed, toes in their ballet slippers tapping against one another in time to the music. The Pogues were playing an instrumental now—"Metropolis"—which sounded like a cross between a Celtic fiddle tune and the old "Dragnet" theme.

"They're really not for me," Sue went on. "I mean if the guy could sing, maybe, but—"

"It's the feeling that he puts into his voice that's important," Jilly said. "But this is an instrumental. He's not even—"

"Supposed to be singing. I know. Only—"

"If you'd just—"

The jangling of the phone sliced through their discussion. Because she was closer—and knew that Jilly would claim some old war wound or any excuse not to get up, now that she was lying down—Sue answered it. She listened for a long moment, an odd expression on her face, then slowly cradled the receiver.

"Wrong number?"

Sue shook her head. "No. It was someone named . . . uh, Zinc? He said that he's been captured by two Elvis Presleys disguised as police officers and would you please come and explain to them that he wasn't stealing bikes, he was just setting them free. Then he hung up."

"Oh, shit!" Jilly stuffed her sketchbook into her shoulderbag and got up.

"This makes sense to you?"

"Zinc's one of the street kids."

Sue rolled her eyes, but she got up as well. "Want me to bring my checkbook?"

"What for?"

"Bail. It's what you have to put up to spring somebody from jail. Don't you *ever* watch TV?"

Jilly shook her head. "What? And let the aliens monitor my brainwaves?"

"What scares me," Sue muttered as they left the loft and started down the stairs, "is that sometimes I don't think you're kidding."

"Who says I am?" Jilly said.

Sue shook her head. "I'm going to pretend I didn't hear that."

Jilly knew people from all over the city, in all walks of life. Socialites and bag ladies. Street kids and university profs. Nobody was too poor, or conversely, too rich for her to strike up a conversation with, no matter where they happened to meet, or under what circumstances. She'd met Detective Lou Fucceri, now of the Crowsea Precinct's General Investigations squad, when he was still a patrolman, walking the Stanton Street Combat Zone beat. He was the reason she'd survived the streets to become an artist instead of just one more statistic to add to all those others who hadn't been so lucky.

"Is it true?" Sue wanted to know as soon as the desk sergeant showed them into Lou's office. "The way you guys met?" Jilly had told her that she'd tried to take his picture one night and he'd arrested her for soliciting.

"You mean UFO-spotting in Butler U. Park?" he replied.

Sue sighed. "I should've known. I must be the only person who's maintained her sanity after meeting Jilly."

She sat down on one of the two wooden chairs that faced Lou's desk in the small cubicle that passed for his office. There was room for a bookcase behind him, crowded with law books and file folders, and a brass coat rack from which hung a lightweight sports jacket. Lou sat at the desk, white shirt sleeves rolled halfway up to his elbows, top collar undone, black tie hanging loose.

His Italian heritage was very much present in the Mediterranean cast to his complexion, his dark brooding eyes and darker hair. As Jilly sat down in the chair Sue had left for her, he shook a cigarette free from a crumpled pack that he dug out from under the litter of files on his desk. He offered the cigarettes around, tossing the pack back down on the desk and lighting his own when there were no takers.

Jilly pulled her chair closer to the desk. "What did he do, Lou? Sue took the call, but I don't know if she got the message right."

"I *can* take a message," Sue began, but Jilly waved a hand in her direction. She wasn't in the mood for banter just now.

Lou blew a stream of blue-grey smoke towards the ceiling. "We've been having a lot of trouble with a bicycle theft ring operating in the city," he said. "They've hit the Beaches, which was bad enough, though with all the Mercedes and BMWs out there, I doubt they're going to miss their bikes a lot. But rich people like to complain, and now the gang's moved their operations into Crowsea."

Jilly nodded. "Where for a lot of people, a bicycle's the only way they *can* get around."

"You got it."

"So what does that have to do with Zinc?"

"The patrol car that picked him up found him standing in the middle of the street with a pair of heavy-duty wire cutters in his hand. The street'd been cleaned right out, Jilly. There wasn't a bike left on the block—just the cut locks and chains left behind."

"So where are the bikes?"

Lou shrugged. "Who knows. Probably in a Foxville chopshop having their serial numbers changed. Jilly, you've got to get Zinc to tell us who he was working with. Christ, they took off, leaving him to hold the bag. He doesn't owe them a thing now."

Jilly shook her head slowly. "This doesn't make any sense. Zinc's not the criminal kind."

"I'll tell you what doesn't make any sense," Lou said. "The kid himself. He's heading straight for the loonie bin with all his talk about Elvis clones and Venusian thought machines and feral fuck—" He glanced at Sue and covered up the profanity with a cough. "Feral bicycles leading the domesticated ones away."

"He said that?"

Lou nodded. "That's why he was clipping the locks—to set the bikes free so that they could follow their, and I quote, 'spiritual leader, home to the place of mystery.' "

"That's a new one," Jilly said.

"You're having me on—right?" Lou said. "That's all you can say? It's a new one? The Elvis clones are old hat now? Christ on a comet. Would you give me a break? Just get the kid to roll over and I'll make sure things go easy for him."

"Christ on a comet?" Sue repeated softly.

"C'mon, Lou," Jilly said. "How can I make Zinc tell you something he doesn't know? Maybe he found those wire cutters on the street—just before the patrol car came. For all we know he could—"

"He *said* he cut the locks."

The air went out of Jilly. "Right," she said. She slouched in her chair. "I forgot you'd said that."

"Maybe the bikes really did just go off on their own," Sue said.

Lou gave her a weary look, but Jilly sat up straighter. "I wonder," she began.

"Oh, for God's sake," Sue said. "I was only joking."

"I know you were," Jilly said. "But I've seen enough odd things in this world that I won't say anything's impossible anymore."

"The police department doesn't see things quite the same way," Lou told Jilly. The dryness of his tone wasn't lost on her.

"I know."

"I want these bike thieves, Jilly."

"Are you arresting Zinc?"

Lou shook his head. "I've got nothing to hold him on except for circumstantial evidence."

"I thought you said he admitted to cutting the locks," Sue said.

Jilly shot her a quick fierce look that plainly said, Don't make waves when he's giving us what we came for.

Lou nodded. "Yeah. He admitted to that. He also admitted to knowing a hobo who was really a spy from Pluto and asked why the patrolmen had traded in their white Vegas suits for uniforms. He wanted to hear them sing 'Heartbreak Hotel.' For next of kin he put down Bigfoot."

"*Gigantopithecus blacki,*" Jilly said.

Lou looked at her. "What?"

"Some guy at Washington State University's given Bigfoot a Latin name now. *Giganto—*"

Lou cut her off. "That's what I thought you said." He turned back to Sue. "So you see, his admitting to cutting the locks isn't really going to amount to much. Not when a lawyer with half a brain can get him off without even having to work up a sweat."

"Does that mean he's free to go then?" Jilly asked.

Lou nodded. "Yeah. He can go. But keep him out of trouble, Jilly. He's in here again, and I'm sending him straight to the Zeb for psychiatric testing. And try to convince him to come clean on this—okay? It's not just for me, it's for him too. We break this case and find out he's involved, nobody's going to go easy on him. We don't give out rain checks."

"Not even for dinner?" Jilly asked brightly, happy now that she knew Zinc was getting out.

"What do you mean?"

Jilly grabbed a pencil and paper from his desk and scrawled "Jilly Coppercorn owes Hotshot Lou one dinner, restaurant of her choice," and passed it over to him.

"I think they call this a bribe," he said.

"I call it keeping in touch with your friends," Jilly replied and gave him a big grin.

Lou glanced at Sue and rolled his eyes.

"Don't look at me like that," she said. "I'm the sane one here."

"You wish," Jilly told her.

Lou heaved himself to his feet with exaggerated weariness. "C'mon, let's get your friend out of here before he decides to sue us because we don't have our coffee flown in from the Twilight Zone," he said as he led the way down to the holding cells.

Zinc had the look of a street kid about two days away from a good meal. His jeans, T-shirt, and cotton jacket were ragged, but clean; his hair was a badly mown lawn, with tufts standing up here and there like exclamation points. The pupils of his dark brown eyes seemed too large for someone who never did drugs. He was seventeen, but acted half his age.

The only home he had was a squat in Upper Foxville that he shared with a couple of performance artists, so that was where Jilly and Sue took him in Sue's Mazda. The living space he shared with the artists was on the upper story of a deserted tenement where someone had put together a makeshift loft by the simple method of removing all the walls, leaving a large empty area cluttered only by support pillars and the squatters' belongings.

Lucia and Ursula were there when they arrived, practicing one of their pieces to the accompaniment of a ghetto blaster pumping out a mixture of electronic music and the sound of breaking glass at a barely audible volume. Lucia was wrapped in plastic and lying on the floor, her black hair spread out in an arc around her head. Every few moments one of her limbs would twitch, the plastic wrap stretching tight against her skin with the movement. Ursula crouched beside the blaster, chanting a poem that consisted only of the line, "There are no patterns." She'd shaved her head since the last time Jilly had seen her.

"What am I doing here?" Sue asked softly. She made no effort to keep the look of astonishment from her features.

"Seeing how the other half lives," Jilly said as she led the way across the loft to where Zinc's junkyard of belongings took up a good third of the available space.

"But just look at this stuff," Sue said. "And how did he get that in here?"

She pointed to a Volkswagen bug that was sitting up on blocks, missing only its wheels and front hood. Scattered all around it was a hodgepodge of metal scraps, old furniture, boxes filled with wiring and God only knew what.

"Piece by piece," Jilly told her.

"And then he reassembled it here?"

Jilly nodded.

"Okay. I'll bite. Why?"

"Why don't you ask him?"

Jilly grinned as Sue quickly shook her head. During the entire trip from the precinct station, Zinc had carefully explained his theory of the world to her, how the planet Earth was actually an asylum for insane aliens, and that was why nothing made sense.

Zinc followed the pair of them across the room, stopping only long enough to greet his squat-mates. "Hi, Luce. Hi, Urse."

Lucia never looked at him.

"There are no patterns," Ursula said.

Zinc nodded thoughtfully.

"Maybe there's a pattern in that," Sue offered.

"Don't start," Jilly said. She turned to Zinc. "Are you going to be all right?"

"You should've seen them go, Jill," Zinc said. "All shiny and wet, just whizzing down the street, heading for the hills."

"I'm sure it was really something, but you've got to promise me to stay off the streets for awhile. Will you do that, Zinc? At least until they catch this gang of bike thieves?"

"But there weren't any thieves. It's like I told Elvis Two, they left on their own."

Sue gave him an odd look. "Elvis too?"

"Don't ask," Jilly said. She touched Zinc's arm. "Just stay in for awhile—okay? Let the bikes take off on their own."

"But I like to watch them go."

"Do it as a favor to me, would you?"

"I'll try."

Jilly gave him a quick smile. "Thanks. Is there anything you need? Do you need money for some food?"

Zinc shook his head. Jilly gave him a quick kiss on the cheek and tousled the exclamation point hair tufts sticking up from his head.

"I'll drop by to see you tomorrow, then—okay?" At his nod, Jilly started back across the room. "C'mon, Sue," she said when her companion paused beside the tape machine where Ursula was still chanting.

"So what about this stock market stuff?" she asked the poet.

"There are no patterns," Ursula said.

"That's what I thought," Sue said, but then Jilly was tugging her arm.

"Couldn't resist, could you?" Jilly said.

Sue just grinned.

"Why do you humor him?" Sue asked when she pulled up in front of Jilly's loft.

"What makes you think I am?"

"I'm being serious, Jilly."

"So am I. He believes in what he's talking about. That's good enough for me."

"But all this stuff he goes on about . . . Elvis clones and insane aliens—"

"Don't forget animated bicycles."

Sue gave Jilly a pained look. "I'm not. That's just what I mean—it's all so crazy."

"What if it's not?"

Sue shook her head. "I can't buy it."

"It's not hurting anybody." Jilly leaned over and gave Sue a quick kiss on the cheek. "Gotta run. Thanks for everything."

"Maybe it's hurting him," Sue said as Jilly opened the door to get out. "Maybe it's closing the door on any chance he has of living a normal life. You know—opportunity comes knocking, but there's nobody home? He's not just eccentric, Jilly. He's crazy."

Jilly sighed. "His mother was a hooker, Sue. The reason he's a little flaky is her pimp threw him down two flights of stairs when he was six years old—not because Zinc did anything, or because his mother didn't trick enough johns that night, but just because the creep felt like doing it. That's what normal was for Zinc. He's happy now—a lot happier than when Social Services tried to put him in a foster home where they only wanted him for the support check they got once a month for taking him in. And a lot happier than he'd be in the Zeb, all doped up or sitting around in a padded cell whenever he tried to tell people about the things he sees.

"He's got his own life now. It's not much—not by your standards, maybe not even by mine, but it's his and I don't want anybody to take it away from him."

"But—"

"I know you mean well," Jilly said, "but things don't always work out the way we'd like them to. Nobody's got time for a kid like Zinc in Social Services. There he's just a statistic that they shuffle around with all the rest of their files and red tape. Out here on the street, we've got a system that works. We take care of our own. It's that simple. Doesn't matter if it's the Cat Lady, sleeping in an alleyway with a half dozen mangy toms, or Rude Ruthie, haranguing the commuters on the subway, we take care of each other."

"Utopia," Sue said.

A corner of Jilly's mouth twitched with the shadow of a humorless smile. "Yeah. I know. We've got a high asshole quotient, but what can you do? You try to get by—that's all. You just try to get by."

"I wish I could understand it better," Sue said.

"Don't worry about it. You're good people, but this just isn't your world. You can visit, but you wouldn't want to live in it, Sue."

"I guess."

Jilly started to add something more, but then just smiled encouragingly and got out of the car.

"See you Friday?" she asked, leaning in the door.

Sue nodded.

Jilly stood on the pavement and watched the Mazda until it turned the corner and its rear lights were lost from view, then she went upstairs to her apartment. The big room seemed too quiet and she felt too wound up to sleep, so she put a cassette in the tape player— Lynn Harrell playing a Schumann concerto—and started to prepare a new canvas to work on in the morning when the light would be better.

2

It was raining again, a soft drizzle that put a glistening sheen on the streets and lampposts, on porch handrails and street signs. Zinc stood in the shadows that had gathered in the mouth of an alleyway, his

new pair of wire cutters a comfortable weight in his hand. His eyes
sparked with reflected lights. His hair was damp against his scalp. He
licked his lips, tasting mountains heights and distant forests within
the drizzle's slightly metallic tang.

Jilly knew a lot about things that were, he thought, and things that
might be, and she always meant well, but there was one thing she
just couldn't get right. You didn't make art by capturing an image
on paper, or canvas, or in stone. You didn't make it by writing down
stories and poems. Music and dance came closest to what real art
was—but only so long as you didn't try to record or film it. Musical
notation was only so much dead ink on paper. Choreography was
planning, not art.

You could only make art by setting it free. Anything else was just
a memory, no matter how you stored it. On film or paper, sculpted
or recorded.

Everything that existed, existed in a captured state. Animate or
inanimate, everything wanted to be free.

That's what the lights said; that was their secret. Wild lights in the
night skies, and domesticated lights, right here on the street, they all
told the same tale. It was so plain to see when you knew *how* to look.
Didn't neon and streetlights yearn to be starlight?

To be free.

He bent down and picked up a stone, smiling at the satisfying
crack it made when it broke the glass protection of the streetlight,
his grin widening as the light inside flickered, then died.

It was part of the secret now, part of the voices that spoke in the
night sky.

Free.

Still smiling, he set out across the street to where a bicycle was
chained to the railing of a porch.

"Let me tell you about art," he said to it as he mounted the stairs.

Psycho Puppies were playing at the YoMan on Gracie Street near
the corner of Landis Avenue that Friday night. They weren't anywhere near as punkish as their name implied. If they had been, Jilly
would never have been able to get Sue out to see them.

"I don't care if they damage themselves," she'd told Jilly the one
and only time she'd gone out to one of the punk clubs further west

on Gracie, "but I refuse to pay good money just to have someone spit at me and do their best to rupture my eardrums."

The Puppies were positively tame compared to how that punk band had been. Their music was loud, but melodic, and while there was an undercurrent of social conscience to their lyrics, you could dance to them as well. Jilly couldn't help but smile to see Sue stepping it up to a chorus of, "You can take my job, but you can't take me, ain't nobody gonna steal my dignity."

The crowd was an even mix of slumming uptowners, Crowsea artistes and the neighborhood kids from surrounding Foxville. Jilly and Sue danced with each other, not from lack of offers, but because they didn't want to feel obligated to any guy that night. Too many men felt that one dance entitled them to ownership—for the night, at least, if not forever—and neither of them felt like going through the ritual repartee that the whole business required.

Sue was on the right side of a bad relationship at the moment, while Jilly was simply eschewing relationships on general principal these days. Relationships required changes, and she wasn't ready for changes in her life just now. And besides, all the men she'd ever cared for were already taken and she didn't think it likely that she'd run into her own particular Prince Charming in a Foxville night club.

"I like this band," Sue confided to her when they took a break to finish the beers they'd ordered at the beginning of the set.

Jilly nodded, but she didn't have anything to say. A glance across the room caught a glimpse of a head with hair enough like Zinc's badly-mown lawn scalp to remind her that he hadn't been home when she'd dropped by his place on the way to the club tonight.

Don't be out setting bicycles free, Zinc, she thought.

"Hey, Tomas. Check this out."

There were two of them, one Anglo, one Hispanic, neither of them much more than a year or so older than Zinc. They both wore leather jackets and jeans, dark hair greased back in ducktails. The drizzle put a sheen on their jackets and hair. The Hispanic moved closer to see what his companion was pointing out.

Zinc had melted into the shadows at their approach. The street-lights that he had yet to free whispered, *careful, careful,* as they wrapped him in darkness, their electric light illuminating the pair on the street.

"Well, shit," the Hispanic said. "Somebody's doing our work for us."

As he picked up the lock that Zinc had just snipped, the chain holding the bike to the railing fell to the pavement with a clatter. Both teenagers froze, one checking out one end of the street, his companion the other.

" 'Scool," the Anglo said. "Nobody here but you, me and your cooties."

"Chew on a big one."

"I don't do myself, *puto.*"

"That's 'cos it's too small to find."

The pair of them laughed—a quick nervous sound that belied their bravado—then the Anglo wheeled the bike away from the railing.

"Hey, Bobby-o," the Hispanic said. "Got another one over here."

"Well, what're you waiting for, man? Wheel her down to the van."

They were setting bicycles free, Zinc realized—just like he was. He'd gotten almost all the way down the block, painstakingly snipping the shackle of each lock, before the pair had arrived.

Careful, careful, the streetlights were still whispering, but Zinc was already moving out of the shadows.

"Hi, guys," he said.

The teenagers froze, then the Anglo's gaze took in the wire cutters in Zinc's hand.

"Well, well," he said. "What've we got here? What're you doing on the night side of the street, kid?"

Before Zinc could reply, the sound of a siren cut the air. A lone siren, approaching fast.

The Chinese waitress looked great in her leather miniskirt and fishnet stockings. She wore a blood-red camisole tucked into the waist of the skirt which made her pale skin seem even paler. Her hair was the black of polished jet, pulled up in a loose bun that spilled stray strands across her neck and shoulders. Blue-black eye shadow made her dark eyes darker. Her lips were the same red as her camisole.

"How come she looks so good," Sue wanted to know, "when I'd just look like a tart if I dressed like that?"

"She's inscrutable," Jilly replied. "You're just obvious."

"How sweet of you to point that out," Sue said with a grin. She stood up from their table. "C'mon. Let's dance."

Jilly shook her head. "You go ahead. I'll sit this one out."

"Uh-uh. I'm not going out there alone."

"There's LaDonna," Jilly said, pointing out a girl they both knew. "Dance with her."

"Are you feeling all right, Jilly?"

"I'm fine—just a little pooped. Give me a chance to catch my breath."

But she wasn't all right, she thought as Sue crossed over to where LaDonna da Costa and her brother Pipo were sitting. Not when she had Zinc to worry about. If he was out there, cutting off the locks of more bicycles . . .

You're not his mother, she told herself. Except—

Out here on the streets we take care of our own.

That's what she'd told Sue. And maybe it wasn't true for a lot of people who hit the skids—the winos and the losers and the bag people who were just too screwed up to take care of themselves, little say look after anyone else—but it was true for her.

Someone like Zinc—he was an in-betweener. Most days he could take care of himself just fine, but there was a fey streak in him so that sometimes he carried a touch of the magic that ran wild in the streets, the magic that was loose late at night when the straights were in bed and the city belonged to the night people. That magic took up lodgings in people like Zinc. For a week. A day. An hour. Didn't matter if it was real or not, if it couldn't be measured or catalogued, it was real to them. It existed all the same.

Did that make it true?

Jilly shook her head. It wasn't her kind of question and it didn't matter anyway. Real or not, it could still be driving Zinc into breaking corporeal laws—the kind that'd have Lou breathing down his neck, real fast. The kind that'd put him in jail with a whole different kind of loser.

Zinc wouldn't last out a week inside.

Jilly got up from the table and headed across the dance floor to where Sue and LaDonna were jitterbugging to a tune that sounded as though Buddy Holly could have penned the melody, if not the words.

"Fuck this, man!" the Anglo said.

He threw down the bike and took off at a run, his companion right on his heels, scattering puddles with the impact of their boots. Zinc watched them go. There was a buzzing in the back of his head. The streetlights were telling him to run too, but he saw the bike lying there on the pavement like a wounded animal, one wheel spinning forlornly, and he couldn't just take off.

Bikes were like turtles. Turn 'em on their backs—or a bike on its side—and they couldn't get up on their own again.

He tossed down the wire cutters and ran to the bike. Just as he was leaning it up against the railing from which the Anglo had taken it, a police cruiser came around the corner, skidding on the wet pavement, cherry light gyrating—screaming, *Run, run!* in its urgent high-pitched voice—headlights pinning Zinc where he stood.

Almost before the cruiser came to a halt, the passenger door popped open and a uniformed officer had stepped out. He drew his gun. Using the cruiser as a shield, he aimed across its roof at where Zinc was standing.

"Hold it right there, kid!" he shouted. "Don't even blink."

Zinc was privy to secrets. He could hear voices in lights. He knew that there was more to be seen in the world if you watched it from the corner of your eye than head on. It was a simple truth that every policeman he ever saw looked just like Elvis. But he hadn't survived all his years on the streets without protection.

He had a lucky charm. A little tin monkey pendant that had originally lived in a box of Crackerjacks—back when Crackerjacks had real prizes in them. Lucia had given it to him. He'd forgotten to bring it out with him the other night when the Elvises had taken him in. But he wasn't stupid. He'd remembered it tonight.

He reached into his pocket to get it out and wake its magic.

"You're just being silly," Sue said as they collected their jackets from their chairs.

"So humor me," Jilly asked.

"I'm coming, aren't I?"

Jilly nodded. She could hear the voice of Zinc's roommate Ursula in the back of her head—

There are no patterns.

—but she could feel one right now, growing tight as a drawn bowstring, humming with its urgency to be loosed.

"C'mon," she said, almost running from the club.

Police officer Mario Hidalgo was still a rookie—tonight was only the beginning of his third month of active duty—and while he'd drawn his sidearm before, he had yet to fire it in the line of duty. He had the makings of a good cop. He was steady, he was conscientious. The street hadn't had a chance to harden him yet, though it had already thrown him more than a couple of serious uglies in his first eight weeks of active duty.

But steady though he'd proved himself to be so far, when he saw the kid reaching into his pocket of his baggy jacket, Hidalgo had a single moment of unreasoning panic.

The kid's got a gun, that panic told him. The kid's going for a weapon.

One moment was all it took.

His finger was already tightening on the trigger of his regulation .38 as the kid's hand came out of his pocket. Hidalgo wanted to stop the pressure he was putting on the gun's trigger, but it was like there was a broken circuit between his brain and his hand.

The gun went off with a deafening roar.

Got it, Zinc thought as his fingers closed on the little tin monkey charm. Got my luck.

He started to take it out of his pocket, but then something hit him straight in the chest. It lifted him off his feet and threw him against the wall behind him with enough force to knock all the wind out of his lungs. There was a raw pain firing every one of his nerve ends. His hands opened and closed spastically, the charm falling out of his grip to hit the ground moments before his body slid down the wall to join it on the wet pavement.

Goodbye, goodbye, sweet friend, the streetlights cried.

He could sense the spin of the stars as they wheeled high above the city streets, their voices joining the electric voices of the street-lights.

My turn to go free, he thought as a white tunnel opened in his mind. He could feel it draw him in, and then he was falling, falling, falling. . . .

"Goodbye. . . ." he said, thought he said, but no words came forth from between his lips.

Just a trickle of blood that mingled with the rain that now began to fall in earnest, as though it, too, was saying its own farewell.

All Jilly had to see was the red spinning cherries of the police cruisers to know where the pattern she'd felt in the club was taking her. There were a lot of cars here—cruisers and unmarked vehicles, an ambulance—all on official business, their presence coinciding with her business. She didn't see Lou approach until he laid his hand on her shoulder.

"You don't want to see," he told her.

Jilly never even looked at him. One moment he was holding her shoulder, the next she'd shrugged herself free of his grip and just kept on walking.

"Is it . . . is it Zinc?" Sue asked the detective.

Jilly didn't have to ask. She knew. Without being told. Without having to see the body.

An officer stepped in front of her to stop her, but Lou waved him aside. In her peripheral vision she saw another officer sitting inside a cruiser, weeping, but it didn't really register.

"I thought he had a gun," the policeman was saying as she went by. "Oh, Jesus. I thought the kid was going for a gun. . . ."

And then she was standing over Zinc's body, looking down at his slender frame, limbs flung awkwardly like those of a rag doll that had been tossed into a corner and forgotten. She knelt down at Zinc's side. Something glinted on the wet pavement. A small tin monkey charm. She picked it up, closed it tightly in her fist before anyone could see what she'd done.

"C'mon, Jilly," Lou said as he came up behind her. He helped her to her feet.

It didn't seem possible that anyone as vibrant—as *alive*—as Zinc had been could have any relation whatsoever with that empty shell of a body that lay there on the pavement.

As Lou led her away from the body, Jilly's tears finally came, welling up from her eyes to salt the rain on her cheek.

"He . . . he wasn't . . . stealing bikes, Lou. . . ." she said.

"It doesn't look good," Lou said.

Often when she'd been with Zinc, Jilly had had a sense of that magic that touched him. A feeling that even if she couldn't see the marvels he told her about, they still existed just beyond the reach of her sight.

That feeling should be gone now, she thought.

"He was just . . . setting them free," she said.

The magic should have died, when he died. But she felt, if she just looked hard enough, that she'd see him, riding a maverick bike at the head of a pack of riderless bicycles—metal frames glistening, reflector lights glinting red, wheels throwing up arcs of fine spray, as they went off down the wet street.

Around the corner and out of sight.

"Nice friends the kid had," a plainclothes detective who was standing near them said to the uniformed officer beside him. "Took off with just about every bike on the street and left him holding the bag."

Jilly didn't think so. Not this time.

This time they'd gone free.

✷ THAT EXPLAINS POLAND ✷

1

Maybe that explains Poland.

Lori's mother used to say that. In the fullness of her Stalinism, the great hamster (as Lori called her) was convinced that every radical twitch to come from Poland and Solidarity was in fact inspired by the CIA, drug addicts, M&Ms, reruns of "The Honeymooners" ("To the moon, Alice!") . . . in fact, just about everything except the possibility of real dissension among the Polish people with their less than democratic regime. It got to the point where she was forever saying "That explains Poland!", regardless of how absurd or incomprehensible the connection.

It became a family joke—*a proposito* to any and all situations and shared by sundry and all, in and about the Snelling clan. You still don't get it?

Maybe you just had to be there.

2

"Listen to this: BIGFOOT SPIED IN UPPER FOXVILLE," Lori read from the Friday edition of *The Daily Journal*. "Bigfoot. Can you believe it? I mean, can you *believe* it?"

Ruth and I feigned indifference. We were used to Lori's outbursts by now and even though half the *clientela* in The Monkey Woman's Nest lifted their heads from whatever had been occupying them to look our way, we merely sipped our beer and looked out onto Williamson Street, watching the commuters hustle down into the subways or jockeying for position at the bus stop.

Lori was an eventful sort of a person. You could always count on something happening around her, with a ninety-nine percent chance that she'd been the catalyst. On a Friday afternoon, with the week's work behind us and two glorious days off ahead, we didn't need an event. Just a quiet moment and a few beers in *la Hora*

Frontera before the streets woke up and the clubs opened their doors.

"Who's playing at Your Second Home this weekend?" Ruth asked.

I wasn't sure, but I had other plans anyway. "I was thinking of taking in that new Rob Lowe movie if it's still playing."

Ruth got a gleam in her eye. "He is *so* dreamy. Every time I see him I just want to take him home and—"

"Don't be such a pair of old poops," Lori interrupted. "This is important. It's history in the making. Just listen to what it says." She gave the paper a snap to keep our attention, which set off another round of lifting heads throughout the restaurant, and started to read.

"The recent sighting of a large, hairy, human-like creature in the back alleys of Upper Foxville has prompted Councilman Cohen to renew his demands for increased police patrols in that section of the city. Eyewitness Barry Jack spotted the huge beast about 1 A.M. last night. He estimated it stood between seven and eight feet tall and weighed about 300 to 400 pounds."

"Lori . . ."

"Let me finish."

" *'While I doubt that the creature seen by Mr. Jack—that a* Bigfoot—*exists,' Cohen is quoted as saying, 'it does emphasize the increased proliferation of transients and the homeless in this area of the city, a problem that the City Council is doing very little about, despite continual requests by residents and this Council member.' "*

"Right." Lori gave us a quick grin. "Well, *that's* stretching a point way beyond *my* credibility."

"Lori, what are you talking about?" I asked.

"The way Cohen's dragging in this business of police patrols." She went back to the article.

"Could such a creature exist? According to archaeology professor Helmet Goddin of Butler University, 'Not in the city. Sightings of Bigfoot or the Sasquatch are usually relegated to wilderness areas, a description that doesn't apply to Upper Foxville, regardless of its resemblance to an archaeological dig.'

"Which is just his way of saying the place is a disaster area," Lori added. "No surprises there."

She held up a hand before either Ruth or I could speak and plunged on.

"Goddin says that the Sasquatch possibly resulted from some division in the homonid line, which evolved separately from humans. He speculates that they are 'more intelligent than apes . . . and apes can be very intelligent. If it does exist, then it is a very, very important biological and anthropological discovery.' "

Lori laid the paper down and sipped some of her beer. "So," she said as she set the glass back down precisely in its ring of condensation on the table. "What do you think?"

"Think about what?" Ruth asked.

Lori tapped the newspaper. "Of this." At our blank looks, she added, "It's something we can do this weekend. We can go hunting for Bigfoot in Upper Foxville."

I could tell from Ruth's expression that the idea had about as much appeal for her as it did for me. Spend the weekend crawling about the rubble of Upper Foxville and risk getting jumped by some junkie or hobo? No thanks.

Lori's studied Shotokan karate and could probably have held her own against Bruce Lee, but Ruth and I were just a couple of Crowsea punkettes, about as useful in a confrontation as a handful of wet noodles. And going into Upper Foxville to chase down some big *muchacho* who'd been mistaken for a Sasquatch was not my idea of fun. I'm way too young for suicide.

"Hunting?" I said. "With what?"

Lori pulled a small Instamatic from her purse. "With this, LaDonna. What else?"

I lifted my brows and looked to Ruth for help, but she was too busy laughing at the look on my face.

Right, I thought. Goodbye, Rob Lowe—it could've been *mucho primo*. Instead I'm going on a *gaza de grillos* with Crowsea's resident madwomen. Who said a weekend had to be boring?

3

I do a lot of thinking about decisions—not so much trying to make up my mind about something as just wondering, *¿que si?* Like if I hadn't decided to skip school that day with my brother Pipo and taken El Sub to the Pier, then I'd never have met Ruth. Ruth introduced me to Lori and Lori introduced me to more trouble than I could ever have gotten into on my own.

Not that I was a Little Miss Innocent before I met Lori. I looked like the kind of *muchacha* that your mother warned you not to hang around with. I liked my black jeans tight and my leather skirt short, but I wasn't a *puta* or anything. It was just for fun. The kind of trouble I got into was for staying out too late, or skipping school, or getting caught having a cigarette with the other girls behind the gym, or coming home with the smell of beer on my breath.

Little troubles. Ordinary ones.

The kind of trouble I got into with Lori was always *mucho* weird. Like the time we went looking for pirate treasure in the storm sewers under the Beaches—the ritzy area where Lori's parents lived before they got divorced. We were down there for hours, all dressed up in her father's spelunking gear, and just about drowned when it started to rain and the sewers filled up. Needless to say, her *papa* was *not* pleased at the mess we made of his gear.

And then there was the time that we hid in the washrooms at the Watley's Department Store downtown and spent the whole night trying on dresses, rearranging the mannequins, eating chocolates from the candy department. . . . If it had been just me on my own—coming from the barrios and all—I'd've ended up in jail. But being with Lori, her *papa* bailed us out and paid for the chocolates and one broken mannequin. We didn't do much for the rest of that summer except for gardening and odd jobs until we'd worked off what we owed him.

¿No muy loco? Verdad, we were only thirteen, and it was just the start. But that's all in the past. I'm grown up now—just turned twenty-one last week. Been on my own for four years, working steady. But I still wonder sometimes.

About decisions.

How different everything might have been if I hadn't done this, or if I *had* done that.

I've never been to Poland. I wonder what it's like.

4

"We'll set it up like a scavenger hunt," Lori said. She paused as the waitress brought another round—Heinekin for Lori, Miller Lites for Ruth and I—then leaned forward, elbows on the table, the palms of her hands cupping her chin. "With a prize and everything."

"What kind of a prize?" Ruth wanted to know.

"Losers take the winner out for dinner to the restaurant of her choice."

"Hold everything," I said. "Are you saying we each go out by ourselves to try to snap a shot of this thing?"

I had visions of the three of us in Upper Foxville, each of us wandering along our own street, the deserted tenements on all sides, the only company being the bums, junkies and *cabrones* that hung out there.

"I don't want to end up as just another statistic," I said.

"Oh, come on. We're around there all the time, hitting the clubs. When's the last time you heard of any trouble?"

"Give me the paper and I'll tell you," I said, reaching for the *Journal*.

"You want to go at *night*?" Ruth asked.

"We go whenever we choose," Lori replied. "The first one with a genuine picture wins."

"I can just see the three of us disappearing in there," I said. " 'The lost women of Foxville flats.' "

"Beats being remembered as loose women," Lori said.

"We'd be just another urban legend."

Ruth nodded. "Like in one of Christy Riddell's stories."

I shook my head. "No thanks. He makes the unreal too real. Anyway, I was thinking more of that Brunvand guy with his choking Doberman and Mexican pets."

"Those are all just stories," Lori said, trying to sound like Christopher Lee. She came off like a bad Elvira. "This could be real."

"Do you *really* believe that?" I asked.

"No. But I think it'll be a bit of fun. Are you scared?"

"I'm sane, aren't I? Of course I'm scared."

"Oh, poop."

"That doesn't mean I'm not up for it."

I wondered if it wasn't too late to have my head examined. Did the hospital handle that kind of thing in their emergency ward?

"Good for you, LaDonna," Lori was saying. "What about you, Ruth?"

"Not at night."

"We'll get the jump on you."

"Not at night," she repeated.

"Not at night," I agreed.

Lori's eyes had that mad little gleam in them that let me know that we'd been had again. She'd never planned on going at night either.

"A toast," she said, raising her beer. "May the best woman win."

We clinked our mugs against each other's and made plans for the night while we finished our beer. I don't think anyone in the restaurant was sorry to see us go when we finally left. First up was the early show at the Oxford (you didn't really think I'd stand you up, did you, Rob?), then the last couple of sets at the Zorb, where the Fat Man Blues Band was playing, because Ruth was crazy about their bass player and Lori and I liked to egg her on.

5

By now you're probably thinking that we're just a bunch of air-heads, out for laughs and not concerned with anything important. Well, it isn't true. I think about things all the time. Like how hanging around with Anglos so much has got me to the point where half the time I sound like one myself. I can hardly speak to my grandmother these days. I don't even think in Spanish anymore and it bothers me.

It's only in the barrio that I still speak it, but I don't go there much—just to visit the family on birthdays and holidays. I worked hard to get out, but sometimes when I'm in my apartment on Lee Street in Crowsea, sitting in the windowseat and looking out at the park, I wonder why. I've got a nice place there, a decent job, some good friends. But I don't have any roots. There's nothing connecting me to this part of the city.

I could vanish overnight (disappear in Upper Foxville on a *caza de grillos*), and it wouldn't cause much more than a ripple. Back home, the *abuelas* are *still* talking about how Donita's youngest girl moved to Crowsea and when was she going to settle down?

I don't really know anybody I can talk to about this kind of thing. Neither my Anglo friends nor my own people would understand. But I think about it. Not a lot, but I think about it. And about decisions. About all kinds of things.

Ruth says I think too much.

Lori just wonders why I'm always trying to explain Poland. You'd think I was her mother or something.

6

Saturday morning, bright and early, and only a little hungover, we got off the Yoors Street subway and followed the stairs up from the underground station to where they spat us out on the corner of Gracie Street and Yoors. Gracie Street's the *frontera* between Upper Foxville and Foxville proper. South of Gracie it's all low-rent apartment buildings and tenements, shabby old *viviendas* that manage to hang on to an old world feel, mostly because it's still families living here, just like it's been for a hundred years. The people take care of their neighborhood, no differently than their parents did before them.

North of Gracie a bunch of developers got together and planned to give the area a new facelift. I've seen the plans—condominiums, shopping malls, parks. Basically what they wanted to do was shove a high class suburb into the middle of the city. Only what happened was their backers pulled out while they were in the middle of leveling about a square mile of city blocks, so now the whole area's just a mess of empty buildings and rubble-strewn lots.

It's creepy, looking out on it from Gracie Street. It's like standing on the line of a map that divides civilization from no-man's-land. You almost expect some graffiti to say, "Here there be dragons."

And maybe they wouldn't be so far off. Because you can find dragons in Upper Foxville—the *muy malo* kind that ride chopped-down Harleys. The Devil's Dragon. Bikers making deals with their junkies. I think I'd prefer the kind that breathe fire.

I don't like the open spaces of rubble in Upper Foxville. My true self—the way I see me—is like an alley cat, crouching for shelter under a car, watching the world go by. I'm comfortable in Crowsea's narrow streets and alleyways. They're like the barrio where I got my street smarts. It's easy to duck away from trouble, to get lost in the shadows. To hang out and watch, but not be seen. Out there, in those desolate blocks north of Gracie, there's no place to hide, and too many places—all at the same time.

If that kind of thing bothered Lori, she sure wasn't showing it. She was all decked out in fatigues, hiking boots and a khaki-colored shoulderbag like she was in the Army Reserves and going out on maneuvers or something. Ruth was almost as bad, only she went to the other extreme. She was wearing baggy white cotton pants with a puffed sleeve blouse and a trendy vest, low-heeled sandals and a matching purse.

Me? That morning I dressed with survival in mind, not fashion. I had my yellow jeans and my red hightops, an old black Motorhead T-shirt and a scuffed leather jacket that I hoped would make me look tough. I had some of my hair up in a top-knot, the rest all *loco,* and went heavy on the makeup. My camera—a *barato* little Vitoret that I'd borrowed from Pipo last fall and still hadn't returned yet— was stuffed in a shapeless canvas shoulderbag. All I wanted to do was fit in.

Checking out the skateboarders and other kids already clogging up Gracie's sidewalks, I didn't think I was doing too bad a job. Especially when this little *muchacho* with a pink Mohawk came whipping over on his board and tried to put the moves on me. I felt like I was sixteen again.

"Well, I'm going straight up Yoors," Lori said. "Everybody got their cameras and some film?"

Ruth and I dutifully patted our purse and shoulderbag respectively.

"I guess I'll try the Tombs," I said.

It only took a week after the machines stopped pushing over the buildings for people to start dumping everything from old car parts to bags of trash in the blocks between Lanois and Flood north of MacNeil. People took to calling it the Tombs because of all the wrecked vehicles.

I'd had some time to think things through over a breakfast of black coffee this morning—a strangely lucid moment, considering the night before. I'd almost decided on getting my friend Izzy from the apartment downstairs to hide out in an ape suit somewhere in the rubble, and then it hit me. Lori probably had something similar planned. She'd have Ruth and I tramping around through the rubble, getting all hot and sweaty, and more than a little tense, and then she'd produce a photo of some friend of *hers* in an ape suit, snapped slightly out of focus as he was ducking into some run-down old building. It'd be good for a laugh and a free dinner and it was just the kind of stunt Lori'd pull. I mean, we could have been doing some serious shopping today. . . .

My new plan was to head out towards the Tombs, then work my way over to Yoors where I'd follow Lori and take my picture of her and her pal in his monkeysuit. *Mama* didn't raise any stupid kids, no matter what her neighbors thought.

So I gave them both a jaunty wave and set off down Gracie to where Lanois would take me north into the Tombs. Lori went up Yoors. Ruth was still standing by the stairs going down to the subway station by the time I lost sight of her, looking back through the crowds. My pink Mohawked admirer followed me until I turned up towards the Tombs, then he went whizzing back to his friends, expertly guiding his skateboard down the congested sidewalk like the pro he was. He couldn't have been more than thirteen.

7

When you're a *niña*—and maybe twenty-one is still being a kid to some people—it's not so weird to be worrying about who you are and how you're ever going to fit in. But then you're supposed to get a handle on things and by the time you're my age, you've got it all pretty well figured out. At least that's the impression I got when I was a *niña* and twenty-one looked like it was about as old as you ever wanted to get.

Verdad, I still don't know who I am or where I fit in. I stand in front of the mirror and the *muchacha* I see studying me just as carefully as I'm studying her *looks* older. But I don't feel any different from when I was fifteen.

So when does it happen?

Maybe it never does.

Maybe that explains Poland.

8

All things considered—I mean, this *was* Upper Foxville—it wasn't a bad day to be scuffling around in the Tombs. The sun was bright in a sky so blue it hurt to look at it. Good thing I hadn't forgotten my shades. Broken glass shimmered and gleamed in the light and crunched underfoot.

What's this thing people have for busting windows and bottles and the like? It seems like all you need is an unbroken piece of glass and rocks just sort of pop into people's hands. Of course it makes such an interesting sound when it breaks. And it gives you such a feeling of . . . oh, I don't know. Having *cojones,* I suppose. What's that song by Nick Lowe? "I Love the Sound of Breaking Glass." Not that I'm into that kind of thing—okay, at least not anymore. And better it be in a place like this than on the sidewalk or streets where people have to walk or go wheeling by on their bikes.

I was feeling pretty punky by the time I'd been in the Tombs for an hour or so. That always happens when I wear my leather jacket. I may not be a real *machona*—or at least not capable of violence, let's say—but the jacket makes me *feel* tough anyway. It says don't mess with me all over it. Not that there was anybody there to mess around with me.

I spotted a few dogs—feral, mangy-looking *perros* that kept their distance. The rat that surprised me as I came around a corner was a lot less forgiving about having its morning disturbed. It stood its ground until I pitched a rock at it, then it just sort of melted away, slinky and fast.

It was early for the junkies and other lowlifes that were out in full force come late afternoon, but the bag ladies were making their rounds, all bundled up in layers of coats and dresses, pushing their homes and belongings around in shopping carts or carrying it all about in plastic shopping bags. I passed winos, sleeping off last night's booze, and hoboes huddled around small fires, taking their time about waking up before they hit the streets of Foxville and Crowsea to panhandle the Saturday crowds. They gave me the creeps, staring at me like I didn't belong—fair enough, I guess, since I didn't—obviously thinking what the hell was I doing here? Would you believe looking for Bigfoot? Didn't think so.

Did I mention the smell? If you've ever been to a dump, you'll know what I mean. It's a sweet-sour cloying smell that gets into your clothes and hair and just hangs in there. You could get used to it, I guess—it stopped bothering me after the first fifteen minutes or so—but I wouldn't want to have to be sitting next to me on El Sub going home.

I guess I killed an hour or so before I worked my way west towards Yoors Street to look for Lori. It was kind of fun, playing Indian scout in the rubble. I got so involved in sneaking around that I almost ran right into them.

Them. Yeah, I was right. Lori was sitting on what was left of some building's front steps, sharing a beer with a guy named Byron Murphy. Near Byron's knee was a plastic shopping bag out of which spilled something that looked remarkably like a flat ape's arm. I mean the arm was flat, because it was part of a costume and there was nobody in it at the moment. Come to think of it, that *would* make it a flat ape, wouldn't it?

Byron worked at the sports clinic at Butler U. as a therapist. Like most of Lori's old boyfriends, he'd stayed her friend after they broke up. That kind of thing never happens to me. When I break up with a guy it usually involves various household objects flying through the air aimed for his head. You'd think I had a Latin temper or something.

I backed up quickly, but I shouldn't have worried. Neither of them had spotted me. I thought about trying to find Ruth, then realized that I'd have to wait until later to let her in on the joke. What I didn't want to do was miss getting this all down on film.

Byron putting on the apesuit. The two of them setting up the shot. I wanted the whole thing. Maybe I could even sell my photos to *The Daily Journal*—"BIGFOOT HOAXERS CAUGHT IN THE ACT"—and really play the trick back on her.

Circling around them, I made my way to an old deserted brownstone and went in. After checking around first to make sure I was alone, I got comfortable by a window where I had a perfect view of Lori and Byron and settled down to wait.

Gotcha now, Lori.

9

The best kinds of practical jokes are those that backfire on whoever's playing the trick. Didn't you ever want to get a camera on Alan Funt and catch *him* looking silly for a change? I didn't get many opportunities to catch Lori—and don't think I haven't tried. (Remind me to tell you the story of the thirty-five pizzas and the priest sometime.) The trouble with Lori is that she doesn't think linearly or even in intuitive leaps. Her mind tends to move sideways in its thinking, which makes it hard to catch her out, since you haven't a clue what she's on about in the first place.

She gets it from her mother, I guess.

It might not explain Poland, but it says volumes about genetics.

10

I had to wait a half hour before they finally pulled the gorilla suit out of the bag. It didn't fit Byron all that well, but did an okay job from a distance. I figured Lori would put him in the shadows of the building on the other side of the street and move the camera a bit while she was taking her shot. Nothing's quite so effective as a slightly blurry, dark shot when you're dealing with whacko things like a Bigfoot or flying saucers.

Me, I was wishing for a telephoto lens and a decent camera, but I was pretty sure the Vitoret would work fine. We weren't talking high art here. Anyway, I could always have the prints blown up— and no, smart guy, I'm not talking about dynamite.

I got the whole thing on film. Byron putting on the costume. Lori posing him, taking her shots. Byron taking the costume off and stashing it away. The two of them leaving. All I wanted to do was lean out the window and shout, "Nya nya!", but I kept my mouth shut and let them go. Then, camera in hand, I left the building by the back, heading for the Tombs.

There were no steps, so I had to jump down a three-foot drop. I paused at the top to put away my camera, and then I froze.

Not twenty yards away, a huge figure in a bulky overcoat and slouched down hat was shuffling through the rubble. Before I could duck away, the figure turned and I was looking straight into this hairy face.

I don't quite know how to describe him to you. You're not going to believe me anyway and words just don't quite do justice to the *feeling* of the moment.

He wasn't wearing anything under the overcoat and the sun was bright enough so that I could see he was covered with hair all over. It was a fine pelt—more like an ape's than a bear's—a rich dark brown that was glossy where it caught the sun. His feet were huge, his chest like a barrel, his arms like a weightlifter's. But his face . . . It was human, and it wasn't. It was like an ape's, but it wasn't. The nose was flat, but the cheekbones were delicate under the fine covering of hair. His lips were thin, chin square. And his eyes . . . They were a warm brown liquid color, full of smarts, no question about it. And they were looking straight at me, thinking about what kind of a threat I posed for him.

Let me tell you, my heart stopped dead in my chest. It was all a joke, right? Lori's gag that I was playing back on her. Except there *had* been that article in the newspaper, and right now I was staring at Bigfoot and there were no ifs, ands, or buts about it. I had my camera in my hand. All I had to do was lift it, snap a shot, and take off running.

But I thought about what it would mean if I did that. If there was a photo to *really* prove this guy existed, they'd be sending in teams to track him down. When they caught him, they'd keep him locked up, maybe dissect him to see what made him work. . . . Like everybody else, I've seen *E.T.*

I don't want to sound all mushy or anything, but there was

something in those eyes that I didn't ever want to see locked away. I moved really slowly, putting the camera away in my bag, then I held my hands out to him so that he could see that I wasn't going to hurt him.

(Me hurt *him*—there's a laugh. The *size* of him . . .)

"You don't want to hang around this city too long," I told him. "If they catch you, nobody's going to be nice about it."

I was surprised at how calm I sounded.

He didn't say anything. He just stood there, looking at me with those big browns of his. Then he grinned—proof positive, as if I needed it, that he wasn't some guy in a suit like Byron, because there was no way they'd made a mask yet that could move like his features did right then. His whole face was animated—filled with a big silly lopsided grin that made me grin right back when it reached his eyes. He tipped a hairy finger to the brim of his hat, and then he just sort of faded away into the rubble—as quick and smooth as the rat had earlier, but there was nothing sneaky or sly about the way he moved.

One minute he was there, grinning like a loon, and the next he was gone.

I sank down and sat in the doorway, my legs swinging in the space below, and looked at where he'd been. I guess I was there for awhile, just trying to take it all in. I remembered a time when I'd been camping with my brother and a couple of friends from the neighborhood. I woke early the first morning and stuck my head out of the tent to find myself face to face with a deer. We both held our breath for what seemed like hours. When I finally breathed, she took off like a shot, but left me with a warm feeling that stayed with me for the rest of that weekend.

That's kind of what I was feeling right now. Like I'd lucked into a peek at one of the big mysteries of the world and if I kept it to myself, then I'd always be a part of it. It'd be our secret. Something nobody could ever take away from me.

11

So we all survived our *casa de grillos* in Upper Foxville. Ruth had gotten bored walking around in the rubble and gone back to Gracie

Street, where she'd spent the better part of the day hanging around with some graffiti artists that she'd met while she was waiting for us. I got my film processed at one of those one-hour places and we made Lori pay up with a fancy dinner for trying to pull another one over on us.

Some reporters were in the area too, we found out later, trying to do a follow-up on the piece in the *Journal* yesterday, but nobody came back with a photo of Bigfoot, except for me, and mine's just a snapshot sitting there in the back of my head where I can take it out from time to time whenever I'm feeling blue and looking for a good memory.

It's absurd when you think about it—Bigfoot wandering around in the city, poorly disguised in an oversized trenchcoat and battered slouch hat—but I like the idea of it. Maybe he was trying to figure out who he was and where he fit in. Maybe it was all a laugh for him too. Maybe he really was just this hairy *muchacho,* making do in the Tombs. I don't know. I just think of him and smile.

Maybe that explains Poland.

≈ ROMANO DROM ≈

THE ROAD LEADING TO A GOAL DOES NOT SEPARATE
YOU FROM THE DESTINATION; IT IS ESSENTIALLY A
PART OF IT.   —ROMANY SAYING

A light Friday night drizzle had left a glistening sheen on Yoors Street when Lorio Munn stepped out of the club. She hefted her guitar case and looked down at her running shoes with a frown. The door opened and closed behind her and Terry Dixon joined her on the sidewalk, carrying his bass.

"What's the problem?" he asked.

Lorio lifted a shoe to show him the hole in its sole. "It's going to be a wet walk."

"You want a lift? Jane's meeting me at the Fan—we can give you a lift home after, if you want."

"No. I'm not much in the mood for socializing tonight."

"Hey, come on. It was a great night. We packed the place."

"Yeah. But they weren't really listening."

"They were dancing, weren't they? All of a sudden, that's not enough? You used to complain that all they'd do is just sit there."

"I know. I like it when they dance. It's just—"

Terry caught her arm. Putting a finger to his lips, he nodded to a pair of women who were walking by, neither of whom noticed Lorio and Terry standing in the club's doorway. One of them was humming the chorus to the band's last number under her breath:

> *I don't need nobody staring at me,*
> *stripping me down with their 1-2-3,*
> *I got a right to my own dignity*
> *—who needs pornography?*

"Okay," Lorio said when the women had passed them. "So somebody's listening. But when I went to get our money, Slimy Ted—"

"Slimy Toad."

Lorio smiled briefly. "He told me I could make a few extra bucks if I'd go out with a couple of his friends who, quote, 'liked my moves,' unquote. What does that tell you?"

"That I ought to break his head."

"It means the people that I want to reach *aren't* listening."

"Maybe we should be singing louder?"

"Sure." Lorio shook her head. "Look, say hi to Jane for me, would you? Maybe I'll make it next time."

She watched him go, then set off in the opposite direction towards Stanton Street. Maybe she shouldn't be complaining. No Nuns Here was starting to get the decent gigs. *In the City* had run an article on them—even spent a paragraph or two on what was behind the band, instead of just dismissing what they were trying to say as post-punk jingoism like their one two-line review in *The Newford Star* had.

Oh, it was still very in to sing about women's rights, gay rights, *people*'s rights, for God's sake, but the band still got the "aren't you limiting yourselves?" thrown at them by people who should know better. Still, at least they were getting some attention and, more importantly, what they were trying to say was getting some attention. It might bore the pants off of Joe Average Jock—but that was just the person they were trying to reach. So where did you go? If they could only get a decent gig. A big one where they could really reach more—

She paused in mid-step, certain she'd heard a moan from the alleyway she was passing. As she peered into it, the sound was repeated. Definitely a moan. She looked up and down Yoors Street, but there was no one close to her.

"Hey!" she called softly into the alley. "Is there someone in there?"

She caught a glimpse of eyes, gleaming like a cat's caught in the headbeams of a car—just a shivery flash and they were gone. Animal's eyes. But the sound she'd heard had seemed human.

"Hey!"

Swallowing thickly, she edged into the alley, her guitar case held out in front of her. As she moved down its length, her eyes began to adjust to the poor light.

Why was she doing this? She had to be nuts.

The moan came a third time then and she saw what she took to be a small man lying in some refuse.

"Oh, jeez." She moved forward, fear forgotten. "Are you okay?"

She laid her guitar case down and knelt beside the figure, but when she reached out a hand to his shoulder, she touched fur instead of clothing. Muscles moved under her fingers—weakly, but enough to tell her that it wasn't a fur coat. She snatched back her hand as a broad face turned towards her.

She froze, looking into that face. The first thing she thought of were the orangutans in the Metro Zoo. The features had a simian cast with their close-set eyes, broad overhanging brow and protruding lower jaw. Reddish fur surrounded the face—the same fur that covered the creature's body.

It had to be a costume, she thought. Except it was too real. She began to back away.

"Help . . . me. . . ."

This *couldn't* be real.

"When they track me down again . . . this time . . . they will . . . they will kill me. . . ."

The gaze that met her own was cloudy with pain, but it wasn't an animal's. Intelligence lay in its depth, behind the pain. But this wasn't a man wearing a costume either.

"Who will?" she asked at last.

For the first time, the gaze appeared to really focus on her.

"You . . . you're a Gypsy," the creature said. *"Sarishan, Romani chi."*

Lorio shook her head, unable to accept what she was hearing.

"The blood's awfully thin," she said finally. "And I don't speak Romany."

Though she knew it to hear it and remembered the odd word. The last person to speak it in her presence had been her uncle Palko, but that was a long time ago now.

"You are strangely garbed," the creature said, "but I know a Gypsy when I see one."

Strangely garbed? Well, it all depended, Lorio thought.

Her long curly hair was dyed a black too deep to be natural and grew from a three-inch swatch down the center of her head. Light brown stubble grew on either side of the mohawk where the sides of her head had been shaved. She wore a brown leather bomber's jacket over a bright red and black Forties dress, net stockings, and her running shoes. A strand of plastic pearls hung around her neck.

Six earrings, from a rhinestone stud to threaded beads, hung from her right ear. In her left lobe was a stud in the shape of an Anarchy symbol.

"My mother was a Gypsy," she said, "but my father—"

She shook her head. What was she doing? Arguing with a ragged bundle of orange fur did not make much bloody sense.

"Your people know the roads," the creature said. "The roads of this world and those roads beyond that bind the balance. You . . . you can help me. Take my place. The hound caught me before—before I could complete my journey. The boundaries grow thin . . . frail. You must—"

"I don't know what you're talking about," Lorio said. "God, I don't even know what you are."

"My name is Elderee and this time Mahail's hound did its job too well. It will be back . . . once it scents my weakness. . . ." He coughed and Lorio stared at the blood speckling the hand-like paw that went up to his mouth.

"Look, you shouldn't be talking. You need a doctor."

Right. Maybe a vet would be more like it. She started to take off her jacket to lay it over him, but Elderee reached out and touched her arm.

"You need only walk it," he said. "That's all it takes. Walk it with intent. An old straight track . . . there for those who know to see it. Like a Gypsy road—*un Romano drom*. It will take you home."

"How do you know where I live?"

And why, she asked herself, am I taking this all so calmly? Probably because any minute she expected Steven Spielberg to step out and say, "Cut! That's a take."

"Not where you live—but *home*. Where all roads meet. Jacca calls it Lankelly—because of the sacred grove in the heart of the valley— but I just think of it as the Wood."

Lorio shook her head. "This is a joke, right? You're just wearing a . . . a costume, right? A really good one."

"No, I—"

"Sure. It's almost Halloween. You were at a party and you got mugged. The Gypsy bit was a good guess. I can handle this—no problem. Now we've got to get you to a hospital."

"Too . . . too late. . . ."

"Jeez, don't fade out on me now. I can . . ."

Her voice trailed off as she realized that the man in the monkey suit was looking behind her. She turned just in time to see a dog-like creature materialize out of nowhere. It came with a *whufft* of displaced air, bringing an unpleasant reek in its wake. Crouching on powerful legs, it looked like a cross between a hyena and a wolf, except for the protruding canines that Lorio had only seen in zoological texts on extinct species such as the saber-toothed tiger.

"Flee!" Elderee croaked. "You can't hope to face a polrech. . . ."

His warning came too late. With a rumbling growl that came from deep in its chest, the creature charged. Lorio didn't even stop to think of what she was doing. She just hoisted her guitar case and swung it in a flailing arc as hard as she could. The end of the case holding the body of her guitar struck the creature with such force that it snapped the beast's neck with an audible crack.

Lorio lost her hold on the case and it flew from her hands to land in a skidding crash well beyond the polrech that had dropped in its tracks. She stared at the dying creature, numb with fright. Adrenaline roared through her, bringing a buzz to her ears.

Saliva dripped from the creature's open mouth. The pavement of the alley smoked at its acidic touch. A pair of red fiery eyes glared at her. Taloned paws twitched, trying to reach her. When the light died in the creature's eyes, its shape wavered, then came apart, drifting away like smoke. A spark or two, like coals in a dying fire, hissed on the pavement, then there was nothing except for the small hole where the creature's saliva had pooled.

Lorio hugged herself to keep from shaking. Slowly she turned to look at her companion, but he lay very still now.

"Uh . . . Elderee?" she tried.

She moved forward, keeping half an eye on the alley behind her in case there were more of the hounds coming. Gingerly she touched Elderee. His eyes flickered open and something sparked between them, leaving Lorio momentarily dizzy. When her gaze cleared, she saw that the life-light was fading in his eyes now.

He had been holding his left arm across his lower torso. It fell free, revealing a gaping wound. Blood had matted in the fur around it. A queasy feeling started up in Lorio's stomach, but she forced it down. She tried to be calm. Something weird was going on—no doubt about that—but first things first.

"You must . . ." Elderee began in a weak voice.

"Uh-uh," Lorio interrupted. "You listen to me. You're hurt. I don't know what you are and I can't take you to a regular hospital, but you look enough like a . . . like an orangutan that the Zoo might take you in and hopefully patch you up. Now what I want you to do is keep your mouth shut and pretend you're an animal, okay? Otherwise they'll probably dissect you, just to see what makes you tick. We'll figure out how to get you out of the Zoo again when that problem comes up."

"But . . ."

"Take it easy. I'm going to get us a ride."

Without letting him reply, she bolted from the alleyway and ran down Yoors Street. She didn't know how she was going to explain this to Terry—she wasn't sure she could explain it to herself—but that didn't matter. First she had to get Elderee to a place where his injury could be treated. Everything else had to wait until then. The Fan loomed up on her left and she charged into the restaurant, ignoring the stares she was getting as she pushed her way to Terry and Jane's table.

"Lorio!" Terry said, looking up with a smile. "So you changed your—"

"No time to talk, Terry. I'm taking you up on that offer of a ride—only I need it right away."

"What's the big—"

"We're talking desperate here, Terry. Please?"

The bass player of No Nuns Here exchanged a glance with his girlfriend. Jane shrugged, so he dumped a handful of bills on the table and hurried out of the restaurant with her, trying to catch up to Lorio who was already running back to the alleyway where she'd left her monkeyman.

It was a twenty minute drive from downtown Newford to the Metro Zoo, and another twenty minutes back again. Terry pulled his Toyota over to the curb in front of Lorio's apartment building on Lee Street in Crowsea. She shared a second floor loft with a traditional musician named Angie Tichell in the old three-story brick building. The loft retained a consistent smell of Chinese food because of the ground floor that specialized in Mainland dishes.

Terry looked back between the bucket seats and studied Lorio for a moment.

"Are you going to be okay?" he asked.

Lorio nodded. "At least they took him in," she said.

They'd stayed in the Zoo parking lot long enough to be sure of that.

"I'm sure they'll do the best they can for him."

"But what if they can't help him? I mean, he *looks* like an orang-utan, but what if he's too alien for them to help him?"

Terry had no answer for her. He'd been shocked enough to see the ape with its orange-red fur lying there in the alleyway, but when he'd heard it talk . . .

"Just what *is* he?" Jane asked.

Lorio wore a mournful expression. "I don't know." She sat there a moment longer, then stepped out of the car. "Thanks for the lift," she told Terry as he got her guitar out of the back for her. "I'll see you tomorrow night. You too, Jane," she added, leaning into the open window on the passenger's side of the car for a moment.

Jane touched her arm. "You take care of yourself," she said.

Lorio nodded. She stepped back as the Toyota pulled away and stood watching its taillights until it turned west on McKennitt and was lost from view. Turning, she faced the door to her building and wished her roommate wasn't away for the weekend. Being on her own in the loft tonight didn't hold very much appeal.

That's because you're scared, she chided herself. Don't be a baby. Just go to sleep.

She gave the night street one last look. A cab went by, but then the street was quiet again. No pedestrians at this time of night; everybody was sensibly in bed and asleep. The rain had stopped, the streetlights reflected in the puddles that it had left behind. Up and down the street the second floor windows were dark above the soft glow of the lit-up display windows of the stores on the ground floors.

Everything seemed normal. There wasn't even a hint that behind the facade there was another world that held talking monkeymen and bizarre dogs that appeared out of nowhere.

Sighing, Lorio squared her shoulders and went upstairs to bed, trying not to think about the weird turn the night had taken. She didn't have much luck.

She kept seeing that dog-like creature and worried about one finding its way into her apartment. Or to the Zoo where Elderee was. Then she worried about Elderee. When she finally nodded off, she fell into a fitful sleep, all too full of disturbing dreams.

At first she was in the alleyway again. For all that it was very real around her, there was a distancing sense, a feeling of dislocation in her being there. As she looked around, the pavement underfoot began to fracture. Cracks went up and down its length, then webbed the sides of the buildings. She started to back away onto Yoors Street when everything shattered like a piece of dropped glass.

Shards of the alley, like images reflected in a broken mirror, whirled and spun around her. When they settled down, drifting slowly around her like feathers after a pillow fight, she found herself on a roadway—more of a farmer's track, really—that stretched on to either horizon. On both sides of the track were rolling hills dotted with stands of trees.

"A pretty scene," a voice said from behind her. "Though not for long."

The man she saw, when she turned around, was a good head taller than her own five-four. His hair was black, his eyes glittery bright, his mouth an arrogant slash in a pale face. He was dressed all in browns and blacks, his clothing hanging in a poor fit from his too-thin frame.

"Who're—" Lorio began, but the man cut her off.

"This I claim for the Dark, while you—" he shook his head, taking in her hair, her clothes, with a disdainful look "—will be my gift to Mahail."

He made a motion towards her with his hand and sparks flew from his fingertips. She stumbled as the road dissolved under her and she began to drop through grey space. There was light far below her. In it was a writhing mass of tentacles that reached up for her from a dark heart of shadow. As she rushed down to meet it, the darkness resolved into a monstrous bloated shape with coal-eyes and a gaping maw.

It didn't take much speculation to realize that this thing had to be Mahail.

"Tell him Dorn sent you!" the pale-faced man cried after her.

She dropped like a bullet, straight for Mahail, her mouth open, but the scream dying before it left her throat. The monster's oozing tentacles snatched her out of the air. They squeezed her, shook her, held her up for inspection to one eye, then the other.

The soul studying her behind those eyes was like something dead. The air was filled with a reek of decay and rot. The tentacles tightened around her chest and lower torso, squeezing the breath from her as they brought her up to the monster's mouth. Slime covered her, burning and painful where it touched her bare skin. She flailed her arms, slapped at the creature's rubbery lips. The scream building up in her throat finally broke free, shrill and rattling and—

—it woke her to a tangle of bedclothes that were wrapped around her. Cold sweat covered her from head to toe.

She lay gasping, pushed aside the sheet and blankets, and stared up at the dark ceiling of her bedroom. Her heart beat a wild tattoo. Slowly the fear drained away.

Just a dream, she thought. That was all. Maybe the whole night had been just a dream. But as she finally drifted off again, she remembered Elderee's warm eyes and the long winding track of a road that went uphill and down, and this time she smiled and her sleep was dreamless.

The next day it all did seem like a dream. She checked the papers, tried the news on both TV and radio, but there was no mention of the Zoo acquiring a mysterious new animal. It wasn't until she called Terry to confirm that they *had* taken Elderee to the Zoo that she was willing to believe that she hadn't gone crazy. Things were weird, sure, but at least she hadn't totally lost it herself.

She spent the day in a state of anxiety that didn't go away until she got on stage at the club and No Nuns Here went into their first set. The chopping rhythms of the music, her guitar humming in her hands, her voice soaring over the blast of the instruments, let her escape that feeling of being lost. By the time they got to the last song of the night, she was filled with a crackling energy that let her rip through the song and make it not just a statement, but an anthem.

I hear your whistle when I cross the park,
you make me nervous when I walk in the dark,
but I won't listen—I won't scream,
you won't find me in your magazines
    'cos
I don't need nobody staring at me,
stripping me down with their 1-2-3. . . .

The song ended with a thunderous chord that shook the stage underfoot. She helped pack up the gear once the crowd was gone, but left on her own, not even taking her guitar with her. Terry promised to drop it off on Sunday afternoon, but she only nodded and made her way out onto Yoors Street.

The sidewalks were crowded, overfilled with a strutting array of humanity from the trendy to punks to burnouts, everyone on their own personal course and all of them the same. They made the city come to life, but at the same time they drowned it with postures, and images like costumes. It was all artifice, lacking depth. Lorio turned to look at her own reflection in a store window. She was no different. Any meaning she meant to communicate was lost behind a shuffle of makeup, styling and pose.

Mahail fed on hearts, she thought, not knowing where the thought had come from. He fed on them and left the shells to walk around just like we walk around.

She turned from the window and made her way through the people to the alley where she'd found Elderee. Without a pause, she turned into it and walked straight to its end. There she stopped and looked back at the sidewalk she'd just left. Cars flickered by on the street beyond it. On the sidewalk itself, every size and shape of Yoors Street poseur walked by the mouth of the alley, leaving echoing spills of conversation or laughter in their wake. But here it was quiet, like a world apart. Here it was . . . different.

Your people know the roads. . . .
You need only walk it . . . with intent. . . .

She sighed. Maybe the Rom of old had known hidden roads, but nobody had taken the time to show her any—not even Palko. Besides, her Gypsy blood was thin, a matter of chance rather than upbringing, and these days there were as many Gypsies in business suits as there were those following the old ways. Gypsy magic was just something the Rom used to baffle the *Gaje,* the non-Gypsies. Magic itself was just parlor tricks. Except . . .

She remembered the polrech, appearing out of nowhere, dissolving into smoke when she'd killed it. And Elderee . . . like an orangutan, only he could talk.

Magic.

She moved closer to one side of the alley, studying the brick wall of the building there. This alleyway was the last place in the world that she would ever expect to find a marvel. The grime and the dirt, the plastic garbage bags torn open in their corners, the refuse heaped against the walls—this wasn't the stuff of magic. Magic was Tolkien's Middle Earth. Cat Midhir's Borderlands. This was . . . She ran a hand down the side of the wall and looked at the smudge it left on her fingers. This was an armpit of the real world.

Turning, she faced the mouth of the alley again, only to find a tall figure standing there, watching her. Fear made her blood pump quicker through her veins and for the first time in her life she knew what it meant to have one's heart in one's mouth. She knew who this was.

"Dorn."

The name came out of her mouth in a spidery croak. The man's face was in shadow, but she could still see, no, sense his grin.

"I warned you not to involve yourself further in what doesn't concern you."

He'd warned her? Then she remembered the dream. The thought of his sending her that dream, of his being inside her head like that, made her skin crawl.

"You should not have come back," he said.

"You don't . . . you don't scare me," she said.

No. He terrified her. How could something she'd only dreamed be real? She took a step back and the heel of her shoe came up against a garbage bag.

"Elderee's road is *mine,*" he said, moving closer. "*I* took it from him. *I* set the hound on him."

"You—"

"But I felt you drawing on its power, and then I knew you would try to take it from me."

"I think you're making a—"

"No mistake." He touched his chest. "I can *feel* the bond between you and that damned monkey. He gave it to you, didn't he? Heart's shadow, look at you!"

He stood very close to her now. A hand went up and flicked a finger against the stubble on the shaved part of her scalp. Lorio flinched at the touch, but couldn't seem to move away. She was weak with fear. Spark's flickered around Dorn's fingers. She stared at them with widening eyes.

"You're nothing better than an animal yourself," he told her.

Strangely enough, Lorio took comfort in that remark. She looked up into his eyes and saw that they were as dead as Mahail's had been in her nightmare. Nightmare. If Dorn was real, did that mean the road was too? Could she shatter this alleyway, as she had in her dream, to find the road lying underfoot—behind its facade?

An old straight track . . . there for those who know to see it.

Something sparked in his eyes. It wasn't until he spoke that Lorio realized it had been amusement.

"You don't know, do you?" he mocked. "You couldn't find a road if your life depended on it."

"I . . ."

"Let me show you."

Before she could do anything, he grabbed her, one hand on either lapel of her bomber's jacket, and slammed her against the wall of the alley. The impact knocked the breath out of her and brought tears to her eyes.

"Watch," he grinned, his face inches from hers.

He held her straight-armed and slowly turned from the wall. He made one full circuit, then dumped her on the ground. Lorio's legs gave away from under her and she tumbled to the dirt.

Dirt?

Slowly the realization settled in her. He'd taken her back into her dream.

The silence came to her first, a sudden cessation of all sound so that her breathing sounded ragged to her ears. Then she looked around. The city was gone. She was crouching on a dirt road, under a starry sky. The hills of her dream were on either side, the road running between them like a straight white ribbon.

Dorn grabbed a handful of her hair and hauled her to her feet. She blinked with the pain, eyes tearing, but as she turned slowly to face her captor she could feel something shift inside her. She had no more doubt that magic was real, that the road existed, that Elderee had offered her something precious beyond compare. There was no way she was going to let Dorn with his dead eyes take this from her.

On the heels of that realization, knowledge filled her like a flower sprouting from a seed in time-lapse photography. Eye to eye, mind to mind, Elderee had left that seed in her mind until something—the promise of this place, the magic of this road, her own understanding of it, perhaps—woke it and set it spinning through her.

There was not one road, but a countless number of them. They made a pattern that webbed not only her own world, but all worlds; not only her own time, but all times. They upheld a fragile balance between light and dark, order and chaos, while at the center of the web lay a sacred grove in that valley that Elderee had called Lankelly.

And I know how to get there, she realized.

I know that Wood. And it was home.

Her understanding of the roads and all they meant took only a moment to flash through her. In the same breath she knew that the magic that Elderee and others like him used was drawn from the pattern of the roads. A being like Dorn was a destroyer and gained his power from what he destroyed. It was a power that came quickly, draining as it ravaged, leaving the user hungry for more, while the power Elderee used worked in harmony with the pattern, built on it, drew from it, then gave back more than it took. It was a slower magic, but a more enduring one.

Dorn saw the understanding come into her eyes. Its suddenness, the depth of it filling her, shocked him. His grip on her hair slackened for a moment and Lorio brought her knee up into his groin. His hand dropped from her hair as he folded over.

Lorio stood over him, staring at his bent figure. She raised her hands and gold sparks flickered between her fingers. But she didn't need magic to deal with him. She brought doubled fists down on the nape of his neck and he sprawled face forward in the dirt. He turned pained eyes to her, hands scrabbling at the surface of the road. His magic glimmered dully between his fingers, but Lorio shook her head.

He wouldn't look at her. Instead he concentrated, brow furrowed, as he called up his magic. Whatever spell he was trying to work made the light between his fingers gleam more sharply. Lorio stepped quickly forward and stamped down hard on his hand. She was wearing boots tonight. Bones crunched under the impact of her heel.

"That's for Elderee," she said, her voice soft but grim.

Dorn bit back a scream and glared at her. He sat up and scuttled a few paces away, moving on two bent legs and one arm, sideways like a crab. When he stopped, he cradled his hurt hand against his chest.

Silently they faced each other. Dorn knew that she was stronger than he was at this moment. Her will was too focused, the cloak of knowledge that Elderee had given her was too powerful in its newness. She'd hurt him. Among humanoids, hands were needed to spark spells—fingers and voice. She'd effectively cut him off from the use of his own spells, from calling up a polrech, from anything he might have done to hurt her. In her eyes, he could see that she knew too.

She took a step towards him and he called up the one magic he could use, that which would take him from the road to safety in any one of the myriad worlds touched by the roads.

"There will be another time," he muttered, and then he was gone.

Displaced air *whuffed* where he'd stood and Lorio found herself alone on the road.

She let out a long breath and looked around.

The road. The Chinese called it a dragon track. Alfred Watkins, in England, had discovered the old straight tracks there and called them leys. Secret ways, hidden roads. The Native Americans had them. African tribesmen and the aborigines of Australia. Even her own people had secret roads unknown to the non-Gypsy. In every culture, the wise people, the shamans and magicians and the outsiders knew these ways, and it made sense, didn't it? It was by following such roads that they could grow strong themselves.

But not like Dorn, she thought. Not the kind of strength that destroys, but rather the kind of strength that gives back more than it takes. Like . . . like playing on stage with No Nuns Here. Having something to say and putting it across as honestly as possible. When it worked, when something sparked between herself and the audience, a strength went back and forth between them, each of them feeding the other, the sensation so intense that she often came off the stage just vibrating.

Lorio smiled. She started to walk the road, giving herself to it as step followed step. She walked and a hum built up in her mind. Time went spilling down other corridors, leaving her to stride through a place where hours moved to a different step. The stars in their unfamiliar constellations wheeled above her. The landscape on either side of the road changed from hills to woodlands to deserts to mountainsides to seashores until she found herself back in the hills once more.

She paused there. A thrumming sensation filled her, giving her surroundings a sparkle. Rich scents filled her nostrils. The wind coming down from the hills was a sigh like a synthesizer, dreamy and distant. And underfoot, the road glimmered faintly as though in response to what she'd given it by walking its length.

There's no end to it, she realized. It just goes around and around. Sometimes it'll be longer, sometimes shorter. It just goes on. Because it wasn't where she was coming from, nor where she was going to that was important, but the road itself and how she walked it. And it would never be the same.

She ruffled through the knowledge that Elderee had planted in her and found a way to step off the road. But when she moved back into her own world, she didn't return to the alleyway where it had all begun. Instead she chose a different exit point and stepped towards it. The road and surrounding hills shimmered around her and then were gone.

It was more a room than a cage, the concrete floor and walls smelling strongly of disinfectant and the unmistakable odor of a zoo's monkey house. The only light came through the barred front of the cage, but it was enough for Lorio to see Elderee glance up at her sudden appearance. A look of fatherly pride came over his simian features. Lorio stood self-consciously in the middle of the floor for a long moment, then after a quick look around to make sure they were alone, she walked over to where Elderee lay, her boots scuffing quietly on the concrete.

"Hi," she said, crouching down beside him.

"Hello, yourself."

"How're you feeling?"

A faint smile touched his lips. "I've felt better."

"The doctors fixed you up?"

"Oh, yes. And a remarkable job they've done. I'm alive, am I not?" He paused, then laid a hand gently on her shoulder. "You found the road?"

Lorio smiled. "Along with everything else you stuck in my head. How did you do that?"

She didn't ask why. Having walked the road, she knew that someone had to assume his responsibility of it. He'd chosen her.

"I'll show you sometime—when I'm better. Did you go to the Wood?"

"No. I thought I'd save that for when I could go with you."

"Did you have any . . . trouble?"

Her dream of Mahail flashed into her mind. And Dorn's very real presence. The hounds that he could have called down on her if he hadn't been so sure of himself.

"Ah," Elderee said, catching the images. "Dorn. I wish I'd been there to see you deal with him."

"Are you reading my mind?"

"Only what you're projecting to me."

"Oh." Lorio settled down into a more comfortable position. "He folded pretty easily, didn't he? Just like the polrech that attacked us in the alley."

Elderee shrugged. "Dorn is a lesser evil. He could control one hound at a time, no more. But like most of his kind, he liked to think of himself as far more than he was. You did well. As for the polrech—you were simply stronger. And quicker."

Lorio flushed at the praise.

"And now?" Elderee asked. "What will you do?"

"Jeez, I . . . I don't know. Take care of your part of the road until you get better, I guess."

"I'm getting old," Elderee said. "I could use your help—even when I'm better. There are more of them—" he didn't need to name Mahail and his minions for Lorio to know whom he meant "—than there ever are of us. And there are many roads."

"We'll handle it," Lorio said, still buzzing from her time on the road. "No problem."

"It can be dangerous," Elderee warned, "if a polrech catches you unaware—or if you run into a pack of them. And there are others like Dorn—only stronger, fiercer. But," he added as Lorio's humor began to drain away, "there are good things, too. Wait until you see the monkey puzzle tree—there are more birds in it, and from stranger worlds, than you could ever imagine. And there are friends in the Wood that I'd like you to meet—Jacca and Mabena and . . ."

His voice began to drift a bit.

"You're wearing yourself out," Lorio said.

Elderee nodded.

"I'll come back and see you tomorrow night," she said. "You should rest now. There'll be time enough to meet all your friends and for us to get to know each other better later on."

She stood up and smiled down at him. Elderee's gaze lifted to meet hers.

"Bahtalo drom," he said in Romany. Roughly translated it meant, follow a good road.

"I will," Lorio said. "Maybe not a Gypsy road, but a good road all the same."

"Not a Gypsy road? Then what are you?"

"Part Rom," Lorio replied with a grin. "But mostly just a punker."

Elderee shook his head. Lorio lifted a hand in farewell, then reached for and found the road that would take her home. She stepped onto it and disappeared. Elderee lay back with a contented smile on his lips and let sleep rise up to claim him once again.

⨯ THE SACRED FIRE ⨯

There were ten thousand maniacs on the radio—the band, not a bunch of lunatics; playing their latest single, Natalie Merchant's distinctive voice rising from the music like a soothing balm.

Trouble me. . . .

Sharing your problems . . . sometimes talking a thing through was enough to ease the burden. You didn't need to be a shrink to know it could work. You just had to find someone to listen to you.

Nicky Straw had tried talking. He'd try anything if it would work, but nothing did. There was only one way to deal with his problems and it took him a long time to accept that. But it was hard, because the job was never done. Every time he put one of them down, another of the freaks would come buzzing in his face like a fly on a corpse.

He was getting tired of fixing things. Tired of running. Tired of being on his own.

Trouble me. . . .

He could hear the music clearly from where he crouched in the bushes. The boom box pumped out the song from one corner of the blanket on which she was sitting, reading a paperback edition of Christy Riddell's *How to Make the Wind Blow*. She even looked a little like Natalie Merchant. Same dark eyes, same dark hair; same slight build. Better taste in clothes, though. None of those thrift shop dresses and the like that made Merchant look like she was old before her time; just a nice white Butler U. T-shirt and a pair of bright yellow jogging shorts. White Reeboks with laces to match the shorts; a red headband.

The light was leaking from the sky. Be too dark to read soon. Maybe she'd get up and go.

Nicky sat back on his haunches. He shifted his weight from one leg to the other.

Maybe nothing would happen, but he didn't see things working out that way. Not with how his luck was running.

All bad.

Trouble me. . . .

I did, he thought. I tried. But it didn't work out, did it?

So now he was back to fixing things the only way he knew how.

Her name was Luann. Luann Somerson.

She'd picked him up in the Tombs—about as far from the green harbor of Fitzhenry Park as you could get in Newford. It was the lost part of the city—a wilderness of urban decay stolen back from the neon and glitter. Block on block of decaying tenements and run-down buildings. The kind of place to which the homeless gravitated, looking for squats; where the kids hung out to sneak beers and junkies made their deals, hands twitching as they exchanged rumpled bills for little packets of short-lived empyrean; where winos slept in doorways that reeked of puke and urine and the cops only went if they were on the take and meeting the moneyman.

It was also the kind of place where the freaks hid out, waiting for Lady Night to start her prowl. Waiting for dark. The freaks liked her shadows and he did too, because he could hide in them as well as they could. Maybe better. He was still alive, wasn't he?

He was looking for the freaks to show when Luann approached him, sitting with his back against the wall, right on the edge of the Tombs, watching the rush hour slow to a trickle on Gracie Street. He had his legs splayed out on the sidewalk in front of him, playing the drunk, the bum. Three-days' stubble, hair getting ragged, scruffy clothes, two dimes in his pocket—it wasn't hard to look the part. Commuters stepped over him or went around him, but nobody gave him a second glance. Their gazes just touched him, then slid on by. Until she showed up.

She stopped, then crouched down so that she wasn't standing over him. She looked too healthy and clean to be hanging around this part of town.

"You look like you could use a meal," she said.

"I suppose you're buying?"

She nodded.

Nicky just shook his head. "What? You like to live dangerously or something, lady? I could be anybody."

She nodded again, a half smile playing on her lips.

"Sure," she said. "Anybody at all. Except you're Nicky Straw. We used to take English 201 together, remember?"

He'd recognized her as well, just hoped she hadn't. The guy she remembered didn't exist anymore.

"I know about being down on your luck," she added when he didn't respond. "Believe me, I've been there."

You haven't been anywhere, he thought. You don't want to know about the places I've been.

"You're Luann Somerson," he said finally.

Again that smile. "Let me buy you a meal, Nicky."

He'd wanted to avoid this kind of a thing, but he supposed he'd known all along that he couldn't. This was what happened when the hunt took you into your hometown. You didn't disappear into the background like all the other bums. Someone was always there to remember.

Hey, Nicky. How's it going? How's the wife and that kid of yours?

Like they cared. Maybe he should just tell the truth for a change. You know those things we used to think were hiding in the closet when we were too young to know any better? Well, surprise. One night one of those monsters came out of the closet and chewed off their faces. . . .

"C'mon," Luann was saying.

She stood up, waiting for him. He gave it a heartbeat, then another. When he saw she wasn't going without him, he finally got to his feet.

"You do this a lot?" he asked.

She shook her head. "First time," she said.

All it took was one time. . . .

"I'm like everyone else," she said. "I pretend there's no one there, lying half-starved in the gutter, you know? But when I recognized you, I couldn't just walk by."

You should have, he thought.

His silence was making her nervous and she began to chatter as they headed slowly down Yoors Street.

"Why don't we just go back to my place?" she said. "It'll give you a chance to clean up. Chad—that's my ex—left some clothes behind that might fit you. . . ."

Her voice trailed off. She was embarrassed now, finally realizing how he must feel, having her see him like this.

"Uh . . ."

"That'd be great," he said, relenting.

He got that smile of hers as a reward. A man could get lost in its warmth, he thought. It'd feed a freak for a month.

"So this guy," he said. "Chad. He been gone long?"

The smile faltered.

"Three and a half weeks now," she said.

That explained a lot. Nothing made you forget your own troubles so much as running into someone who had them worse.

"Not too bright a guy, I guess," he said.

"That's . . . Thank you, Nicky. I guess I need to hear that kind of thing."

"Hey, I'm a bum. We've got nothing better to do than to think up nice things to say."

"You were never a bum, Nicky."

"Yeah. Well, things change."

She took the hint. As they walked on, she talked about the book she'd started reading last night instead.

It took them fifteen minutes or so to reach her apartment on McKennitt, right in the heart of Lower Crowsea. It was a walk-up with its own stairwell—a narrow, winding affair that started on the pavement by the entrance of a small Lebanese groceteria and then deposited you on a balcony overlooking the street.

Inside, the apartment had the look of a recent split-up. There was an amplifier on a wooden orange crate by the front window, but no turntable or speakers. The bookcase to the right of the window had gaps where apparently random volumes had been removed. A pair of rattan chairs with bright slipcovers stood in the middle of the room, but there were no end tables to go with them, nor a coffee table. She was making do with another orange crate, this one cluttered with magazines, a couple of plates stacked on top of each other and what looked like every coffee mug she owned squeezed into the remaining space. A small portable black-and-white Zenith TV stood at the base of the bookcase, alongside a portable cassette deck. There were a couple of rectangles on the wall where paintings had obviously been removed. A couple of weeks' worth of newspapers were in a pile on the floor by one of the chairs.

She started to apologize for the mess, then smiled and shrugged.

Nicky had to smile with her. Like he was going to complain about the place, looking like he did.

She showed him to the bathroom. By the time he came out again, showered and shaved, dressed in a pair of Chad's corduroys and a white linen shirt, both of which were at least a size too big, she had a salad on the tiny table in the kitchen, wine glasses out, the bottle waiting for him to open it, breaded pork chops and potatoes on the stove, still cooking.

Nicky's stomach grumbled at the rich smell that filled the air.

She talked a little about her failed marriage over dinner—sounding sad rather than bitter—but more about old times at the university. As she spoke, Nicky realized that the only thing they had shared back then had been that English class; still he let her ramble on about campus events he only half-remembered and people who'd meant nothing to him then and even less now.

But at least they hadn't been freaks.

He corrected himself. He hadn't been able to *recognize* the freaks among them back then.

"God, listen to me," Luann said suddenly.

They were finished their meal and sitting in her living room having coffee. He'd been wrong; there were still two clean mugs in her cupboard.

"I am," he said.

She gave him that smile of hers again—this time it had a wistfulness about it.

"I know you are," she said. "It's just that all I've been talking about is myself. What about you, Nicky? What happened to you?"

"I . . ."

Where did he start? Which lie did he give her?

That was the one good thing about street people. They didn't ask questions. Whatever put you there, that was your business. But citizens always wanted whys and hows and wherefores.

As he hesitated, she seemed to realize her faux pas.

"I'm sorry," she said. "If you don't want to talk about it . . ."

"It's not that," Nicky told her. "It's just . . ."

"Hard to open up?"

Try impossible. But oddly enough, Nicky found himself wanting to talk to her about it. To explain. To ease the burden. Even to warn her, because she was just the kind of person the freaks went for.

The fire inside her shimmered off her skin like a high voltage aura, sending shadows skittering. It was a bright shatter of light and a deep golden glow like honey, all at the same time. It sparked in her eyes; blazed when she smiled. Sooner or later it was going to draw a nest of the freaks to her, just as surely as a junkie could sniff out a fix.

"There's these . . . things," he said slowly. "They look enough like you or me to walk among us—especially at night—but they're . . . they're not human."

She got a puzzled look on her face which didn't surprise him in the least.

"They're freaks," he said. "I don't know what they are, or where they came from, but they're not natural. They feed on us, on our hopes and our dreams, on our vitality. They're like . . . I guess the best analogy would be that they're like vampires. Once they're on to you, you can't shake them. They'll keep after you until they've bled you dry."

Her puzzlement was turning to a mild alarm, but now that he'd started, Nicky was determined to tell it all through, right to the end.

"What," she began.

"What I do," he said, interrupting her, "is hunt them down."

The song by 10,000 Maniacs ended and the boom box's speakers offered up another to the fading day. Nicky couldn't name the band this time, but he was familiar with the song's punchy rhythm. The lead singer was talking about burning beds. . . .

Beside the machine, Luann put down her book and stretched.

Do it, Nicky thought. Get out of here. Now. While you still can.

Instead, she lay down on the blanket, hands behind her head, and looked up into the darkening sky, listening to the music. Maybe she was looking for the first star of the night.

Something to wish upon.

The fire burned in her brighter than any star. Flaring and ebbing to the pulse of her thoughts.

Calling to the freaks.

Nicky's fingers clenched into fists. He made himself look away. But even closing his eyes, he couldn't ignore the fire. Its heat sparked the distance between them as though he lay beside her on the blanket, skin pressed to skin. His pulse drummed, twinning her heartbeat.

This was how the freaks felt. This was what they wanted, what they hungered for, what they fed on. This was what he denied them.

The spark of life.

The sacred fire.

He couldn't look away any longer. He had to see her one more time, her fire burning, burning . . .

He opened his eyes to find that the twilight had finally found Fitzhenry Park. And Luann—she was blazing like a bonfire in its dusky shadows.

"What do you mean, you hunt them down?" she asked.

"I kill them," Nicky told her.

"But—"

"Understand, they're not human. They just *look* like us, but their faces don't fit quite right and they wear our kind of a body like they've put on an unfamiliar suit of loose clothing."

He touched his borrowed shirt as he spoke. She just stared at him—all trace of that earlier smile gone. Fear lived in her eyes now.

That's it, he told himself. You've done enough. Get out of here.

But once started, he didn't seem to be able to stop. All the lonely years of the endless hunt came spilling out of him.

"They're out there in the night," he said. "That's when they can get away with moving among us. When their shambling walk makes you think of drunks or some feeble old homeless bag lady—not of monsters. They're freaks and they live on the fire that makes us human."

"The . . . the fire . . . ?

He touched his chest.

"The one in here," he said. "They're drawn to the ones whose fires burn the brightest," he added. "Like yours does."

She edged her chair back from the table, ready to bolt. Then he saw her realize that there was no place to bolt to. The knowledge sat there in her eyes, fanning the fear into an ever-more debilitating panic. Where was she going to go that he couldn't get to her first?

"I know what you're thinking," he said. "If someone had come to me with this story before I . . . found out about them—"

("Momma! Daddy!" he could hear his daughter crying. "The monsters are coming for me!"

Soothing her. Showing her that the closet was empty. But never thinking about the window and the fire escape outside it. Never thinking for a minute that the freaks would come in through the window and take them both when he was at work.

But that was before he'd known about the freaks, wasn't it?)

He looked down at the table and cleared his throat. There was pain in his eyes when his gaze lifted to meet hers again—pain as intense as her fear.

"If someone had told me," he went on, "I'd have recommended him for the Zeb, too—just lock him up in a padded cell and throw away the key. But I don't think that way now. Because I can see them. I can recognize them. All it takes is one time and you'll never disbelieve again.

"And you'll never forget."

"You . . . you just kill these people . . . ?" she asked.

Her voice was tiny—no more than a whisper. Her mind was tape looped around the one fact. She wasn't hearing anything else.

"I told you—they're not people," he began, then shook his head.

What was the point? What had he thought was going to happen? She'd go, yeah, right, and jump in to help him? Here, honey, let me hold the stake. Would you like another garlic clove in your lunch?

But they weren't vampires. He didn't know what they were, just that they were dangerous.

Freaks.

"They know about me," he said. "They've been hunting me for as long as I've been hunting them, but I move too fast for them. One day, though, I'll make a mistake and then they'll have me. It's that, or the cops'll pick me up and I wouldn't last the night in a cell. The freaks'd be on me so fast . . ."

He let his voice trail off. Her lower lip was trembling. Her eyes looked like those of some small panicked creature, caught in a trap, the hunter almost upon her.

"Maybe I should go," he said.

He rose from the table, pretending he didn't see the astonished relief in her eyes. He paused at the door that would let him out onto the balcony.

"I didn't mean to scare you," he said.

"I . . . you . . ."

He shook his head. "I should never have come."

"I . . ."

She still couldn't string two words together. Still didn't believe that she was getting out of this alive. He felt bad for unsettling her the way he had, but maybe it was for the best. Maybe she wouldn't bring any more strays home the way she had him. Maybe the freaks'd never get to her.

"Just think about this," he said, before he left. "What if I'm right?"

Then he stepped outside and closed the door behind him.

He could move fast when he had to—it was what had kept him alive through all these years. By the time she reached her living room window, he was down the stairs and across the street, looking back at her from the darkened mouth of an alleyway nestled between a yuppie restaurant and a bookstore, both of which were closed. He could see her, studying the street, looking for him.

But she couldn't see him.

And that was the way he'd keep it.

He came out of the bushes, the mask of his face shifting and unsettled in the poor light. Luann was sitting up, fiddling with the dial on her boom box, flipping through the channels. She didn't hear him until he was almost upon her. When she turned, her face drained of color. She sprawled backwards in her attempt to escape and then could only lie there and stare, mouth working, but no sound coming out. He lunged for her—

But then Nicky was there. The hunting knife that he carried in a sheath under his shirt was in his hand, cutting edge up. He grabbed the freak by the back of his collar and hauled him around. Before the freak could make a move, Nicky rammed the knife home in the freak's stomach and ripped it up. Blood sprayed, showering them both.

He could hear Luann screaming. He could feel the freak jerking in his grip as he died. He could taste the freak's blood on his lips. But his mind was years and miles away, falling back and back to a small apartment where his wife and daughter had fallen prey to the monsters his daughter told him were living in the closet. . . .

The freak slipped from his grip and sprawled on the grass. The knife fell from Nicky's hand. He looked at Luann, finally focusing on her. She was on her knees, staring at him and the freak like they were both aliens.

"He . . . his face . . . he . . ."

She could barely speak.

"I can't do it anymore," he told her.

He was empty inside. Couldn't feel a thing. It was as though all those years of hunting down the freaks had finally extinguished his own fire.

In the distance he could hear a siren. Someone must have seen what went down. Had to have been a citizen, because street people minded their own business, didn't matter what they saw.

"It ends here," he said.

He sat down beside the freak's corpse to wait for the police to arrive.

"For me, it ends here."

Late the following day, Luann was still in shock.

She'd finally escaped the endless barrage of questions from both the police and the press, only to find that being alone brought no relief. She kept seeing the face of the man who had attacked her. Had it really seemed to *shift* about like an ill-fitting mask, or had that just been something she'd seen as a result of the poor light and what Nicky had told her?

Their faces don't fit quite right. . . .

She couldn't get it out of her mind. The face. The blood. The police dragging Nicky away. And all those things he'd told her last night.

They're freaks. . . .

Crazy things.

They live on the fire that makes us human.

Words that seemed to well up out of some great pain he was carrying around inside him.

They're not human . . . they just look *like us. . . .*

A thump on her balcony had her jumping nervously out of her chair until she realized that it was just the paperboy tossing up today's newspaper. She didn't want to look at what *The Daily Journal* had to say, but couldn't seem to stop herself from going out to get it. She took the paper back inside and spread it out on her lap.

Naturally enough, the story had made the front page. There was a picture of her, looking washed out and stunned. A shot of the corpse being taking away in a body bag. A head and shoulders shot of Nicky . . .

She stopped, her pulse doubling its tempo as the headline under Nicky's picture sank in.

"KILLER FOUND DEAD IN CELL—POLICE BAFFLED."

"No," she said.

They know about me.

She pushed the paper away from her until it fell to the floor. But Nicky's picture continued to look up at her from where the paper lay.

They've been hunting me.

None of what he'd told her could be true. It had just been the pitiful ravings of a very disturbed man.

I wouldn't last the night in a cell. The freaks'd be on me so fast . . .

But she'd known him once—a long time ago—and he'd been as normal as anybody then. Still, people changed. . . .

She picked up the paper and quickly scanned the story, looking for a reasonable explanation to put to rest the irrational fears that were reawakening her panic. But the police knew nothing. Nobody knew a thing.

"I suppose that at this point, only Nicky Straw knows what really happened," the police spokesman was quoted as saying.

Nicky and you, a small worried voice said in the back of Luann's mind.

She shook her head, unwilling to accept it.

They're drawn to the ones whose fires burn the brightest.

She looked to her window. Beyond its smudged panes, the night was gathering. Soon it would be dark. Soon it would be night. Light showed a long way in the dark; a bright light would show further.

The ones whose fires burn the brightest . . . like yours does.

"It . . . it wasn't true," she said, her voice ringing hollowly in the room. "None of it. Tell me it wasn't true, Nicky."

But Nicky was dead.

She let the paper fall again and rose to her feet, drifting across the room to the window like a ghost. She just didn't seem to feel connected to anything anymore.

It seemed oddly quiet on the street below. Less traffic than usual—both vehicular and pedestrian. There was a figure standing in front of the bookstore across the street, back to the window display, leaning against the glass. He seemed to be looking up at her window, but it was hard to tell because the brim of his hat cast a shadow on his face.

Once they're on to you, you can't shake them.

That man in the park. His face. Shifting. The skin seeming too loose.

They'll keep after you until they bleed you dry.

It wasn't real.

She turned from the window and shivered, hugging her arms around herself as she remembered what Nicky had said when he'd left the apartment last night.

What if I'm right?

She couldn't accept that. She looked back across the street, but the figure was gone. She listened for a footstep on the narrow, winding stairwell that led up to her balcony. Waited for the movement of a shadow across the window.

❧ WINTER WAS HARD ❧

*I PRETTY MUCH TRY TO STAY IN A CONSTANT STATE OF
CONFUSION JUST BECAUSE OF THE EXPRESSION IT LEAVES
ON MY FACE.*   —JOHNNY DEPP

It was the coldest December since they'd first started keeping records at the turn of the century, though warmer, Jilly thought, than it must have been in the ice ages of the Pleistocene. The veracity of that extraneous bit of trivia gave her small comfort, for it did nothing to lessen the impact of the night's bitter weather. The wind shrieked through the tunnel-like streets created by the abandoned buildings of the Tombs, carrying with it a deep, arctic chill. It spun the granular snow into dervishing whirligigs that made it almost impossible to see at times and packed drifts up against the sides of the buildings and derelict cars.

Jilly felt like a little kid, bundled up in her boots and parka, with longjohns under her jeans, a woolen cap pushing down her unruly curls and a long scarf wrapped about fifty times around her neck and face, cocooning her so completely that only her eyes peered out through a narrow slit. Turtle-like, she hunched her shoulders, trying to make her neck disappear into her parka, and stuffed her mittened hands deep in its pockets.

It didn't help. The wind bit through it all as though unhindered, and she just grew colder with each step she took as she plodded on through the deepening drifts. The work crews were already out with their carnival of flashing blue and amber lights, removing the snow on Gracie Street and Williamson, but here in the Tombs it would just lie where it fell until the spring melt. The only signs of humanity were the odd little trails that the derelicts and other inhabitants of the Tombs made as they went about their business, but even those were being swallowed by the storm.

Only fools or those who had no choice were out tonight. Jilly thought she should be counted among the latter, though Geordie had called her the former when she'd left the loft earlier in the evening.

"This is just craziness, Jilly," he'd said. "Look at the bloody weather."

"I've got to go. It's important."

"To you and the penguins, but nobody else."

Still, she'd had to come. It was the eve of the solstice, one year exactly since the gemmin went away, and she didn't feel as though she had any choice in the matter. She was driven to walk the Tombs tonight, never mind the storm. What sent her out from the warm comfort of her loft was like what Professor Dapple said they used to call a geas in the old days—something you just had to do.

So she left Geordie sitting on her Murphy bed, playing his new Copeland whistle, surrounded by finished and unfinished canvases and the rest of the clutter that her motley collection of possessions had created in the loft, and went out into the storm.

She didn't pause until she reached the mouth of the alley that ran along the south side of the old Clark Building. There, under the suspicious gaze of the building's snow-swept gargoyles, she hunched her back against the storm and pulled her scarf down a little, widening the eye-slit so that she could have a clearer look down the length of the alley. She could almost see Babe, leaning casually against the side of the old Buick that was still sitting there, dressed in her raggedy T-shirt, black body stocking and raincoat, Doc Martin's dark against the snow that lay underfoot. She could almost hear the high husky voices of the other gemmin, chanting an eerie version of a rap song that had been popular at the time.

She could almost—

But no. She blinked as the wind shifted, blinding her with snow. She saw only snow, heard only the wind. But in her memory . . .

By night they nested in one of those abandoned cars that could be found on any street or alley of the Tombs—a handful of gangly teenagers burrowed under blankets, burlap sacks and tattered jackets, bodies snugly fit into holes that seemed to have been chewed from the ragged upholstery. This morning they had built a fire in the trunk of the Buick, scavenging fuel from the buildings, and one of them was cooking their breakfast on the heated metal of its hood.

Babe was the oldest. She looked about seventeen—it was something in the way she carried herself—but otherwise had the same thin androgynous body as her companions. The other gemmin all had dark complexions and feminine features, but none of them had Babe's short mauve hair, nor her luminous violet eyes. The hair coloring of the others ran more to various shades of henna red; their eyes were mostly the same electric blue that Jilly's were.

That December had been as unnaturally warm as this one was cold, but Babe's open raincoat with the thin T-shirt and body stocking underneath still made Jilly pause with concern. There was such a thing as carrying fashion too far, she thought—had they never heard of pneumonia?—but then Babe lifted her head, her large violet eyes fixing their gaze as curiously on Jilly as Jilly's did on her. Concern fell by the wayside, shifting into a sense of frustration as Jilly realized that all she had in the pocket of her coat that day was a stub of charcoal and her sketchbook instead of the oils and canvas which was the only medium that could really do justice in capturing the startling picture Babe and her companions made.

For long moments none of them spoke. Babe watched her, a half-smile teasing one corner of her mouth. Behind her, the cook stood motionless, a makeshift spatula held negligently in a delicate hand. Eggs and bacon sizzled on the trunk hood in front of her, filling the air with their unmistakable aroma. The other gemmin peered up over the dash of the Buick, supporting their narrow chins on their folded arms.

All Jilly could do was look back. A kind of vertigo licked at the edges of her mind, making her feel as though she'd just stepped into one of her own paintings—the ones that made up her last show, an urban faerie series: twelve enormous canvases, all in oils, one for each month, each depicting a different kind of mythological being transposed from its traditional folkloric rural surroundings onto a cityscape.

Her vague dizziness wasn't caused by the promise of magic that seemed to decorate the moment with a sparkling sense of impossible possibilities as surely as the bacon filled the air with its come-hither smell. It was rather the unexpectedness of coming across a moment like this—in the Tombs, of all places, where winos and junkies were the norm.

It took her awhile to collect her thoughts.

"Interesting stove you've got there," she said finally.

Babe's brow furrowed for a moment, then cleared as a radiant smile first lifted the corners of her mouth, then put an infectious humor into those amazing eyes of hers.

"Interesting, yes," she said. Her voice had an accent Jilly couldn't place and an odd tonality that was at once both husky and high-pitched. "But we—" she frowned prettily, searching for what she wanted to say "—make do."

It was obvious to Jilly that English wasn't her first language. It was also obvious, the more Jilly looked, that while the girl and her companions weren't at all properly dressed for the weather, it really didn't seem to bother them. Even with the fire in the trunk of the Buick, and mild winter or not, they should still have been shivering, but she couldn't spot one goosebump.

"And you're not cold?" she asked.

"Cold is . . . ?" Babe began, frowning again, but before Jilly could elaborate, that dazzling smile returned. "No, we have comfort. Cold is no trouble for us. We like the winter; we like any weather."

Jilly couldn't help but laugh.

"I suppose you're all snow elves," she said, "so the cold doesn't bother you?"

"Not elves—but we are good neighbors. Would you like some breakfast?"

A year and three days later, the memory of that first meeting brought a touch of warmth to Jilly where she stood shivering in the mouth of the alleyway. Gemmin. She'd always liked the taste of words and that one had sounded just right for Babe and her companions. It reminded Jilly of gummy bears, thick cotton quilts and the sound that the bass strings of Geordie's fiddle made when he was playing a fast reel. It reminded her of tiny bunches of fresh violets, touched with dew, that still couldn't hope to match the incandescent hue of Babe's eyes.

She had met the gemmin at a perfect time. She was in need of something warm and happy just then, being on the wrong end of a three-month relationship with a guy who, throughout the time they'd been together, turned out to have been married all along. He wouldn't leave his wife, and Jilly had no taste to be someone's—anyone's—mistress, all of which had been discussed in increasingly raised voices in The Monkey Woman's Nest the last time she saw him. She'd been mortified when she realized that a whole restaurant full of people had been listening to their breaking-up argument, but unrepentant.

She missed Jeff—missed him desperately—but refused to listen to any of the subsequent phonecalls or answer any of the letters that had deluged her loft over the next couple of weeks, explaining how they could "work things out." She wasn't interested in working things out. It wasn't just the fact that he had a wife, but that he'd kept it from her. The thing she kept asking her friend Sue was: having been with him for all that time, how could she not have *known*?

So she wasn't a happy camper, traipsing aimlessly through the Tombs that day. Her normally high-spirited view of the world was overhung with gloominess and there was a sick feeling in the pit of her stomach that just wouldn't go away.

Until she met Babe and her friends.

Gemmin wasn't a name that they used; they had no name for themselves. It was Frank Hodgers who told Jilly what they were.

Breakfast with the gemmin on that long gone morning was . . . odd. Jilly sat behind the driver's wheel of the Buick, with the door propped open and her feet dangling outside. Babe sat on a steel drum set a few feet from the car, facing her. Four of the other gemmin were crowded in the back seat; the fifth was beside Jilly in the front, her back against the passenger's door. The eggs were tasty, flavored with herbs that Jilly couldn't recognize; the tea had a similarly odd tang about it. The bacon was fried to a perfect crisp. The toast was actually muffins, neatly sliced in two and toasted on coat hangers rebent into new shapes for that purpose.

The gemmin acted like they were having a picnic. When Jilly introduced herself, a chorus of odd names echoed back in reply: Nita, Emmie, Callio, Yoon, Purspie. And Babe.

"Babe?" Jilly repeated.

"It was a present—from Johnny Defalco."

Jilly had seen Defalco around and talked to him once or twice. He was a hash dealer who'd had himself a squat in the Clark Building up until the end of the summer when he'd made the mistake of selling to a narc and had to leave the city just one step ahead of a warrant. Somehow, she couldn't see him keeping company with this odd little gaggle of street girls. Defalco's taste seemed to run more to what her bouncer friend Percy called the three B's—bold, blonde and built—or at least it had whenever she'd seen him in the clubs.

"He gave all of you your names?" Jilly asked.

Babe shook her head. "He only ever saw me, and whenever he did, he'd say, 'Hey Babe, how're ya doin'?' "

Babe's speech patterns seemed to change the longer they talked, Jilly remembered thinking later. She no longer sounded like a foreigner struggling with the language; instead, the words came easily, sentences peppered with conjunctions and slang.

"We miss him," Purspie—or perhaps it was Nita—said. Except for Babe, Jilly was still having trouble telling them all apart.

"He talked in the dark." That was definitely Emmie—her voice was slightly higher than those of the others.

"He told stories to the walls," Babe explained, "and we'd creep close and listen to him."

"You've lived around here for awhile?" Jilly asked.

Yoon—or was it Callio?—nodded. "All our lives."

Jilly had to smile at the seriousness with which that line was delivered. As though, except for Babe, there was one of them older than thirteen.

She spent the rest of the morning with them, chatting, listening to their odd songs, sketching them whenever she could get them to sit still for longer than five seconds. Thanks goodness, she thought more than once as she bent over her sketchbook, for life drawing classes and Albert Choira, one of her arts instructor at Butler U., who had instilled in her and every one of his students the ability to capture shape and form in just a few quick strokes of charcoal.

Her depression and the sick feeling in her stomach had gone away, and her heart didn't feel nearly so fragile anymore, but all too soon it was noon and time for her to go. She had Christmas presents to deliver at St. Vincent's Home for the Aged, where she did volunteer work twice a week. Some of her favorites were going to stay with family during the holidays and today would be her last chance to see them.

"We'll be going soon, too," Babe told her when Jilly explained she had to leave.

"Going?" Jilly repeated, feeling an odd tightness in her chest. It wasn't the same kind of a feeling that Jeff had left in her, but it was discomforting all the same.

Babe nodded. "When the moon's full, we'll sail away."

"Away, away, away," the others chorused.

There was something both sweet and sad in the way they half spoke, half chanted the words. The tightness in Jilly's chest grew more pronounced. She wanted to ask, Away to where?, but found herself only saying, "But you'll be here tomorrow?"

Babe lifted a delicate hand to push back the unruly curls that were forever falling in Jilly's eyes. There was something so maternal in the motion that it made Jilly wish she could just rest her head on Babe's breast, to be protected from all that was fierce and mean and dangerous in the world beyond the enfolding comfort that that motherly embrace would offer.

"We'll be here," Babe said.

Then, giggling like schoolgirls, the little band ran off through the ruins, leaving Jilly to stand alone on the deserted street. She felt giddy and lost, all at once. She wanted to run with them, imagining Babe as a kind of archetypal Peter Pan who could take her away to a place where she could be forever young. Then she shook her head, and headed back downtown to St. Vincent's.

She saved her visit with Frank for last, as she always did. He was sitting in a wheelchair by the small window in his room that overlooked the alley between St. Vincent's and the office building next door. It wasn't much of a view, but Frank never seemed to mind.

"I'd rather stare at a brick wall, anytime, than watch that damn TV in the lounge," he'd told Jilly more than once. "That's when things started to go wrong—with the invention of television. Wasn't till then that we found out there was so much wrong in the world."

Jilly was one of those who preferred to know what was going on and try to do something about it, rather than pretend it wasn't happening and hoping that, by ignoring what was wrong, it would just go away. Truth was, Jilly had long ago learned, trouble never went away. It just got worse—unless you fixed it. But at eighty-seven, she felt that Frank was entitled to his opinions.

His face lit up when she came in the door. He was all lines and bones, as he liked to say; a skinny man, made almost cadaverous by age. His cheeks were hollowed, eyes sunken, torso collapsed in on itself. His skin was wrinkled and dry, his hair just a few white tufts around his ears. But whatever ruin the years had brought to his body, they hadn't managed to get even a fingerhold on his spirit. He could be cantankerous, but he was never bitter.

She'd first met him last spring. His son had died, and with nowhere else to go, he'd come to live at St. Vincent's. From the first afternoon that she met him in his room, he'd become one of her favorite people.

"You've got that look," he said after she'd kissed his cheek and sat down on the edge of his bed.

"What look?" Jilly asked, pretending ignorance.

She often gave the impression of being in a constant state of confusion—which was what gave her her charm, Sue had told her more than once—but she knew that Frank wasn't referring to that. It was that strange occurrences tended to gather around her; mystery clung to her like burrs on an old sweater.

At one time when she was younger, she just collected folktales and odd stories, magical rumors and mythologies—much like Geordie's brother Christy did, although she never published them. She couldn't have explained why she was drawn to that kind of story; she just liked the idea of what they had to say. But then one day she discovered that there *was* an alternate reality, and her view of the world was forever changed.

It had felt like a curse at first, knowing that magic was real, but that if she spoke of it, people would think her mad. But the wonder it woke in her could never be considered a curse and she merely learned to be careful with whom she spoke. It was in her art that she allowed herself total freedom to express what she saw from the corner of her eye. An endless stream of faerie folk paraded from her easel and sketchbook, making new homes for themselves in back alleys and city parks, on the wharves down by the waterfront or in the twisty lanes of Lower Crowsea.

In that way, she and Frank were much alike. He'd been a writer once, but, "I've told all the tales I have to tell by now," he explained to Jilly when she asked him why he'd stopped. She disagreed, but knew that his arthritis was so bad that he could neither hold a pencil nor work a keyboard for any length of time.

"You've seen something magic," he said to her now.

"I have," she replied with a grin and told him of her morning.

"Show me your sketches," Frank said when she was done.

Jilly dutifully handed them over, apologizing for the rough state they were in until Frank told her to shush. He turned the pages of the sketchbook, studying each quick drawing carefully before going on to the next one.

"They're gemmin," he pronounced finally.

"I've never heard of them."

"Most people haven't. It was my grandmother who told me about them—she saw them one night, dancing in Fitzhenry Park—but I never did."

The wistfulness in his voice made Jilly want to stage a breakout from the old folk's home and carry him off to the Tombs to meet Babe, but she knew she couldn't. She couldn't even bring him home to her own loft for the holidays because he was too dependent on the care that he could only get here. She'd never even be able to carry him up the steep stairs to her loft.

"How do you know that they're gemmin and whatever *are* gemmin?" she asked.

Frank tapped the sketchbook. "I know they're gemmin because they look just like the way my gran described them to me. And didn't you say they had violet eyes?"

"But only Babe's got them."

Frank smiled, enjoying himself. "Do you know what violet's made up of?"

"Sure. Blue and red."

"Which, symbolically, stand for devotion and passion; blended into violet, they're a symbol of memory."

"That still doesn't explain anything."

"Gemmin are the spirits of place, just like hobs are spirits of a house. They're what make a place feel good and safeguard its positive memories. When they leave, that's when a place gets a haunted feeling. And then only the bad feelings are left—or no feelings, which is just about the same difference."

"So what makes them go?" Jilly asked, remembering what Babe had said earlier.

"Nasty things happening. In the old days, it might be a murder or a battle. Nowadays we can add pollution and the like to that list."

"But—"

"They store memories you see," Frank went on. "The one you call Babe is the oldest, so her eyes have turned violet."

"So," Jilly asked with a grin. "Does it make their hair go mauve, too?"

"Don't be impudent."

They talked some more about the gemmin, going back and forth between, "Were they really?" and "What else could they be?" until it was time for Frank's supper and Jilly had to go. But first she made him open his Christmas present. His eyes filmed when he saw the tiny painting of his old house that Jilly had done for him. Sitting on the stoop was a younger version of himself with a small faun standing jauntily behind him, elbow resting on his shoulder.

"Got something in my eye," he muttered as he brought his sleeve up to his eyes.

"I just wanted you to have this today, because I brought every-body else their presents," Jilly said, "but I'm coming back on Christmas—we'll do something fun. I'd come Christmas eve, but I've got to work at the restaurant that night."

Frank nodded. His tears were gone, but his eyes were still shiny.

"The solstice is coming," he said. "In two days."

Jilly nodded, but didn't say anything.

"That's when they'll be going," Frank explained. "The gemmin. The moon'll be full, just like Babe said. Solstices are like May Eve and Halloween—the borders between this world and others are thinnest then." He gave Jilly a sad smile. "Wouldn't I love to see them before they go."

Jilly thought quickly, but she still couldn't think of any way she could maneuver him into the Tombs in his chair. She couldn't even borrow Sue's car, because the streets there were too choked with rubble and refuse. So she picked up her sketchbook and put it on his lap.

"Keep this," she said.

Then she wheeled him off to the dining room, refusing to listen to his protests that he couldn't.

★   ★   ★

A sad smile touched Jilly's lips as she stood in the storm, remembering. She walked down the alleyway and ran her mittened hand along
the windshield of the Buick, dislodging the snow that had gathered
there. She tried the door, but it was rusted shut. A back window was
open, so she crawled in through it, then clambered into the front
seat, which was relatively free of snow.

It was warmer inside—probably because she was out of the wind.
She sat looking out the windshield until the snow covered it again.
It was like being in a cocoon, she thought. Protected. A person
could almost imagine that the gemmin were still around, not yet
ready to leave. And when they did, maybe they'd take her with
them. . . .

A dreamy feeling stole over her and her eyes fluttered, grew
heavy, then closed. Outside the wind continued to howl, driving the
snow against the car; inside, Jilly slept, dreaming of the past.

The gemmin were waiting for her the day after she saw Frank,
lounging around the abandoned Buick beside the old Clark Building. She wanted to talk to them about what they were and why they
were going away and a hundred other things, but somehow she just
never got around to any of it. She was too busy laughing at their
antics and trying to capture their portraits with the pastels she'd
brought that day. Once they all sang a long song that sounded like
a cross between a traditional ballad and rap, but was in some foreign
language that was both flutelike and gritty. Babe later explained that
it was one of their traditional song cycles, a part of their oral tradition
that kept alive the histories and genealogies of their people and the
places where they lived.

Gemmin, Jilly thought. Storing memories. And then she was
clearheaded long enough to ask if they would come with her to visit
Frank.

Babe shook her head, honest regret in her luminous eyes.

"It's too far," she said.

"Too far, too far," the other gemmin chorused.

"From home," Babe explained.

"But," Jilly began, except she couldn't find the words for what
she wanted to say.

There were people who just made other people feel good. Just being around them, made you feel better, creative, uplifted, happy. Geordie said that she was like that herself, though Jilly wasn't so sure of that. She tried to be, but she was subject to the same bad moods as anybody else, the same impatience with stupidity and ignorance which, parenthetically speaking, were to her mind the prime causes of all the world's ills.

The gemmin didn't seem to have those flaws. Even better, beyond that, there was magic about them. It lay thick in the air, filling your eyes and ears and nose and heart with its wild tang. Jilly desperately wanted Frank to share this with her, but when she tried to explain it to Babe, she just couldn't seem to make herself understood.

And then she realized the time and knew she had to go to work. Art was well and fine to feed the heart and mind, and so was magic, but if she wanted to pay the rent on the loft and have anything to eat next month—never mind the endless drain that art supplies made on her meager budget—she had to go.

As though sensing her imminent departure, the gemmin bounded around her in an abandoned display of wild monkeyshines, and then vanished like so many will-o'-the-wisps in among the snowy rubble of the Tombs, leaving her alone once again.

The next day was much the same, except that tonight was the night they were leaving. Babe never made mention of it, but the knowledge hung ever heavier on Jilly as the hours progressed, coloring her enjoyment of their company.

The gemmin had washed away most of the residue of her bad breakup with Jeff, and for that Jilly was grateful. She could look on it now with that kind of wistful remembering one held for high school romances, long past and distanced. But in its place they had left a sense of abandonment. They were going, would soon be gone, and the world would be that much the emptier for their departure.

Jilly tried to find words to express what she was feeling, but as had happened yesterday when she'd tried to explain Frank's need, she couldn't get the first one past her tongue.

And then again, it was time to go. The gemmin started acting wilder again, dancing and singing around her like a pack of mad imps, but before they could all vanish once more, Jilly caught Babe's arm. Don't go, don't go, she wanted to say, but all that came out was, "I . . . I don't . . . I want . . ."

Jilly, normally never at a loss for something to say, sighed with frustration.

"We won't be gone forever," Babe said, understanding Jilly's unspoken need. She touched a long delicate finger to her temple. "We'll always be with you in here, in your memories of us, and in here—" she tapped the pocket in Jilly's coat that held her sketchbook "—in your pictures. If you don't forget us, we'll never be gone."

"It . . . it won't be the same," Jilly said.

Babe smiled sadly. "Nothing is ever the same. That's why we must go now."

She ruffled Jilly's hair—again the motion was like one made by a mother, rather than someone who appeared to be a girl only half Jilly's age—then stepped back. The other gemmin approached, and touched her as well—featherlight fingers brushing against her arms, tousling her hair like a breeze—and then they all began their mad dancing and pirouetting like so many scruffy ballerinas.

Until they were gone.

Jilly thought she would just stay here, never mind going in to work, but somehow she couldn't face a second parting. Slowly, she headed south, towards Gracie Street and the subway that would take her to work. And oddly enough, though she was sad at their leaving, it wasn't the kind of sadness that hurt. It was the kind that was like a singing in the soul.

Frank died that night, on the winter solstice, but Jilly didn't find out until the next day. He died in his sleep, Jilly's painting propped up on the night table beside him, her sketchbook with her initial rough drawings of the gemmin in it held against his thin chest. On the first blank page after her sketches of the gemmin, in an awkward script that must have taken him hours to write, he'd left her a short note:

"I have to tell you this, Jilly. I never saw any real magic—I just pretended that I did. I only knew it through the stories I got from my gran and from you. But I always believed. That's why I wrote all those stories when I was younger, because I wanted others to believe. I thought if enough of us did, if we learned to care again about the wild places from which we'd driven the magic away, then maybe it would return.

"I didn't think it ever would, but I'm going to open my window tonight and call to them. I'm going to ask them to take me with them when they go. I'm all used up—at least the man I am in this world is—but maybe in another world I'll have something to give. I hope they'll give me the chance.

"The faerie folk used to do that in the old days, you know. That was what a lot of the stories were about—people like us, going away, beyond the fields we know.

"If they take me, don't be sad, Jilly. I'll be waiting for you there."

The script was almost illegible by the time it got near the end, but Jilly managed to decipher it all. At the very end, he'd just signed the note with an "F" with a small flower drawn beside it. It looked an awful lot like a tiny violet, though maybe that was only because that was what Jilly wanted to see.

You saw real magic, she thought when she looked up from the sketchbook. You *were* real magic.

She gazed out the window of his room to where a soft snow was falling in the alley between St. Vincent's and the building next door. She hoped that on their way to wherever they'd gone, the gemmin had been able to include the tired and lonely spirit of one old man in their company.

Take care of him, Babe, she thought.

That Christmas was a quiet period in Jilly's life. She had gone to a church service for the first time since she was a child to attend the memorial service that St. Vincent's held for Frank. She and Geordie and a few of the staff of the home were the only ones in attendance. She missed Frank and found herself putting him in crowd scenes in the paintings she did over the holidays—Frank in the crowds, and the thin ghostly shapes of gemmin peering out from behind cornices and rooflines and the corners of alleyways.

Often when she went out on her night walks—after the restaurant was closed, when the city was half-asleep—she'd hear a singing in the quiet snow-muffled streets; not an audible singing, something she could hear with her ears, but one that only her heart and spirit could feel. Then she'd wonder if it was the voices of Frank and Babe and the others she heard, singing to her from the faraway, or that of other gemmin, not yet gone.

She never thought of Jeff, except with distance.

Life was subdued. A hiatus between storms. Just thinking of that time, usually brought her a sense of peace, if not completion. So why . . . remembering now . . . this time . . . ?

There was a ringing in her ears—sharp and loud, like thunder-claps erupting directly above her. She felt as though she was in an earthquake, her body being violently shaken. Everything felt topsy-turvy. There was no up and no down, just a sense of vertigo and endless spinning, a roar and whorl of shouting and shaking until—

She snapped her eyes open to find Geordie's worried features peering out at her from the circle that the fur of his parka hood made around his face. He was in the Buick with her, on the front seat beside her. It was his hands on her shoulders, shaking her; his voice that sounded like thunder in the confines of the Buick.

The Buick.

And then she remembered: walking in the Tombs, the storm, climbing into the car, falling asleep . . .

"Jesus, Jilly," Geordie was saying. He sat back from her, giving her a bit of space, but the worry hadn't left his features yet. "You really are nuts, aren't you? I mean, falling asleep out here. Didn't you ever hear of hypothermia?"

She could have died, Jilly realized. She could have just slept on here until she froze to death and nobody'd know until the spring thaw, or until some poor homeless bugger crawled in to get out of the wind and found himself sharing space with Jilly, the Amazing Dead Woman.

She shivered, as much from dread as the storm's chill.

"How . . . how did you find me?" she asked.

Geordie shrugged. "God only knows. I got worried, the longer you were gone, until finally I couldn't stand it and had to come looking for you. It was like there was a nagging in the back of my head—sort of a Lassie kind of a thought, you know?"

Jilly had to smile at the analogy.

"Maybe I'm getting psychic—what do you think?" he asked.

"Finding me the way you did, maybe you are," Jilly said.

She sat up a little straighter, then realized that sometime during her sleep, she had unbuttoned her parka enough to stick a hand in under the coat. She pulled it out and both she and Geordie stared at what she held in her mittened hand.

It was a small violet flower, complete with roots.

"Jilly, where did you . . . ?" Geordie began, but then he shook his head. "Never mind. I don't want to know."

But Jilly knew. Tonight was the anniversary, after all. Babe or Frank, or maybe both of them, had come by as well.

If you don't forget us, we'll never be gone.

She hadn't.

And it looked like they hadn't either, because who else had left her this flower, and maybe sent Geordie out into the storm to find her? How else could he have lucked upon her the way he had with all those blocks upon blocks of the Tombs that he would have to search?

"Are you going to be okay?" Geordie asked.

Jilly stuck the plant back under her parka and nodded.

"Help me home, would you? I feel a little wobbly."

"You've got it."

"And Geordie?"

He looked at her, eyebrows raised.

"Thanks for coming out to look for me."

It was a long trek back to Jilly's loft, but this time the wind was helpful, rather than hindering. It rose up at their backs and hurried them along so that it seemed to only take them half the time it should have to return. While Jilly changed, Geordie made great steaming mugs of hot chocolate for both of them. They sat together on the old sofa by the window, Geordie in his usual rumpled sweater and old jeans, Jilly bundled up in two pairs of sweatpants, fingerless gloves and what seemed like a half-dozen shirts and socks.

Jilly told him her story of finding about the gemmin, and how they went away. When she was done, Geordie just said, "Wow. We should tell Christy about them—he'd put them in one of his books."

"Yes, we should," Jilly said. "Maybe if more people knew about them, they wouldn't be so ready to go away."

"What about Mr. Hodgers?" Geordie asked. "Do you really think they took him away with them?"

Jilly looked at the newly potted flower on her windowsill. It stood jauntily in the dirt and looked an awful lot like a drawing in one of her sketchbooks that she hadn't drawn herself.

"I like to think so," she said. "I like to think that St. Vincent's was on the way to wherever they were going." She gave Geordie a smile, more sweet than bitter. "You couldn't see it to look at him," she added, "but Frank had violet eyes, too; he had all kinds of memories stored away in that old head of his—just like Babe did."

Her own eyes took on a distant look, as though she was looking into the faraway herself, through the gates of dream and beyond the fields we know.

"I like to think they're getting along just fine," she said.

✕ PITY THE MONSTERS ✕

WE ARE STANDING IN THE STORM OF OUR OWN BEING.
——MICHAEL VENTURA

"I was a beauty once," the old woman said. "The neighborhood boys were forever standing outside my parents' home, hoping for a word, a smile, a kiss, as though somehow my unearned beauty gave me an intrinsic worth that far overshadowed Emma's cleverness with her schoolwork, or Betsy's gift for music. It always seemed unfair to me. My value was based on an accident of birth; theirs was earned."

The monster made no reply.

"I would have given anything to be clever or to have had some artistic ability," the old woman added. "Those are assets with which a body can grow old."

She drew her tattery shawl closer, hunching her thin shoulders against the cold. Her gaze went to her companion. The monster was looking at the blank expanse of wall above her head, eyes unfocused, scars almost invisible in the dim light.

"Yes, well," she said. "I suppose we all have our own cross to bear. At least I have good memories to go with the bad."

The snow was coming down so thickly that visibility had already become all but impossible. The fat wet flakes whirled and spun in dervishing clouds, clogging the sidewalks and streets, snarling traffic, making the simple act of walking an epic adventure. One could be anywhere, anywhen. The familiar was suddenly strange; the city transformed. The wind and the snow made even the commonest landmarks unrecognizable.

If she hadn't already been so bloody late, Harriet Pierson would have simply walked her mountain bike through the storm. She only lived a mile or so from the library and the trip wouldn't have taken *that* long by foot. But she was late, desperately late, and being sensible had never been her forte, so there she was, pedaling like a madwoman in her highest gear, the wheels skidding and sliding for purchase on the slippery street as she biked along the narrow passageway between the curb and the crawling traffic.

The so-called waterproof boots that she'd bought on sale last week were already soaked, as were the bottoms of her jeans. Her old camel hair coat was standing up to the cold, however, and her earmuffs kept her ears warm. The same couldn't be said for her hands and face. The wind bit straight through her thin woolen mittens, her cheeks were red with the cold, while her long, brown hair, bound up into a vague bun on the top of her head, was covered with an inch of snow that was already leaking its wet chill into her scalp.

Why did I move to this bloody country? she thought. It's too hot in the summer, too cold in the winter . . .

England looked very good right at that moment, but it hadn't always been so. England hadn't had Brian whom she'd met while on holiday here in Newford three years ago, Brian who'd been just as eager for her to come as she had been to emigrate, Brian who walked out on her not two months after she'd arrived and they had gotten an apartment together. She'd refused to go back. Deciding to make the best of her new homeland, she had stuck it out surprisingly well, not so much because she led such an ordered existence, as that she'd refused to run back home and have her mother tell her, ever so patronizingly, "Well, I told you so, dear."

She had a good job, if not a great one, a lovely little flat that was all her own, a fairly busy social life—that admittedly contained more friends than it did romantic interests—and liked everything about her new home. Except for the weather.

She turned off Yoors Street onto Kelly, navigating more by instinct than vision, and was just starting to congratulate herself on having completed her journey all in one piece, with time to spare, when a tall shape loomed suddenly up out of the whirling snow in front of her. Trying to avoid a collision, she turned the handlebars too quickly—and the wrong way.

Her front wheel hit the curb and she sailed over the handlebars, one more white airborne object defying gravity, except that unlike the lighter snowflakes with which she momentarily shared the sky, her weight brought her immediately down with a jarring impact against a heap of refuse that someone had set out in anticipation of tomorrow's garbage pickup.

She rose spluttering snow and staggered back towards her bike, disoriented, the suddenness of her accident not yet having sunk in. She knelt beside the bike and stared with dismay at the bent wheel frame. Then she remembered what had caused her to veer in the first place.

Her gaze went to the street, but then traveled up, and up, to the face of the tall shape that stood by the curb. The man was a giant. At five-one, Harriet wasn't tall, and perhaps it had something to do with her low perspective, but he seemed to be at least seven feet high. And yet it wasn't his size that brought the small gasp to her lips.

That face . . .

It was set in a squarish head which was itself perched on thick broad shoulders. The big nose was bent, the left eye was slightly higher than the right, the ears were like huge cauliflowers, the hairline high and square. Thick white scars crisscrossed his features, giving the impression that he'd been sewn together by some untalented seamstress who was too deep in her cups to do a proper job. An icon from an old horror movie flashed in Harriet's mind and she found herself looking for the bolts in the man's neck before she even knew what she was doing.

Of course they weren't there, but the size of the man and the way he was just standing there, staring at her, made Harriet unaccountably nervous as though this really was Victor Frankenstein's creation standing over her in the storm. She stood quickly, wanting to lessen the discrepancy of their heights. The sudden movement woke a wave of dizziness.

"I'm dreadfully sorry," she meant to say, but the words slurred, turning to mush in her mouth and what came out was, "Redfolly shurry."

Vertigo jellied her legs and made the street underfoot so wobbly that she couldn't keep her balance. The giant took a quick step towards her, huge hands outstretched, as a black wave swept over her and she pitched forward.

Bloody hell, she had time to think. I'm going all faint. . . .

Water bubbled merrily in the tin can that sat on the Coleman stove's burner. The old woman leaned forward and dropped in a tea bag, then moved the can from the heat with a mittened hand.

Only two more bags left, she thought.

She held her hands out to the stove and savored the warmth.

"I married for money, not love," she told her companion. "My Henry was not a handsome man."

The monster gaze focused and tracked down to her face.

"But I grew to love him. Not for his money, nor for the comfort of his home and the safety it offered to a young woman whose future, for all her beauty, looked to take her no further than the tenements in which she was born and bred."

The monster made a querulous noise, no more than a grunt, but the old woman could hear the question in it. They'd been together for so long that she could read him easily, without his needing to speak.

"It was for his kindness," she said.

Harriet woke to the cold. Shivering, she sat up to find herself in an unfamiliar room, enwrapped in a nest of blankets that carried a pungent, musty odor in their folds. The room itself appeared to be part of some abandoned building. The walls were unadorned except for their chipped paint and plaster and a cheerful bit of graffiti suggesting that the reader of it do something that Harriet didn't think was anatomically possible.

There were no furnishings at all. The only light came from a short, fat candle which sat on the windowsill in a puddle of cooled wax. Outside, the wind howled. In the room, in the building itself, all was still. But as she cocked her head to listen, she could just faintly make out a low murmur of conversation. It appeared to be a monologue, for it was simply one voice, droning on.

She remembered her accident and the seven-foot tall giant as though they were only something she'd experienced in a dream. The vague sense of dislocation she'd felt upon awakening had grown into a dreamy kind of muddled feeling. She was somewhat concerned over her whereabouts, but not in any sort of a pressing way. Her mind seemed to be in a fog.

Getting up, she hesitated for a moment, then wrapped one of the smelly blankets about her shoulders like a shawl against the cold and crossed the room to its one doorway. Stepping outside, she found herself in a hall as disrepaired and empty as the room she'd just quit.

The murmuring voice led her down the length of the hall into what proved to be a foyer. Leaning against the last bit of wall, there where the hallway opened up into the larger space, she studied the odd scene before her.

Seven candles sat in their wax on wooden orange crates that were arranged in a half circle around an old woman. She had her back to the wall, legs tucked up under what appeared to be a half-dozen skirts. A ratty shawl covered her grey hair and hung down over her shoulders. Her face was a spiderweb of lines, all pinched and thin. Water steamed in a large tin can on a Coleman stove that stood on the floor in front of her. She had another, smaller tin can in her hand filled with, judging by the smell that filled the room, some kind of herbal tea. She was talking softly to no one that Harriet could see.

The old woman looked up just as Harriet was trying to decide how to approach her. The candlelight woke an odd glimmer in the woman's eyes, a reflective quality that reminded Harriet of a cat's gaze caught in a car's headbeams.

"And who are you, dear?" the woman asked.

"I . . . my name's Harriet. Harriet Pierson." She got the odd feeling that she should curtsy as she introduced herself.

"You may call me Flora," the old woman said. "My name's actually Anne Boddeker, but I prefer Flora."

Harriet nodded absently. Under the muddle of of her thoughts, the first sharp wedge of concern was beginning to surface. She remembered taking a fall from her bike . . . had she hit her head?

"What am I doing here?" she asked.

The old woman's eyes twinkled with humor. "Now how would I know?"

"But . . ." The fuzz in Harriet's head seemed to thicken. She blinked a couple of times and then cleared her throat. "Where are we?" she tried.

"North of Gracie Street," Flora replied, "in that part of town that, I believe, people your age refer to as Squatland. I'm afraid I don't know the exact address. Vandals have played havoc with the street signs, as I'm sure you know, but I believe we're not far from the corner of Flood and MacNeil where I grew up."

Harriet's heart sank. She was in the Tombs, an area of Newford that had once been a developer's bright dream. The old, tired blocks of tenements, office buildings and factories were to be transformed into a yuppie paradise and work had already begun on tearing down the existing structures when a sudden lack of backing had left the developer scrambling for solvency. All that remained now of the bright dream was block upon block of abandoned buildings and rubble-strewn lots generally referred to as the Tombs. It was home to runaways, the homeless, derelicts, bikers, drug addicts and the like who squatted in its buildings.

It was also probably one of the most dangerous parts of Newford.

"I . . . how did I get here?" Harriet tried again.

"What do you remember?" Flora said.

"I was biking home from work," Harriet began and then proceeded to relate what she remembered of the storm, the giant who'd loomed up so suddenly out of the snow, her accident . . . "And then I suppose I must have fainted."

She lifted a hand to her head and searched about for a tender spot, but couldn't find a lump or a bruise.

"Did he speak to you?" Flora asked. "The . . . man who startled you?"

Harriet shook her head.

"Then it was Frank. He must have brought you here."

Harriet thought about what the old woman had just said.

"Does that mean there's more than one of him?" she asked. She had the feeling that her memory was playing tricks on her when she tried to call up the giant's scarred and misshapen features. She couldn't imagine there being more than one of him.

"In a way," Flora said.

"You're not being very clear."

"I'm sorry."

But she didn't appear to be, Harriet realized.

"So . . . he, this Frank . . . he's mute?" she asked.

"Terrible, isn't it?" Flora said. "A great big strapping lad like that."

Harriet nodded in agreement. "But that doesn't explain what you meant by there being more than one of him. Does he have a brother?"

"He . . ." The old woman hesitated. "Perhaps you should ask him yourself."

"But you just said that he was a mute."

"I think he's down that hall," Flora said, ignoring Harriet. She pointed to a doorway opposite from the one that Harriet had used to enter the foyer. "That's usually where he goes to play."

Harriet stood there for a long moment, just looking at the old woman. Flora, Anne, whatever her name was—she was obviously senile. That had to explain her odd manner.

Harriet lifted her gaze to look in the direction Flora had pointed. Her thoughts still felt muddy. She found standing as long as she had been was far more tiring than it should have been and her tongue felt all fuzzy.

All she wanted to do was to go home. But if this *was* the Tombs, then she'd need directions. Perhaps even protection from some of the more feral characters who were said to inhabit these abandoned buildings. Unless, she thought glumly, this "Frank" was the danger himself. . . .

She looked back at Flora, but the old woman was ignoring her. Flora drew her shawl more tightly around her shoulders and took a sip of tea from her tin can.

Bother, Harriet thought and started across the foyer.

Halfway down the new hallway, she heard a child's voice singing softly. She couldn't make out the words until she'd reached the end of the hall where yet another candlelit room offered up a view of its bizarre occupant.

Frank was sitting cross-legged in the middle of the room, the contents of Harriet's purse scattered on the floor by his knees. Her purse itself had been tossed into a corner. Harriet would have backed right out of the room before Frank looked up except that she was frozen in place by the singing. The child's voice came from Frank's twisted lips—a high, impossibly sweet sound. It was a little girl's voice, singing a skipping song:

> *Frank and Harriet, sitting in a tree*
> *K-I-S-S-I-N-G*
> *First comes love, then comes marriage*
> *Here comes Frank with a baby's carriage*

Frank's features seemed more monstrous than ever with that sweet child's voice issuing from his throat. He tossed the contents of

Harriet's wallet into the air, juggling them. Her ID, a credit card, some photos from back home, scraps of paper with addresses or phone numbers on them, paper money, her bank card . . . they did a fluttering fandango as he sang, the movement of his hands oddly graceful for all the scarred squat bulk of his fingers. Her makeup, keys and loose change were lined up in rows like toy soldiers on parade in front of him. A half-burned ten dollar bill lay beside a candle on the wooden crate to his right. On the crate to his left lay a dead cat, curled up as though it was only sleeping, but the glassy dead eyes and swollen tongue that pushed open its jaws gave lie to the pretense.

Harriet felt a scream build up in her throat. She tried to back away, but bumped into the wall. The child's voice went still and Frank looked up. Photos, paper money, paper scraps and all flittered down upon his knees. His gaze locked on hers.

For one moment, Harriet was sure it was a child's eyes that regarded her from that ruined face. They carried a look of pure, absolute innocence, utterly at odds with the misshapen flesh and scars that surrounded them. But then they changed, gaining a feral, dark intelligence.

Frank scattered the scraps of paper and money in front of him away with a sweep of his hands.

"Mine," he cried in a deep, booming voice. "Girl is mine!"

As he lurched to his feet, Harriet fled back the way she'd come.

"The hardest thing," the old woman said, "is watching everybody die. One by one, they all die: your parents, your friends, your family. . . ."

Her voice trailed off, rheumy eyes going sad. The monster merely regarded her.

"It was hardest when Julie died," she went on after a moment. There was a hitch in her voice as she spoke her daughter's name. "It's not right that parents should outlive their children." Her gaze settled on the monster's face. "But then you'll never know that particular pain, will you?"

The monster threw back his head and a soundless howl tore from his throat.

★　　★　　★

As Harriet ran back into the room where she'd left Flora, she saw that the old woman was gone. Her candles, the crates and stove remained. The tin can half full of tea sat warming on the edge of the stove, not quite on the lit burner.

Harried looked back down the hall where Frank's shambling bulk stumbled towards her.

She had to get out of this place. Never mind the storm still howling outside the building, never mind the confusing maze of abandoned buildings and refuse-choked streets of the Tombs. She just had to—

"There you are," a voice said from directly behind her.

Harriet heart skipped a beat. A sharp, small inadvertent squeak escaped her lips as she flung herself to one side and then backed quickly away from the shadows by the door from which the voice had come. When she realized it was only the old woman, she kept right on backing up. Whoever, whatever, Flora was, Harriet knew she wasn't a friend.

Frank shambled into the foyer then, the queer lopsided set of his gaze fixed hungrily upon her. Harriet's heartbeat kicked into double-time. Her throat went dry. The muscles of her chest tightened, squeezing her lungs so that she found it hard to breathe.

Oh god, she thought. Get out of here while you can.

But she couldn't seem to move. Her limbs were deadened weights and she was starting to feel faint again.

"Now, now," the old woman said. "Don't carry on so, Samson, or you'll frighten her to death."

The monster obediently stopped in the doorway, but his hungry gaze never left Harriet.

"Sam-samson?" Harriet asked in a weak voice.

"Oh, there's all sorts of bits and pieces of people inside that poor ugly head," Flora replied. "Comes from traumas he suffered as a child. He suffers from—what was it that Dr. Adams called him? Dissociation. I think, before the accident, the doctor had documented seventeen people inside him. Some are harmless, such as Frank and little Bessie. Others, like Samson, have an unfortunate capacity for violence when they can't have their way."

"Doctor?" Harriet asked. All she seemed capable of was catching a word from the woman's explanation and repeating it as a question.

"Yes, he was institutionalized as a young boy. The odd thing is that he's somewhat aware of all the different people living inside him. He thinks that when his father sewed him back together, he used parts of all sorts of different people to do so and those bits of alien skin and tissue took hold of his mind and borrowed parts of it for their own use."

"That . . ." Harriet cleared her throat. "That was the . . . accident?"

"Oh, it wasn't any accident," Flora said. "And don't let anyone try to tell you different. His father knew exactly what he was doing when he threw him through that plate glass window."

"But . . ."

"Of course, the father was too poor to be able to afford medical attention for the boy, so he patched him up on his own."

Harriet stared at the monstrous figure with growing horror.

"This . . . none of this can be true," she finally managed.

"It's all documented at the institution," Flora told her. "His father made a full confession before they locked him away. Poor Frank, though. It was too late to do anything to help him by that point, so he ended up being put away as well, for all that his only crime was the misfortune of being born the son of a lunatic."

Harriet tore her gaze from Frank's scarred features and turned to the old woman.

"How do you know all of this?" she asked.

"Why, I lived there as well," Flora said. "Didn't I tell you?"

"No. No, you didn't."

Flora shrugged. "It's old history. Mind you, when you get to be my age, everything's old history."

Harriet wanted to ask why Flora had been in the institution herself, but couldn't find the courage to do so. She wasn't even sure she *wanted* to know. But there was something she had no choice but to ask. She hugged her blanket closer around her, no longer even aware of its smell, but the chill that was in her bones didn't come from the cold.

"What happens now?" she said.

"I'm not sure I understand the question," Flora replied with a sly smile in her eyes that said she understood all too well.

Harriet pressed forward. "What happens to me?"

"Well, now," Flora said. She shot the monster an affectionate look. "Frank wants to start a family."

Harriet shook her head. "No," she said, her voice sounding weak and ineffectual even to her own ears. "No way."

"You don't exactly have a say in the matter, dear. It's not as though there's anyone coming to rescue you—not in this storm. And even if someone did come searching, where would they look? People disappear in this city all of the time. It's a sad, but unavoidable fact in these trying times that we've brought upon ourselves."

Harriet was still shaking her head.

"Oh, think of someone else for a change," the old woman told her. "I know your type. You're filled with your own self-importance; the whole world revolves around you. It's a party here, an evening of dancing there, theatre, clubs, cabaret, with never a thought for those less fortunate. What would it hurt you to give a bit of love and affection to a poor, lonely monster?"

I've gone all demented, Harriet thought. All of this—the monster, the lunatic calm of the old woman—none of it was real. None of it *could* be real.

"Do you think he *likes* being this way?" Flora demanded.

Her voice grew sharp and the monster shifted nervously at the tone of her anger, the way a dog might bristle, catching its master's mood.

"It's got nothing to do with me," Harriet said, surprising herself that she could still find the courage to stand up for herself. "I'm not like you think I am and I had nothing to do with what happened to that—to Frank."

"It's got everything to do with you," the old woman replied. "It's got to do with caring and family and good Samaritanism and decency and long, lasting relationships."

"You can't force a person into something like that," Harriet argued.

Flora sighed. "Sometimes, in *these* times, it's the only way. There's a sickness abroad in the world, child; your denial of what's right and true is as much a cause as a symptom."

"You're the one that's sick!" Harriet cried.

She bolted for the building's front doors, praying they weren't locked. The monster was too far away and moved too slowly to stop her. The old woman was closer and quicker, but in her panic, Harriet found the strength to fling her bodily away. She raced for the glass doors that led out of the foyer and into the storm.

The wind almost drove her back inside when she finally got a door open, but she pressed against it, through the door and out onto the street. The whirling snow, driven by the mad, capricious wind, soon stole away all sense of direction, but she didn't dare stop. She plowed through drifts, blinded by the snow, head bent against the howling wind, determined to put as much distance between herself and what she fled.

Oh god, she thought at one point. My purse was back there. My ID. They know where I live. They can come and get me at home, or at work, anytime they want.

But mostly she fought the snow and wind. How long she fled through the blizzard, she had no way of knowing. It might have been an hour, it might have been the whole night. She was shaking with cold and fear when she stumbled to the ground one last time and couldn't get up.

She lay there, a delicious sense of warmth enveloping her. All she had to do was let go, she realized. Just let go and she could drift away into that dark, warm place that beckoned to her. She rolled over on her side and stared up into the white sky. Snow immediately filmed her face. She rubbed it away with her hand, already half-frozen with the cold.

She was ready to let go. She was ready to just give up the struggle, because she was only so strong and she'd given it her all, hadn't she? She—

A tall dark figure loomed up suddenly, towering over her. Snow blurred her sight so that it was only a shape, an outline, against the white.

No, she pleaded. Don't take me back. I'd rather die than go back.

As the figure bent down beside her, she found the strength to beat at it with her frozen hands.

"Easy now," a kind voice said, blocking her weak blows. "We'll get you out of here."

She stopped trying to fight. It wasn't the monster, but a policeman. Somehow, in her aimless flight, she'd wandered out of the Tombs.

"What are you doing out here?" the policeman said.

Monster, she wanted to say. There's a monster. It attacked me. But all that came out from her frozen lips was, "Muh . . . tacked me . . ."

"First we'll get you out of this weather," he told her, "then we'll deal with the man who assaulted you."

The hours that followed passed in a blur. She was in a hospital, being treated for frostbite. A detective interviewed her, calmly, patiently sifting through her mumbled replies for a description of what had happened to her, and then finally she was left alone.

At one point she came out of her dozing state and thought she saw two policeman standing at the end of her bed. She wasn't sure if they were actually present or not, but like Agatha Christie characters, gathered at the denouement of one of the great mystery writer's stories, their conversation conveniently filled in some details concerning her captors of which she hadn't been aware.

"Maybe it was before your time," one of the policemen was saying, "but that description she gave fits."

"No, I remember," the other replied. "They were residents in the Zeb's criminal ward and Cross killed their shrink during a power failure."

The first officer nodded. "I don't know which of them was worse: Cross with that monstrous face, or Boddeker."

"Poisoned her whole family, didn't she?"

"Yeah, but I remember seeing what Cross did to the shrink—just about tore the poor bastard in two."

"I heard that it was Boddeker who put him up to it. The poor geek doesn't have a mind of his own."

Vaguely, as though observing the action from a vast distance, Harriet could sense the first officer looking in her direction.

"She's lucky she's still alive," he added, looking back at his companion.

In the days that followed, researching old newspapers at the library, Harriet found out that all that the two men had said, or that she'd dreamed they had said, was true, but she couldn't absorb any of it at the moment. For now she just drifted away once more, entering a troubled sleep that was plagued with dreams of ghosts and monsters. The latter wore masks to hide the horror inside them, and they were the worst of all.

She woke much later, desperately needing to pee. It was still dark in her room. Outside she could hear the wind howling.

She fumbled her way into the bathroom and did her business, then stared into the mirror after she'd flushed. There was barely enough light for the mirror to show her reflection. What looked back at her from the glass was a ghostly face that she almost didn't recognize.

"Monsters," she said softly, not sure if what she felt was pity or fear, not sure if she recognized one in herself, or if it was just the old woman's lunatic calm still pointing an accusing finger.

She stared at that spectral reflection for a very long time before she finally went back to bed.

"We'll find you another," the old woman said.

Her tea had gone cold but she was too tired to relight the stove and make herself another cup. Her hand were folded on her lap, her gaze fixed on the tin can of cold water that still sat on the stove. A film of ice was forming on the water.

"You'll see," she added. "We'll find another, but this time we'll put her together ourselves, just the way your father did with you. We'll take a bit from one and a bit from another and we'll make you the perfect mate, just see if we don't. I always was a fair hand with a needle and thread, you know—a necessary quality for a wife in my time. Of course everything's different now, everything's changed. Sometimes I wonder why we bother to go on. . . ."

The monster stared out the window to where the snow still fell, quietly now, the blizzard having moved on, leaving only this calm memory of its storm winds in its wake. He gave no indication that he was listening to the old woman, but she went on talking all the same.

≋ GHOSTS OF WIND ≋
AND SHADOW

THERE MAY BE GREAT AND UNDREAMED OF POSSIBILI-
TIES AWAITING MANKIND; BUT BECAUSE OF OUR LINE
OF DESCENT THERE ARE ALSO QUEER LIMITATIONS.
—CLARENCE DAY, FROM THIS SIMIAN WORLD

Tuesday and Thursday afternoons, from two to four, Meran Kelledy gave flute lessons at the Old Firehall on Lee Street which served as Lower Crowsea's community center. A small room in the basement was set aside for her at those times. The rest of the week it served as an office for the editor of *The Crowsea Times,* the monthly community newspaper.

The room always had a bit of a damp smell about it. The walls were bare except for two old posters: one sponsored a community rummage sale, now long past; the other was an advertisement for a Jilly Coppercorn one-woman show at the The Green Man Gallery featuring a reproduction of the firehall that had been taken from the artist's *In Lower Crowsea* series of street scenes. It, too, was long out of date.

Much of the room was taken up by a sturdy oak desk. A computer sat on its broad surface, always surrounded by a clutter of manuscripts waiting to be put on diskette, spot art, advertisements, sheets of Lettraset, glue sticks, pens, pencils, scratch pads and the like. Its printer was relegated to an apple crate on the floor. A large cork board in easy reach of the desk held a bewildering array of pinned-up slips of paper with almost indecipherable notes and appointments jotted on them. Post-its laureled the frame of the cork board and the sides of the computer like festive yellow decorations. A battered metal filing cabinet held back issues of the newspaper. On top of it was a vase with dried flowers—not so much an arrangement as a forgotten bouquet. One week of the month, the entire desk was covered with the current issue in progress in its various stages of layout.

It was not a room that appeared conducive to music, despite the presence of two small music stands taken from their storage spot behind the filing cabinet and set out in the open space between the desk and door along with a pair of straight-backed wooden chairs, salvaged twice a week from a closet down the hall. But music has its own enchantment and the first few notes of an old tune are all that it requires to transform any site into a place of magic, even if that location is no more than a windowless office cubicle in the Old Firehall's basement.

Meran taught an old style of flute-playing. Her instrument of choice was that enduring cousin of the silver transverse orchestral flute: a simpler wooden instrument, side-blown as well, though it lacked a lip plate to help direct the airstream; keyless with only six holes. It was popularly referred to as an Irish flute since it was used for the playing of traditional Irish and Scottish dance music and the plaintive slow airs native to those same countries, but it had relatives in most countries of the world as well as in baroque orchestras.

In one form or another, it was one of the first implements created by ancient people to give voice to the mysteries that words cannot encompass, but that they had a need to express; only the drum was older.

With her last student of the day just out the door, Meran began the ritual of cleaning her instrument in preparation to packing it away and going home herself. She separated the flute into its three parts, swabbing dry the inside of each piece with a piece of soft cotton attached to a flute-rod. As she was putting the instrument away in its case, she realized that there was a woman standing in the doorway, a hesitant presence, reluctant to disturb the ritual until Meran was ready to notice her.

"Mrs. Batterberry," Meran said. "I'm sorry. I didn't realize you were there."

The mother of her last student was in her late thirties, a striking, well-dressed woman whose attractiveness was undermined by an obvious lack of self-esteem.

"I hope I'm not intruding . . . ?"

"Not at all; I'm just packing up. Please have a seat."

Meran indicated the second chair, which Mrs. Batterberry's daughter had so recently vacated. The woman walked gingerly into the room and perched on the edge of the chair, handbag clutched in both hands. She looked for all the world like a bird that was ready at any moment to erupt into flight and be gone.

"How can I help you, Mrs. Batterberry?" Meran asked.

"Please, call me Anna."

"Anna it is."

Meran waited expectantly.

"I . . . it's about Lesli," Mrs. Batterberry finally began.

Meran nodded encouragingly. "She's doing very well. I think she has a real gift."

"Here perhaps, but . . . well, look at this."

Drawing a handful of folded papers from her handbag, she passed them over to Meran. There were about five sheets of neat, closely-written lines of what appeared to be a school essay. Meran recognized the handwriting as Lesli's. She read the teacher's remarks, written in red ink at the top of the first page—"Well written and imaginative, but the next time, please stick to the assigned topic"—then quickly scanned through the pages. The last two paragraphs bore rereading:

"The old gods and their magics did not dwindle away into murky memories of brownies and little fairies more at home in a Disney cartoon; rather, they changed. The coming of Christ and Christians actually freed them. They were no longer bound to people's expectations but could now become anything that they could imagine themselves to be.

"They are still here, walking among us. We just don't recognize them anymore."

Meran looked up from the paper. "It's quite evocative."

"The essay was supposed to be on one of the ethnic minorities of Newford," Mrs. Batterberry said.

"Then, to a believer in Faerie," Meran said with a smile, "Lesli's essay would seem most apropos."

"I'm sorry," Mrs. Batterberry said, "but I can't find any humor in this situation. This—" she indicated the essay "—it just makes me uncomfortable."

"No, I'm the one who's sorry," Meran said. "I didn't mean to make light of your worries, but I'm also afraid that I don't understand them."

Mrs. Batterberry looked more uncomfortable than ever. "It . . . it just seems so obvious. She must be involved with the occult, or drugs. Perhaps both."

"Just because of this essay?" Meran asked. She only just managed to keep the incredulity from her voice.

"Fairies and magic are all she ever talks about—or did talk about, I should say. We don't seem to have much luck communicating anymore."

Mrs. Batterberry fell silent then. Meran looked down at the essay, reading more of it as she waited for Lesli's mother to go on. After a few moments, she looked up to find Mrs. Batterberry regarding her hopefully.

Meran cleared her throat. "I'm not exactly sure why it is that you've come to me," she said finally.

"I was hoping you'd talk to her—to Lesli. She adores you. I'm sure she'd listen to you."

"And tell her what?"

"That this sort of thinking—" Mrs. Batterberry waved a hand in the general direction of the essay that Meran was holding "—is wrong."

"I'm not sure that I can—"

Before Meran could complete her sentence with "do that," Mrs. Batterberry reached over and gripped her hand.

"Please," the woman said. "I don't know where else to turn. She's going to be sixteen in a few days. Legally, she can live on her own then and I'm afraid she's just going to leave home if we can't get this settled. I won't have drugs or . . . or occult things in my house. But I . . ." Her eyes were suddenly swimming with unshed tears. "I don't want to lose her. . . ."

She drew back. From her handbag, she fished out a handkerchief which she used to dab at her eyes.

Meran sighed. "All right," she said. "Lesli has another lesson with me on Thursday—a makeup one for having missed one last week. I'll talk to her then, but I can't promise you anything."

Mrs. Batterberry looked embarrassed, but relieved. "I'm sure you'll be able to help."

Meran had no such assurances, but Lesli's mother was already on her feet and heading for the door, forestalling any attempt Meran might have tried to muster to back out of the situation. Mrs. Batter-berry paused in the doorway and looked back.

"Thank you so much," she said, and then she was gone.

Meran stared sourly at the space Mrs. Batterberry had occupied.

"Well, isn't this just wonderful," she said.

From Lesli's diary, entry dated October 12th:

I saw another one today! It wasn't at all the same as the one I spied on the Common last week. That one was more like a wizened little monkey, dressed up like an Arthur Rackham leprechaun. If I'd told anybody about him, they'd say that it *was* just a dressed-up monkey, but we know better, don't we?

This is just so wonderful. I've always known they were there, of course. All around. But they were just hints, things I'd see out of the corner of my eye, snatches of music or conversation that I'd hear in a park or the backyard, when no one else was around. But ever since Midsummer's Eve, I've actually been able to see them.

I feel like a birder, noting each new separate species I spot down here on your pages, but was there ever a birdwatcher that could claim to have seen the marvels I have? It's like, all of a sudden, I've finally learned how to *see*.

This one was at the Old Firehall of all places. I was having my weekly lesson with Meran—I get two this week because she was out of town last week. Anyway, we were playing my new tune—the one with the arpeggio bit in the second part that I'm sup-posed to be practicing but can't quite get the hang of. It's easy when Meran's playing along with me, but when I try to do it on my own, my fingers get all fumbly and I keep muddling up the middle D.

I seem to have gotten sidetracked. Where was I? Oh yes. We were playing "Touch Me If You Dare" and it really sounded nice with both of us playing. Meran just seemed to pull my playing along with hers until it got lost in her music and you couldn't tell which instrument was which, or even how many there were play-ing.

It was one of those perfect moments. I felt like I was in a trance or something. I had my eyes closed, but then I felt the air getting all thick. There was this weird sort of pressure on my skin, as though gravity had just doubled or something. I kept on playing, but I opened my eyes and that's when I saw her—hovering up behind Meran's shoulders.

She was the neatest thing I've ever seen—just the tiniest little faerie, ever so pretty, with gossamer wings that moved so quickly to keep her aloft that they were just a blur. They moved like a hummingbird's wings. She looked just like the faeries on a pair of earrings I got a few years ago at a stall in the Market—sort of a Mucha design and all delicate and airy. But she wasn't two-dimensional or just one color.

Her wings were like a rainbow blaze. Her hair was like honey, her skin a soft-burnished gold. She was wearing—now don't blush, diary—nothing at all on top and just a gauzy skirt that seemed to be made of little leaves that kept changing colour, now sort of pink, now mauve, now bluish.

I was so surprised that I almost dropped my flute. I didn't—wouldn't that give Mom something to yell at me for if I broke it!—but I did muddle the tune. As soon as the music faltered—just like that, as though the only thing that was keeping her in this world was that tune—she disappeared.

I didn't pay a whole lot of attention to what Meran was saying for the rest of the lesson, but I don't think she noticed. I couldn't get the faerie out of my mind. I still can't. I wish Mom had been there to see her, or stupid old Mr. Allen. They couldn't say it was just my imagination then!

Of course they probably wouldn't have been able to see her anyway. That's the thing with magic. You've got to know it's still here, all around us, or it just stays invisible for you.

After my lesson, Mom went in to talk to Meran and made me wait in the car. She wouldn't say what they'd talked about, but she seemed to be in a way better mood than usual when she got back. God, I wish she wouldn't get so uptight.

"So," Cerin said finally, setting aside his book. Meran had been moping about the house for the whole of the hour since she'd gotten home from the Firehall. "Do you want to talk about it?"

"You'll just say I told you so."

"Told you so how?"

Meran sighed. "Oh, you know. How did you put it? 'The problem with teaching children is that you have to put up with their parents.' It was something like that."

Cerin joined her in the windowseat, where she'd been staring out at the garden. He looked out at the giant old oaks that surrounded the house and said nothing for a long moment. In the fading afternoon light, he could see little brown men scurrying about in the leaves like so many monkeys.

"But the kids are worth it," he said finally.

"I don't see you teaching children."

"There's just not many parents that can afford a harp for their prodigies."

"But still . . ."

"Still," he agreed. "You're perfectly right. I don't like dealing with their parents; never did. When I see children put into little boxes, their enthusiasms stifled . . . Everything gets regimented into what's proper and what's not, into recitals and passing examinations instead of just playing—" he began to mimic a hoity-toity voice "—I don't care if you want to play in a rock band, you'll learn what I tell you to learn. . . ."

His voice trailed off. In the back of his eyes, a dark light gleamed—not quite anger, more frustration.

"It makes you want to give them a good whack," Meran said.

"Exactly. So did you?"

Meran shook her head. "It wasn't like that, but it was almost as bad. No, maybe it was worse."

She told her husband about what Lesli's mother had asked of her, handing over the English essay when she was done so that he could read it for himself.

"This is quite good, isn't it?" he said when he reached the end.

Meran nodded. "But how can I tell Lesli that none of it's true when I know it is?"

"You can't."

Cerin laid the essay down on the windowsill and looked out at the oaks again. The twilight had crept up on the garden while they were talking. All the trees wore thick mantles of shadow now—poor recompense for the glorious cloaks of leaves that the season had stolen from them over the past few weeks. At the base of one fat trunk, the little monkeymen were roasting skewers of mushrooms and acorns over a small, almost smokeless fire.

"What about Anna Batterberry herself?" he asked. "Does she remember anything?"

Meran shook her head. "I don't think she even realizes that we've met before, that she changed but we never did. She's like most people; if it doesn't make sense, she'd rather convince herself that it simply never happened."

Cerin turned from the window to regard his wife.

"Perhaps the solution would be to remind her, then," he said.

"I don't think that's such a good idea. It'd probably do more harm than good. She's just not the right sort of person . . ."

Meran sighed again.

"But she could have been," Cerin said.

"Oh yes," Meran said, remembering. "She could have been. But it's too late for her now."

Cerin shook his head. "It's never too late."

From Lesli's diary, addendum to the entry dated October 12th:

I hate living in this house! I just hate it! How could she do this to me? It's bad enough that she never lets me so much as breathe without standing there behind me to determine that I'm not making a vulgar display of myself in the process, but this really isn't fair.

I suppose you're wondering what I'm talking about. Well, remember that essay I did on ethnic minorities for Mr. Allen? Mom got her hands on it and it's convinced her that I've turned into a Satan-worshipping drug fiend. The worst thing is that she gave it to Meran and now Meran's supposed to "have a talk with me to set me straight" on Thursday.

I just hate this. She had no right to do that. And how am I supposed to go to my lesson now? It's so embarrassing. Not to mention disappointing. I thought Meran would understand. I never thought she'd take Mom's side—not on something like this.

Meran's always seemed so special. It's not just that she wears all those funky clothes and doesn't talk down to me and looks just like one of those Pre-Raphaelite women, except that she's got those really neat green streaks in her hair. She's just a great person. She makes playing music seem so effortlessly magical and she's got all these really great stories about the origins of the tunes. When she talks about things like where "The Gold Ring" came from, it's like she really believes it was the faeries that gave that piper the tune in exchange for the lost ring he returned to them. The way she tells it, it's like she was there when it happened.

I feel like I've always known her. From the first time I saw her, I felt like I was meeting an old friend. Sometimes I think that she's magic herself—a kind of oak-tree faerie princess who's just spending a few years living in the Fields We Know before she goes back home to the magic place where she really lives.

Why would someone like that involve themselves in my mother's crusade against Faerie?

I guess I was just being naive. She's probably no different from Mom or Mr. Allen and everybody else who doesn't believe. Well, I'm not going to any more stupid flute lessons, that's for sure.

I hate living here. Anything'd be better.

Oh, why couldn't I just have been stolen by the faeries when I was a baby? Then I'd *be* there and there'd just be some changeling living here in my place. Mom could turn *it* into a good little robot instead. Because that's all she wants. She doesn't want a daughter who can think on her own, but a boring, closed-minded junior model of herself. She should have gotten a dog instead of having a kid. Dogs are easy to train and they like being led around on a leash.

I wish Granny Nell was still alive. She would never, ever have tried to tell me that I had to grow up and stop imagining things. Everything seemed magic when she was around. It was like she was magic—just like Meran. Sometimes when Meran's playing her flute, I almost feel as though Granny Nell's sitting there with us, just listening to the music with that sad wise smile of hers.

I know I was only five when she died, but lots of the time she seems more real to me than any of my relatives that are still alive. If she was still alive, I could be living with her right now and everything'd be really great.

Jeez, I miss her.

Anna Batterberry was in an anxious state when she pulled up in front of the Kelledy house on McKennitt Street. She checked the street number that hung beside the wrought-iron gate where the walkway met the sidewalk and compared it against the address she'd hurriedly scribbled down on a scrap of paper before leaving home. When she was sure that they were the same, she slipped out of the car and approached the gate.

Walking up to the house, the sound of her heels was loud on the walkway's flagstones. She frowned at the thick carpet of fallen oak leaves that covered the lawn. The Kelledys had better hurry in cleaning them up, she thought. The city work crews would only be collecting leaves for one more week and they had to be neatly bagged and sitting at the curb for them to do so. It was a shame that such a pretty estate wasn't treated better.

When she reached the porch, she spent a disorienting moment trying to find a doorbell, then realized that there was only the small brass door knocker in the middle of the door. It was shaped like a Cornish piskie.

The sight of it gave her a queer feeling. Where had she seen that before? In one of Lesli's books, she supposed.

Lesli.

At the thought of her daughter, she quickly reached for the knocker, but the door swung open before she could use it. Lesli's flute teacher stood in the open doorway and regarded her with a puzzled look.

"Anna," Meran said, her voice betraying her surprise. "Whatever are you—"

"It's Lesli," Anna said, interrupting. "She's . . . she . . ."

Her voice trailed off as what she could see of the house's interior behind Meran registered. A strange dissonance built up in her mind at the sight of the long hallway, paneled in dark wood, the thick Oriental carpet on the hardwood floor, the old photographs and prints that hung from the walls. It was when she focused on the burnished metal umbrella stand, which was, itself, in the shape of a partially-opened umbrella, and the sidetable on which stood a cast-iron, grinning gargoyle bereft of its roof gutter home, that the curious sense of familiarity she felt delved deep into the secret recesses of her mind and connected with a swell of long-forgotten memories.

She put out a hand against the doorjamb to steady herself as the flood rose up inside her. She saw her mother-in-law standing in that hallway with a kind of glow around her head. She was older than she'd been when Anna had married Peter, years older, her body wreathed in a golden Botticelli nimbus, that beatific smile on her lips, Meran Kelledy standing beside her, the two of them sharing some private joke, and all around them . . . presences seemed to slip and slide across one's vision.

No, she told herself. None of that was real. Not the golden glow, nor the flickering twig-thin figures that teased the mind from the corner of the eye.

But she'd thought she'd seen them. Once. More than once. Many times. Whenever she was with Helen Batterberry . . .

Walking in her mother-in-law's garden and hearing music, turning the corner of the house to see a trio of what she first took to be children, then realized were midgets, playing fiddle and flute and drum, the figures slipping away as they approached, winking out of existence, the music fading, but its echoes lingering on. In the mind. In memory. In dreams.

"Faerie," her mother-in-law explained to her, matter-of-factly.

Lesli as a toddler, playing with her invisible friends that could actually be *seen* when Helen Batterberry was in the room.

No. None of that was possible.

That was when she and Peter were going through a rough period in their marriage. Those sights, those strange ethereal beings, music played on absent instruments, they were all part and parcel of what she later realized had been a nervous breakdown. Her analyst had agreed.

But they'd seemed so real.

In the hospital room where her mother-in-law lay dying, her bed a clutter of strange creatures, tiny wizened men, small perfect women, all of them flickering in and out of sight, the wonder of their presences, the music of their voices, Lesli sitting wide-eyed by the bed as the courts of Faerie came to bid farewell to an old friend.

"Say you're going to live forever," Leslie had said to her grandmother.

"I will," the old woman replied. "But you have to remember me. You have to promise never to close your awareness to the Otherworld around you. If you do that, I'll never be far."

All nonsense.

But there in the hospital room, with the scratchy sound of the IVAC pump, the clean white walls, the incessant beep of the heart monitor, the antiseptic sting in the air, Anna could only shake her head.

"None . . . none of this is real. . . ." she said.

Her mother-in-law turned her head to look at her, an infinite sadness in her dark eyes.

"Maybe not for you," she said sadly, "but for those who will see, it will always be there."

And later, with Lesli at home, when just she and Peter were there, she remembered Meran coming into that hospital room, Meran and her husband, neither of them having aged since the first time Anna had seen them at her mother-in-law's house, years, oh now years ago. The four of them were there when Helen Batterberry died. She and Peter had bent their heads over the body at the moment of death, but the other two, the unaging musicians who claimed Faerie more silently, but as surely and subtly as ever Helen Batterberry had, stood at the window and watched the twilight grow across the hospital lawn as though they could see the old woman's spirit walking off into the night.

They didn't come to the funeral.

They—

She tried to push the memories aside, just as she had when the events had first occurred, but the flood was too strong. And worse, she knew they were true memories. Not the clouded rantings of a stressful mind suffering a mild breakdown.

Meran was speaking to her, but Anna couldn't hear what she was saying. She heard a vague, disturbing music that seemed to come from the ground underfoot. Small figures seemed to caper and dance in the corner of her eye, humming and buzzing like summer bees. Vertigo gripped her and she could feel herself falling. She realized that Meran was stepping forward to catch her, but by then the darkness had grown too seductive and she simply let herself fall into its welcoming depths.

From Lesli's diary, entry dated October 13th:

I've well and truly done it. I got up this morning and instead of my school books, I packed my flute and some clothes and you, of

course, in my knapsack; and then I just left. I couldn't live there
anymore. I just couldn't.

Nobody's going to miss me. Daddy's never home anyway and
Mom won't be looking for me—she'll be looking for her idea of me
and that person doesn't exist. The city's so big that they'll never
find me.

I was kind of worried about where I was going to stay tonight,
especially with the sky getting more and more overcast all day long,
but I met this really neat girl in Fitzhenry Park this morning. Her
name's Susan and even though she's just a year older than me, she
lives with this guy in an apartment in Chinatown. She's gone to ask
him if I can stay with them for a couple of days. His name's Paul.
Susan says he's in his late twenties, but he doesn't act at all like an
old guy. He's really neat and treats her like she's an adult, not a kid.
She's his *girlfriend*!

I'm sitting in the park waiting for her to come back as I write this.
I hope she doesn't take too long because there's some weird-looking
people around here. This one guy sitting over by the War Memorial
keeps giving me the eye like he's going to hit on me or something.
He really gives me the creeps. He's got this kind of dark aura that
flickers around him so I know he's bad news.

I know it's only been one morning since I left home, but I already
feel different. It's like I was dragging around this huge weight and
all of a sudden it's gone. I feel light as a feather. Of course, we all
know what that weight was: neuro-mother.

Once I get settled in at Susan and Paul's, I'm going to go look for
a job. Susan says Paul can get me some fake ID so that I can work
in a club or something and make some real money. That's what
Susan does. She said that there's been times when she's made fifty
bucks in tips in just one night!

I've never met anyone like her before. It's hard to believe she's
almost my age. When I compare the girls at school to her, they just
seem like a bunch of kids. Susan dresses so cool, like she just stepped
out of an MTV video. She's got short funky black hair, a leather
jacket and jeans so tight I don't know how she gets into them. Her
T-shirt's got this really cool picture of a Brian Froud faery on it that
I'd never seen before.

When I asked her if she believes in Faerie, she just gave me this big grin and said, "I'll tell you, Lesli, I'll believe in anything that makes me feel good."

I think I'm going to like living with her.

When Anna Batterberry regained consciousness, it was to find herself inside that disturbingly familiar house. She lay on a soft, overstuffed sofa, surrounded by the crouching presences of far more pieces of comfortable-looking furniture than the room was really meant to hold. The room simply had a too-full look about it, aided and abetted by a bewildering array of knickknacks that ranged from dozens of tiny porcelain miniatures on the mantle, each depicting some anthropomorphized woodland creature playing a harp or a fiddle or a flute, to a life-sized fabric mâché sculpture of a grizzly-bear in top hat and tails that reared up in one corner of the room.

Every square inch of wall space appeared to be taken up with posters, framed photographs, prints and paintings. Old-fashioned curtains—the print was large dusky roses on a black background— stood guard on either side of a window seat. Underfoot was a thick carpet that had been woven into a semblance of the heavily-leafed yard outside.

The more she looked around herself, the more familiar it all looked. And the more her mind filled with memories that she'd spent so many years denying.

The sound of a footstep had her sitting up and half-turning to look behind the sofa at who—or maybe even, what—was approaching. It was only Meran. The movement brought back the vertigo and she lay down once more. Meran sat down on an ottoman that had been pulled up beside the sofa and laid a deliciously cool damp cloth against Anna's brow.

"You gave me a bit of a start," Meran said, "collapsing on my porch like that."

Anna had lost her ability to be polite. Forsaking small talk, she went straight for the heart of the matter.

"I've been here before," she said.

Meran nodded.

"With my mother-in-law—Helen Batterberry."

"Nell," Meran agreed. "She was a good friend."

192 • CHARLES DE LINT

"But why haven't I *remembered* that I'd met you before until today?"

Meran shrugged. "These things happen."

"No," Anna said. "People forget things, yes, but not like this. I didn't just meet you in passing, I knew you for years—from my last year in college when Peter first began dating me. You were at his parents' house the first time he took me home. I remember thinking how odd that you and Helen were such good friends, considering how much younger you were than her."

"Should age make a difference?" Meran asked.

"No. It's just . . . you haven't changed at all. You're still the same age."

"I know," Meran said.

"But . . ." Anna's bewilderment accentuated her nervous bird temperament. "How can that be possible?"

"You said something about Lesli when you first arrived," Meran said, changing the subject.

That was probably the only thing that could have drawn Anna away from the quagmire puzzle of agelessness and hidden music and twitchy shapes moving just beyond the grasp of her vision.

"She's run away from home," Anna said. "I went into her room to get something and found that she'd left all her schoolbooks just sitting on her desk. Then when I called the school, they told me that she'd never arrived. They were about to call me to ask if she was ill. Lesli never misses school, you know."

Meran nodded. She hadn't, but it fit with the image of the relationship between Lesli and her mother that was growing in her mind.

"Have you called the police?" she asked.

"As soon as I got off the phone. They told me it was a little early to start worrying—can you imagine that? The detective I spoke to said that he'd put out her description so that his officers would keep an eye out for her, but basically he told me that she must just be skipping school. Lesli would *never* do that."

"What does your husband say?"

"Peter doesn't know yet. He's on a business trip out east and I won't be able to talk to him until he calls me tonight. I don't even know what hotel he'll be staying in until he calls." Anna reached out with a bird-thin hand and gripped Meran's arm. "What am I going to *do*?"

"We could go looking for her ourselves."

Anna nodded eagerly at the suggestion, but then the futility of that course of action hit home.

"The city's so big," she said. "It's too big. How would we ever find her?"

"There is another way," Cerin said.

Anna started at the new voice. Meran removed the damp cloth from Anna's brow and moved back from the sofa so that Anna could sit up once more. She looked at the tall figure standing in the doorway, recognizing him as Meran's husband. She didn't remember him seeming quite so intimidating before.

"What . . . what way is that?" Anna said.

"You could ask for help from Faerie," Cerin told her.

"So—you're gonna be one of Paulie's girls?"

Lesli looked up from writing in her diary to find that the creepy guy by the War Memorial had sauntered over to stand beside her bench. Up close, he seemed even tougher than he had from a distance. His hair was slicked back on top, long at the back. He had three earrings in his left earlobe, one in the right. Dirty jeans were tucked into tall black cowboy boots, his white shirt was half open under his jean jacket. There was an oily look in his eyes that made her shiver.

She quickly shut the diary, keeping her place with a finger, and looked around hopefully to see if Susan was on her way back, but there was no sign of her new friend. Taking a deep breath, she gave him what she hoped was a look of appropriate streetwise bravado.

"I . . . I don't know what you're talking about," she said.

"I saw you talking to Susie," he said, sitting down beside her on the bench. "She's Paulie's recruiter."

Lesli started to get a bad feeling right about then. It wasn't just that this guy was so awful, but that she might have made a terrible misjudgment when it came to Susan.

"I think I should go," she said.

She started to get up, but he grabbed her arm. Off balance, she fell back onto the bench.

"Hey, look," he said. "I'm doing you a favor. Paulie's got ten or twelve girls in his string and he works them like they're dogs. You look like a nice kid. Do you really want to spend the next ten years peddling your ass for some homeboy who's gonna have you hooked on junk before the week's out?"

"I—"

"See, I run a clean shop. No drugs, nice clothes for the girls, nice apartment that you're gonna share with just one other girl, not a half dozen the way Paulie run his biz. My girls turn maybe two, three tricks a night and that's it. Paulie'll have you on the street nine, ten hours a pop, easy."

His voice was calm, easygoing, but Leslie had never been so scared before in her life.

"Please," she said. "You're making a mistake. I really have to go."

She tried to rise again, but he kept a hand on her shoulder so that she couldn't get up. His voice, so mild before, went hard.

"You go anywhere, babe, you're going with me," he said. "There are no other options. End of conversation."

He stood up and hauled her to her feet. His hand held her in a bruising grip. Her diary fell from her grip, and he let her pick it up and stuff it into her knapsack, but then he pulled her roughly away from the bench.

"You're hurting me!" she cried.

He leaned close to her, his mouth only inches from her ear.

"Keep that up," he warned her, "and you're really gonna find out what pain's all about. Now make nice. You're working for me now."

"I . . ."

"Repeat after me, sweet stuff: I'm Cutter's girl."

Tears welled in Lesli's eyes. She looked around the park, but nobody was paying any attention to what was happening to her. Cutter gave her a painful shake that made her teeth rattle.

"C'mon," he told her. "Say it."

He glared at her with the promise of worse to come in his eyes if she didn't start doing what he said. His grip tightened on her shoulder, fingers digging into the soft flesh of her upper arm.

"Say it!"

"I . . . I'm Cutter's . . . girl."

"See? That wasn't so hard."

He gave her another shove to start her moving again. She wanted desperately to break free of his hand and just run, but as he marched her across the park, she discovered that she was too scared to do anything but let him lead her away.

She'd never felt so helpless or alone in all her life. It made her feel ashamed.

"Please don't joke about this," Anna said in response to Cerin's suggestion that they turn to Faerie for help in finding Lesli.

"Yes," Meran agreed, though she wasn't speaking of jokes. "This isn't the time."

Cerin shook his head. "This seems a particularly appropriate time to me." He turned to Anna. "I don't like to involve myself in private quarrels, but since it's you that's come to us, I feel I have the right to ask you this: Why is it, do you think, that Lesli ran away in the first place?"

"What are you insinuating? That I'm not a good mother?"

"Hardly. I no longer know you well enough to make that sort of a judgment. Besides, it's not really any of my business, is it?"

"Cerin, please," Meran said.

A headache was starting up between Anna's temples.

"I don't understand," Anna said. "What is it that you're saying?"

"Meran and I loved Nell Batterberry," Cerin said. "I don't doubt that you held some affection for her as well, but I do know that you thought her a bit of a daft old woman. She told me once that after her husband—after Philip—died, you tried to convince Peter that she should be put in a home. Not in a home for the elderly, but for the, shall we say, gently mad?"

"But she—"

"Was full of stories that made no sense to you," Cerin said. "She heard and saw what others couldn't, though she had the gift that would allow such people to see into the invisible world of Faerie when they were in her presence. You saw into that world once, Anna. I don't think you ever forgave her for showing it to you."

"It . . . it wasn't real."

Cerin shrugged. "That's not really important at this moment. What's important is that, if I understand the situation correctly, you've been living in the fear that Lesli would grow up just as fey as her grandmother. And if this is so, your denying her belief in Faerie lies at the root of the troubles that the two of you share."

Anna looked to Meran for support, but Meran knew her husband too well and kept her own council. Having begun, Cerin wouldn't stop until he said everything he meant to.

"Why are you doing this to me?" Anna asked. "My daughter's run away. All of . . . all of this . . ." She waved a hand that was perhaps meant to take in just the conversation, perhaps the whole room. "It's not real. Little people and fairies and all the things my mother-in-law reveled in discussing just aren't real. She could make them *seem* real, I'll grant you that, but they could never exist."

"In your world," Cerin said.

"In the real world."

"They're not one and the same," Cerin told her.

Anna began to rise from the sofa. "I don't have to listen to any of this," she said. "My daughter's run away and I thought you might be able to help me. I didn't come here to be mocked."

"The only reason I've said anything at all," Cerin told her, "is for Lesli's sake. Meran talks about her all the time. She sounds like a wonderful, gifted child."

"She is."

"I hate the thought of her being forced into a box that doesn't fit her. Of having her wings cut off, her sight blinded, her hearing muted, her voice stilled."

"I'm not doing any such thing!" Anna cried.

"You just don't realize what you're doing," Cerin replied.

His voice was mild, but dark lights in the back of his eyes were flashing.

Meran realized it was time to intervene. She stepped between the two. Putting her back to her husband, she turned to face Anna.

"We'll find Lesli," she said.

"How? With *magic*?"

"It doesn't matter how. Just trust that we will. What you have to think of is of what you were telling me yesterday: her birthday's coming up in just a few days. Once she turns sixteen, so long as she can prove that she's capable of supporting herself, she can legally leave home and nothing you might do or say then can stop her."

"It's you, isn't it?" Anna cried. "You're the one who's been filling up her head with all these horrible fairy tales. I should never have let her take those lessons."

Her voice rose ever higher in pitch as she lunged forward, arms flailing. Meran slipped to one side, then reached out one quick hand. She pinched a nerve in Anna's neck and the woman suddenly went limp. Cerin caught her before she could fall and carried her back to the sofa.

"Now do you see what I mean about parents?" he said as he laid Anna down.

Meran gave him a mock-serious cuff on the back of his head.

"Go find Lesli," she said.

"But—"

"Or would you rather stay with Anna and continue your silly attempt at converting her when she wakes up again?"

"I'm on my way," Cerin told her and was out the door before she could change her mind.

Thunder cracked almost directly overhead as Cutter dragged Lesli into a brownstone just off Palm Street. The building stood in the heart of what was known as Newford's Combat Zone, a few square blocks of night clubs, strip joints and bars. It was a tough part of town with hookers on every corner, bikers cruising the streets on chopped-down Harleys, bums sleeping in doorways, winos sitting on the curbs, drinking cheap booze from bottles vaguely hidden in paper bags.

Cutter had an apartment on the top floor of the brownstone, three stories up from the street. If he hadn't told her that he lived here, Leslie would have thought that he'd taken her into an abandoned building. There was no furniture except a vinyl-topped table and two chairs in the dirty kitchen. A few mangy pillows were piled up against the wall in what she assumed was the living room.

He led her down to the room at the end of the long hall that ran the length of the apartment and pushed her inside. She lost her balance and went sprawling onto the mattress that lay in the middle of the floor. It smelled of mildew and, vaguely, of old urine. She scrambled away from it and crouched up against the far wall, clutching her knapsack against her chest.

"Now, you just relax, sweet stuff," Cutter told her. "Take things easy. I'm going out for a little while to find you a nice guy to ease you into the trade. I'd do it myself, but there's guys that want to be first with a kid as young and pretty as you are and I sure could use the bread they're willing to pay for the privilege."

Lesli was prepared to beg him to let her go, but her throat was so tight she couldn't make a sound.

"Don't go away now," Cutter told her.

He chuckled at his own wit, then closed the door and locked it. Lesli didn't think she'd ever heard anything so final as the sound of that lock catching. She listened to Cutter's footsteps as they crossed the apartment, the sound of the front door closing, his footsteps receding on the stairs.

As soon as she was sure he was far enough away, she got up and ran to the door, trying it, just in case, but it really was locked and far too solid for her to have any hope of breaking through its panels. Of course there was no phone. She crossed the room to the window and forced it open. The window looked out on the side of another building, with an alleyway below. There was no fire escape outside the window and she was far too high up to think of trying to get down to the alley.

Thunder rumbled again, not quite overhead now, and it started to rain. She leaned by the window, resting her head on its sill. Tears sprang up in her eyes again.

"Please," she sniffed. "Please, somebody help me. . . ."

The rain coming in the window mingled with the tears that streaked her cheek.

Cerin began his search at the Batterberry house, which was in Ferryside, across the Stanton Street Bridge on the west side of the Kickaha river. As Anna Batterberry had remarked, the city was large. To find one teenage girl, hiding somewhere in the confounding labyrinth of its thousands of crisscrossing streets and avenues, was a daunting task, but Cerin was depending on help.

To anyone watching him, he must have appeared to be slightly mad. He wandered back and forth across the streets of Ferryside, stopping under trees to look up into their bare branches, hunkering down at the mouths of alleys or alongside hedges, apparently talking to himself. In truth, he was looking for the city's gossips:

Magpies and crows, sparrows and pigeons saw everything, but listening to their litanies of the day's events was like looking something up in an encyclopedia that was merely a confusing heap of loose pages, gathered together in a basket. All the information you wanted was there, but finding it would take more hours than there were in a day.

Cats were little better. They liked to keep most of what they knew to themselves, so what they did offer him was usually cryptic and sometimes even pointedly unhelpful. Cerin couldn't blame them; they were by nature secretive and, like much of Faerie, capricious.

The most ready to give him a hand were those little sprites commonly known as the flower faeries. They were the little winged spirits of the various trees and bushes, flowers and weeds, that grew tidily in parks and gardens, rioting only in the odd empty lot or wild place, such as the riverbanks that ran down under the Stanton Street Bridge to meet the water. Years ago, Cicely Mary Barker had catalogued any number of them in a loving series of books; more recently the Boston artist, Terri Windling, had taken up the task, specializing in the urban relations of those Barker had already noted.

It was late in the year for the little folk. Most of them were already tucked away in Faerie, sleeping through the winter, or else too busy with their harvests and other seasonal preoccupations to have paid any attention at all to what went on beyond the task at hand. But a few had seen the young girl who could sometimes see them. Meran's cousins were the most helpful. Their small pointed faces would regard Cerin gravely from under acorn caps as they pointed this way down one street, or that way down another.

It took time. The sky grew darker, and then still darker as the clouds thickened with an approaching storm, but slowly and surely, Cerin traced Lesli's passage over the Stanton Street Bridge all the way across town to Fitzhenry Park. It was just as he reached the bench where she'd been sitting that it began to rain.

There, from two of the wizened little monkey-like bodachs that lived in the park, he got the tale of how she'd been accosted and taken away.

"She didn't want to go, sir," said the one, adjusting the brim of his little cap against the rain.

All faerie knew Cerin, but it wasn't just for his bardic harping that they paid him the respect that they did. He was the husband of the oak king's daughter, she who could match them trick for trick and then some, and they'd long since learned to treat her, and those under her protection, with a wary deference.

"No sir, she didn't," added the other, "but he led her off all the same."

Cerin hunkered down beside the bench so that he wasn't towering over them.

"Where did he take her?" he asked.

The first bodach pointed to where two men were standing by the War Memorial, shoulders hunched against the rain, heads bent together as they spoke. One wore a thin raincoat over a suit; the other was dressed in denim jacket, jeans and cowboy boots. They appeared to be discussing a business transaction.

"You could ask him for yourself," the bodach said. "He's the one all in blue."

Cerin's gaze went to the pair and a hard look came over his features. If Meran had been there, she might have laid a hand on his arm, or spoken a calming word, to bank the dangerous fire that grew in behind his eyes. But she was at home, too far away for her quieting influence to be felt.

The bodachs scampered away as Cerin rose to his feet. By the War Memorial, the two men seemed to come to an agreement and left the park together. Cerin fell in behind them, the rain that slicked the pavement underfoot muffling his footsteps. His fingers twitched at his side, as though striking a harp's strings.

From the branches of the tree where they'd taken sanctuary, the bodachs thought they could hear the sound of a harp, its music echoing softly against the rhythm of the rain.

Anna came to once more just as Meran was returning from the kitchen with a pot of herb tea and a pair of mugs. Meran set the mugs and pot down on the table by the sofa and sat down beside Lesli's mother.

"How are you feeling?" she asked as she adjusted the cool cloth she'd laid upon Anna's brow earlier.

Anna's gaze flicked from left to right, over Meran's shoulder and down to the floor, as though tracking invisible presences. Meran tried to shoo away the inquisitive faerie, but it was a useless gesture. In this house, with Anna's presence to fuel their quenchless curiosity, it was like trying to catch the wind.

"I've made us some tea," Meran said. "It'll make you feel better."

Anna appeared docile now, her earlier anger fled as though it had never existed. Outside, rain pattered gently against the window panes. The face of a nosy hob was pressed against one lower pane, its breath clouding the glass, its large eyes glimmering with their own inner light.

"Can . . . can you make them go away?" Anna asked.

Meran shook her head. "But I can make you forget again."

"Forget." Anna's voice grew dreamy. "Is that what you did before? You made me forget?"

"No. You did that on your own. You didn't want to remember, so you simply forgot."

"And you . . . you didn't do a thing?"

"We do have a certain . . . aura," Meran admitted, "which accelerates the process. It's not even something we consciously work at. It just seems to happen when we're around those who'd rather not remember what they see."

"So I'll forget, but they'll all still be there?"

Meran nodded.

"I just won't be able to see them?"

"It'll be like it was before," Meran said.

"I . . . I don't think I like that. . . ."

Her voice slurred. Meran leaned forward with a worried expression. Anna seemed to regard her through blurring vision.

"I think I'm going . . . away . . . now. . . ." she said.

Her eyelids fluttered, then her head lolled to one side and she lay still. Meran called Anna's name and gave her a little shake, but there was no response. She put two fingers to Anna's throat and found her pulse. It was regular and strong, but try though she did, Meran couldn't rouse the woman.

Rising from the sofa, she went into the kitchen to phone for an ambulance. As she was dialing the number, she heard Cerin's harp begin to play by itself up in his study on the second floor.

*   *   *

Lesli's tears lasted until she thought she saw something moving in the rain on the other side of the window. It was a flicker of movement and color, just above the outside windowsill, as though a pigeon had come in for a wet landing, but it had moved with far more grace and deftness than any pigeon she'd ever seen. And that memory of color was all wrong, too. It hadn't been the blue/white/grey of a pigeon; it had been more like a butterfly—

doubtful, she thought, in the rain and this time of year

—or a hummingbird—

even more doubtful

—but then she remembered what the music had woken at her last flute lesson. She rubbed at her eyes with her sleeve to remove the blur of her tears and looked more closely into the rain. Face-on, she couldn't see anything, but as soon as she turned her head, there it was again, she could see it out of the corner of her eye, a dancing dervish of color and movement that flickered out of her line of sight as soon as she concentrated on it.

After a few moments, she turned from the window. She gave the door a considering look and listened hard, but there was still no sound of Cutter's return.

Maybe, she thought, maybe magic can rescue me. . . .

She dug out her flute from her knapsack and quickly put the pieces together. Turning back to the window, she sat on her haunches and tried to start up a tune, but to no avail. She was still too nervous, her chest felt too tight, and she couldn't get the air to come up properly from her diaphragm.

She brought the flute down from her lip and laid it across her knees. Trying not to think of the locked door, of why it was locked and who would be coming through it, she steadied her breathing.

In, slowly now, hold it, let it out, slowly. And again.

She pretended she was with Meran, just the two of them in the basement of the Old Firehall. There. She could almost hear the tune that Meran was playing, except it sounded more like the bell-like tones of a harp than the breathy timbre of a wooden flute. But still, it was there for her to follow, a path marked out on a roadmap of music.

Lifting the flute back up to her lip, she blew again, a narrow channel of air going down into the mouth hole at an angle, all her fingers down, the low D note ringing in the empty room, a deep rich sound, resonant and full. She played it again, then caught the music she heard, that particular path laid out on the roadmap of all tunes that are or yet could be, and followed where it led.

It was easier to do than she would have thought possible, easier than at all those lessons with Meran. The music she followed seemed to allow her instrument to almost play itself. And as the tune woke from her flute, she fixed her gaze on the rain falling just outside the window where a flicker of color appeared, a spin of movement.

Please, she thought. Oh please . . .

And then it was there, hummingbird wings vibrating in the rain, sending incandescent sprays of water arcing away from their movement; the tiny naked upper torso, the lower wrapped in tiny leaves and vines; the dark hair gathered wetly against her miniature cheeks and neck; the eyes, tiny and timeless, watching her as she watched back and all the while, the music played.

Help me, she thought to that little hovering figure. Won't you please—

She had been oblivious to anything but the music and the tiny faerie outside in the rain. She hadn't heard the footsteps on the stairs, nor heard them crossing the apartment. But she heard the door open.

The tune faltered, the faerie flickered out of sight as though it had never been there. She brought the flute down from her lip and turned, her heart drumming wildly in her chest, but she refused to be scared. That's all guys like Cutter wanted. They wanted to see you scared of them. They wanted to be in control. But no more.

I'm not going to go without a fight, she thought. I'll break my flute over his stupid head. I'll . . .

The stranger standing in the doorway brought her train of thought to a scurrying halt. And then she realized that the harping she'd heard, the tune that had led her flute to join it, had grown in volume, rather than diminished.

"Who . . . who are you?" she asked.

Her hands had begun to perspire, making her flute slippery and hard to hold. The stranger had longer hair than Cutter. It was drawn back in a braid that hung down one side of his head and dangled halfway down his chest. He had a full beard and wore clothes that, though they were simple jeans, shirt and jacket, seemed to have a timeless cut to them, as though they could have been worn at any point in history and not seemed out of place. Meran dressed like that as well, she realized.

But it was his eyes that held her—not their startling brightness, but the fire that seemed to flicker in their depths, a rhythmic movement that seemed to keep time to the harping she heard.

"Have you come to . . . rescue me?" she found herself asking before the stranger had time to reply to her first question.

"I'd think," he said, "with a spirit so brave as yours, that you'd simply rescue yourself."

Lesli shook her head. "I'm not really brave at all."

"Braver than you know, fluting here while a darkness stalked you through the storm. My name's Cerin Kelledy; I'm Meran's husband and I've come to take you home."

He waited for her to disassemble her flute and stow it away, then offered her a hand up from the floor. As she stood up, he took the knapsack and slung it over his shoulder and led her towards the door. The sound of the harping was very faint now, Lesli realized.

When they walked by the hall, she stopped in the doorway leading to the living room and looked at the two men that were huddled against the far wall, their eyes wild with terror. One was Cutter; the other a business man in suit and raincoat whom she'd never seen before. She hesitated, fingers tightening on Cerin's hand, as she turned to see what was frightening them so much. There was nothing at all in the spot that their frightened gazes were fixed upon.

"What . . . what's the matter with them?" she asked her companion. "What are they looking at?"

"Night fears," Cerin replied. "Somehow the darkness that lies in their hearts has given those fears substance and made them real."

The way he said "somehow" let Lesli know that he'd been responsible for what the two men were undergoing.

"Are they going to die?" she asked.

She didn't think she was the first girl to fall prey to Cutter so she wasn't exactly feeling sorry for him at that point.

Cerin shook his head. "But they will always have the *sight*. Unless they change their ways, it will show them only the dark side of Faerie."

Lesli shivered.

"There are no happy endings," Cerin told her. "There are no real endings ever—happy or otherwise. We all have our own stories which are just a part of the one Story that binds both this world and Faerie. Sometimes we step into each others' stories—perhaps just for a few minutes, perhaps for years—and then we step out of them again. But all the while, the Story just goes on."

That day, his explanation only served to confuse her.

From Lesli's diary, entry dated November 24th:

Nothing turned out the way I thought it would.

Something happened to Mom. Everybody tells me it's not my fault, but it happened when I ran away, so I can't help but feel that I'm to blame. Daddy says she had a nervous breakdown and that's why she's in the sanitarium. It happened to her before and it had been coming again for a long time. But that's not the way Mom tells it.

I go by to see her every day after school. Sometimes she's pretty spaced from the drugs they give her to keep her calm, but on one of her good days, she told me about Granny Nell and the Kelledys and Faerie. She says the world's just like I said it was in that essay I did for English. Faerie's real and it didn't go away; it just got freed from people's preconceptions of it and now it's just whatever it wants to be.

And that's what scares her.

She also thinks the Kelledys are some kind of earth spirits.

"I can't forget this time," she told me.

"But if you know," I asked her, "if you believe, then why are you in this place? Maybe I should be in here, too."

And you know what she told me? "I don't want to believe in any of it; it just makes me feel sick. But at the same time, I can't stop knowing it's all out there: every kind of magic being and nightmare. They're all real."

I remember thinking of Cutter and that other guy in his apartment and what Cerin said about them. Did that make my Mom a bad person? I couldn't believe that.

"But they're not *supposed* to be real," Mom said. "That's what's got me feeling so crazy. In a sane world, in the world that was the way I'd grown up believing it to be, that *wouldn't* be real. The Kelledys could fix it so that I'd forget again, but then I'd be back to going through life always feeling like there was something important that I couldn't remember. And that just leaves you with another kind of craziness—an ache that you can't explain and it doesn't ever go away. It's better this way, and my medicine keeps me from feeling too crazy."

She looked away then, out the window of her room. I looked, too, and saw the little monkeyman that was crossing the lawn of the sanitarium, pulling a pig behind him. The pig had a load of gear on its back like it was a pack horse.

"Could you . . . could you ask the nurse to bring my medicine," Mom said.

I tried to tell her that all she had to do was accept it, but she wouldn't listen. She just kept asking for the nurse, so finally I went and got one.

I still think it's my fault.

I live with the Kelledys now. Daddy was going to send me away to a boarding school, because he felt that he couldn't be home enough to take care of me. I never really thought about it before, but when he said that, I realized that he didn't know me at all.

Meran offered to let me live at their place. I moved in on my birthday.

There's a book in their library—ha! There's like ten million books in there. But the one I'm thinking of is by a local writer, this guy named Christy Riddell.

In it, he talks about Faerie, how everybody just thinks of them as ghosts of wind and shadow.

"Faerie music is the wind," he says, "and their movement is the play of shadow cast by moonlight, or starlight, or no light at all. Faerie lives like a ghost beside us, but only the city remembers. But then the city never forgets anything."

I don't know if the Kelledys are part of that ghostliness. What I do know is that, seeing how they live for each other, how they care so much about each other, I find myself feeling more hopeful about things. My parents and I didn't so much not get along, as lack interest in each other. It got to the point where I figured that's how everybody was in the world, because I never knew any different.

So I'm trying harder with Mom. I don't talk about things she doesn't want to hear, but I don't stop believing in them either. Like Cerin said, we're just two threads of the Story. Sometimes we come together for awhile and sometimes we're apart. And no matter how much one or the other of us might want it to be different, both our stories are true.

But I can't stop wishing for a happy ending.

≈ THE CONJURE MAN ≈

I DO NOT THINK IT HAD ANY FRIENDS, OR MOURNERS,
EXCEPT MYSELF AND A PAIR OF OWLS.

> —J. R. R. TOLKIEN, FROM THE INTRODUCTORY
> NOTE TO *TREE AND LEAF*

YOU ONLY SEE THE TREE BY THE LIGHT OF THE LAMP. I
WONDER WHEN YOU WOULD EVER SEE THE LAMP BY THE
LIGHT OF THE TREE.

> —G. K. CHESTERTON, FROM
> *THE MAN WHO WAS THURSDAY*

The conjure man rode a red, old-fashioned bicycle with fat tires and only one, fixed gear. A wicker basket in front contained a small mongrel dog that seemed mostly terrier. Behind the seat, tied to the carrier, was a battered brown satchel that hid from prying eyes the sum total of all his worldly possessions.

What he had was not much, but he needed little. He was, after all, the conjure man, and what he didn't have, he could conjure for himself.

He was more stout than slim, with a long grizzled beard and a halo of frizzy grey hair that protruded from under his tall black hat like ivy tangled under an eave. Nesting in the hatband were a posy of dried wildflowers and three feathers: one white, from a swan; one black, from a crow; one brown, from an owl. His jacket was an exhilarating shade of blue, the color of the sky on a perfect summer's morning. Under it he wore a shirt that was as green as a fresh-cut lawn. His trousers were brown corduroy, patched with leather and plaid squares; his boots were a deep golden yellow, the color of buttercups past their prime.

His age was a puzzle, somewhere between fifty and seventy. Most people assumed he was one of the homeless—more colorful than most, and certainly more cheerful, but a derelict all the same—so the scent of apples that seemed to follow him was always a surprise, as was the good humor that walked hand in hand with a keen intelligence in his bright blue eyes. When he raised his head, hat brim lifting, and he met one's gaze, the impact of those eyes was a sudden shock, a diamond in the rough.

His name was John Windle, which could mean, if you were one to ascribe meaning to names, "favored of god" for his given name, while his surname was variously defined as "basket," "the red-winged thrush," or "to lose vigor and strength, to dwindle." They could all be true, for he led a charmed life; his mind was a treasure trove storing equal amounts of experience, rumor and history; he had a high clear singing voice; and though he wasn't tall—he stood five-ten in his boots—he had once been a much larger man.

"I was a giant once," he liked to explain, "when the world was young. But conjuring takes its toll. Now John's just an old man, pretty well all used up. Just like the world," he'd add with a sigh and a nod, bright eyes holding a tired sorrow. "Just like the world."

There were some things even the conjure man couldn't fix.

Living in the city, one grew used to its more outlandish characters, eventually noting them in passing with an almost familial affection: The pigeon lady in her faded Laura Ashley dresses with her shopping cart filled with sacks of birdseed and bread crumbs. Paperjack, the old black man with his Chinese fortune-teller and deft origami sculptures. The German cowboy who dressed like an extra from a spaghetti western and made long declamatory speeches in his native language to which no one listened.

And, of course, the conjure man.

Wendy St. James had seen him dozens of times—she lived and worked downtown, which was the conjure man's principle haunt—but she'd never actually spoken to him until one day in the fall when the trees were just beginning to change into their cheerful autumnal party dresses.

She was sitting on a bench on the Ferryside bank of the Kickaha River, a small, almost waif-like woman in jeans and a white T-shirt, with an unzipped brown leather bomber's jacket and hightops. In lieu of a purse, she had a small, worn knapsack sitting on the bench beside her and she was bent over a hardcover journal which she spent more time staring at than actually writing in. Her hair was thick and blonde, hanging down past her collar in a grown-out pageboy with a half-inch of dark roots showing. She was chewing on the end of her pen, worrying the plastic for inspiration.

It was a poem that had stopped her in mid-stroll and plunked her down on the bench. It had glimmered and shone in her head until she got out her journal and pen. Then it fled, as impossible to catch as a fading dream. The more she tried to recapture the impulse that had set her wanting to put pen to paper, the less it seemed to have ever existed in the first place. The annoying presence of three teenage boys clowning around on the lawn a half-dozen yards from where she sat didn't help at all.

She was giving them a dirty stare when she saw one of the boys pick up a stick and throw it into the wheel of the conjure man's bike as he came riding up on the park path that followed the river. The small dog in the bike's wicker basket jumped free, but the conjure man himself fell in a tangle of limbs and spinning wheels. The boys took off, laughing, the dog chasing them for a few feet, yapping shrilly, before it hurried back to where its master had fallen.

Wendy had already put down her journal and pen and reached the fallen man by the time the dog got back to its master's side.

"Are you okay?" Wendy asked the conjure man as she helped him untangle himself from the bike.

She'd taken a fall herself in the summer. The front wheel of her ten-speed struck a pebble, the bike wobbled dangerously and she'd grabbed at the brakes, but her fingers closed over the front ones first, and too hard. The back of the bike went up, flipping her right over the handlebars, and she'd had the worst headache for at least a week afterwards.

The conjure man didn't answer her immediately. His gaze followed the escaping boys.

"As you sow," he muttered.

Following his gaze, Wendy saw the boy who'd thrown the stick trip and go sprawling in the grass. An odd chill danced up her spine. The boy's tumble came so quickly on the heels of the conjure man's words, for a moment it felt to her as though he'd actually caused the boy's fall.

As you sow, so shall you reap.

She looked back at the conjure man, but he was sitting up now, fingering a tear in his corduroys, which already had a quiltwork of patches on them. He gave her a quick smile that traveled all the way up to his eyes and she found herself thinking of Santa Claus. The little dog pressed its nose up against the conjure man's hand, pushing it away from the tear. But the tear was gone.

It had just been a fold in the cloth, Wendy realized. That was all. She helped the conjure man limp to her bench, then went back and got his bike. She righted it and wheeled it over to lean against the back of the bench before sitting down herself. The little dog leaped up onto the conjure man's lap.

"What a cute dog," Wendy said, giving it a pat. "What's her name?"

"Ginger," the conjure man replied as though it was so obvious that he couldn't understand her having to ask.

Wendy looked at the dog. Ginger's fur was as grey and grizzled as her master's beard without a hint of the spice's strong brown hue.

"But she's not at all brown," Wendy found herself saying.

The conjure man shook his head. "It's what she's made of—she's a gingerbread dog. Here." He plucked a hair from Ginger's back which made the dog start and give him a sour look. He offered the hair to Wendy. "Taste it."

Wendy grimaced. "I don't think so."

"Suit yourself," the conjure man said. He shrugged and popped the hair into his own mouth, chewing it with relish.

Oh boy, Wendy thought. She had a live one on her hands.

"Where do you think ginger comes from?" the conjure man asked her.

"What, do you mean your dog?"

"No, the spice."

Wendy shrugged. "I don't know. Some kind of plant, I suppose."

"And that's where you're wrong. They shave gingerbread dogs like our Ginger here and grind up the hair until all that's left is a powder that's ever so fine. Then they leave it out in the hot sun for a day and half—which is where it gets its brownish colour."

Wendy only just stopped herself from rolling her eyes. It was time to extract herself from this encounter, she realized. Well past the time. She'd done her bit to make sure he was all right and since the conjure man didn't seem any worse for the wear from his fall—

"Hey!" she said as he picked up her journal and started to leaf through it. "That's personal."

He fended off her reaching hand with his own and continued to look through it.

"Poetry," he said. "And lovely verses they are, too."

"Please . . ."

"Ever had any published?"

Wendy let her hand drop and leaned back against the bench with a sigh.

"Two collections," she said, adding, "and a few sales to some of the literary magazines."

Although, she corrected herself, "sales" was perhaps a misnomer since most of the magazines only paid in copies. And while she did have two collections in print, they were published by the East Street Press, a small local publisher, which meant the bookstores of New-ford were probably the only places in the world where either of her books could be found.

"Romantic, but with a very optimistic flavor," the conjure man remarked as he continued to look through her journal where all her false starts and incomplete drafts were laid out for him to see. "None of that *Sturm und drang* of the earlier romantic era and more like Yeats' Celtic twilight or, what did Chesteron call it? *Mooreeffoc*—that queerness that comes when familiar things are seen from a new angle."

Wendy couldn't believe she was having this conversation. What was he? A renegade English professor living on the street like some hedgerow philosopher of old? It seemed absurd to be sitting here, listening to his discourse.

The conjure man turned to give her a charming smile. "Because that's our hope for the future, isn't it? That the imagination reaches beyond the present to glimpse not so much a sense of meaning in what lies all around us, but to let us simply see it in the first place?"

"I . . . I don't know what to say," Wendy replied.

Ginger had fallen asleep on his lap. He closed her journal and regarded her for a long moment, eyes impossibly blue and bright under the brim of his odd hat.

"John has something he wants to show you," he said.

Wendy blinked. "John?" she asked, looking around.

The conjure man tapped his chest. "John Windle is what those who know my name call me."

"Oh."

She found it odd how his speech shifted from that of a learned man to a much simpler idiom, even referring to himself in the third person. But then, if she stopped to consider it, everything about him was odd.

"What kind of something?" Wendy asked cautiously.

"It's not far."

Wendy looked at her watch. Her shift started at four, which was still a couple of hours away, so there was plenty of time. But she was fairly certain that interesting though her companion was, he wasn't at all the sort of person with whom she wanted to involve herself any more than she already had. The dichotomy between the nonsense and substance that peppered his conversation made her uncomfortable.

It wasn't so much that she thought him dangerous. She just felt as though she was walking on boggy ground that might at any minute dissolve into quicksand with a wrong turn. Despite hardly knowing him at all, she was already sure that listening to him would be full of the potential for wrong turns.

"I'm sorry," she said, "but I don't have the time."

"It's something that I think only you can, if not understand, then at least appreciate."

"I'm sure it's fascinating, whatever it is, but—"

"Come along, then," he said.

He handed her back her journal and stood up, dislodging Ginger, who leapt to the ground with a sharp yap of protest. Scooping the dog up, he returned her to the wicker basket that hung from his handlebars, then wheeled the bike in front of the bench where he stood waiting for Wendy.

Wendy opened her mouth to continue her protest, but then simply shrugged. Well, why not? He really didn't look at all dangerous and she'd just make sure that she stayed in public places.

She stuffed her journal back into her knapsack and then followed as he led the way south along the park path up to where the City Commission's lawns gave way to Butler University's common. She started to ask him how his leg felt, since he'd been limping before, but he walked at a quick, easy pace—that of someone half his apparent age—so she just assumed he hadn't been hurt that badly by his fall after all.

They crossed the common, eschewing the path now to walk straight across the lawn towards the G. Smithers Memorial Library, weaving their way in between islands of students involved in any number of activities, none of which included studying. When they reached the library, they followed its ivy hung walls to the rear of the building, where the conjure man stopped.

"There," he said, waving his arm in a gesture that took in the entire area behind the library. "What do you see?"

The view they had was of an open space of land backed by a number of other buildings. Having attended the university herself, Wendy recognized all three: the Student Center, the Science Building and one of the dorms, though she couldn't remember which one. The landscape enclosed by their various bulking presences had the look of recently having undergone a complete overhaul. All the lilacs and hawthorns had been cut back, brush and weeds were now just an uneven stubble of ground covering, there were clumps of raw dirt, scattered here and there, where trees had obviously been removed, and right in the middle was enormous stump.

It had been at least fifteen years since Wendy had had any reason to come here in behind the library. But it was so different now. She found herself looking around with a "what's wrong with this picture?" caption floating in her mind. This had been a little cranny of wild wood when she'd attended Butler, hidden away from all the trimmed lawns and shrubbery that made the rest of the university so picturesque. But she could remember slipping back here, journal in hand, and sitting under that huge . . .

"It's all changed," she said slowly. "They cleaned out all the brush and cut down the oak tree. . . ."

Someone had once told her that this particular tree was—had been—a rarity. It had belonged to a species not native to North America—the *Quercus robur,* or common oak of Europe—and was supposed to be over four hundred years old, which made it older than the university, older than Newford itself.

"How could they just . . . cut it down . . . ?" she asked.

The conjure man jerked a thumb over his shoulder towards the library.

"Your man with the books had the work done—didn't like the shade it was throwing on his office. Didn't like to look out and see an untamed bit of the wild hidden in here disturbing his sense of order."

"The head librarian?" Wendy asked.

The conjure man just shrugged.

"But—didn't anyone complain? Surely the students . . ."

In her day there would have been protests. Students would have formed a human chain around the tree, refusing to let anyone near it. They would have camped out, day and night. They . . .

She looked at the stump and felt a tightness in her chest as though someone had wrapped her in wet leather that was now starting to dry out and shrink.

"That tree was John's friend," the conjure man said. "The last friend I ever had. She was ten thousand years old and they just cut her down."

Wendy gave him an odd look. Ten thousand years old? Were we exaggerating now or what?

"Her death is a symbol," the conjure man went on. "The world has no more time for stories."

"I'm not sure I follow you," Wendy said.

He turned to look at her, eyes glittering with a strange light under the dark brim of his hat.

"She was a Tree of Tales," he said. "There are very few of them left, just as there are very few of me. She held stories, all the stories the wind brought to her that were of any worth, and with each such story she heard, she grew."

"But there's always going to be stories," Wendy said, falling into the spirit of the conversation even if she didn't quite understand its relevance to the situation at hand. "There are more books being published today than there ever have been in the history of the world."

The conjure man gave her a sour frown and hooked his thumb towards the library again. "Now you sound like him."

"But—"

"There's stories and then there's stories," he said, interrupting her. "The ones with any worth change your life forever, perhaps only in a small way, but once you've heard them, they are forever a part of you. You nurture them and pass them on and the giving only makes you feel better.

"The others are just words on a page."

"I know that," Wendy said.

And on some level she did, though it wasn't something she'd ever really stopped to think about. It was more an instinctive sort of knowledge that had always been present inside her, rising up into her awareness now as though called forth by the conjure man's words.

"It's all machines now," the conjure man went on. "It's a—what do they call it?—high-tech world. Fascinating, to be sure, but John thinks that it estranges many people, cheapens the human experience. There's no more room for the stories that matter, and that's wrong, for stories are a part of the language of dream—they grow not from one writer, but from a people. They become the voice of a country, or a race. Without them, people lose touch with themselves."

"You're talking about myths," Wendy said.

The conjure man shook his head. "Not specifically—not in the classical sense of the word. Such myths are only a part of the collective story that is harvested in a Tree of Tales. In a world as pessimistic as this has become, that collective story is all that's left to guide people through the encroaching dark. It serves to create a sense of options, the possibility of permanence out of nothing."

Wendy was really beginning to lose the thread of his argument now.

"What exactly is it that you're saying?" she asked.

"A Tree of Tales is an act of magic, of faith. It's existence becomes an affirmation of the power that the human spirit can have over its own destiny. The stories are just stories—they entertain, they make one laugh or cry—but if they have any worth, they carry within them a deeper resonance that remains long after the final page is turned, or the storyteller has come to the end of her tale. Both aspects of the story are necessary for it to have any worth."

He was silent for a long moment, then added, "Otherwise the story goes on without you."

Wendy gave him a questioning look.

"Do you know what 'ever after' means?" he asked.

"I suppose."

"It's one bookend of a tale—the kind that begins with 'once upon a time.' It's the end of the story when everybody goes home. That's what they said at the end of the story John was in, but John wasn't paying attention, so he got left behind."

"I'm not sure I know what you're talking about," Wendy said.

Not sure? she thought. She was positive. It was all so much . . . well, not exactly nonsense, as queer. And unrelated to any working of the world with which she was familiar. But the oddest thing was that everything he said continued to pull a kind of tickle out from deep in her mind so that while she didn't completely understand him, some part of her did. Some part, hidden behind the person who took care of all the day-to-day business of her life, perhaps the same part of her that pulled a poem into the empty page where no words had ever existed before. The part of her that was a conjurer.

"John took care of the Tale of Trees," the conjure man went on. "Because John got left behind in his own story, he wanted to make sure that the stories themselves would at least live on. But one day he went wandering too far—just like he did when his story was ending—and when he got back she was gone. When he got back, they'd done *this* to her."

Wendy said nothing. For all that he was a comical figure in his bright clothes and with his Santa Clause air, there was nothing even faintly humorous about the sudden anguish in his voice.

"I'm sorry," she said.

And she was. Not just in sympathy with him, but because in her own way she'd loved that old oak tree as well. And—just like the conjure man, she supposed—she'd wandered away as well.

"Well then," the conjure man said. He rubbed a sleeve up against his nose and looked away from her. "John just wanted you to see."

He got on his bike and reached forward to tousle the fur around Ginger's ears. When he looked back to Wendy, his eyes glittered like tiny blue fires.

"I knew you'd understand," he said.

Before Wendy could respond, he pushed off and pedaled away, bumping across the uneven lawn to leave her standing alone in that once wild place that was now so dispiriting. But then she saw something stir in the middle of the broad stump.

At first it was no more than a small flicker in the air like a heat ripple. Wendy took a step forward, stopping when the flicker resolved into a tiny sapling. As she watched, it took on the slow stately dance of time-lapse photography: budded, unfurled leaves, grew taller, its growth like a rondo, a basic theme that brackets two completely separate tunes. Growth was the theme, while the tunes on either end began with the tiny sapling and ended with a full-grown oak tree as majestic as the behemoth that had originally stood there. When it reached its full height, light seemed to emanate from its trunk, from the roots underground, from each stalkless, broad saw-toothed leaf.

Wendy stared, wide-eyed, then stepped forward with an outstretched hand. As soon as her fingers touched the glowing tree, it came apart, drifting like mist until every trace of it was gone. Once more, all that remained was the stump of the original tree.

The vision, combined with the tightness in her chest and the sadness the conjure man had left her, transformed itself into words that rolled across her mind, but she didn't write them down. All she could do was stand and look at the tree stump for a very long time, before she finally turned and walked away.

Kathryn's Cafe was on Battersfield Road in Lower Crowsea, not far from the university but across the river and far enough that Wendy had to hurry to make it to work on time. But it was as though a black hole had swallowed the two hours from when she'd met the conjure man to when her shift began. She was late getting to work—not by much, but she could see that Jilly had already taken orders from two tables that were supposed to be her responsibility.

She dashed into the restaurant's washroom and changed from her jeans into a short black skirt. She tucked her T-shirt in, pulled her hair back into a loose bun, then bustled out to stash her knapsack and pick up her order pad from the storage shelf behind the employee's coat rack.

"You're looking peaked," Jilly said as she finally got out into the dining area.

Jilly Coppercorn and Wendy were spiritual sisters and could almost pass as physical ones as well. Both women were small, with slender frames and attractive delicate features, though Jilly's hair was a dark curly brown—the same as Wendy's natural hair color. They both moonlighted as waitresses, saving their true energy for creative pursuits: Jilly for her art, Wendy her poetry.

Neither had known the other until they began to work at the restaurant together, but they'd become fast friends from the very first shift they shared.

"I'm feeling confused," Wendy said in response to Jilly's comment.

"You're confused? Check out table five—he's changed his mind three times since he first ordered. I'm going to stand here and wait five minutes before I give Frank his latest order, just in case he decides he wants to change it again."

Wendy smiled. "And then he'll complain about slow service and won't leave you much of a tip."

"If he leaves one at all."

Wendy laid a hand on Jilly's arm. "Are you busy tonight?"

Jilly shook her head. "What's up?"

"I need to talk to someone."

"I'm yours to command," Jilly said. She made a little curtsy which had Wendy quickly stifle a giggle, then shifted her gaze to table five. "Oh bother, he's signaling me again."

"Give me his order," Wendy said. "I'll take care of him."

It was such a nice night that they just went around back of the restaurant when their shift was over. Walking the length of a short alley, they came out on small strip of lawn and made their way down to the river. There they sat on a stone wall, dangling their feet above the sluggish water. The night felt still. Through some trick of the air, the traffic on nearby Battersfield Road was no more than a distant murmur, as though there was more of a sound baffle between where they sat and the busy street than just the building that housed their workplace.

"Remember that time we went camping?" Wendy said after they'd been sitting for awhile in a companionable silence. "It was just me, you and LaDonna. We sat around the campfire telling ghost stories that first night."

"Sure," Jilly said with a smile in her voice. "You kept telling us ones by Robert Aickman and the like—they were all taken from books."

"While you and LaDonna claimed that the ones you told were real and no matter how much I tried to get either of you to admit they weren't, you wouldn't."

"But they were true," Jilly said.

Wendy thought of LaDonna telling them that she'd seen Bigfoot in the Tombs and Jilly's stories about a kind of earth spirit called a gemmin that she'd met in the same part of the city and of a race of goblin-like creatures living in the subterranean remains of the old city that lay beneath Newford's subway system.

She turned from the river to regard her friend. "Do you really believe those things you told me?"

Jilly nodded. "Of course I do. They're true." She paused a moment, leaning closer to Wendy as though trying to read her features in the gloom. "Why? What's happened, Wendy?"

"I think I just had my own close encounter of the weird kind this afternoon."

When Jilly said nothing, Wendy went on to tell her of her meeting with the conjure man earlier in the day.

"I mean, I know why he's called the conjure man," she finished up. "I've seen him pulling flowers out of people's ears and all those other stage tricks he does, but this was different. The whole time I was with him I kept feeling like there really was a kind of magic in the air, a *real* magic just sort of humming around him, and then when I saw the . . . I guess it was a vision of the tree . . .

"Well, I don't know what to think."

She'd been looking across the river while she spoke, gaze fixed on the darkness of the far bank. Now she turned to Jilly.

"Who is he?" she asked. "Or maybe I should be asking *what* is he?"

"I've always thought of him as a kind of anima," Jilly said. "A loose bit of myth that got left behind when all the others went on to wherever it is that myths go when we don't believe in them anymore."

"That's sort of what he said. But what does it mean? What is he really?"

Jilly shrugged. "Maybe what he is isn't so important as *that* he is."
At Wendy's puzzled look, she added, "I can't explain it any better.
I . . . Look, it's like it's not so important that he is or isn't what he
says he is, but *that* he says it. That he believes it."

"Why?"

"Because it's just like he told you," Jilly said. "People are losing
touch with themselves and with each other. They need stories
because they really are the only thing that brings us together. Gossip,
anecdotes, jokes, stories—these are the things that we used to exchange with each other. It kept the lines of communication open,
let us touch each other on a regular basis.

"That's what art's all about, too. My paintings and your poems,
the books Christy writes, the music Geordie plays—they're all lines
of communication. But they're harder to keep open now because
it's so much easier for most people to relate to a TV set than it is to
another person. They get all this data fed into them, but they don't
know what to do with it anymore. When they talk to other people,
it's all surface. How ya doing, what about the weather. The only
opinions they have are those that they've gotten from people on the
TV. They think they're informed, but all they're doing is repeating
the views of talk show hosts and news commentators.

"They don't know how to listen to real people anymore."

"I know all that," Wendy said. "But what does any of it have to
do with what the conjure man was showing me this afternoon?"

"I guess what I'm trying to say is that he validates an older kind
of value, that's all."

"Okay, but what did he want from me?"

Jilly didn't say anything for a long time. She looked out across the
river, her gaze caught by the same darkness as Wendy's had earlier
when she was relating her afternoon encounter. Twice Wendy
started to ask Jilly what she was thinking, but both times she forbore.
Then finally Jilly turned to her.

"Maybe he wants you to plant a new tree," she said.

"But that's silly. I wouldn't know how to begin to go about
something like that." Wendy sighed. "I don't even know if I believe
in a Tree of Tales."

But then she remembered the feeling that had risen in her
when the conjure man spoke to her, that sense of familiarity as

though she was being reminded of something she already knew, rather than being told what she didn't. And then there was the vision of the tree . . .

She sighed again.

"Why me?" she asked.

Her words were directed almost to the night at large, rather than just her companion, but it was Jilly who replied. The night held its own counsel.

"I'm going to ask you something," Jilly said, "and I don't want you to think about the answer. Just tell me the first thing that comes to mind—okay?"

Wendy nodded uncertainly. "I guess."

"If you could be granted one wish—anything at all, no limits—what would you ask for?"

With the state the world was in at the moment, Wendy had no hesitation in answering: "World peace."

"Well, there you go," Jilly told her.

"I don't get it."

"You were asking why the conjure man picked you and there's your reason. Most people would have started out thinking of what they wanted for themselves. You know, tons of money, or to live forever—that kind of thing."

Wendy shook her head. "But he doesn't even know me."

Jilly got up and pulled Wendy to her feet.

"Come on," she said. "Let's go look at the tree."

"It's just a stump."

"Let's go anyway."

Wendy wasn't sure why she felt reluctant, but just as she had this afternoon, she allowed herself to be led back to the campus.

Nothing had changed, except that this time it was dark, which gave the scene, at least to Wendy's way of thinking, an even more desolate feeling.

Jilly was very quiet beside her. She stepped ahead of Wendy and crouched down beside the stump, running her hand along the top of it.

"I'd forgotten all about this place," she said softly.

That's right, Wendy thought. Jilly'd gone to Butler U. just as she had—around the same time, too, though they hadn't known each other then.

She crouched down beside Jilly, starting slightly when Jilly took her hand and laid it on the stump.

"Listen," Jilly said. "You can almost feel the whisper of a story . . . a last echo . . ."

Wendy shivered, though the night was mild. Jilly turned to her. At that moment, the starlight flickering in her companion's blue eyes reminded Wendy very much of the conjure man.

"You've got to do it," Jilly said. "You've got to plant a new tree. It wasn't just the conjure man choosing you—the tree chose you, too."

Wendy wasn't sure what was what anymore. It all seemed more than a little mad, yet as she listened to Jilly, she could almost believe in it all. But then that was one of Jilly's gifts: she could make the oddest thing seem normal. Wendy wasn't sure if you could call a thing like that a gift, but whatever it was, Jilly had it.

"Maybe we should get Christy to do it," she said. "After all, he's the story writer."

"Christy is a lovely man," Jilly said, "but sometimes he's far more concerned with how he says a thing, rather than with the story itself."

"Well, I'm not much better. I've been known to worry for hours over a stanza—or even just a line."

"For the sake of being clever?" Jilly asked.

"No. So that it's right."

Jilly raked her fingers through the short stubble of the weeds that passed for a lawn around the base of the oak stump. She found something and pressed it into Wendy's hand. Wendy didn't have to look at it to know that it was an acorn.

"You have to do it," Jilly said. "Plant a new Tree of Tales and feed it with stories. It's really up to you."

Wendy looked from the glow of her friend's eyes to the stump. She remembered her conversation with the conjure man and her vision of the tree. She closed her fingers around the acorn, feeling the press of the cap's bristles indent her skin.

Maybe it *was* up to her, she found herself thinking.

★   ★   ★

The poem that came to her that night after she left Jilly and got back to her little apartment in Ferryside, came all at once, fully formed and complete. The act of putting it to paper was a mere formality.

She sat by her window for a long time afterward, her journal on her lap, the acorn in her hand. She rolled it slowly back and forth on her palm. Finally, she laid both journal and acorn on the windowsill and went into her tiny kitchen. She rummaged around in the cupboard under the sink until she came up with an old flowerpot which she took into the backyard and filled with dirt—rich loam, as dark and mysterious as that indefinable place inside herself that was the source of the words that filled her poetry and had risen in recognition to the conjure man's words.

When she returned to the window, she put the pot between her knees. Tearing the new poem out of her journal, she wrapped the acorn up in it and buried it in the pot. She watered it until the surface of the dirt was slick with mud, then placed the flowerpot on her windowsill and went to bed.

That night she dreamed of Jilly's gemmin—slender earth spirits that appeared outside the old three-story building that housed her apartment and peered in at the flowerpot on the windowsill. In the morning, she got up and told the buried acorn her dream.

Autumn turned to winter and Wendy's life went pretty much the way it always had. She took turns working at the restaurant and on her poems, she saw her friends, she started a relationship with a fellow she met at a party in Jilly's loft, but it floundered after a month.

Life went on.

The only change was centered around the contents of the pot on her windowsill. As though the tiny green sprig that pushed up through the dark soil was her lover, every day she told it all the things that had happened to her and around her. Sometimes she read it her favorite stories from anthologies and collections, or interesting bits from magazines and newspapers. She badgered her friends for stories, sometimes passing them on, speaking to the tiny plant in a low, but animated voice, other times convincing her friends to come over and tell the stories themselves.

Except for Jilly, LaDonna and the two Riddell brothers, Geordie and Christy, most people thought she'd gone just a little daft. Nothing serious, mind you, but strange all the same.

Wendy didn't care.

Somewhere out in the world, there were other Trees of Tales, but they were few—if the conjure man was to be believed. And she believed him now. She had no proof, only faith, but oddly enough, faith seemed enough. But since she believed, she knew it was more important than ever that her charge should flourish.

With the coming of winter, there were less and less of the street people to be found. They were indoors, if they had such an option, or perhaps they migrated to warmer climes like the swallows. But Wendy still spied the more regular ones in their usual haunts. Paperjack had gone, but the pigeon lady still fed her charges every day, the German cowboy continued his bombastic monologues—though mostly on the subway platforms now. She saw the conjure man, too, but he was never near enough for her to get a chance to talk to him.

By the springtime, the sprig of green in the flowerpot grew into a sapling that stood almost a foot high. On warmer days, Wendy put the pot out on the backporch steps, where it could taste the air and catch the growing warmth of the afternoon sun. She still wasn't sure what she was going to do with it once it outgrew its pot.

But she had some ideas. There was a part of Fitzhenry Park called the Silenus Gardens that was dedicated to the poet Joshua Stanhold. She thought it might be appropriate to plant the sapling there.

One day in late April, she was leaning on the handlebars of her ten-speed in front of the public library in Lower Crowsea, admiring the yellow splash the daffodils made against the building's grey stone walls, when she sensed, more than saw, a red bicycle pull up onto the sidewalk behind her. She turned around to find herself looking into the conjure man's merry features.

"It's spring, isn't it just," the conjure man said. "A time to finally forget the cold and bluster and think of summer. John can feel the leaf buds stir, the flowers blossoming. There's a grand smile in the air for all the growing."

Wendy gave Ginger a pat, before letting her gaze meet the blue shock of his eyes.

"What about a Tree of Tales?" she asked. "Can you feel her growing?"

The conjure man gave her a wide smile. "Especially her." He paused to adjust the brim of his hat, then gave her a sly look. "Your man Stanhold," he added. "Now there was a fine poet—and a fine storyteller."

Wendy didn't bother to ask how he knew of her plan. She just returned the conjure man's smile and then asked, "Do you have a story to tell me?"

The conjure man polished one of the buttons of his bright blue jacket.

"I believe I do," he said. He patted the brown satchel that rode on his back carrier. "John has a thermos filled with the very best tea, right here in his bag. Why don't we find ourselves a comfortable place to sit and he'll tell you how he got this bicycle of his over a hot cuppa."

He started to pedal off down the street, without waiting for her response. Wendy stared after him, her gaze catching the little terrier, sitting erect in her basket and looking back at her.

There seemed to be a humming in the air that woke a kind of singing feeling in her chest. The wind rose up and caught her hair, pushing it playfully into her eyes. As she swept it back from her face with her hand, she thought of the sapling sitting in its pot on her back steps, thought of the wind, and knew that stories were already being harvested without the necessity of her having to pass them on.

But she wanted to hear them all the same.

Getting on her ten-speed, she hurried to catch up with the conjure man.

⨳ SMALL DEATHS ⨳

*WHAT UNITES US UNIVERSALLY IS OUR EMO-
TIONS, OUR FEELINGS IN THE FACE OF EXPERI-
ENCE, AND NOT NECESSARILY THE ACTUAL
EXPERIENCES THEMSELVES.* —ANAIS NIN

"I feel like I should know you."

Zoe Brill looked up. The line was familiar, but it usually came only after she'd spoken—that was the down side of being an all-night DJ in a city with too many people awake and having nothing to do between midnight and dawn. Everybody felt they knew you, everybody was your friend. Most of the time that suited her fine, since she genuinely liked people, but as her mother used to tell her, every family has its black sheep. Sometimes it seemed that every one of them tended to gravitate to her at one point or another in their lives.

The man who'd paused by the cafe railing to speak to Zoe this evening reminded her of a fox. He had lean, pointy features, dark eyes, the corners of his lips constantly lifted in a sly smile, hair as red as her own, if not as long. Unlike her, he had a dark complexion, as though swimming somewhere back in the gene pool of his fore-bears was an Italian, an Arab, or a Native American. His self-assurance radiated a touch too shrill for Zoe's taste, but he seemed basically harmless. Just your average single male yuppie on the prowl, heading out for an evening in clubland—she could almost hear the Full Force–produced dance number kick up as a soundtrack to the moment. Move your body all night long.

He was well-dressed, as all Lotharios should be, casual, but with flair; she doubted there was a single item in his wardrobe worth under two hundred dollars. Maybe the socks.

"I think I'd remember if we'd met before," she said.

He ignored the wryness in her voice and took what she'd said as a compliment.

"Most people do," he agreed.

"Lucky them."

It was one of those rare, supernaturally perfect November evenings, warm with a light breeze, wedged in between a week of
sub-zero temperatures with similar weather to follow. All up and
down Lee Street, from one end of the Market to the other, the
restaurants and cafes had opened their patios for one last outdoor
fling.

"No, no," the man said, finally picking up on her lack of interest.
"it's not like what you're thinking."

Zoe tapped a long finger lightly against the page of the opened
book that lay on her table beside a glass of red wine.

"I'm kind of busy," she said. "Maybe some other time."

He leaned closer to read the running head at the top of the book's
left-hand page: *Disappearing Through the Skylight.*

"That's by O. B. Hardison, isn't it?" he asked. "Didn't he also
write *Entering the Maze?*"

Zoe gave a reluctant nod and upgraded her opinion of him. Fine.
So he was a well-read single male yuppie on the prowl, but she still
wasn't interested.

"Technology," he said, "is a perfect example of evolution, don't
you think? Take the camera. If you compare present models to the
best they had just thirty years ago, you can see—"

"Look," Zoe said. "This is all very interesting, and I don't mean
to sound rude, but why don't you go hit on someone else? If I'd
wanted company, I would've gone out with a friend."

He shook his head. "No, no. I told you, I'm not trying to pick
you up." He put out his hand. "My name's Gordon Wolfe."

He gave her his name with the simple assurance inherent in his
voice that it was impossible that she wouldn't recognize it.

Zoe ignored the hand. As an attractive woman living on her own
in a city the size of Newford, she'd long ago acquired a highly
developed sense of radar, a kind of mental dah-*dum,* dah-*dum*
straight out of *Jaws,* that kicked in whenever that sixth sense hiding
somewhere in her subconscious decided that the situation carried
too much of a possibility of turning weird, or a little too intense.

Gordon Wolfe had done nothing yet, but the warning bell was
sounding faintly in her mind.

"Then what do you want?" she asked.

He lifted his hand and ran it through his hair, the movement so casual it was as though he'd never been rebuffed. "I'm just trying to figure out why I feel like I should know you."

So they were back to that again.

"The world's full of mysteries," Zoe told him. "I guess that's just going to be another one."

She turned back to her book, but he didn't leave the railing. Looking up, she tried to catch the eye of the waiter, to let him know that she was being bothered, but naturally neither he nor the two waitresses were anywhere in sight. The patio held only the usual bohemian mix of Lower Crowsea's inhabitants and hangers-on—a well-stirred stew of actors, poets, artists, musicians and those who aspired, through their clothing or attitude, to be counted in that number. Sometimes it was all just a little too trendy.

She turned back to her unwelcome visitor who still stood on the other side of the cafe's railing.

"It's nothing personal," she began. "I just don't—"

"You shouldn't mock me," he said, cutting in. "I'm the bringer of small deaths." His dark eyes flashed. "Remember me the next time you die a little."

Then he turned and walked away, losing himself in among the crowd of pedestrians that filled the sidewalk on either side of Lee Street.

Zoe sighed. Why were they always drawn to her? The weird and the wacky. Why not the wonderful for a change? When was the last time a nice normal guy had tried to chat her up?

It wasn't as though she looked particularly exotic: skin a little too pale, perhaps, due to the same genes that had given her her shoulder-length red hair and green eyes, but certainly not the extreme vampiric pallor affected by so many fans of the various British Gothic bands that jostled for position on the album charts of college radio and independent record stores; clothing less thrift-shop than most of those with whom she shared the patio this evening: ankle-high black lace-up boots, dark stockings, a black dress that was somewhat tight and a little short, a faded jean jacket that was a couple of sizes too big.

Just your basic semi-hip working girl, relaxing over a glass of wine and a book before she had to head over to the studio. So where were all the nice semi-hip guys for her to meet?

She took a sip of her wine and went back to her book, but found herself unable to concentrate on what she was reading. Gordon Wolfe's parting shot kept intruding on the words that filled the page before her.

Remember me the next time you die a little.

She couldn't suppress the small shiver that slithered up her spine.

Congratulations, she thought to her now-absent irritant. You've succeeded in screwing up my evening anyway.

Paying her bill, she decided to go home and walk Rupert, then head in to work early. An electronic score with lots of deep, low bass notes echoed in her head as she went home, Tangerine Dream crossed with B-movie horror themes. She kept thinking Wolfe was lurking about, following her home, although whenever she turned, there was no one there. She hated this mild anxiety he'd bestowed upon her like some spiteful parting gift.

Her relief at finally getting home to where Rupert waited for her far outweighed the dog's slobbery enthusiasm at the thought of going out for their evening ramble earlier than usual. Zoe took a long roundabout way to the station, letting Rupert's ingenuous affection work its magic. With the big galoot at her side, it was easy to put the bad taste of her encounter with Wolfe to rest.

An old Lovin' Spoonful song provided backdrop to the walk, bouncing and cheerful. It wasn't summer yet, but it was warmer than usual and Newford had always been a hot town.

The phone call came in during the fourth hour of her show, "Nightnoise." As usual, the music was an eclectic mix. An Italian aria by Kiri Te Kanawa was segueing into a cut by the New Age Celtic group from which the show had gotten its name, with Steve Earle's "The Hard Way" cued up next, when the yellow light on the studio's phone began to blink with an incoming call.

"Nightnoise," she said into the receiver. "Zoe B. here."

"Are we on the air?"

It was a man's voice—an unfamiliar voice, warm and friendly with just the vaguest undercurrent of tension.

"I'm sorry," she said. "We don't take call-ins after three."

From one to three A.M. she took on-air calls for requests, commentaries, sometimes just to chat; during that time period she also conducted interviews, if she had any slated. Experience had proven that the real fruitcakes didn't come out of the woodwork until the show was into its fourth hour, creeping up on dawn.

"That's all right," her caller said. "It's you I wanted to talk to."

Zoe cradled the receiver between her shoulder and ear and checked the studio clock. As the instrumental she was playing ended, she brought up the beginning of the Steve Earle cut and began to cue up her next choice, Concrete Blonde's cover of a Leonard Cohen song from the *Pump Up the Volume* soundtrack.

"So talk," she said, shifting the receiver back to her hand.

She could almost feel the caller's hesitation. It happened a lot. They got up the nerve to make the call, but once they were connected, their mouths went dry and all their words turned to sand.

"What's your name?" she added, trying to make it easier on him.

"Bob."

"Not the one from *Twin Peaks* I hope."

"I'm sorry?"

Obviously not a David Lynch fan, Zoe thought.

"Nothing," she said. "What can I do for you tonight, Bob?" Maybe she'd make an exception, she thought, and added: "Did you have a special song you wanted me to play for you?"

"No, I . . . It's about Gordon."

Zoe went blank for a moment. The first Gordon that came to mind was Gordon Waller from the old UK band, Peter & Gordon, rapidly followed by rockabilly great Robert Gordon and then Jim Gordon, the drummer who'd played with everybody from Baez to Clapton, including a short stint with Bread.

"Gordon Wolfe," Bob said, filling in the blank for her. "You were talking to him earlier tonight on the patio of The Rusty Lion."

Zoe shivered. From his blanket beside the studio door, Rupert lifted his head and gave an anxious whine, sensing her distress.

"You . . ." she began. "How could you know? What were you doing, following me?"

"No. I was following him."

"Oh."

Recovering her equilibrium, Zoe glanced at the studio clock and cued up the first cut from her next set in the CD player, her fingers going through the procedure on automatic.

"Why?" she asked.

"Because he's dangerous."

He'd given her the creeps, Zoe remembered, but she hadn't really thought of him as dangerous—at least not until his parting shot.

Remember me the next time you die a little.

"Who is he?" she asked. "Better yet, who are you? Why are you following this Wolfe guy around?"

"That's not his real name," Bob said.

"Then what is?"

"I can't tell you."

"Why the hell not?"

"Not won't," Bob said quickly. "*Can't.* I don't know it myself. All I know is he's dangerous and you shouldn't have gotten him mad at you."

"Jesus," Zoe said. "I really need this." Her gaze flicked back to the studio clock; the Steve Earle cut was heading into its fade-out. "Hang on a sec, Bob. I've got to run some commercials."

She put him on hold and brought up the volume on her mike.

"That was Steve Earle," she said, "with the title cut from his latest album, and you're listening to Nightnoise on WKPN. Zoe B. here, spinning the tunes for all you night birds and birdettes. Coming up we've got a hot and heavy metal set, starting off with the classic 'Ace of Spades' by Motorhead. These are *not* new kids on the block, my friends. But first, oh yes, even at this time of night, a word from some sponsors."

She punched up the cassette with its minute of ads for this half hour and brought the volume down off her mike again. But when she turned back to the phone, the on-line light was dead. She tried it anyway, but Bob had hung up.

"Shit," she said. "Why are you doing this to me?"

Rupert looked up again, then got up from his blanket and padded across the floor to press his wet nose up against her hand. He was a cross between a golden lab and a German shepherd, seventy pounds of big-hearted mush.

"No, not you," she told him, taking his head in both of her hands and rubbing her nose against the tip of his muzzle. "You're Zoe's big baby, aren't you?"

The ads cassette ran its course and she brought up Motorhead. As she cued up the rest of the pieces for this set, she kept looking at the phone, but the on-line light stayed dead.

"Weird," Hilary Carlisle agreed. She brushed a stray lock of hair away from her face and gave Zoe a quick smile. "But par for the course, don't you think?"

"Thanks a lot."

"I didn't say you egged them on, but it seems to be the story of your life: put you in a roomful of strangers and you can almost guarantee that the most oddball guy there will be standing beside you within ten minutes. It's—" she grinned "—just a gift you have."

"Well, this guy's really given me a case of the creeps."

"Which one—Gordon or Bob?"

"Both of them, if you want the truth."

Hilary's smile faded. "This is really getting to you, isn't it?"

"I could've just forgotten my delightful encounter at The Rusty Lion if it hadn't been for the follow-up call."

"You think it's connected?"

"Well, of course it's connected."

"No, not like that," Hilary said. "I mean, do you think the two of them have worked this thing up together?"

That was just what Zoe had been thinking. She didn't really believe in coincidence. To her mind, there was always connections; they just weren't always that easy to work out.

"But what would be the point?" she asked.

"You've got me," Hilary said. "You can stay here with me for a few days if you like," she added.

They were sitting in the front room of Hilary's downstairs apartment which was in the front half of one of the old Tudor buildings on the south side of Stanton Street facing the estates. Hilary in this room always reminded Zoe of Mendelssohn's "Concerto in E Minor," a perfect dialogue between soloist and orchestra. Paintings, curtains, carpet and furniture all reflected Hilary's slightly askew worldview so that Impressionists hung side-by-side with paintings that seemed more the work of a camera; an antique sideboard housed a state-of-the-art stereo, glass shelves held old books; the curtains were dark antique flower prints, with sheers trimmed in lace, the carpet a riot of symmetrical designs and primary colors. The recamier on which Hilary was lounging had a glory of leaf and scrollwork in its wood; Zoe's club chair looked as though a bear had been hibernating in it.

Hilary herself was as tall as Zoe's five-ten, but where Zoe was more angular and big-boned, Hilary was all graceful lines with tanned skin that accentuated her blue eyes and the waterfall of her long straight blonde hair. She was dressed in white this morning, wearing a simple cotton shirt and trousers with the casual elegance of a model, and appeared, as she always did, as the perfect centerpiece to the room.

"I think I'll be okay," Zoe said. "Besides, I've always got Rupert to protect me."

At the sound of his name, Rupert lifted his head from the floor by Zoe's feet and gave her a quick, searching glance.

Hilary laughed. "Right. Like he isn't scared of his own shadow."

"He can't help being nervous. He's just—"

"I know. High-strung."

"Did I ever tell you how he jumped right—"

"Into the canal and saved Tommy's dog from drowning when it fell in? Only about a hundred times since it happened."

Zoe lips shaped a moue.

"Oh God," Hilary said, starting to laugh. "Don't pout. You know what it does to me when you pout."

Hilary was a talent scout for WEA Records. They'd met three years ago at a record launch party when Hilary had made a pass at her. Once they got past the fact that Zoe preferred men and wasn't planning on changing that preference, they discovered that they had far too much in common not to be good friends. But that didn't stop Hilary from occasionally teasing her, especially when Zoe was complaining about man troubles.

Such troubles were usually far simpler than the one currently in hand.

"What do you think he meant by small deaths?" Zoe asked. "The more I think of it, the more it gives me the creeps."

Hilary nodded. "Isn't sleep sometimes referred to as the little death?"

Zoe could hear Wolfe's voice in her head. *I'm the bringer of small deaths.*

"I don't think that's what he was talking about," she said.

"Maybe it's just his way of saying you're going to have bad dreams. You know, he freaks you out a little, makes you nervous, then bingo—he's a success."

"But why?"

"Creeps don't need reasons for what they do; that's why they're creeps."

Remember me the next time you die a little.

Zoe was back to shivering again.

"Maybe I will stay here," she said, "if you're sure I won't be in your way."

"Be in my way?" Hilary glanced at her watch. "I'm supposed to be at work right now—I've got a meeting in an hour—so you'll have the place to yourself."

"I just hope I can get to sleep."

"Do you want something to help you relax?"

"What, like a sleeping pill?"

Hilary shook her head. "I was thinking more along the lines of some hot milk."

"That'd be lovely."

Zoe didn't sleep well. It wasn't her own bed and the daytime street noises were different from the ones outside her own apartment, but it was mostly the constant replay of last night's two conversations that kept her turning restlessly from one side of the bed to the other. Finally, she just gave up and decided to face the day on less sleep than she normally needed.

She knew she'd been having bad dreams during the few times when she had managed to sleep, but couldn't remember one of them. Padding through the apartment in an oversize T-shirt, she found herself drawn to the front window. She peeked out through the curtains, gaze traveling up and down the length of Stanton Street. When she realized what she was doing—looking for a shock of red hair, dark eyes watching the house—she felt more irritable than ever.

She was not going to let it get to her, she decided. At least not anymore.

A shower woke her up, while breakfast and a long afternoon

ramble with Rupert through the grounds of Butler University made her feel a little better, but by the time she got to work at a quarter to twelve that night and started to go through the station's library to collect the music she needed for the show, she was back to being tense and irritable. Halfway through the first hour of the show, she interrupted a Bobby Brown/Ice T/Living Colour set and brought up her voice mike.

"Here's a song for Gordon Wolfe," she said as she cued up an album cut by the local band No Nuns Here. "Memories are made of this, Wolfe."

The long wail of an electric guitar went out over the air waves, a primal screech as the high E string was fingered down around the fourteenth fret and pushed up past the G string, then the bass and drums caught and settled into a driving back beat. The wailing guitar broke into chunky bar chords as Lorio Munn's voice cut across the music like the punch of a fist.

> I don't want your love, baby
>> So don't come on so sweet
> I don't need a man, baby
>> Treats me like I'm meat

> I'm coming to your house, baby
>> Coming to your door
> Gonna knock you down, right where you stand
>> And stomp you on the floor

Zoe eyed the studio phone. She picked up the handset as soon as the on-line light began to flash. Which one was it going to be? she thought as she spoke into the phone.

"Nightnoise. Zoe B. here."

She kept the call off the air, just in case.

"What the hell do you think you're doing?"

Bingo. It was Bob.

"Tell me about small deaths," she said.

"I *told* you he was dangerous, but you just—"

"You'll get your chance to natter on," Zoe interrupted, "but first I want to know about these small deaths."

Silence on the line was the only reply.

"I don't hear a dial tone," she said, "so I know you're still there. Talk to me."

"I . . . Jesus," Bob said finally.

"Small deaths," Zoe repeated.

After another long hesitation, she heard Bob sigh. "They're those pivotal moments in a person's life that change it forever: a love affair gone wrong, not getting into the right post-graduate program, stealing a car on a dare and getting caught, that kind of thing. They're the moments that some people brood on forever; right now they could have the most successful marriage or career, but they can't stop thinking about the past, about what might have happened if things had gone differently.

"It sours their success, makes them bitter. And usually it leads to more small deaths: depression, stress, heavy drinking or drug use, abusing their spouse or children."

"What are you saying?" Zoe asked. "That a small death's like disappointment?"

"More like a pain, a sorrow, an anger. It doesn't have to be something you do to yourself. Maybe one of your parents died when you were just a kid, or you were abused as a child; that kind of trauma changes a person forever. You can't go through such an experience and grow up to be the same person you would have been without it."

"It sounds like you're just talking about life," Zoe said. "It's got its ups and its downs; to stay sane, you've got to take what it hands you. Ride the punches and maybe try to leave the place in a little better shape than it was before you got there."

What was *with* this conversation? Zoe thought as she was speaking.

As the No Nuns Here cut came to an end, she cued in a version of Carly Simon's "You're So Vain" by Faster Pussycat.

"Jesus," Bob said as the song went out over the air. "You really have a death wish, don't you?"

"Tell me about Gordon Wolfe."

The man's voice echoed in her mind as she spoke his name.

I'm the bringer of small deaths.

"What's he got to do with all of this?" she added.

Remember me the next time you die a little.

"He's a catalyst for bad luck," Bob said. "It's like, being in his company—just being in proximity to him—can bring on a small death. It's like . . . do you remember that character in the *L'il Abner* comic strip—the one who always had a cloud hanging over his head. What was his name?"

"I can't remember."

"Everywhere he went he brought bad luck."

"What about him?" Zoe asked.

"Gordon Wolfe's like that, except you don't see the cloud. You don't get any warning at all. I guess the worst thing is that his effects are completely random—unless he happens to take a dislike to you. Then it's personal."

"A serial killer of people's hopes," Zoe said, half jokingly.

"Exactly."

"Oh, give me a break."

"I'm trying to."

"Yeah, right," Zoe said. "You feed me a crock of shit and then expect me to—"

"I don't think he's human," Bob said then.

Zoe wasn't sure what she'd been expecting from this conversation—a confession, perhaps, or even just an apology, but it wasn't this.

"And I don't think you are either," he added.

"Oh, please."

"Why else do you think he was so attracted to you? He recognized something in you—I'm sure of it."

Wolfe's voice was back in her head.

I feel like I should know you.

"I think we've taken this about as far as it can go," Zoe said.

This time she was the one to cut the connection.

The phone's on-line light immediately lit up once more. She hesitated for a long moment, then brought the handset up to her ear.

"I am not bullshitting you," Bob said.

"Look, why don't you take it the tabloids—they'd eat it up."

"You don't think I've tried? I'd do anything to see him stopped."

"Why?"

"Because the world's tough enough without having something

like him wandering through it, randomly shooting down people's hopes. He's the father of fear. You know what fear stands for? Fuck Everything And Run. You want the whole world to be like that? People screw up their lives enough on their own; they don't need a . . . a *thing* like Wolfe to add to their grief."

The scariest thing, Zoe realized, was that he really sounded sincere.

"So what am I then?" she asked. "The mother of hope?"

"I don't know. But I think you scare *him*."

Zoe had to laugh. Wolfe had her so creeped out she hadn't even been able to go to her own apartment last night, and Bob thought she was the scary one?

"Look, could we meet somewhere?" Bob said.

"I don't think so."

"Somewhere public. Bring along a friend—bring a dozen friends. Face to face, I know I can make you understand."

Zoe thought about it.

"It's important," Bob said. "Look at it this way: if I'm a nut, you've got nothing to lose except some time. But if I'm right, then you'd really be—how did you put it?—leaving the world in a little better shape than it was before you got there. A lot better shape."

"Okay," Zoe said. "Tomorrow noon. I'll be at the main entrance of the Williamson Street Mall."

"Great." Zoe started to hang up, pausing when he added: "And Zoe, cool it with the on-air digs at Wolfe, would you? You don't want to see him pissed."

Zoe hung up.

"Your problem," Hilary said as the two of them sat on the edge of the indoor fountain just inside the main entrance of the Williamson Street Mall, "is that you keep expecting to find a man who's going to solve all of your problems for you."

"Of course. Why didn't I realize that was the problem?"

"You know," Hilary went on, ignoring Zoe's sarcasm. "Like who you are, where you're going, who you want to be."

Rupert sat on his haunches by Zoe's knee, head leaning in towards her as she absently played with the hair on the top of his head.

"So what're you saying?" she asked. "That I should be looking for a woman instead?"

Hilary shook her head. "You've got to find yourself first. Everything else'll follow."

"I'm not looking for a man."

"Right."

"Well, not actively. And besides, what's that got to with anything?"

"Everything. You wouldn't be in this situation, you wouldn't have all these weird guys coming on to you, if you didn't exude a kind of confusion about your identity. People pick up on that kind of thing, even if the signals are just subliminal. Look at yourself: You're a nice normal-looking woman with terrific skin and hair and great posture. The loony squad shouldn't be hitting on you. Who's that actor you like so much?"

"Mel Gibson."

"Guys like him should be hitting on you. Or at least, guys like your idolized version of him. Who knows what Gibson's really like?"

Over an early breakfast, Zoe had laid out the whole story for her friend. Hilary had been skeptical about meeting with Bob, but when she realized that Zoe was going to keep the rendezvous, with or without her, she'd allowed herself to be talked into coming along. She'd left work early enough to return to her apartment to wake Zoe and then the two of them had taken the subway over to the Mall.

"You think this is all a waste of time, don't you?" Zoe said.

"Don't you?"

Zoe shrugged. A young security guard walked by and eyed the three of them, his gaze lingering longest on Rupert, but he didn't ask them to leave. Maybe he thought Rupert was a seeing-eye dog, Zoe thought. Maybe he just liked the look of Hilary. Most guys did.

Hilary glanced at her watch. "He's five minutes late. Want to bet he's a no-show?"

But Zoe wasn't listening to her. Her gaze was locked on the red-haired man who had just come in off the street.

"What's the matter?" Hilary asked.

"That's him—the red-haired guy."

"I thought you'd never met this Bob."

"I haven't," Zoe said. "That's Gordon Wolfe."

Or was it? Wolfe was still decked out like a highroller on the make, but there was something subtly different about him this afternoon. His carriage, his whole body language had changed.

Zoe was struck with a sudden insight. A long shiver went up her spine. It started out as a low thrum and climbed into a high-pitched, almost piercing note, like Mariah Carey running through all seven of her octaves.

"Hello, Zoe," Wolfe said as he joined them.

Zoe looked up at him, trying to find a physical difference. It was Wolfe, but it wasn't. The voice was the same as the one on the phone, but people could change their voices; a good actor could look like an entirely different person just through the use of his body language.

Wolfe glanced at Hilary, raising his eyebrows questioningly.

"You . . . you're Bob?" Zoe asked.

He nodded. "I know what you're thinking."

"You're twins?"

"It's a little more complicated than that." His gaze flicked to Hilary again. "How much does your friend know?"

"My name's Hilary and Zoe's pretty well filled me in on the whole sorry business."

"That's good."

Hilary shook her head. "No, it isn't. The whole thing sucks. Why don't just pack up your silly game and take it someplace else?"

Rupert stirred by Zoe's feet. The sharpness in Hilary's voice and Zoe's tension brought the rumbling start of a growl to his chest.

"I didn't start anything," Bob said. "Keep your anger for someone who deserves it."

"Like Wolfe," Zoe said.

Bob nodded.

"Your twin."

"It's more like he's my other half," Bob said. "We share the same body, except he doesn't know it. Only I'm aware of the relationship."

"Jesus, would you give us a break," Hilary said. "This is about as lame as that episode of—"

Zoe laid a hand on her friend's knee. "Wait a minute," she said. "You're saying Wolfe's a schizophrene?"

"I'm not sure if that's technically correct," Bob replied.

He sat down on the marble floor in front of them. It made for an incongruous image: an obviously well-heeled executive type sitting cross-legged on the floor like some panhandler.

"I just know that there's two of us in here," he added, touched a hand to his chest.

"You said you went to the tabloids with this story, didn't you?" Zoe asked.

"I tried."

"I can't believe that they weren't interested. When you think of the stuff that they do print . . ."

"Something . . . happened to every reporter I approached. I gave up after the third one."

"What kind of something?" Hilary asked.

Bob sighed. He lifted a hand and began to count on his fingers. "The first one's wife died in a freak traffic accident; the second had a miscarriage; the third lost his job in disgrace."

"That kind of thing just happens," Zoe said. "It's awful, but there's no way you or Wolfe could be to blame for any of it."

"I'd like to believe you, but I know better."

"Wait a sec," Hilary said. "This happened after you talked to these reporters? What's to stop something from happening to us?"

Zoe glanced at her. "I thought you didn't believe any of this."

"I don't. Do you?"

Zoe just didn't know anymore. The whole thing sounded preposterous, but she couldn't shake the nagging possibility that he wasn't lying to her. It was the complete sincerity with which he—Bob, Wolfe, whatever his name was—spoke that had her mistrusting her logic. Somehow she just couldn't see that sincerity as being faked. She felt that she was too good a judge of character to be taken in so easily by an act, no matter how good; ludicrous as the situation was, she realized that she'd actually feel better if it was true. At least her judgment wouldn't be in question then.

Of course, if Bob was telling the truth, then that changed all the rules. The world could never be the same again.

"I don't know," she said finally.

"Yeah, well better safe than sorry," Hilary said. She turned her attention back to Bob. "Well?" she asked. "*Are* we in danger?"

"Not at the moment. Zoe negates Wolfe's abilities."

"Whoa," Hilary said. "I can already see where this is going. You want her to be your shadow so that the big bad Wolfe won't hurt anybody else—right? Jesus, I've heard some lame pick-up lines in my time, but this beats them all, hands down."

"That's not it at all," Bob said. "He can't hurt Zoe, that's true. And he's already tried. He's exerted tremendous amounts of time and energy since last night in making her life miserable and hasn't seen any success."

"I don't know about that," Zoe said. "I haven't exactly been having a fun time since I ran into him last night."

"What I'm worried about," Bob said, going on as though Zoe hadn't spoken, "is that he's now going to turn his attention on her friends."

"Okay," Zoe said. "This has gone far enough. I'm going to the cops."

"I'm not threatening you," Bob said as she started to stand up. "I'm just warning you."

"It sounds like a threat to me, pal."

"I've spent years looking for some way to stop Wolfe," Bob said. The desperation in his eyes held Zoe captive. "You're the first ray of hope I've found in all that time. He's scared of you."

"Why? I'm nobody special."

"I could give you a lecture on how we're all unique individuals, each important in his or her own way," Bob said, "but that's not what we're talking about here. What you are goes beyond that. In some ways, you and Wolfe are much the same, except where he brings pain into people's lives, you heal."

Zoe shook her head. "Oh, please."

"I don't think the world is the way we like to think it is," Bob went on. "I don't think it's one solid world, but many, thousands upon thousands of them—as many as there are people—because each person perceives the world in his or her own way; each lives in his or her own world. Sometimes they connect, for a moment, or more rarely, for a lifetime, but mostly we are alone, each living in our own world, suffering our small deaths."

"This is stupid," Zoe said.

But she was still held captive by his sincerity. She heard a kind of mystical backdrop to what he was saying, a breathy sound that reminded her of an LP they had in the station's library of R. Carlos Nakai playing a traditional Native American flute.

"I believe you're an easy person to meet," Bob said. "The kind of person that people are drawn to talk to—especially by those who are confused, or hurt, or lost. You give them hope. You help them heal."

Zoe continued to shake her head. "I'm not any of that."

"I'm not so sure he's wrong," Hilary said.

Zoe gave her friend a sour look.

"Well, think about it," Hilary said. "The weird and the wacky are always drawn to you. And that show of yours. There's no way that Nightnoise should work—it's just too bizarre a mix. I can't see headbangers sitting through the opera you play, classical buffs putting up with rap, but they do. It's the most popular show in its time slot."

"Yeah, right. Like it's got so much competition at that hour of the night."

"That's just it," Hilary said. "It does have competition, but people still tune in to you."

"Not fifteen minutes ago, you were telling me that the reason I get all these weird people coming on to me is because I'm putting out confused vibes."

Hilary nodded. "I think I was wrong."

"Oh, for God's sake."

"You do help people," Hilary said. "I've seen some of your fan mail and then there's all of those people who are constantly calling in. You help them, Zoe. You really do."

This was just too much for Zoe.

"Why are you saying all of this?" she asked Hilary. "Can't you hear what it sounds like?"

"I know. It sounds ridiculous. But at the same time, I think it makes its own kind of sense. All those people are turning to you for help. I don't think they expect you to solve all of their problems; they just want that touch of hope that you give them."

"I think Wolfe's asking for your help, too," Bob said.

"Oh, really?" Zoe said. "And how am I supposed to do that? Find you and him a good shrink?"

"In the old days," Hilary said, "there were people who could drive out demons just by a laying on of the hands."

Zoe looked from Hilary to Bob and realized that they were both serious. A smartass remark was on the tip of her tongue, but this time she just let it die unspoken.

A surreal quality had taken hold of the afternoon, as though the Academy of St. Martin-in-the-Fields was playing Hendrix, or Captain Beefheart was doing a duet with Tiffany. The light in the Mall seemed incandescent. The air was hot on her skin, but she could feel a chill all the way down to the marrow of her bones.

I don't want this to be real, she realized.

But she knelt down in front of Bob and reached out her hands, laying a palm on either temple.

What now? she thought. Am I supposed to reel off some gibberish to make it sound like a genuine exorcism?

She felt so dumb, she—

The change caught her completely by surprise, stunning her thoughts and the ever-playing soundtrack that ran through her mind into silence. A tingle like static electricity built up in her fingers.

She was looking directly at Bob, but suddenly it seemed as though she was looking through him, directly into him, into the essence of him. It was flesh and blood that lay under her hands, but rainbowing swirls of light were all she could see. A small sound of wonder sighed from between her lips at the sight.

We're all made of light, she thought. Sounds and light, cells vibrating . . .

But when she looked more closely, she could see that under her hands the play of lights was threaded with discordances. As soon as she noticed them, the webwork of dark threads coalesced into a pebble-sized oval of shadow that fell through the swirl of lights, down, down, until it was gone. The rainbowing pattern of the lights was unblemished now, the lights faded, became flesh and bone and skin, and then she was just holding Bob's head in her hands once more.

The tingle left her fingers and she dropped her hands. Bob smiled at her.

"Thank you," he said.

That sense of sincerity remained, but it wasn't Bob's voice anymore. It was Wolfe's.

"Be careful," he added.

"What do you mean?" she asked.

"I was like you once."

"Like me how?"

"Just be careful," he said.

She tilted her head back as he rose to his feet, gaze tracking him as he walked away, across the marble floor and through the doors of the Mall. He didn't open the doors, he just stepped through the glass and steel out into the street and continued off across the pavement. A half-dozen yards from the entrance, he simply faded away like a video effect and was gone.

Zoe shook her head.

"No," she said softly. "I don't want to believe this."

"Believe what?" Hilary asked.

Zoe turned to look at her. "You didn't see what happened?"

"Happened where?"

"Bob."

"He's finally here?" Hilary looked around at the passersby. "I was so sure he was going to pull a no-show."

"No, he's not here," Zoe said. "He . . ."

Her voice trailed off as the realization hit home. She was on her own with this. What had happened? If she took it all at face value, she realized that meeting Wolfe *had* brought her a small death after all—the death of the world the way it had been to the way she now knew it to be. It was changed forever. *She* was changed forever. She carried a responsibility now of which she'd never been aware before.

Why didn't Hilary remember the encounter? Probably because it would have been the same small death for her as it had been for Zoe herself; her world would have been changed forever.

But *I've* negated that for her, Zoe thought. Just like I did for Wolfe, or Bob, or whoever he really was.

Her gaze dropped to the floor where he'd been sitting and saw a small black pebble lying on the marble. She hesitated for a moment, then reached over and picked it up. Her fingers tingled again and she watched in wonder as the pebble went from black, through grey, until it was a milky white.

"What've you got there?" Hilary asked.

Zoe shook her head. She closed her fingers around the small smooth stone, savoring its odd warmth.

"Nothing," she said. "Just a pebble."

She got up and sat beside Hilary again.

"Excuse me, miss?"

The security guard had returned and this time he wasn't ignoring Rupert.

"I'm sorry," he said, "but I'm afraid you'll have to take your dog outside. It's the mall management's rules."

"Yes," Zoe said. "Of course."

She gave him a quick smile which the guard returned with more warmth than Zoe thought was warranted. It was as though she'd propositioned him or something.

Jesus, she thought. Was she going to go through the rest of her life second-guessing every encounter she ever had? Does he know, does she? Life was tough enough without having to feel self-conscious every time she met somebody. Maybe this was what Wolfe had meant when he said that he had been just like her once. Maybe the pressure just got to be too much for him and it turned him from healing to hurting.

Just be careful.

It seemed possible. It seemed more than possible when she remembered the gratitude she'd seen in his eyes when he'd thanked her.

Beside her, Hilary looked at her watch. "We might as well go," she said. "This whole thing's a washout. It's almost twelve-thirty. If he was going to come, he'd've been here by now."

Zoe nodded her head.

"See the thing is," Hilary said as they started for the door, Rupert walking in between them, "a guy like that can't face an actual confrontation. If you ask me, you're never going to hear from him again."

"I think you're right," Zoe said.

But there might be others, changing, already changed. She might become one of them herself if she wasn't—

just be

Her fingers tightened around the white pebble she'd picked up.

She stuck it in the front pocket of her jeans as a token to remind her of what had happened to Wolfe, of how it could just as easily happen to her if she wasn't

—*careful.*

⚹ THE MOON IS DROWNING ⚹ WHILE I SLEEP

IF YOU KEEP YOUR MIND SUFFICIENTLY OPEN, PEOPLE WILL THROW A LOT OF RUBBISH INTO IT. —WILLIAM A. ORTON

1

Once upon a time there was what there was, and if nothing had happened there would be nothing to tell.

2

It was my father who told me that dreams want to be real. When you start to wake up, he said, they hang on and try to slip out into the waking world when you don't notice. Very strong dreams, he added, can almost do it; they can last for almost half a day, but not much longer.

I asked him if any ever made it. If any of the people our subconscious minds toss up and make real while we're sleeping had ever actually stolen out into this world from the dream world.

He knew of at least one that had, he said.

He had that kind of lost look in his eyes that made me think of my mother. He always looked like that when he talked about her, which wasn't often.

Who was it? I asked, hoping he'd dole out another little tidbit about my mother. Is it someone I know?

Even as I asked, I was wondering how he related my mother to a dream. He'd at least known her. I didn't have any memories, just imaginings. Dreams.

But he only shook his head. Not really, he told me. It happened a long time ago. But I often wondered, he added almost to himself, what did *she* dream of?

★   ★   ★

That was a long time ago and I don't know if he ever found out. If he did, he never told me. But lately I've been wondering about it. I think maybe they don't dream. I think that if they do, they get pulled back into the dream world.

And if we're not too careful, they can pull us back with them.

3

"I've been having the strangest dreams," Sophie Etoile said, more as an observation than a conversational opener.

She and Jilly Coppercorn had been enjoying a companionable silence while they sat on the stone river wall in the old part of Lower Crowsea's Market. The wall is by a small public courtyard, surrounded on three sides by old three-story brick and stone town houses, peaked with mansard roofs, the dormer windows thrusting out from the walls like hooded eyes with heavy brows. The buildings date back over a hundred years, leaning against each other like old friends too tired to talk, just taking comfort from each other's presence.

The cobblestoned streets that web out from the courtyard are narrow, too tight a fit for a car, even the small imported makes. They twist and turn, winding in and around the buildings more like back alleys than thoroughfares. If you have any sort of familiarity with the area you can maze your way by those lanes to find still smaller courtyards, hidden and private, and deeper still, secret gardens.

There are more cats in Old Market than anywhere else in Newford and the air smells different. Though it sits just a few blocks west of some of the city's principal thoroughfares, you can hardly hear the traffic, and you can't smell it at all. No exhaust, no refuse, no dead air. In Old Market it always seems to smell of fresh bread baking, cabbage soups, frying fish, roses and those tart, sharp-tasting apples that make the best strudels.

Sophie and Jilly were bookended by stairs going down to the Kickaha River on either side of them. Pale yellow light from the streetlamp behind them put a glow on their hair, haloing each with her own nimbus of light—Jilly's darker, all loose tangled curls,

Sophie's a soft auburn, hanging in ringlets. They each had a similar slim build, though Sophie was somewhat bustier.

In the half-dark of the streetlamp's murky light, their small figures could almost be taken for each other, but when the light touched their features as they turned to talk to each other, Jilly could be seen to have the quick, clever features of a Rackham pixie, while Sophie's were softer, as though rendered by Rossetti or Burne-Jones.

Though similarly dressed with paint-stained smocks over loose T-shirts and baggy cotton pants, Sophie still managed to look tidy, while Jilly could never seem to help a slight tendency towards scruffiness. She was the only one of the two with paint in her hair.

"What sort of dreams?" she asked.

It was almost four o'clock in the morning. The narrow streets of Old Market lay empty and still about them, except for the odd prowling cat, and cats can be like the hint of a whisper when they want, ghosting and silent, invisible presences. The two women had been working at Sophie's studio on a joint painting, a collaboration that was going to combine Jilly's precise delicate work with Sophie's current penchant for bright flaring colors and loosely rendered figures.

Neither was sure the experiment would work, but they'd been enjoying themselves immensely with it, so it really didn't matter.

"Well, they're sort of serial," Sophie said. "You know, where you keep dreaming about the same place, the same people, the same events, except each night you're a little further along in the story."

Jilly gave her an envious look. "I've always wanted to have that kind of dream. Christy's had them. I think he told me that it's called lucid dreaming."

"They're anything but lucid," Sophie said. "If you ask me, they're downright strange."

"No, no. It just means that you know you're dreaming, *when* you're dreaming, and have some kind of control over what happens in the dream."

Sophie laughed. "I wish."

4

I'm wearing a long pleated skirt and one of those white cotton peasant blouses that's cut way too low in the bodice. I don't know why. I hate that kind of bodice. I keep feeling like I'm going to fall out whenever I bend over. Definitely designed by a man. Wendy likes to wear that kind of thing from time to time, but it's not for me.

Nor is going barefoot. Especially not here. I'm standing on a path, but it's muddy underfoot, all squishy between my toes. It's sort of nice in some ways, but I keep getting the feeling that something's going to sidle up to me, under the mud, and brush against my foot, so I don't want to move, but I don't want to just stand here either.

Everywhere I look it's all marsh. Low flat fens, with just the odd crack willow or alder trailing raggedy vines the way you see Spanish moss do in pictures of the Everglades, but this definitely isn't Florida. It feels more Englishy, if that makes sense.

I know if I step off the path I'll be in muck up to my knees.

I can see a dim kind of light off in the distance, way off the path. I'm attracted to it, the way any light in the darkness seems to call out, welcoming you, but I don't want to brave the deeper mud or the pools of still water that glimmer in the pale starlight.

It's all mud and reeds, cattails, bulrushes and swamp grass and I just want to be back home in bed, but I can't wake up. There's a funny smell in the air, a mix of things rotting and stagnant water. I feel like there's something horrible in the shadows under those strange over-hung trees—especially the willows, the tall sharp leaves of sedge and water plantain growing thick around their trunks. It's like there are eyes watching me from all sides, dark misshapen heads floating frog-like in the water, only the eyes showing, staring. Quicks and bogles and dark things.

I hear something move in the tangle of bulrushes and bur-reeds just a few feet away. My heart's in my throat, but I move a little closer to see that it's only a bird caught in some kind of a net.

Hush, I tell it and move closer.

The bird gets fanatic when I put my hand on the netting. It starts to peck at my fingers, but I keep talking softly to it until it finally settles down. The net's a mess of knots and tangles and I can't work too quickly because I don't want to hurt the bird.

You should leave him be, a voice says, and I turn to find an old woman standing on the path beside me. I don't know where she came from. Every time I lift one of my feet it makes this creepy sucking sound, but I never even heard her approach.

She looks like the wizened old crone in that painting Jilly did for Geordie when he got onto this kick of learning fiddle tunes with the word "hag" in the title: "The Hag in the Kiln," "Old Hag You Have Killed Me," "The Hag With the Money" and god knows how many more.

Just like in the painting, she's wizened and small and bent over and . . . dry. Like kindling, like the pages of an old book. Like she's almost all used up. Hair thin, body thinner. But then you look into her eyes and they're so alive it makes you feel a little dizzy.

Helping such as he will only bring you grief, she says.

I tell her that I can't just leave it.

She looks at me for a long moment, then shrugs. So be it, she says.

I wait a moment, but she doesn't seem to have anything else to say, so I go back to freeing the bird. But now, where a moment ago the netting was a hopeless tangle, it just seems to unknot itself as soon as I lay my hand on it. I'm careful when I put my fingers around the bird and pull it free. I get it out of the tangle and then toss it up in the air. It circles above me in the air, once, twice, three times, cawing. Then it flies away.

It's not safe here, the old lady says then.

I'd forgotten all about her. I get back onto the path, my legs smeared with smelly dark mud.

What do you mean? I ask her.

When the Moon still walked the sky, she says, why it was safe then. The dark things didn't like her light and fair fell over themselves to get away when she shone. But they're bold now, tricked and trapped her, they have, and no one's safe. Not you, not me. Best we were away.

Trapped her? I repeat like an echo. The moon?

She nods.

Where?

She points to the light I saw earlier, far out in the fens.

They've drowned her under the Black Snag, she says. I will show you.

She takes my hand before I realize what she's doing and pulls me through the rushes and reeds, the mud squishing awfully under my bare feet, but it doesn't seem to bother her at all. She stops when we're at the edge of some open water.

Watch now, she says.

She takes something from the pocket of her apron and tosses it into the water. It's like a small stone, or a pebble or something, and it enters the water without a sound, without making a ripple. Then the water starts to glow and a picture forms in the dim flickering light.

It's like we have a bird's eye view of the fens for a moment, then the focus comes in sharp on the edge of a big still pool, sentried by a huge dead willow. I don't know how I know it, because the light's still poor, but the mud's black around its shore. It almost swallows the pale wan glow coming up from out of the water.

Drowning, the old woman says. The moon is drowning.

I look down at the image that's formed on the surface and I see a woman floating there. Her hair's all spread out from her, drifting in the water like lily roots. There's a great big stone on top of her torso so she's only really visible from the breasts up. Her shoulders are slightly sloped, neck slender, with a swan's curve, but not so long. Her face is in repose, as though she's sleeping, but she's underwater, so I know she's dead.

She looks like me.

I turn to the old woman, but before I can say anything, there's movement all around us. Shadows pull away from trees, rise from the stagnant pools, change from vague blotches of darkness, into moving shapes, limbed and headed, pale eyes glowing with menace. The old woman pulls me back onto the path.

Wake quick! she cries.

She pinches my arm—hard, sharp. It really hurts. And then I'm sitting up in my bed.

5

"And did you have a bruise on your arm from where she pinched you?" Jilly asked.

Sophie shook her head and smiled. Trust Jilly. Who else was always looking for the magic in a situation?

"Of course not," she said. "It was just a dream."

"But . . ."

"Wait," Sophie said. "There's more."

Something suddenly hopped onto the wall between them and they both started, until they realized it was only a cat.

"Silly puss," Sophie said as it walked towards her and began to butt its head against her arm. She gave it a pat.

6

The next night I'm standing by my window, looking out at the street, when I hear movement behind me. I turn and it isn't my apartment any more. It's like the inside of an old barn, heaped up with straw in a big tidy pile against one wall. There's a lit lantern swinging from a low rafter beam, a dusty but pleasant smell in the air, a cow or maybe a horse making some kind of nickering sound in a stall at the far end.

And there's a guy standing there in the lantern light, a half dozen feet away from me, not doing anything, just looking at me. He's drop-down gorgeous. Not too thin, not too muscle-bound. A friendly open face with a wide smile and eyes to kill for—long moody lashes, and the irises are the color of violets. His hair's thick and dark, long in the back with a cowlick hanging down over his brow that I just want to reach out and brush back.

I'm sorry, he says. I didn't mean to startle you.

That's okay, I tell him.

And it is. I think maybe I'm already getting used to all the to-and-froing.

He smiles. My name's Jeck Crow, he says.

I don't know why, but all of a sudden I'm feeling a little weak in the knees. Ah, who am I kidding? I know why.

What are you doing here? he asks.

I tell him I was standing in my apartment, looking for the moon, but then I remembered that I'd just seen the last quarter a few nights ago and I wouldn't be able to see it tonight.

He nods. She's drowning, he says, and then I remember the old woman from last night.

I look out the window and see the fens are out there. It's dark and creepy and I can't see the distant glow of the woman drowned in the pool from here the way I could last night. I shiver and Jeck comes over all concerned. He's picked up a blanket that was hanging from one of the support beams and he lays it across my shoulders. He leaves his arm there, to keep it in place, and I don't mind. I just sort of lean into him, like we've always been together. It's weird. I'm feeling drowsy and safe and incredibly aroused, all at the same time.

He looks out the window with me, his hip against mine, the press of his arm on my shoulder a comfortable weight, his body radiating heat.

It used to be, he says, that she would walk every night until she grew so weak that her light was almost failing. Then she would leave the world to go to another, into Faerie, it's said, or at least to a place where the darkness doesn't hide quicks and bogles, and there she would rejuvenate herself for her return. We would have three nights of darkness, when evil owned the night, but then we'd see the glow of her lantern approaching and the haunts would flee her light and we could visit with one another again when the day's work was done.

He leans his head against mine, his voice going dreamy.

I remember my mam saying once, how the Moon lived another life in those three days. How time moves differently in Faerie so that what was a day for us, might be a month for her in that place.

He pauses, then adds, I wonder if they miss her in that other world.

I don't know what to say. But then I realize it's not the kind of conversation in which I have to say anything.

He turns to me, head lowering until we're looking straight into each other's eyes. I get lost in the violet and suddenly I'm in his arms and we're kissing. He guides me, step by sweet step, backward towards that heap of straw. We've got the blanket under us and this time I'm glad I'm wearing the long skirt and peasant blouse again, because they come off so easily.

His hands and his mouth are so gentle and they're all over me like moth wings brushing my skin. I don't know how to describe what he's doing to me. It isn't anything that other lovers haven't done to me before, but the way Jeck does it has me glowing, my skin all warm and tingling with this deep slow burn starting up deep between my legs and just firing up along every one of my nerve ends.

I can hear myself making moaning sounds and then he's inside me, his breathing heavy in my ear. All I can feel and smell is him. My hips are grinding against his and we're synched into this perfect rhythm and then I wake up in my own bed and I'm all tangled up in the sheets with my hand between my legs, finger tip right on the spot, moving back and forth and back and forth. . . .

7

Sophie fell silent.

"Steamy," Jilly said after a moment.

Sophie gave a little bit of an embarrassed laugh. "You're telling me. I get a little squirmy just thinking about it. And that night—I was still so fired up when I woke that I couldn't think straight. I just went ahead and finished and then lay there afterwards, completely spent. I couldn't even move."

"You know a guy named Jack Crow, don't you?" Jilly asked.

"Yeah, he's the one who's got that tattoo parlor down on Palm Street. I went out with him a couple of times, but—" Sophie shrugged "—you know. Things just didn't work out."

"That's right. You told me that all he ever wanted to do was to give you tattoos."

Sophie shook her head, remembering. "In private places so only he and I would know they were there. Boy."

The cat had fallen asleep, body sprawled out on her lap, head pressed tight up against her stomach. A deep resonant purr rose up from him. Sophie just hoped he didn't have fleas.

"But the guy in my dream was nothing like Jack," she said. "And besides, his name was Jeck."

"What kind of a name *is* that?"

"A dream name."

"So did you see him again—the next night?"

Sophie shook her head. "Though not from lack of interest on my part."

8

The third night I find myself in this one-room cottage out of a fairy tale. You know, there's dried herbs hanging everywhere, a big hearth considering the size of the place, with black iron pots and a kettle sitting on the hearth stones, thick hand-woven rugs underfoot, a small tidy little bed in one corner, a cloak hanging by the door, a rough set of a table and two chairs by a shuttered window.

The old lady is sitting on one of the chairs.

There you are, she says. I looked for you to come last night, but I couldn't find you.

I'm getting so used to this dreaming business by now that I'm not at all weirded out, just kind of accepting it all, but I am a little disappointed to find myself here, instead of in the barn.

I was with Jeck, I say and then she frowns, but she doesn't say anything.

Do you know him? I ask.

Too well.

Is there something wrong with him?

I'm feeling a little flushed, just talking about him. So far as I'm concerned, there's nothing wrong with him at all.

He's not trustworthy, the old lady finally says.

I shake my head. He seems to be just as upset about the drowned lady as you are. He told me all about her—how she used to go into Faerie and that kind of thing.

She never went into Faerie.

Well then, where did she go?

The old lady shakes her head. Crows talk too much, she says and I can't tell if she means the birds, or a whole bunch of Jecks.

Thinking about the latter gives me goosebumps. I can barely stay clear-headed around Jeck; a whole crowd of him would probably overload all my circuits and leave me lying on the floor like a little pool of jelly.

I don't tell the old lady any of this. Jeck inspired confidences, as much as sensuality; she does neither.

Will you help us? she says instead.

I sit down at the table with her and ask, Help with what?

The Moon, she says.

I shake my head. I don't understand. You mean the drowned lady in the pool?

Drowned, the old lady says, but not dead. Not yet.

I start to argue the point, but then realize where I am. It's a dream and anything can happen, right?

It needs you to break the bogles' spell, the old lady goes on.

Me? But—

Tomorrow night, go to sleep with a stone in your mouth and a hazel twig in your hands. Now mayhap, you'll find yourself back here, mayhap with your crow, but guard you don't say a word, not one word. Go out into the fen until you find a coffin, and on that coffin a candle, and then look sideways and you'll see that you're in the place I showed you yesternight.

She falls silent.

And then what am I supposed to do? I ask.

What needs to be done.

But—

I'm tired, she says.

She waves her hand at me and I'm back in my own bed again.

9

"And so?" Jilly asked. "Did you do it?"

"Would you have?"

"In a moment," Jilly said. She sidled closer along the wall until she was right beside Sophie and peered into her friend's face. "Oh don't tell me you didn't do it. Don't tell me that's the whole story."

"The whole thing just seemed silly," Sophie said.

"Oh, please!"

"Well, it did. It was all too oblique and riddlish. I know it was just a dream, so that it didn't have to make sense, but there was so much of a coherence to a lot of it that when it did get incomprehensible, it just didn't seem . . . oh, I don't know. Didn't seem fair, I suppose."

"But you *did* do it?"

Sophie finally relented.

"Yes," she said.

10

I go to sleep with a small smooth stone in my mouth and have the hardest time getting to sleep because I'm sure I'm going to swallow it during the night and choke. And I have the hazel twig as well, though I don't know what help either of them is going to be.

Hazel twig to ward you from quicks and bogles, I hear Jeck say. And the stone to remind you of your own world, of the difference between waking and dream, else you might find yourself sharing the Moon's fate.

We're standing on a sort of grassy knoll, an island of semi-solid ground, but the footing's still spongy. I start to say hello, but he puts his finger to his lips.

She's old, is Granny Weather, he says, and cranky, too, but there's more magic in one of her toenails than most of us will find in a lifetime.

I never really thought about his voice before. It's like velvet, soft and smooth, but not effeminate. It's too resonant for that.

He puts his hands on my shoulders and I feel like melting. I close my eyes, lift my face to his, but he turns me around until I'm leaning against his back. He cups his hands around my breasts and kisses me on the nape of my neck. I lean back against him, but he lifts his mouth to my ear.

You must go, he says softly, his breath tickling the inside of my ear. Into the fens.

I pull free from his embrace and face him. I start to say, Why me? Why do I have to go alone? But before I can get a word out he has his hand across my mouth.

Trust Granny Weather, he says. And trust me. This is something only you can do. Whether you do it or not, is your choice. But if you mean to try tonight, you mustn't speak. You must go out into the fens and find her. They will tempt you and torment you, but you must ignore them, else they'll have you drowning too, under the Black Snag.

I look at him and I know he can see the need I have for him because in his eyes I can see the same need for me reflected in their violet depths.

I will wait for you, he says. If I can.

I don't like the sound of that. I don't like the sound of any of it, but I tell myself again, it's just a dream, so I finally nod. I start to turn away, but he catches hold of me for a last moment and kisses me. There's a hot rush of tongues touching, arms tight around each other, before he finally steps back.

I love the strength of you, he says.

I don't want to go, I want to change the rules of the dream, but I get this feeling that if I do, if I change one thing, everything'll change, and maybe he won't even exist in whatever comes along to replace it. So I lift my hand and run it along the side of his face, I take a long last drink of those deep violet eyes that just want to swallow me, then I get brave and turn away again.

And this time I go into the fens.

I'm nervous, but I guess that goes without saying. I look back, but I can't see Jeck anymore. I can just feel I'm being watched, and it's not by him. I clutch my little hazel twig tighter, roll the stone around from one side of my mouth to the other, and keep going.

It's not easy. I have to test each step to make sure I'm not just going to sink away forever into the muck. I start thinking of what you hear about dreams, how if you die in a dream, you die for real, that's why you always wake up just in time. Except for those people who die in their sleep, I guess.

I don't know how long I'm slogging through the muck. My arms and legs have dozens of little nicks and cuts—you never think of how sharp the edge of a reed can be until your skin slides across one. It's like a paper cut, sharp and quick, and it stings like hell. I don't suppose all the muck's doing the cuts much good either. The only thing I can be happy about is that there aren't any bugs.

Actually, there doesn't seem to be the sense of anything living at all in the fens, just me, on my own. But I know I'm not alone. It's like a word sitting on the tip of your tongue. I can't see or hear or sense anything, but I'm being watched.

I think of Jeck and Granny Weather, of what they say the darkness hides. Quicks and bogles and haunts.

After awhile I almost forget what I'm doing out here. I'm just stumbling along with a feeling of dread hanging over me that just won't go away. Bogbean and water mint leaves feel like cold wet fingers sliding along my legs. I hear the occasional flutter of wings, and sometimes a deep kind of sighing moan, but I never see anything.

I'm just about played out when suddenly I come up upon this tall rock under the biggest crack willow I've seen so far. The tree's dead, drooping leafless branches into the still water around the stone. The stone rises out of the water at a slant, the mud's all really black underfoot, the marsh is, if anything, even quieter here, expectant, almost, and I get the feeling like something—some*things* are closing in all around me.

I start to walk across the dark mud to the other side of the rock until I hit a certain vantage point. I stop when I can see that it's shaped like a big strange coffin and I remember what Granny Weather told me. I look for the candle and I see a tiny light flickering at the very top of the black stone, right where it's pushed up and snagged among the dangling branches of the dead willow. It's no brighter than a firefly's glow, but it burns steady.

I do what Granny Weather told me and look around myself using my peripheral vision. I don't see anything at first, but as I slowly turn towards the water, I catch just a hint of a glow in the water. I stop and then I wonder what to do. Is it still going to be there if I turn to face it?

Eventually, I move sideways towards it, always keeping it in the corner of my eye. The closer I get, the brighter it starts to glow, until I'm standing hip deep in the cold water, the mud sucking at my feet, and it's all around me, this dim eerie glowing. I look down into the water and I see my own face reflected back at me, but then I realize that it's not me I'm seeing, it's the drowned woman, the moon, trapped under the stone.

I stick my hazel twig down the bodice of my blouse and reach into the water. I have to bend down, the dark water licking at my shoulders and chin and smelling something awful, but I finally touch the woman's shoulder. Her skin's warm against my fingers and for some reason that makes me feel braver. I get a grip with one hand on her shoulder, then the other, and give a pull.

Nothing budges.

I try some more, moving a little deeper into the water. Finally I plunge my head under and get a really good hold, but she simply won't move. The rock's got her pressed down tight, and the willow's got the rock snagged, and dream or no dream, I'm not some kind of superwoman. I'm only so strong and I have to breathe.

I come up spluttering and choking on the foul water.

And then I hear the laughter.

I look up and there's these things all around the edge of the pool. Quicks and bogles and small monsters. All eyes and teeth and spindly black limbs and crooked hands with too many joints to the fingers. The tree is full of crows and their cawing adds to the mocking hubbub of sound.

First got one, now got two, a pair of voices chant. Boil her up in a tiddy stew.

I'm starting to shiver—not just because I'm scared, which I am, but because the water's so damn cold. The haunts just keep on laughing and making up these creepy little rhymes that mostly have to do with little stews and barbecues. And then suddenly, they all fall silent and these three figures come swinging down from the willow's boughs.

I don't know where they came from, they're just there all of a sudden. These aren't haunts, nor quicks nor bogles. They're men and they look all too familiar.

Ask for anything, one of them says, and it will be yours.

It's Jeck, I realize. Jeck talking to me, except the voice doesn't sound right. But it looks just like him. All three look like him.

I remember Granny Weather telling me that Jeck was untrustworthy, but then Jeck told me to trust her. And to trust him. Looking at these three Jecks, I don't know what to think anymore. My head starts to hurt and I just wish I could wake up.

You need only tell us what it is you want, one of the Jecks says, and we will give it to you. There should be no enmity between us. The woman is drowned. She is dead. You have come too late. There is nothing you can do for her now. But you can do something for yourself. Let us gift you with your heart's desire.

My heart's desire, I think.

I tell myself, again, it's just a dream, but I can't help the way I start thinking about what I'd ask for if I could really have anything I wanted, anything at all.

I look down into the water at the drowned woman and I think about my dad. He never liked to talk about my mother. It's like she was just a dream, he said once.

And maybe she was, I find myself thinking as my gaze goes down into the water and I study the features of the drowned woman who looks so much like me. Maybe she was the Moon in this world and she came to ours to rejuvenate, but when the time came for her to go back, she didn't want to leave because she loved me and dad too much. Except she didn't have a choice.

So when she returned, she was weaker, instead of stronger like she was supposed to be, because she was so sad. And that's how the quicks and the bogles trapped her.

I laugh then. What I'm making up, as I stand here waist-deep in smelly dream water, is the classic abandoned child's scenario. They always figure that there was just a mix-up, that one day their real parents are going to show up and take them away to some place where everything's magical and loving and perfect.

I used to feel real guilty about my mother leaving us—that's something else that happens when you're just a kid in that kind of a situation. You just automatically feel guilty when something bad happens, like it's got to be your fault. But I got older. I learned to deal with it. I learned that I was a good person, that it hadn't been my fault, that my dad was a good person, too, and it wasn't his fault either.

I'd still like to know why my mother left us, but I came to understand that whatever the reasons were for her going, they had to do with her, not with us. Just like I know this is only a dream and the drowned woman might look like me, but that's just something I'm projecting onto her. I *want* her to be my mother. I want her having abandoned me and dad not to have been her fault either. I want to come to her rescue and bring us all back together again.

Except it isn't going to happen. Pretend and real just don't mix. But it's tempting all the same. It's tempting to let it all play out. I know the haunts just want me to talk so that they can trap me as well, that they wouldn't follow through on any promise they made, but this is *my* dream. I can *make* them keep to their promise. All I have to do is say what I want.

And then I understand that it's all real after all. Not real in the sense that I can be physically harmed in this place, but real in that if I make a selfish choice, even if it's just in a dream, I'll still have to live with the fact of it when I wake up. It doesn't matter that I'm dreaming, I'll *still* have done it.

What the bogles are offering is my heart's desire, if I just leave the Moon to drown. But if I do that, I'm responsible for her death. She might not be real, but it doesn't change anything at all. It'll still mean that I'm willing to let someone die, just so I can have my own way.

I suck on the stone and move it back and forth from one cheek to the other. I reach down into my wet bodice and pluck out the hazel twig from where it got pushed down between my breasts. I lift a hand to my hair and brush it back from my face and then I look at those sham copies of my Jeck Crow and I smile at them.

My dream, I think. What I say goes.

I don't if it's going to work, but I'm fed up with having everyone else decide what happens in my dream. I turn to the stone and I put my hands upon it, the hazel twig sticking out between the fingers of my right hand, and I give the stone a shove. There's this great big outcry among the quicks and bogles and haunts as the stone starts to topple over. I look down at the drowned woman and I see her eyes open, I see her smile, but then there's too much light and I'm blinded.

When my vision finally clears, I'm alone by the pool. There's a big fat full moon hanging in the sky, making the fens almost as bright as day. They've all fled, the monsters, the quicks and bogles and things. The dead willow's still full of crows, but as soon as I look up, they lift from the tree in an explosion of dark wings, a circling murder, cawing and crying, until they finally go away. The stone's lying on its side, half in the water, half out.

And I'm still dreaming.

I'm standing here, up to my waist in the smelly water, with a hazel twig in my hand and a stone in my mouth, and I stare up at that big full moon until it seems I can feel her light just singing through my veins. For a moment it's like being back in the barn with Jeck, I'm just on fire, but it's a different kind of fire, it burns away the darknesses that have gotten lodged in me over the years, just like they get lodged in everybody, and just for that moment, I'm solid light, innocent and newborn, a burning Midsummer fire in the shape of a woman.

And then I wake up, back home again.

I lie there in my bed and look out the window, but it's still the dark of the moon in our world. The streets are quiet outside, there's a hush over the whole city, and I'm lying here with a hazel twig in my hand, a stone in my mouth, pushed up into one cheek, and a warm burning glow deep inside.

I sit up and spit the stone out into my hand. I walk over to the window. I'm not in some magical dream now; I'm in the real world. I know the lighted moon glows with light borrowed from the sun. That she's still out there in the dark of the moon, we just can't see her tonight because the earth is between her and the sun.

Or maybe she's gone into some other world, to replenish her lantern before she begins her nightly trek across the sky once more.

I feel like I've learned something, but I'm not sure what. I'm not sure what any of it means.

11

"How can you say that?" Jilly said. "God, Sophie, it's so obvious. She really *was* your mother and you really *did* save her. As for Jeck, he was the bird you rescued in your first dream. Jeck *Crow*—don't you get it? One of the bad guys, only you won him over with an act of kindness. It all makes perfect sense."

Sophie slowly shook her head. "I suppose I'd like to believe that, too," she said, "but what we want and what really is aren't always the same thing."

"But what about Jeck? He'll be waiting for you. And Granny Weather? They both knew you were the Moon's daughter all along. It all means something."

Sophie sighed. She stroked the sleeping cat on her lap, imagining for a moment that it was the soft dark curls of a crow that could be a man, in a land that only existed in her dreams.

"I guess," she said, "it means I need a new boyfriend."

12

Jilly's a real sweetheart, and I love her dearly, but she's naive in some ways. Or maybe it's just that she wants to play the ingenue. She's always so ready to believe anything that anyone tells her, so long as it's magical.

Well, I believe in magic, too, but it's the magic that can turn a caterpillar into a butterfly, the natural wonder and beauty of the world that's all around me. I can't believe in some dreamland being real. I can't believe what Jilly now insists is true: that I've got faerie blood, because I'm the daughter of the Moon.

Though I have to admit that I'd like to.

I never do get to sleep that night. I prowl around the apartment, drinking coffee to keep me awake. I'm afraid to go to sleep, afraid I'll dream and that it'll all be real.

Or maybe that it won't.

When it starts to get light, I take a long cold shower, because I've been thinking about Jeck again. I guess if my making the wrong decision in a dream would've had ramifications in the waking world, then there's no reason that a rampaging libido shouldn't carry over as well.

I get dressed in some old clothes I haven't worn in years, just to try to recapture a more innocent time. White blouse, faded jeans, and hightops with this smoking jacket overtop that used to belong to my dad. It's made of burgundy velvet with black satin lapels. A black hat, with a flat top and a bit of a curl to its brim, completes the picture.

I look in the mirror and I feel like I'm auditioning to be a stage magician's assistant, but I don't much care.

As soon as the hour gets civilized, I head over to Christy Riddell's house. I'm knocking on his door at nine o'clock, but when he comes to let me in, he's all sleepy-eyed and disheveled and I realize that I should've given him another couple of hours. Too late for that now.

I just come right out with it. I tell him that Jilly said he knew all about lucid dreaming and what I want to know is, is any of it real—the place you dream of, the people you meet there?

He stands there in the doorway, blinking like an owl, but I guess he's used to stranger things, because after a moment he leans against the door jamb and asks me what I know about consensual reality.

It's where everything that we see around us only exists because we all agree it does, I say.

Well, maybe it's the same in a dream, he replies. If everyone in the dream agrees that what's around them is real, then why shouldn't it be?

I want to ask him about what my dad had to say about dreams trying to escape into the waking world, but I decide I've already pushed my luck.

Thanks, I say.

He gives me a funny look. That's it? he asks.

I'll explain it some other time, I tell him.

Please do, he says without a whole lot of enthusiasm, then goes back inside.

When I get home, I go and lie down on the old sofa that's out on my balcony. I close my eyes. I'm still not so sure about any of this, but I figure it can't hurt to see if Jeck and I can't find ourselves one of those happily-ever-afters with which fairy tales usually end.

Who knows? Maybe I really am the daughter of the Moon. If not here, then someplace.

≈ IN THE HOUSE ≈ OF MY ENEMY

WE HAVE NOT INHERITED THE EARTH FROM OUR FATHERS, WE ARE BORROWING IT FROM OUR CHILDREN. —NATIVE AMERICAN SAYING

1

The past scampers like an alleycat through the present, leaving the pawprints of memories scattered helter-skelter—here ink is smeared on a page, there lies an old photograph with a chewed corner, elsewhere still, a nest has been made of old newspapers, the headlines running one into the other to make strange declarations. There is no order to what we recall, the wheel of time follows no straight line as it turns in our heads. In the dark attics of our minds, all times mingle, sometimes literally.

I get so confused. I've been so many people; some I didn't like at all. I wonder that anyone could. Victim, hooker, junkie, liar, thief. But without them, I wouldn't be who I am today. I'm no one special, but I like who I am, lost childhood and all.

Did I have to be all those people to become the person I am today? Are they still living inside me, hiding in some dark corner of my mind, waiting for me to slip and stumble and fall and give them life again?

I tell myself not to remember, but that's wrong, too. Not remembering makes them stronger.

2

The morning sun came in through the window of Jilly Copper-corn's loft, playing across the features of her guest. The girl was still asleep on the Murphy bed, sheets all tangled around her skinny limbs, pulled tight and smooth over the rounded swell of her abdomen. Sleep had gentled her features. Her hair clouded the pillow around her head. The soft morning sunlight gave her a Madonna quality, a nimbus of Botticelli purity that the harsher light of the later day would steal away once she woke.

She was fifteen years old. And eight months pregnant.

Jilly sat in the windowseat, feet propped up on the sill, sketchpad on her lap. She caught the scene in charcoal, smudging the lines with the pad of her middle finger to soften them. On the fire escape outside, a stray cat climbed up the last few metal steps until it was level with where she was sitting and gave a plaintive meow.

Jilly had been expecting the black and white tabby. She reached under her knees and picked up a small plastic margarine container filled with dried kibbles, which she set down on the fire escape in front of the cat. As the tabby contentedly crunched its breakfast, Jilly returned to her portrait.

"My name's Annie," her guest had told her last night when she stopped Jilly on Yoors Street just a few blocks south of the loft. "Could you spare some change? I really need to get some decent food. It's not so much for me. . . ."

She put her hand on the swell of her stomach as she spoke. Jilly had looked at her, taking in the stringy hair, the ragged clothes, the unhealthy color of her complexion, the too-thin body that seemed barely capable of sustaining the girl herself, little say nourishing the child she carried.

"Are you all on your own?" Jilly asked.

The girl nodded.

Jilly put her arm around the girl's shoulder and steered her back to the loft. She let her take a shower while she cooked a meal, gave her a clean smock to wear, and tried not to be patronizing while she did it all.

The girl had lost enough dignity as it was and Jilly knew that dignity was almost as hard to recover as innocence. She knew all too well.

3

Stolen Childhood, by Sophie Etoile. Copperplate engraving. Five Coyotes Singing Studio, Newford, 1988.

A child in a ragged dress stands in front of a ramshackle farmhouse. In one hand she holds a doll—a stick with a ball stuck in one end and a skirt on the other. She wears a lost expression, holding the doll as though she doesn't quite know what to do with it.

A shadowed figure stands behind the screen door, watching her.

I guess I was around three years old when my oldest brother started molesting me. That'd make him eleven. He used to touch me down between my legs while my parents were out drinking or sobering up down in the kitchen. I tried to fight him off, but I didn't really know that what he was doing was wrong—even when he started to put his cock inside me.

I was eight when my mother walked in on one of his rapes and you know what she did? She walked right out again until my brother was finished and we both had our clothes on again. She waited until he'd left the room, then she came back in and started screaming at me.

"You little slut! Why are you doing this to your own brother?"

Like it was my fault. Like I *wanted* him to rape me. Like the three-year-old I was when he started molesting me had any idea about what he was doing.

I think my other brothers knew what was going on all along, but they never said anything about it—they didn't want to break that macho code-of-honor bullshit. When my dad found out about, he beat the crap out of my brother, but in some ways it just got worse after that.

My brother didn't molest me anymore, but he'd glare at me all the time, like he was going to pay me back for the beating he got soon as he got a chance. My mother and my other brothers, every time I'd come into a room, they'd all just stop talking and look at me like I was some kind of bug.

I think at first my dad wanted to do something to help me, but in the end he really wasn't any better than my mother. I could see it in his eyes: he blamed me for it, too. He kept me at a distance, never came close to me anymore, never let me feel like I was normal.

He's the one who had me see a psychiatrist. I'd have to go and sit in his office all alone, just a little kid in this big leather chair. The psychiatrist would lean across his desk, all smiles and smarmy under-standing, and try to get me to talk, but I never told him a thing. I didn't trust him. I'd already learned that I couldn't trust men. Couldn't trust women either, thanks to my mother. Her idea of working things out was to send me to confession, like the same God who let my brother rape me was now going to make everything okay so long as I owned up to seducing him in the first place.

What kind of a way is that for a kid to grow up?

4

"Forgive me, Father, for I have sinned. I let my brother . . ."

5

Jilly laid her sketchpad aside when her guest began to stir. She swung her legs down so that they dangled from the windowsill, heels banging lightly against the wall, toes almost touching the ground. She pushed an unruly lock of hair from her brow, leaving behind a charcoal smudge on her temple.

Small and slender, with pixie features and a mass of curly dark hair, she looked almost as young as the girl on her bed. Jeans and sneakers, a dark T-shirt and an oversized peach-colored smock only added to her air of slightness and youth. But she was halfway through her thirties, her own teenage years long gone; she could have been Annie's mother.

"What were you doing?" Annie asked as she sat up, tugging the sheets up around herself.

"Sketching you while you slept. I hope you don't mind."

"Can I see?"

Jilly passed the sketchpad over and watched Annie study it. On the fire escape behind her, two more cats had joined the black and white tabby at the margarine container. One was an old alleycat, its left ear ragged and torn, ribs showing like so many hills and valleys against the matted landscape of its fur. The other belonged to an upstairs neighbor; it was making its usual morning rounds.

"You made me look a lot better than I really am," Annie said finally.

Jilly shook her head. "I only drew what was there."

"Yeah, right."

Jilly didn't bother to contradict her. The self-worth speech would keep.

"So is this how you make your living?" Annie asked.

"Pretty well. I do a little waitressing on the side."

"Beats being a hooker, I guess."

She gave Jilly a challenging look as she spoke, obviously anticipating a reaction.

Jilly only shrugged. "Tell me about it," she said.

Annie didn't say anything for a long moment. She looked down at the rough portrait with an unreadable expression, then finally met Jilly's gaze again.

"I've heard about you," she said. "On the street. Seems like everybody knows you. They say . . ."

Her voice trailed off.

Jilly smiled. "What do they say?"

"Oh, all kinds of stuff." She shrugged. "You know. That you used to live on the street, that you're kind of like a one-woman social service, but you don't lecture. And that you're—" she hesitated, looked away for a moment "—you know, a witch."

Jilly laughed. "A witch?"

That was a new one on her.

Annie waved a hand towards the wall across from the window where Jilly was sitting. Paintings leaned up against each other in untidy stacks. Above them, the wall held more, a careless gallery hung frame to frame to save space. They were part of Jilly's ongoing "Urban Faerie" series, realistic city scenes and characters to which were added the curious little denizens of lands which never were. Hobs and fairies, little elf men and goblins.

"They say you think all that stuff's real," Annie said.

"What do you think?"

When Annie gave her a "give me a break" look, Jilly just smiled again.

"How about some breakfast?" she asked to change the subject.

"Look," Annie said. "I really appreciate your taking me in and feeding me and everything last night, but I don't want to be free-loader."

"One more meal's not freeloading."

Jilly pretended to pay no attention as Annie's pride fought with her baby's need.

"Well, if you're sure it's okay," Annie said hesitantly.

"I wouldn't have offered if it wasn't," Jilly said.

She dropped down from the windowsill and went across the loft to the kitchen corner. She normally didn't eat a big breakfast, but twenty minutes later they were both sitting down to fried eggs and bacon, home fries and toast, coffee for Jilly and herb tea for Annie.

"Got any plans for today?" Jilly asked as they were finishing up.

"Why?" Annie replied, immediately suspicious.

"I thought you might want to come visit a friend of mine."

"A social worker, right?"

The tone in her voice was the same as though she was talking about a cockroach or maggot.

Jilly shook her head. "More like a storefront counselor. Her name's Angelina Marceau. She runs that drop-in center on Grasso Street. It's privately funded, no political connections."

"I've heard of her. The Grasso Street Angel."

"You don't have to come," Jilly said, "but I know she'd like to meet you."

"I'm sure."

Jilly shrugged. When she started to clean up, Annie stopped her. "Please," she said. "Let me do it."

Jilly retrieved her sketchpad from the bed and returned to the windowseat while Annie washed up. She was just adding the finishing touches to the rough portrait she'd started earlier when Annie came to sit on the edge of the Murphy bed.

"That painting on the easel," Annie said. "Is that something new you're working on?"

Jilly nodded.

"It's not like your other stuff at all."

"I'm part of an artist's group that calls itself the Five Coyotes Singing Studio," Jilly explained. "The actual studio's owned by a friend of mine named Sophie Etoile, but we all work in it from time to time. There's five of us, all women, and we're doing a group show with a theme of child abuse at the Green Man Gallery next month."

"And that painting's going to be in it?" Annie asked.

"It's one of three I'm doing for the show."

"What's that one called?"

" 'I Don't Know How To Laugh Anymore.' "

Annie put her hands on top of her swollen stomach.

"Me, neither," she said.

6

I Don't Know How to Laugh Anymore, *by Jilly Coppercorn.*
Oils and mixed media. Yoors Street Studio, Newford, 1991.

A life-sized female subject leans against an inner city wall in the classic pose of a prostitute waiting for a customer. She wears high heels, a micro-miniskirt, tube-top and short jacket, with a purse slung over one shoulder, hanging against her hip from a narrow strap. Her hands are thrust into the pockets of her jacket. Her features are tired, the lost look of a junkie in her eyes undermining her attempt to appear sultry.

Near her feet, a condom is attached to the painting, stiffened with gesso.

The subject is thirteen years old.

I started running away from home when I was ten. The summer I turned eleven I managed to make it to Newford and lived on its streets for six months. I ate what I could find in the dumpsters behind the McDonald's and other fast food places on Williamson Street—there was nothing wrong with the food. It was just dried out from having been under the heating lamps for too long.

I spent those six months walking the streets all night. I was afraid to sleep when it was dark because I was just a kid and who knows what could've happened to me. At least being awake I could hide whenever I saw something that made me nervous. In the daytime I slept where I could—in parks, in the back seats of abandoned cars, wherever I didn't think I'd get caught. I tried to keep myself clean, washed up in restaurant bathrooms and at this gas bar on Yoors Street where the guy running the pumps took a liking to me. Paydays he'd spot me for lunch at the grill down the street.

I started drawing back then and for awhile I tried to hawk my pictures to the tourists down by the Pier, but the stuff wasn't all that good and I was drawing with pencils on foolscap or pages torn out of old school notebooks—not exactly the kind of art that looks good in a frame, if you know what I mean. I did a lot better panhandling and shoplifting.

I finally got busted trying to boost a tape deck from Kreiger's Stereo—it used to be where Gypsy Records is. Now it's out on the strip past the Tombs. I've always been small for my age, which didn't help when I tried to to convince the cops that I was older than I really was. I figured juvie would be better than going back to my parents' place, but it didn't work. My parents had a missing persons out on me, God knows why. It's not like they could've missed me.

But I didn't go back home. My mother didn't want me and my dad didn't argue, so I guess he didn't either. I figured that was great until I started making the rounds of foster homes, bouncing back and forth them and the Home for Wayward Girls. It's just juvie with an old-fashioned name.

I guess there must be some good foster parents, but I never saw any. All mine ever wanted was to collect their check and treat me like I was a piece of shit unless my case worker was coming by for a visit. Then I got moved up from the mattress in the basement to one of their kids' rooms. The first time I tried to tell the worker what was going down, she didn't believe me and then my foster parents beat the crap out of me once she was gone. I didn't make that mistake again.

I was thirteen and in my fourth or fifth foster home when I got molested again. This time I didn't take any crap. I booted the old pervert in the balls and just took off out of there, back to Newford.

I was older and knew better now. Girls I talked to in juvie told me how to get around, who to trust and who was just out to peddle your ass.

See, I never planned on being a hooker. I don't know what I thought I'd do when I got to the city—I wasn't exactly thinking straight. Anyway, I ended up with this guy—Robert Carson. He was fifteen.

I met him in back of the Convention Center on the beach where all the kids used to all hang out in the summer and we ended up getting a room together on Grasso Street, near the high school. I was still pretty fucked up about getting physical with a guy but we ended up doing so many drugs—acid, MDA, coke, smack, you name it—that half the time I didn't know when he was putting it to me.

We ran out of money one day, rent was due, no food in the place, no dope, both of us too fucked up to panhandle, when Rob gets the big idea of selling my ass to bring in a little money. Well, I was screwed up, but not that screwed up. But then he got some guy to front him some smack and next thing I know I'm in this car with some guy I never saw before and he's expecting a blow job and I'm crying and all fucked up from the dope and then I'm doing it and standing out on the street corner where he's dumped me some ten minutes later with forty bucks in my hand and Rob's laughing, saying how we got it made, and all I can do is crouch on the sidewalk and puke, trying to get the taste of that guy's come out of my mouth.

So Rob thinks I'm being, like, so fucking weird—I mean, it's easy money, he tells me. Easy for him maybe. We have this big fight and then he hits me. Tells me if I don't get my ass out on the street and make some more money, he's going to do worse, like cut me.

My luck, I guess. Of all the guys to hang out with, I've got to pick one who suddenly realizes it's his ambition in life to be a pimp. Three years later he's running a string of five girls, but he lets me pay my respect—two grand which I got by skimming what I was paying him—and I'm out of the scene.

Except I'm not, because I'm still a junkie and I'm too fucked up to work, I've got no ID, I've got no skills except I can draw a little when I'm not fucked up on smack which is just about all the time. I start muling for a couple of dealers in Fitzhenry Park, just to get my fixes, and then one night I'm so out of it, I just collapse in a doorway of a pawn shop up on Perry Street.

I haven't eaten in, like, three days. I'm shaking because I need a fix so bad I can't see straight. I haven't washed in Christ knows how long, so I smell and the clothes I'm wearing are worse. I'm at the end of the line and I know it, when I hear footsteps coming down the street and I know it's the local cop on his beat, doing his rounds.

I try to crawl deeper into the shadows but the doorway's only so deep and the cop's coming closer and then he's standing there, blocking what little light the streetlamps were throwing and I know

I'm screwed. But there's no way I'm going back into juvie or a foster home. I'm thinking of offering him a blow job to let me go—so far as the cops're concerned, hookers're just scum, but they'll take a freebie all the same—but I see something in this guy's face, when he turns his head and the streetlight touches it, that tells me he's an honest joe. A rookie, true blue, probably his first week on the beat and full of wanting to help everybody and I know for sure I'm screwed. With my luck running true, he's going to be the kind of guy who thinks social workers really want to help someone like me instead of playing bureaucratic mind-fuck games with my head.

I don't think I can take anymore.

I find myself wishing I had Rob's switchblade—the one he liked to push up against my face when he didn't think I was bringing in enough. I just want to cut something. The cop. Myself. I don't really give a fuck. I just want out.

He crouches down so he's kind of level with me, lying there scrunched up against the door, and says, "How bad is it?"

I just look at him like he's from another planet. How bad is it? Can it get any worse I wonder?

"I . . . I'm doing fine," I tell him.

He nods like we're discussing the weather. "What's your name?"

"Jilly," I say.

"Jilly what?"

"Uh. . . ."

I think of my parents, who've turned their backs on me. I think of juvie and foster homes. I look over his shoulder and there's a pair of billboards on the building behind me. One's advertising a suntan lotion—you know the one with the dog pulling the kid's pants down? I'll bet some old pervert thought that one up. The other's got the Jolly Green Giant himself selling vegetables. I pull a word from each ad and give it to the cop.

"Jilly Coppercorn."

"Think you can stand, Jilly?"

I'm thinking, If I could stand, would I be lying here? But I give it a try. He helps me the rest of the way up, supports me when I start to sway.

"So . . . so am I busted?" I ask him.

"Have you committed a crime?"

I don't know where the laugh comes from, but it falls out of my mouth all the same. There's no humor in it.

"Sure," I tell him. "I was born."

He sees my bag still lying on the ground. He picks it up while I lean against the wall and a bunch of my drawings fall out. He looks at them as he stuffs them back in the bag.

"Did you do those?"

I want to sneer at him, ask him why the fuck should he care, but I've got nothing left in me. It's all I can do to stand. So I tell him, yeah, they're mine.

"They're very good."

Right. I'm actually this fucking brilliant artist, slumming just to get material for my art.

"Do you have a place to stay?" he asks.

Whoops, did I read him wrong? Maybe he's planning to get me home, clean me up, and then put it to me.

"Jilly?" he asks when I don't answer.

Sure, I want to tell him. I've got my pick of the city's alleyways and doorways. I'm welcome wherever I go. World treats me like a fucking princess. But all I do is shake my head.

"I want to take you to see a friend of mine," he says.

I wonder how he can stand to touch me. I can't stand myself. I'm like a walking sewer. And now he wants to bring me to meet a friend?

"Am I busted?" I ask him again.

He shakes his head. I think of where I am, what I got ahead of me, then I just shrug. If I'm not busted, then whatever's he's got planned for me's got to be better. Who knows, maybe his friend'll front me with a fix to get me through the night.

"Okay," I tell him. "Whatever."

"C'mon," he says.

He puts an arm around my shoulder and steers me off down the street and that's how I met Lou Fucceri and his girlfriend, the Grasso Street Angel.

7

Jilly sat on the stoop of Angel's office on Grasso Street, watching the passersby. She had her sketchpad on her knee, but she hadn't opened it yet. Instead, she was amusing herself with one of her favorite pastimes: making up stories about the people walking by. The young woman with the child in a stroller, she was a princess in exile, disguising herself as a nanny in a far distant land until she could regain her rightful station in some suitably romantic dukedom in Europe. The old black man with the cane was a physicist studying the effects of Chaos theory in the Grasso Street traffic. The Hispanic girl on her skateboard was actually a mermaid, having exchanged the waves of her ocean for concrete.

She didn't turn around when she heard the door open behind her. There was a scuffle of sneakers on the stoop, then the sound of the door closing again. After a moment, Annie sat down beside her.

"How're you doing?" Jilly asked.

"It was weird."

"Good weird, or bad?" Jilly asked when Annie didn't go on. "Or just uncomfortable?"

"Good weird, I guess. She played the tape you did for her book. She said you knew, that you'd said it was okay."

Jilly nodded.

"I couldn't believe it was you. I mean, I recognized your voice and everything, but you sounded so different."

"I was just a kid," Jilly said. "A punky street kid."

"But look at you now."

"I'm nothing special," Jilly said, suddenly feeling self-conscious. She ran a hand through her hair. "Did Angel tell you about the sponsorship program?"

Annie nodded. "Sort of. She said you'd tell me more."

"What Angel does is coordinate a relationship between kids that need help and people who want to help. It's different every time, because everybody's different. I didn't meet my sponsor for the longest time; he just put up the money while Angel was my contact. My lifeline, if you want to know the truth. I can't remember how many times I'd show up at her door and spend the night crying on her shoulder."

"How did you get, you know, cleaned up?" Annie asked. Her voice was shy.

"The first thing is I went into detox. When I finally got out, my sponsor paid for my room and board at the Chelsea Arms while I went through an accelerated high school program. I told Angel I wanted to go on to college, so he cosigned my student loan and helped me out with my books and supplies and stuff. I was working by that point. I had part-time jobs at a couple of stores and with the Post Office, and then I started waitressing, but that kind of money doesn't go far—not when you're carrying a full course load."

"When did you find out who your sponsor was?"

"When I graduated. He was at the ceremony."

"Was it weird finally meeting him?"

Jilly laughed. "Yes and no. I'd already known him for years—he was my art history professor. We got along really well and he used to let me use the sunroom at the back of his house for a studio. Angel and Lou had shown him some of that bad art I'd been doing when I was still on the street and that's why he sponsored me—because he thought I had a lot of talent, he told me later. But he didn't want me to know it was him putting up the money because he thought it might affect our relationship at Butler U." She shook her head. "He said he *knew* I'd be going the first time Angel and Lou showed him the stuff I was doing."

"It's sort of like a fairy tale, isn't it?" Annie said.

"I guess it is. I never thought of it that way."

"And it really works, doesn't it?"

"If you want it to," Jilly said. "I'm not saying it's easy. There's ups and downs—lots more downs at the start."

"How many kids make it?"

"This hasn't got anything to do with statistics," Jilly said. "You can only look at it on a person to person basis. But Angel's been doing this for a long, long time. You can trust her to do her best for you. She takes a lot of flak for what she does. Parents get mad at her because she won't tell them where their kids are. Social services says she's undermining their authority. She's been to jail twice on contempt of court charges because she wouldn't tell where some kid was."

"Even with her boyfriend being a cop?"

"That was a long time ago," Jilly said. "And it didn't work out. They're still friends but—Angel went through an awful bad time when she was a kid. That changes a person, no matter how much they learn to take control of their life. Angel's great with people, especially kids, and she's got a million friends, but she's not good at maintaining a personal relationship with a guy. When it comes down to the crunch, she just can't learn to trust them. As friends, sure, but not as lovers."

"She said something along the same lines about you," Annie said. "She said you were full of love, but it wasn't sexual or romantic so much as a general kindness towards everything and everybody."

"Yeah, well . . . I guess both Angel and I talk too much."

Annie hesitated for a few heartbeats, then said, "She also told me that you want to sponsor me."

Jilly nodded. "I'd like to."

"I don't get it."

"What's to get?"

"Well, I'm not like you or your professor friend. I'm not, you know, all that creative. I couldn't make something beautiful if my life depended on it. I'm not much good at anything."

Jilly shook her head. "That's not what it's about. Beauty isn't what you see on TV or in magazine ads or even necessarily in art galleries. It's a lot deeper and a lot simpler than that. It's realizing the goodness of things, it's leaving the world a little better than it was before you got here. It's appreciating the inspiration of the world around you and trying to inspire others.

"Sculptors, poets, painters, musicians—they're the traditional purveyors of Beauty. But it can as easily be created by a gardener, a farmer, a plumber, a careworker. It's the intent you put into your work, the pride you take in it—whatever it is."

"But still. . . . I really don't have anything to offer."

Annie's statement was all the more painful for Jilly because it held no self-pity, it was just a laying out of facts as Annie saw them.

"Giving birth is an act of Beauty," Jilly said.

"I don't even know if I want a kid. I . . . I don't know what I want. I don't know who I am."

She turned to Jilly. There seemed to be years of pain and confusion in her eyes, far more years than she had lived in the world. When had that pain begun? Jilly thought. Who could have done it to her, beautiful child that she must have been? Father, brother, uncle, family friend?

Jilly wanted to just reach out and hold her, but knew too well how the physical contact of comfort could too easily be miscon-strued as an invasion of the private space an abused victim sometimes so desperately needed to maintain.

"I need help," Annie said softly. "I know that. But I don't want charity."

"Don't think of this sponsorship program as charity," Jilly said. "What Angel does is simply what we all should be doing all of the time—taking care of each other."

Annie sighed, but fell silent. Jilly didn't push it any further. They sat for awhile longer on the stoop while the world bustled by on Grasso Street.

"What was the hardest part?" Annie asked. "You know, when you first came off the street."

"Thinking of myself as normal."

8

Daddy's Home, *by Isabelle Copley. Painted Wood. Adjani Farm, Wren Island, 1990.*

The sculpture is three feet high, a flat rectangle of solid wood, standing on end with a child's face, upper torso and hands protruding from one side, as though the wood is gauze against which the subject is pressing.

The child wears a look of terror.

Annie's sleeping again. She needs the rest as much as she needs regular meals and the knowledge that she's got a safe place to stay. I took my Walkman out onto the fire escape and listened to a copy of the tape that Angel played for her today. I don't much recognize that kid either, but I know it's me.

It's funny, me talking about Angel, Angel talking about me, both of us knowing what the other needs, but neither able to help herself. I like to see my friends as couples. I like to see them in love with each other. But it's not the same for me.

Except who am I kidding? I want the same thing, but I just choke when a man gets too close to me. I can't let down that final barrier, I can't even tell them why.

Sophie says I expect them to just instinctively know. That I'm waiting for them to be understanding and caring without ever opening up to them. If I want them to follow the script I've got written out my head, she says I have to let them in on it.

I know she's right, but I can't do anything about it.

I see a dog slink into the alleyway beside the building. He's skinny as a whippet, but he's just a mongrel that no one's taken care of for awhile. He's got dried blood on his shoulders, so I guess someone's been beating him.

I go down with some cat food in a bowl, but he won't come near me, no matter how soothingly I call to him. I know he can smell the food, but he's more scared of me than he's hungry. Finally I just leave the bowl and go back up the fire escape. He waits until I'm sitting outside my window again before he goes up to the bowl. He wolfs the food down and then he takes off like he's done something wrong.

I guess that's the way I am when I meet a man I like. I'm really happy with him until he's nice to me, until he wants to kiss me and hold me, and then I just run off like I've done something wrong.

9

Annie woke while Jilly was starting dinner. She helped chop up vegetables for the vegetarian stew Jilly was making, then drifted over to the long worktable that ran along the back wall near Jilly's easel. She found a brochure for the Five Coyotes Singing Studio show in amongst the litter of paper, magazines, sketches and old paint brushes and brought it over to the kitchen table where she leafed through it while Jilly finished up the dinner preparations.

"Do you really think something like this is going to make a difference?" Annie asked after she'd read through the brochure.

"Depends on how big a difference you're talking about," Jilly said. "Sophie's arranged for a series of lectures to run in association with the show and she's also organized a couple of discussion evenings at the gallery where people who come to the show can talk to us—about their reactions to the show, about their feelings, maybe even share their own experiences if that's something that feels right to them at the time."

"Yeah, but what about the kids that this is all about?" Annie asked.

Jilly turned from the stove. Annie didn't look at all like a young expectant mother, glowing with her pregnancy. She just looked like a hurt and confused kid with a distended stomach, a kind of Ralph Steadman aura of frantic anxiety splattered around her.

"The way we see it," Jilly said, "is if only one kid gets spared the kind of hell we all went through, then the show'll be worth it."

"Yeah, but the only kind of people who are going to go to this kind of thing are those who already know about it. You're preaching to the converted."

"Maybe. But there'll be media coverage—in the papers for sure, maybe a spot on the news. That's where—if we're going to reach out and wake someone up—that's where it's going to happen."

"I suppose."

Annie flipped over the brochure and looked at the four photographs on the back.

"How come there isn't a picture of Sophie?" she asked.

"Cameras don't seem to work all that well around her," Jilly said. "It's like—" she smiled "—an enchantment."

The corner of Annie's mouth twitched in response.

"Tell me about, you know . . ." She pointed to Jilly's Urban Faerie paintings. "Magic. Enchanted stuff."

Jilly put the stew on low to simmer then fetched a sketchbook that held some of the preliminary pencil drawings for the finished paintings that were leaning up against the wall. The urban settings were barely realized—just rough outlines and shapes—but the faerie were painstakingly detailed.

As they flipped through the sketchbook, Jilly talked about where she'd done the sketches, what she'd seen, or more properly glimpsed, that led her to make the drawings she had.

"You've really seen all these . . . little magic people?" Annie asked.

Her tone of voice was incredulous, but Jilly could tell that she wanted to believe.

"Not all of them," Jilly said. "Some I've only imagined, but others . . . like this one." She pointed to a sketch that had been done in the Tombs where a number of fey figures were hanging out around an abandoned car, pre-Raphaelite features at odds with their raggedy clothing and setting. "They're real."

"But they could just be people. It's not like they're tiny or have wings like some of the others."

Jilly shrugged. "Maybe, but they weren't just people."

"Do you have to be magic yourself to see them?"

Jilly shook her head. "You just have to pay attention. If you don't you'll miss them, or see something else—something you expected to see rather than what was really there. Fairy voices become just the wind, a bodach, like this little man here—" she flipped to another page and pointed out a small gnomish figure the size of a cat, darting off a sidewalk "—scurrying across the street becomes just a piece of litter caught in the backwash of a bus."

"Pay attention," Annie repeated dubiously.

Jilly nodded. "Just like we have to pay attention to each other, or we miss the important things that are going on there as well."

Annie turned another page, but she didn't look at the drawing. Instead she studied Jilly's pixie features.

"You really, really believe in magic, don't you?" she said.

"I really, really do," Jilly told her. "But it's not something I just take on faith. For me, art is an act of magic. I pass on the spirits that I see—of people, of places, mysteries."

"So what if you're not an artist? Where's the magic then?"

"Life's an act of magic, too. Claire Hamill sings a line in one of her songs that really sums it up for me: 'If there's no magic, there's no meaning.' Without magic—or call it wonder, mystery, natural wisdom—nothing has any depth. It's all just surface. You know: what you see is what you get. I honestly believe there's more to everything than that, whether it's a Monet hanging in a gallery or some old vagrant sleeping in an alley."

"I don't know," Annie said. "I understand what you're saying, about people and things, but this other stuff—it sounds more like the kinds of things you see when you're tripping."

Jilly shook her head. "I've done drugs and I've seen Faerie. They're not the same."

She got up to stir the stew. When she sat down again, Annie had closed the sketchbook and was sitting with her hands flat against her stomach.

"Can you feel the baby?" Jilly asked.

Annie nodded.

"Have you thought about what you want to do?"

"I guess. I'm just not sure I even want to keep the baby."

"That's your decision," Jilly said. "Whatever you want to do, we'll stand by you. Either way we'll get you a place to stay. If you keep the baby and want to work, we'll see about arranging daycare. If you want to stay home with the baby, we'll work something out for that as well. That's what this sponsorship's all about. It's not us telling you what to do; we just want to help you be the person you were meant to be."

"I don't know if that's such a good person," Annie said.

"Don't think like that. It's not true."

Annie shrugged. "I guess I'm scared I'll do the same thing to my baby that my mother did to me. That's how it happens, doesn't it? My mom used to beat the crap out of me all the time, didn't matter if I did something wrong or not, and I'm just going to end up doing the same thing to my kid."

"You're only hurting yourself with that kind of thinking," Jilly said.

"But it *can* happen, can't it? Jesus, I . . . You know I've been gone from her for two years now, but I still feel like she's standing right next to me half the time, or waiting around the corner for me. It's like I'll never escape. When I lived at home, it was like I was living in the house of an enemy. But running away didn't change that. I still feel like that, except now it's like everybody's my enemy."

Jilly reached over and laid a hand on hers.

"Not everybody," she said. "You've got to believe that."

"It's hard not to."

"I know."

10

This Is Where We Dump Them, *by Meg Mullally. Tinted photograph. The Tombs, Newford, 1991.*

Two children sit on the stoop of one of the abandoned buildings in the Tombs. Their hair is matted, faces smudged, clothing dirty and ill-fitting. They look like turn-of-the-century Irish tinkers. There's litter all around them: torn garbage bags spewing their contents on the sidewalk, broken bottles, a rotting mattress on the street, half-crushed pop cans, soggy newspapers, used condoms.

The children are seven and thirteen, a boy and a girl. They have no home, no family. They only have each other.

The next month went by awfully fast. Annie stayed with me—it was what she wanted. Angel and I did get her a place, a one-bedroom on Landis that she's going to move into after she's had the baby. It's right behind the loft—you can see her back window from mine. But for now she's going to stay here with me.

She's really a great kid. No artistic leanings, but really bright. She could be anything she wants to be if she can just learn to deal with all the baggage her parents dumped on her.

She's kind of shy around Angel and some of my other friends—I guess they're all too old for her or something—but she gets along really well with Sophie and me. Probably because, whenever you put Sophie and me together in the same room for more than two minutes, we just start giggling and acting about half our respective ages, which would make us, mentally at least, just a few years Annie's senior.

"You two could be sisters," Annie told me one day when we got back from Sophie's studio. "Her hair's lighter, and she's a little chestier, and she's *definitely* more organized than you are, but I get a real sense of family when I'm with the two of you. The way families are supposed to be."

"Even though Sophie's got faerie blood?" I asked her.

She thought I was joking.

"If she's got magic in her," Annie said, "then so do you. Maybe that's what makes you seem so much like sisters."

"I just pay attention to things," I told her. "That's all."

"Yeah, right."

The baby came right on schedule—three-thirty, Sunday morning. I probably would've panicked if Annie hadn't been doing enough of that for both of us. Instead I got on the phone, called Angel, and then saw about helping Annie get dressed.

The contractions were really close by the time Angel arrived with the car. But everything worked out fine. Jillian Sophia Mackle was born two hours and forty-five minutes later at the Newford General Hospital. Six pounds and five ounces of red-faced wonder. There were no complications.

Those came later.

11

The last week before the show was simple chaos. There seemed to be a hundred and one things that none of them had thought of, all of which had to be done at the last moment. And to make matters worse, Jilly still had one unfinished canvas haunting her by Friday night.

It stood on her easel, untitled, barely-sketched in images, still in monochrome. The colors eluded her. She knew what she wanted, but every time she stood before her easel, her mind went blank. She seemed to forget everything she'd ever known about art. The inner essence of the canvas rose up inside her like a ghost, so close she could almost touch it, but then fled daily, like a dream lost upon waking. The outside world intruded. A knock on the door. The ringing of the phone.

The show opened in exactly seven days.

Annie's baby was almost two weeks old. She was a happy, satisfied infant, the kind of baby that was forever making contented little gurgling sounds, as though talking to herself; she never cried. Annie herself was a nervous wreck.

"I'm scared," she told Jilly when she came over to the loft that afternoon. "Everything's going too well. I don't deserve it."

They were sitting at the kitchen table, the baby propped up on the

Murphy bed between two pillows. Annie kept fidgeting. Finally she picked up a pencil and started drawing stick figures on pieces of paper.

"Don't say that," Jilly said. "Don't even think it."

"But it's true. Look at me. I'm not like you or Sophie. I'm not like Angel. What have I got to offer my baby? What's she going to have to look up to when she looks at me?"

"A kind, caring mother."

Annie shook her head. "I don't feel like that. I feel like everything's sort of fuzzy and it's like pushing through cobwebs to just to make it through the day."

"We'd better make an appointment with you to see a doctor."

"Make it a shrink," Annie said. She continued to doodle, then looked down at what she was doing. "Look at this. It's just crap."

Before Jilly could see, Annie swept the sheaf of papers to the floor.

"Oh, jeez," she said as they went fluttering all over the place. "I'm sorry. I didn't mean to do that."

She got up before Jilly could and tossed the lot of them in the garbage container beside the stove. She stood there for a long moment, taking deep breaths, holding them, slowly letting them out.

"Annie . . . ?"

She turned as Jilly approached her. The glow of motherhood that had seemed to revitalize her in the month before the baby was born had slowly worn away. She was pale again. Wan. She looked so lost that all Jilly could do was put her arms around her and offer a wordless comfort.

"I'm sorry," Annie said against Jilly's hair. "I don't know what's going on. I just . . . I know I should be really happy, but I just feel scared and confused." She rubbed at her eyes with a knuckle. "God, listen to me. All it seems I can do is complain about my life."

"It's not like you've had a great one," Jilly said.

"Yeah, but when I compare it to what it was like before I met you, it's like I moved up into heaven."

"Why don't you stay here tonight?" Jilly said.

Annie stepped back out of her arms. "Maybe I will—if you really don't mind . . . ?"

"I really don't mind."

"Thanks."

Annie glanced towards the bed, her gaze pausing on the clock on the wall above the stove.

"You're going to be late for work," she said.

"That's all right. I don't think I'll go in tonight."

Annie shook her head. "No, go on. You've told me how busy it gets on a Friday night."

Jilly still worked part-time at Kathryn's Cafe on Battersfield Road. She could just imagine what Wendy would say if she called in sick. There was no one else in town this weekend to take her shift, so that would leave Wendy working all the tables on her own.

"If you're sure," Jilly said.

"We'll be okay," Annie said. "Honestly."

She went over to the bed and picked up the baby, cradling her gently in her arms.

"Look at her," she said, almost to herself. "It's hard to believe something so beautiful came out of me." She turned to Jilly, adding before Jilly could speak, "That's a kind of magic all by itself, isn't it?"

"Maybe one of the best we can make," Jilly said.

12

How Can You Call This Love? by Claudia Feder. Oils. Old Market Studio, Newford, 1990.

A fat man sits on a bed in a cheap hotel room. He's removing his shirt. Through the ajar door of the bathroom behind him, a thin girl in bra and panties can be seen sitting on the toilet, shooting up.

She appears to be about fourteen.

I just pay attention to things, I told her. I guess that's why, when I got off my shift and came back to the loft, Annie was gone. Because I pay such good attention. The baby was still on the bed, lying between the pillows, sleeping. There was a note on the kitchen table:

I don't know what's wrong with me. I just keep wanting to hit something. I look at little Jilly and I think about my mother and I get so scared. Take care of her for me. Teach her magic.

Please don't hate me.

I don't know how long I sat and stared at those sad, piteous words, tears streaming from my eyes.

I should never have gone to work. I should never have left her alone. She really thought she was just going to replay her own childhood. She told me, I don't know how many times she told me, but I just wasn't paying attention, was I?

Finally I got on the phone. I called Angel. I called Sophie. I called Lou Fucceri. I called everybody I could think of to go out and look for Annie. Angel was at the loft with me when we finally heard. I was the one who picked up the phone.

I heard what Lou said: "A patrolman brought her into the General not fifteen minutes ago, ODing on Christ knows what. She was just trying to self-destruct, is what he said. I'm sorry, Jilly. But she died before I got there."

I didn't say anything. I just passed the phone to Angel and went to sit on the bed. I held little Jilly in my arms and then I cried some more.

I was never joking about Sophie. She really does have faerie blood. It's something I can't explain, something we've never really talked about, something I just know and she's never denied. But she did promise me that she'd bless Annie's baby, just the way fairy god-mothers would do it in all those old stories.

"I gave her the gift of a happy life," she told me later. "I never dreamed it wouldn't include Annie."

But that's the way it works in fairy tales, too, isn't it? Something always goes wrong, or there wouldn't be a story. You have to be strong, you have to earn your happily ever after.

Annie was strong enough to go away from her baby when she felt like all she could do was just lash out, but she wasn't strong enough to help herself. That was the awful gift her parents gave her.

I never finished that last painting in time for the show, but I found something to take its place. Something that said more to me in just a few rough lines than anything I've ever done.

I was about to throw out my garbage when I saw those crude little drawings that Annie had been doodling on my kitchen table the night she died. They were like the work of a child.

I framed one of them and hung it in the show.

"I guess we're five coyotes and one coyote ghost now," was all Sophie said when she saw what I had done.

13

In the House of My Enemy, *by Annie Mackle. Pencils. Yoors Street Studio, Newford, 1991.*

The images are crudely rendered. In a house that is merely a square with a triangle on top, are three stick figures, one plain, two with small "skirt" triangles to represent their gender. The two larger figures are beating the smaller one with what might be crooked sticks, or might be belts.

The small figure is cringing away.

14

In the visitor's book set out at the show, someone wrote: "I can never forgive those responsible for what's been done to us. I don't even want to try."

"Neither do I," Jilly said when she read it. "God help me, but neither do I."

⊰ BUT FOR THE GRACE ⊱ GO I

*YOU CAN ONLY PREDICT THINGS
AFTER THEY'VE HAPPENED.*
—EUGENE IONESCO

I inherited Tommy the same way I did the dogs. Found him wandering lost and alone, so I took him home. I've always taken in strays—maybe because a long time ago I used to hope that someone'd take me in. I grew out of that idea pretty fast.

Tommy's kind of like a pet, I guess, except he can talk. He doesn't make a whole lot of sense, but then I don't find what most people have to say makes much sense. At least Tommy's honest. What you see is what you get. No games, no hidden agendas. He's only Tommy, a big guy who wouldn't hurt you even if you took a stick to him. Likes to smile, likes to laugh—a regular guy. He's just a few bricks short of a load, is all. Hell, sometimes I figure all he's got is bricks sitting back in there behind his eyes.

I know what you're thinking. A guy like him should be in an institution, and I suppose you're right, except they pronounced him cured at the Zeb when they needed his bed for somebody whose family had money to pay for the space he was taking up and they're not exactly falling over themselves to get him back.

We live right in the middle of that part of Newford that some people call the Tombs and some call Squatland. It's the dead part of the city—a jungle of empty lots filled with trash and abandoned cars, gutted buildings and rubble. I've seen it described in the papers as a blight, a disgrace, a breeding ground for criminals and racial strife, though we've got every color you can think of living in here and we get along pretty well together, mostly because we just leave each other alone. And we're not so much criminals as losers.

Sitting in their fancy apartments and houses, with running water and electricity and no worry about where the next meal's coming from, the good citizens of Newford have got a lot of names and ways to describe this place and us, but those of us who actually live here just call it home. I think of it as one of those outlaw roosts like they used to have in the Old West—some little ramshackle town, way back in the badlands, where only the outlaws lived. Of course those guys like L'Amour and Short who wrote about places like that probably just made them up. I find that a lot of people have this thing about making crap romantic, the way they like to blur outlaws and heroes, the good with the bad.

I know that feeling all too well, but I broke the only pair of rose-colored glasses I had the chance to own a long time ago. Sometimes I pretend I'm here because I want to be, because it's the only place I can be free, because I'm judged by who I am and what I can do, not by how screwed up my family is and how dirt poor looked pretty good from the position we were in.

I'm not saying this part of town's pretty. I'm not even saying I like living here. We're all just putting in time, trying to make do. Every time I hear about some kid ODing, somebody getting knifed, somebody taking that long step off a building or wrapping their belt around their neck, I figure that's just one more of us who finally got out. It's a war zone in here, and just like in Vietnam, they either carry you out in a box, or you leave under your own steam carrying a piece of the place with you—a kind of cold shadow that sits inside your soul and has you waking up in a cold sweat some nights, or feeling closed in and crazy in your new work place, home, social life, whatever, for no good reason except that it's the Tombs calling to you, telling you that maybe you don't deserve what you've got now, reminding you of all those people you left behind who didn't get the break you did.

I don't know why we bother. Let's be honest. I don't know why *I* bother. I just don't know any better, I guess. Or maybe I'm just too damn stubborn to give up.

Angel—you know, the do-gooder who runs that program out of her Grasso Street office to get kids like me off the streets? She tells me I've got a nihilistic attitude. Once she explained what that meant, all I could do was laugh.

"Look at where I'm coming from," I told her. "What do you expect?"

"I can help you."

I just shook my head. "You want a piece of me, that's all, but I've got nothing left to give."

That's only partly true. See, I've got responsibilities, just like a regular citizen. I've got the dogs. And I've got Tommy. I was joking about calling him my pet. That's just what the bikers who're squatting down the street from us call him. I think of us all—me, the dogs and Tommy—as family. Or about as close to family as any of us are ever going to get. I can't leave, because what would they do without me? And who'd take the whole pack of us, which is the only way I'd go?

Tommy's got this thing about magazines, though he can't read a word. Me, I love to read. I've got thousands of books. I get them all from the dump bins in back of bookstores—you know, where they tear off the covers to get their money back for the ones they don't sell and just throw the book away? Never made any sense to me, but you won't catch me complaining.

I'm not that particular about what I read. I just like the stories. Danielle Steel or Dostoyevsky, Somerset Maugham or King—doesn't make much difference. Just so long as I can get away in the words.

But Tommy likes his magazines, and he likes them with his name on the cover—you know, the subscription sticker? There's two words he can read: Thomas and Flood. I know his first name's Tommy, because he knows that much and that's what he told me. I made up the last name. The building we live in is on Flood Street.

He likes *People* and *Us* and *Entertainment Weekly* and *Life* and stuff like that. Lots of pictures, not too many words. He gets me to cut out the pictures of the people and animals and ads and stuff he likes and then he plays with them like they were paper dolls. That's how he gets away, I guess. Whatever works.

Anyway, I've got a post office box down on Grasso Street near Angel's office and that's where I have the subscriptions sent. I go down once a week to pick them up—usually on Thursday afternoons. It's all a little more than I can afford—makes me work a little harder at my garbage picking, you know?—but what am I going to do? Cut him off from his only pleasure? People think I'm hard—when they don't just think I'm crazy—and maybe I am, but I'm not mean.

The thing about having a post office box is that you get some pretty interesting junk mail—well at least Tommy finds it interesting. I used to throw it out, but he came down with me to the box one time and got all weirded out when he saw me throwing it out so I bring most of it back now. He calls them his surprises. First thing he asks when I get back is, "Were there any surprises?"

I went in the Thursday this all started and gave the clerk my usual glare, hoping that one day he'll finally get the message, but he never does. He was the one who sicced Angel on me in the first place. Thought nineteen was too young to be a bag lady, pretty girl like me. Thought he could help.

I didn't bother to explain that I'd chosen to live this way. I've been living on my own since I was twelve. I don't sell my bod' and I don't do drugs. My clothes may be worn down and patched, but they're clean. I wash every day, which is more than I can say for some of the real citizens I pass by on the street. You can smell their B.O. a half block away. I look pretty regular except on garbage day when Tommy and I hit the streets with our shopping carts, the dogs all strung out around us like our own special honor guard.

There's nothing wrong with garbage picking. Where do you think all those fancy antique shops get most of their high-priced merchandise?

I do okay, without either Angel's help or his. He was probably just hard up for a girlfriend.

"How's it going, Maisie?" he asked when I came in, all friendly, like we're pals. I guess he got my name from the form I filled out when I rented the box.

I ignored him, like I always do, and gathered the week's pile up. It was a fairly thick stack—lots of surprises for Tommy. I took it all outside where Rexy was waiting for me. He's the smallest of the dogs, just a small little mutt with wiry brown hair and a real insecurity problem. He's the only one who comes everywhere with me because he just falls apart if I leave him at home.

I gave Rexy a quick pat, then sat on the curb, sorting through Tommy's surprises. If the junk mail doesn't have pictures, I toss it. I only want to carry so much of this crap back with me.

It was while I was going through the stack that this envelope fell out. I just sat and stared at it for the longest time. It looked like one of those ornate invitations they're always making a fuss over in the romance novels I read: almost square, the paper really thick and cream-colored, ornate lettering on the outside that was real high-class calligraphy, it was so pretty. But that wasn't what had me staring at it, unwilling to pick it up.

The lettering spelled out my name. Not the one I use, but my real name. Margaret. Maisie's just a diminutive of it that I read about in this book about Scotland. That was all that was there, just "Margaret," no surname. I never use one except for when the cops decide to roust the squatters in the Tombs, like they do from time to time—I think it's like some kind of training exercise for them—and then I use Flood, same as I gave Tommy.

I shot a glance back in through the glass doors because I figured it had to be from the postal clerk—who else knew me?—but he wasn't even looking at me. I sat and stared at it a little longer, but then I finally picked it up. I took out my pen knife and slit the envelope open, and carefully pulled out this card. All it said on it was, "Allow the dark-robed access tonight and they will kill you."

I didn't have a clue what it meant, but it gave me a royal case of the creeps. If it wasn't a joke—which I figured it had to be—then who were these black-robed and why would they want to kill me?

Every big city like this is really two worlds. You could say it's divided up between the haves and the have-nots, but it's not that simple. It's more like some people are citizens of the day and others of the night. Someone like me belongs to the night. Not because I'm bad, but because I'm invisible. People don't know I exist. They don't know and they don't care, except for Angel and the postal clerk, I guess.

But now someone did.

Unless it was a joke. I tried to laugh it off, but it just didn't work. I looked at the envelope again, checking it out for a return address, and that's when I realized something I should have noticed straight-away. The envelope didn't have my box number on it, it didn't have anything at all except for my name. So how the hell did it end up in my box? There was only one way.

I left Rexy guarding Tommy's mail—just to keep him occupied—and went back inside. When the clerk finished with the customer ahead of me, he gave me a big smile but I laid the envelope down on the counter between us and didn't smile back.

Actually, he's a pretty good-looking guy. He's got one of those flat-top haircuts—shaved sides, kinky black hair standing straight up on top. His skin's the color of coffee and he's got dark eyes with the longest lashes I ever saw on a guy. I could like him just fine, but the trouble is he's a regular citizen. It'd just never work out.

"How'd this get in my box?" I asked him. "All it's got is my name on it, no box number, no address, nothing."

He looked down at the envelope. "You found it in your box?"

I nodded.

"I didn't put it in there and I'm the one who sorts all the mail for the boxes."

"I still found it in there."

He picked it up and turned it over in his hands.

"This is really weird," he said.

"You into occult shit?" I asked him.

I was thinking of dark robes. The only people I ever saw wear them were priests or people dabbling in the occult.

He blinked with surprise. "What do you mean?"

"Nothing."

I grabbed the envelope back and headed back to where Rexy was waiting for me.

"Maisie!" the clerk called after me, but I just ignored him.

Great, I thought as I collected the mail Rexy'd been guarding for me. First Joe postal clerk's got a good Samaritan complex over me—probably fueled by his dick—now he's going downright weird. I wondered if he knew where I lived. I wondered if he knew about the dogs. I wondered about magicians in dark robes and whether he thought he had some kind of magic that was going to deal with the dogs and make me go all gooshy for him—just before he killed me.

The more I thought about it, the more screwed up I got. I wasn't so much scared as confused. And angry. How was I supposed to keep coming back to get Tommy's mail, knowing he was there? What would he put in the box next? A dead rat? It wasn't like I could complain to anybody. People like me, we don't have any rights.

Finally I just started for home, but I paused as I passed the door to Angel's office.

Angel's a little cool with me these days. She still says she wanted to help me, but she doesn't quite trust me anymore. It's not really her fault.

She had me in her office one time—I finally went, just to get her off my back—and we sat there for awhile, looking at each other, drinking this crappy coffee from the machine that someone donated to her a few years ago. I wouldn't have picked it up on a dare if I'd come across it on my rounds.

"What do you want from me?" I finally asked her.

"I'm just trying to understand you."

"There's nothing to understand. What you see is what I am. No more, no less."

"But why do you live the way you do?"

Understand, I admire what Angel does. She's helped a lot of kids that were in a really bad way and that's a good thing. Some people need help because they can't help themselves.

She's an attractive woman with a heart-shaped face, the kind of eyes that always look really warm and caring and long dark hair that seems to go on forever down her back. I always figured something really bad must have happened to her as a kid, for her to do what she does. It's not like she makes much of a living. I think the only thing she really and honestly cares about is helping people through this sponsorship program she's developed where straights put up money and time to help the down-and-outers get a second chance.

I don't need that kind of help. I'm never going to be much more than what I am, but that's okay. It beats what I had before I hit the streets.

I've told Angel all of this a dozen times, but she sat there behind her desk, looking at me with those sad eyes of hers, and I knew she wanted a piece of me, so I gave her one. I figured maybe she'd leave me alone then.

"I was in high school," I told her, "and there was this girl who wanted to get back at one of the teachers—a really nice guy named Mr. Hammond. He taught math. So she made up this story about how he'd molested her and the shit really hit the van. He got suspended while the cops and the school board looked into the matter and all the time this girl's laughing her head off behind everybody's back, but looking real sad and screwed up whenever the cops and the social workers are talking to her.

"But I knew he didn't do it. I knew where she was, the night she said it happened, and it wasn't with Mr. Hammond. Now I wasn't exactly the best-liked kid in that school, and I knew what this girl's gang was going to do to me, but I went ahead and told the truth anyway.

"Things worked out pretty much the way I expected. I got the cold shoulder from everybody, but at least Mr. Hammond got his name cleared and his job back.

"One afternoon he asks me to see him after school and I figure it's to thank me for what I've done, so I go to his classroom. The building's pretty well empty and the scuff of my shoes in the hallway is the only sound I hear as I go to see him. I get to the math room and he takes me back into his office. Then he locks the door and he rapes me. Not just once, but over and over again. And you know what he says to me while he's doing it?

" 'Nobody's going to believe a thing you say,' he says. 'You try to talk about this and they're just going to laugh in your face.' "

I looked over at Angel and there were tears swimming in her eyes.

"And you know what?" I said. "I knew he was right. I was the one that cleared his name. There was *nobody* going to believe me and I didn't even try."

"Oh, Jesus," Angel said. "You poor kid."

"Don't take it so hard," I told her. "It's past history. Besides, it never really happened. I just made it up because I figured it was the kind of thing you wanted to hear."

I'll give her this: she took it well. Didn't yell at me, didn't pitch me out onto the street. But you can see why maybe I'm not on her list of favorite people these days. On the other hand, she doesn't hold a grudge—I know that too.

I felt like a hypocrite going in to see her with this problem, but I didn't have anyone else to turn to. It's not like Tommy or the dogs could give me any advice. I hesitated for the longest moment in the doorway, but then she looked up and saw me standing there, so I went ahead in.

I took off my hat—it's this fedora that I actually bought new because it was just too cool to pass up. I wear it all the time, my light brown hair hanging down from it, long and straight, though not as long as Angel's. I like the way it looks with my jeans and sneakers and this cotton shirt I found at a rummage sale that only needed a tear fixed on one of its shirttails.

I know what you're thinking, but hey, I never said I wasn't vain. I may be a squatter, but I like to look my best. It gets me into places where they don't let in bums.

Anyway I took off my hat and slouched in the chair on this side of Angel's desk.

"Which one's that?" she asked, pointing to Rexy who was sitting outside by the door like the good little dog he is.

"Rexy."

"He can come in if you'd like."

I shook my head. "No. I'm not staying long. I just had this thing I wanted to ask you about. It's . . ."

I didn't know where to begin, but finally I just started in with finding the envelope. It got easier as I went along. That's one thing you got to hand to Angel—there's nobody can listen like she does. You take up *all* of her attention when you're talking to her. You never get the feeling she's thinking of something else, or of what she's going to say back to you, or anything like that.

Angel didn't speak for a long time after I was done. When I stopped talking, she looked past me, out at the traffic going by on Grasso Street.

"Maisie," she said finally. "Have you ever heard the story of the boy who cried wolf?"

"Sure, but what's that got to do with—oh, I get it." I took out the envelope and slid it across the desk to her. "I didn't have to come in here," I added.

And I was wishing I hadn't, but Angel seemed to give herself a kind of mental shake. She opened the envelope and read the message, then her gaze came back to me.

"No," she said. "I'm glad you did. Do you want me to have a talk with Franklin?"

"Who's that?"

"The fellow behind the counter at the post office. I don't mind doing it, although I have to admit that it doesn't sound like the kind of thing he'd do."

So that was his name. Franklin. Franklin the creep.

I shrugged. "What good would that do? Even if he did do it—" and the odds looked good so far as I was concerned "—he's not going to admit to it."

"Maybe we can talk to his supervisor." She looked at her watch. "I think it's too late to do it today, but I can try first thing tomorrow morning."

Great. In the meantime, I could be dead.

Angel must have guessed what I was thinking, because she added, "Do you need a place to stay for tonight? Some place where you'll feel safe?"

I thought of Tommy and the dogs and shook my head.

"No, I'll be okay," I said as I collected my envelope and stuck it back in with Tommy's mail. "Thanks for, you know, listening and everything."

I waited for her to roll into some spiel about how she could do more, could get me off the street, that kind of thing, but it was like she was tuned right into my wavelength because she didn't say a word about any of that. She just knew, I guess, that I'd never come back if every time I talked to her that was all I could look forward to.

"Come see me tomorrow," was all she said as I got to my feet. "And Maisie?"

I paused in the doorway where Rexy was ready to start bouncing off my legs as if he hadn't seen me in weeks.

"Be careful," Angel added.

"I will."

I took a long route back to the squat, watching my back the whole time, but I never saw anybody that looked like he was following me, and not a single person in a dark robe. I almost laughed at myself by the time I got back. There were Tommy and the dogs, all sprawled out on the steps of our building until Rexy yelped and then the whole pack of them were racing down the street towards me.

Okay, big as he was, Tommy still couldn't hurt a flea even if his life depended on it and the dogs were all small and old and pretty well used up, but Franklin would still have to be crazy to think he could mess with us. He didn't *know* my family. You get a guy as big as Tommy and all those dogs . . . well, they just looked dangerous. What did I have to worry about?

The dogs were all over me then with Tommy right behind them. He grinned from ear to ear as I handed him his mail.

"Surprises!" he cried happily, in that weird high voice of his. "Maisie bring surprises!"

We went inside to our place up on the second floor. It's got this big open space that we use in the summer when we want the air to have a chance to move around. There's books everywhere. Tommy's got his own corner with his magazines and all the little cut-out people and stuff that he plays with. There's a couple of mismatched kitchen chairs and a card table. A kind of old cabinet that some hoboes helped me move up the one flight from the street holds our food and the Coleman stove I use for cooking.

We sleep on the mattresses over in another corner, the whole pack together, except for Chuckie. He's this old lab that likes to guard the doorway. I usually think he's crazy for doing so, but I wouldn't mind tonight. Chuckie can look real fierce when he wants to. There's a couple of chests by the bed area. I keep our clothes in one and dry kibbles for the dogs in another. They're pretty good scavengers, but I like to see that they're eating the right kind of food. I wouldn't want anything to happen to them. One thing I can't afford is vet bills.

First off I fed the dogs, then I made supper for Tommy and me—lentil soup with day-old buns I'd picked up behind a bakery in Crowsea. We'd been eating the soup for a few days, but we had to use it up because, with the spring finally here, it was getting too warm for food to keep. In the winter we've got smaller quarters down the hall, complete with a cast-iron stove that I salvaged from this place they were wrecking over in Foxville. Tommy and I pretty near killed ourselves hauling it back. One of the bikers helped us bring it upstairs.

We fell into our usual Thursday night ritual once we'd finished supper. After hauling down tomorrow's water from the tank I'd set up on the roof to catch rainwater, I lit the oil lamp, then Tommy and I sat down at the table and went through his new magazines and ads. Every time he'd point out something that he liked in a picture, I'd cut it out for him. I do a pretty tidy job, if I say so myself. Getting to be an old hand at it. By the time we finished, he had a big stack of new cut-out people and stuff for his games that he just had to go try out right away. I went and got the book I'd started this morning and brought it back to the table, but I couldn't read.

I could hear Tommy talking to his new little friends. The dogs shifting and moving about the way they do. Down the street a Harley kicked over and I listened to it go through the Tombs until it faded in the distance. Then there was only the sound of the wind outside the window.

I'd been able to keep that stupid envelope with its message out of my head just by staying busy, but now it was all I could think about. I looked out the window. It was barely eight, but it was dark already. The real long days of summer were still to come.

So is Franklin out there? I asked myself. Is he watching the building, scoping things out, getting ready to make his move? Maybe dressed up in some black robe, him and a bunch of his pals?

I didn't really believe it. I didn't know him, but like Angel had said, it didn't seem like him and I could believe it. He might bug me, being all friendly and wanting to play Pygmalion to my Eliza Doolittle, but I didn't think he had a mean streak in him.

So where *did* the damn message come from? What was it supposed to mean? And, here was the scary part: if it wasn't a joke, and if Franklin wasn't responsible for it, then who was?

I kept turning that around and around in my mind until my head felt like it was spinning. Everybody started picking up on my mood. The dogs became all anxious and when I walked near them got to whining and shrinking away like I was going to hit them. Tommy got the shakes and his little people started tearing and then he was crying and the dogs started in howling and I just wanted to get the hell out of there.

But I didn't. It took me a couple of hours to calm Tommy down and finally get him to fall asleep. I told him the story he likes the best, the one where this count from some place far away shows up and tells us that we're really his kids and he takes us away, dogs and all, to our real home where we all live happily ever after. Sometimes I use his little cut-outs to tell the story, but I didn't do that tonight. I didn't want to remind him of how a bunch'd gotten torn.

By the time Tommy was sleeping, the dogs had calmed down

again and were sleeping too. I couldn't. I sat up all night worrying about that damned message, about what would happen to Tommy and the dogs if anything ever did happen to me, about all kinds of crap that I usually don't let myself think about.

Come the morning, I felt like I'd crawled up out of a sewer. You know what it's like when you pull an all-nighter? Your eyes have this burning behind them, you'd kill for a shower and everything seems a little on edge? I saw about getting breakfast for everyone, let the dogs out for a run, then I told Tommy I had to go back downtown.

"You don't go out today," I told him. "You understand? You don't go out and you don't let anybody in. You and the dogs play inside today, okay? Can you do that for Maisie?"

"Sure," Tommy said, like I was the one with bricks for brains. "No problem, Maisie."

God I love him.

I gave him a big hug and a kiss, patted each of the dogs, then headed back down to Grasso Street with Rexy. I was about half a block from Angel's office when the headlines of a newspaper outside a drugstore caught my eye. I stopped dead in my tracks and just stared at it. The words swam in my sight, headlines blurring with the subheadings. I picked up the paper and unfolded it so that I could see the whole front page, then I started reading from the top.

GRIERSON SLAIN BY SATANISTS.

DIRECTOR OF THE CITY'S NEW AIDS CLINIC FOUND DEAD IN FERRY-SIDE GRAVEYARD AMID OCCULT PARAPHERNALIA.

POLICE BAFFLED.

MAYOR SAYS, 'THIS IS AN OUTRAGE.'

"Hey, this isn't a library, kid."

Rexy growled and I looked up to find the drugstore owner standing over me. I dug in my pocket until it coughed up a quarter, then handed it over to him. I took the paper over to the curb and sat down.

It was the picture that got to me. It looked like one of the buildings in the Tombs in which kids had been playing at ritual magic a few years ago. All the same kinds of candles and inverted pentacles and weird graffiti. Nobody squatted in that building any-more, though the kids hadn't been back for over a year. There was still something wrong about the place, like the miasma of whatever the hell it was that they'd been doing was still there, hanging on.

It was a place to give you the creeps. But this picture had something worse. It had a body, covered up by a blanket, right in the middle of it. The tombstones around it were all scorched and in pieces, like someone had set off a bomb. The police couldn't explain what had happened, except they did say it hadn't been a bomb, because no one nearby had heard a thing.

Pinpricks of dread went crawling up my spine as I reread the first paragraph. The victim, Grierson. Her first name was Margaret.

I folded the paper and got up, heading for the post office. Franklin was alone behind the counter when I got inside.

"The woman who died last night," I said before he had a chance to even say hello. "Margaret Grierson. The Director of the AIDS Clinic. Did she have a box here?"

Franklin nodded. "It's terrible, isn't it? One of my friends says the whole clinic's going to fall apart without her there to run it. God, I hope it doesn't change anything. I know a half-dozen people that are going to it."

I gave him a considering look. A half dozen friends? He had this real sad look in his eyes, like . . . Jesus, I thought. Was Franklin gay? Had he really been just making nice and not trying to jump my bones?

I reached across the counter and put my hand on his arm.

"They won't let this screw it up," I told him. "The clinic's too important."

The look of surprise in his face had me backing out the door fast. What the hell was I doing?

"Maisie!" he cried.

I guess I felt like a bit of a shit for having misjudged him, but all the same, I couldn't stick around. I followed my usual rule of thumb when things get heavy or weird: I fled.

I just started wandering aimlessly, thinking about what I'd learned. That message hadn't been for me, it had been for Grierson. Margaret, yeah, but Margaret *Grierson,* not Flood. Not me. Somehow it had gotten in the wrong box. I don't know who put it there, or how he knew what was going to happen last night before it happened, but whoever he was, he'd screwed up royally.

Better it had been me, I thought. Better a loser from the Tombs, than someone like Grierson who was really doing something worthwhile.

When I thought that, I realized something that I guess I'd always known, but I just didn't ever let myself think about. You get called a loser often enough and you start to believe it. I know I did. But it didn't have to be true.

I guess I had what they call an epiphany in some of the older books I've read. Everything came together and made sense—except for what I was doing with myself.

I unfolded the paper again. There was a picture of Grierson near the bottom—one of those shots they keep on file for important people and run whenever they haven't got anything else. It was cropped down from one that had been taken when she cut the ribbon at the new clinic a few months back. I remembered seeing it when they ran coverage of the ceremony.

"This isn't going to mean a whole lot to you," I told her picture, "but I'm sorry about what happened to you. Maybe it should've been me, but it wasn't. There's not much I can do about that. But I can do something about the rest of *my* life."

I left the paper on a bench near a bus stop and walked back to Grasso Street to Angel's office. I sat down in the chair across from her desk, holding Rexy on my lap to give me courage, and I told her about Tommy and the dogs, about how they needed me and that was why I'd never wanted to take her up on her offers to help.

She shook her head sadly when I was done. She was looking a little weepy again—like she had when I told her that story before—but I was feeling a little weepy myself this time.

"Why didn't you tell me?" she asked.

I shrugged. "I guess I thought you'd take them away from me."

I surprised myself. I hadn't lied, or made a joke. Instead I'd told her the truth. It wasn't much, but it was a start.

"Oh, Maisie," she said. "We can work something out."

She came around the desk and I let her hold me. It's funny. I didn't mean to cry, but I did. And so did she. It felt good, having someone else be strong for a change. I haven't had someone be there for me since my grandma died in 1971, the year I turned eight. I hung in for a long time, all things considered, but the day that Mr.

Hammond asked me to come see him after school was the day I finally gave up my nice little regulated slot as a citizen of the day and became a part of the night world instead.

I knew it wasn't going to be easy, trying to fit into the day world—I'd probably never fit in completely, and I don't think I'd want to. I also knew that I was going to have a lot of crap to go through and to put up with in the days to come, and maybe I'd regret the decision I'd made today, but right now it felt good to be back.

≫ BRIDGES ≫

She watched the taillights dwindle until, far down the dirt road, the car went around a curve. The two red dots winked out and then she was alone.

Stones crunched underfoot as she shifted from one foot to another, looking around herself. Trees, mostly cedar and pine, crowded the narrow verge on either side. Above her, the sky held too many stars, but for all their number, they shed too little light. She was used to city streets and pavement, to neon and streetlights. Even in the 'burbs there was always some manmade light.

The darkness and silence, the loneliness of the night as it crouched in the trees, spooked her. It chipped at the veneer of her streetsmart toughness. She was twenty miles out of the city, up in the hills that backed onto the Kickaha Reserve. Attitude counted for nothing out here.

She didn't bother cursing Eddie. She conserved her breath for the long walk back to the city, just hoping she wouldn't run into some pickup truck full of redneck hillbillies who might not be quite as ready to just cut her loose as Eddie had when he realized he wasn't going to get his way. For too many men, no meant yes. And she'd heard stories about some of the good old boys who lived in these hills.

She didn't even hate Eddie, for all that he was eminently hateful. She saved that hatred for herself, for being so trusting when she knew—when she *knew*—how it always turned out.

"Stupid bloody cow," she muttered as she began to walk.

High school was where it had started.

She'd liked to party, she'd liked to have a good time, she hadn't seen anything wrong with making out because it was fun. Once you got a guy to slow down, sex was the best thing around.

She went with a lot of guys, but it took her a long time to realize just how many and that they only wanted one thing from her. She was slow on the uptake because she didn't see a problem until that night with Dave. Before that, she'd just seen herself as popular. She always had a date; someone was always ready to take her out and have some fun. The guy she'd gone out with on the weekend might ignore her the next Monday at school, but there was always someone else there, leaning up against her locker, asking her what was she doing tonight, so that she never really had time to think it through.

Never *wanted* to think it through, she'd realized in retrospect.

Until Dave wanted her to go to the drive-in that Saturday night.

"I'd rather go to the dance," she told him.

It was just a disco with a DJ, but she was in the mood for loud music and stepping out, not a movie. First Dave tried to convince her to go to the drive-in, then he said that if she wanted to go dancing, he knew some good clubs. She didn't know where the flash of insight came from—it just flared there inside her head, leaving a sick feeling in the pit of her stomach, a tightness in her chest.

"You don't want to be seen with me at the dance," she said.

"It's not that. It's just . . . well, all the guys . . ."

"Told you what? That I'm a cheap lay?"

"No, it's just, well . . ."

The knowing looks she got in the hall, the way guys would talk to her before they went out, but avoided her later—it all came together.

Jesus, how could she have been so stupid?

She got out of his car, which was still parked in front of her dad's house. Tears were burning the back of her eyes, but she refused to let them come. She never talked to Dave again. She swore that things were going to change.

It didn't matter that she didn't go out with another guy for her whole senior year; everyone still thought of her as the school tramp. Two months ago, she'd finally finished school. She didn't even wait to get her grades. With money she'd saved up through the years, she moved from her dad's place in the 'burbs to her own apartment in Lower Crowsea, got a job as a receptionist in an office on Yoors Street and was determined that things were going to be different. She had no history where she lived or where she worked; no one to snigger at her when she went down a hall.

It was a new start and it wasn't easy. She didn't have any friends, but then she hadn't really had any before either—she just hadn't had the time or good sense to realize that. But she was working on it now. She'd gotten to know Sandra who lived down the hall in her building, and they'd hung out together, watching videos or going to one of the bars in the Market—girls night out, men need not apply.

She liked having a girl for a friend. She hadn't had one since she lost her virginity just a few days before her fifteenth birthday and discovered that boys could make her feel really good in ways that a girl couldn't.

Besides Sandra, she was starting to get to know the people at work, too—which was where she met Eddie. He was the building's mail clerk, dropping off a bundle of mail on her desk every morning, hanging out for a couple of minutes, finally getting the courage up to ask her for a date. Her first one in a very long time.

He seemed like a nice guy, so she said yes. A friend of his was having a party at his cottage, not far from town. There'd be a bonfire on the beach, some people would be bringing their guitars and they'd sing old Buddy Holly and Beatles tunes. They'd barbecue hamburgers and hotdogs. It'd be fun.

Fifteen minutes ago, Eddie had pulled the car over to the side of the road. Killing the engine, he leaned back against the driver's door, gaze lingering on how her T-shirt molded to her chest. He gave her a goofy grin.

"Why are we stopping?" she'd asked, knowing it sounded dumb, knowing what was coming next.

"I was thinking," Eddie said. "We could have our private party."

"No thanks."

"Come on. Chuck said—"

"Chuck? Chuck who?"

"Anderson. He used to go to Mawson High with you."

A ghost from the past, rising to haunt her. She knew Chuck Anderson.

"He just moved into my building. We were talking and when I mentioned your name, he told me all about you. He said you liked to party."

"Well, he's full of shit. I think you'd better take me home."

"You don't have to play hard to get," Eddie said.

He started to reach for her, but her hand was quicker. It went into her purse and came out with a switchblade. She touched the release button and its blade came out of the handle with a wicked-sounding *snick*. Eddie moved back to his own side of the car.

"What the hell are you trying to prove?" he demanded.

"Just take me home."

"Screw you. Either you come across, or you walk."

She gave him a long hard stare, then nodded. "Then I walk."

The car's wheels spat gravel as soon as she was out, engine gunning as Eddie maneuvered a tight one-eighty. She closed up her knife and dropped it back into her purse as she watched the tail lights recede.

Her legs were aching by the time she reached the covered bridge that crossed Stickers Creek just before it ran into the Kickaha River. She'd walked about three miles since Eddie had dumped her; only another seventeen to go.

Twice she'd hidden in the trees as a vehicle passed her. The first one had looked so innocent that she'd berated herself for not trying to thumb a ride. The second was a pickup with a couple of yahoos in it. One of them had tossed out a beer bottle that just missed hitting her—he hadn't known she was hiding in the cedars there and she was happy that it had stayed that way. Thankfully, she had let nervous caution overrule the desire to just get the hell out of here and home.

She sat down on this side of the bridge to rest. She couldn't see much of the quick-moving creek below her—just white tops that flashed in the starlight—but she could hear it. It was a soothing sound.

She thought about Eddie.

She should have been able to see it in him, shouldn't she? It wasn't as though she didn't know what to be looking out for.

And Chuck Anderson. Jesus.

What was the point in trying to make a new start when nobody gave you a break?

She sighed and rose to her feet. There was no sense in railing against it. The world wasn't fair, and that was that. But god it was lonely. How could you carry on, always by yourself? What was the *point*?

Her footsteps had a hollow ring as she walked across the covered bridge and she started to get spooked again. What if a car came, right *now*? There was nowhere to run to, nowhere to hide. Just the dusty insides of the covered bridge, its wood so old she was surprised it was still standing.

Halfway across she felt an odd dropping sensation in her stomach, like being in an elevator that was going down too quickly. Vertigo had her leaning against the wooden planks that sided the bridge. She knew a moment's panic—oh, Jesus, she was falling—but then the feeling went away and she could walk without feeling dizzy to the far end of the bridge.

She stepped outside and stopped dead in her tracks. Her earlier panic was mild in comparison to what she felt now as she stared ahead in disbelief.

Everything familiar was gone. Road, trees, hills—all gone. She wasn't in the same country anymore—wasn't in the country at all. A city like something out of an Escher painting lay spread out in front of her. Odd buildings, angles all awry, leaned against and pushed away from each other, all at the same time. Halfway up their lengths, there seemed to be a kind of vortal shift so that the top halves appeared to be reflections of the lower.

And then there were the bridges.

Everywhere she looked there were bridges. Bridges connecting the buildings, bridges connecting bridges, bridges that went nowhere, bridges that folded back on themselves so that you couldn't tell where they started or ended. Too many bridges to count.

She started to back up the way she'd come but got no further than two steps when a hand reached out of the shadows and pulled her forward. She flailed against her attacker who swung her about and then held her with her arms pinned against her body.

"Easy, easy," a male voice said in her ear.

It had a dry, dusty sound to it, like the kind you could imagine old books in a library's stacks have when they talk to each other late at night.

"Let me go, let me *GO!*" she cried.

Still holding her, her assailant walked her to the mouth of the covered bridge.

"Look," he said.

For a moment she was still too panicked to know what he was

talking about. But then it registered. The bridge she'd walked across to get to this nightmare city no longer had a roadway. There was just empty space between its wooden walls now. If her captor hadn't grabbed her when he did, she would have fallen god knew how far.

She stopped struggling and he let her go. She moved gingerly away from the mouth of the covered bridge, then stopped again, not knowing where to go, what to do. Everywhere she looked there were weird tilting buildings and bridges.

It was impossible. None of this was happening, she decided. She'd fallen asleep on the other side of the bridge and was just dreaming all of this.

"Will you be all right?" her benefactor asked.

"I . . . I . . ."

She turned to look at him. The moonlight made him out to be a harmless-looking guy. He was dressed in faded jeans and an off-white flannel shirt, cowboy boots and a jean jacket. His hair was dark and short. It was hard to make out his features, except for his eyes. They seemed to take in the moonlight and then send it back out again, twice as bright.

Something about him calmed her—until she tried to speak.

"Whoareyou?" she asked. "Whatisthisplacehowdidlgethere?"

As soon as the first question came out, a hundred others came clamoring into her mind, each demanding to be voiced, to be answered. She shut her mouth after the first few burst out in a breathless spurt, realizing that they would just feed the panic that she was only barely keeping in check.

She took a deep breath, then tried again.

"Thank you," she said. "For saving me."

"You're welcome."

Again that dry, dusty voice. But the air itself was dry, she realized. She could almost feel the moisture leaving her skin.

"Who are you?" she asked.

"You can call me Jack."

"My name's Moira—Moira Jones."

Jack inclined his head in a slight nod. "Are you all right now, Moira Jones?" he asked.

"I think so."

"Good, well—"

"Wait!" she cried, realizing that he was about to leave her. "What is this place? Why did you bring me here?"

He shook his head. "I didn't," he said. "No one comes to the City of Bridges unless it's their fate to do so. In that sense, you brought yourself."

"But . . . ?"

"I know. It's all strange and different. You don't know where to turn, who to trust."

There was the faintest hint of mockery under the dry tones of his voice.

"Something like that," Moira said.

He seemed to consider her for the longest time.

"I don't know you," he said finally. "I don't know why you brought yourself here or where you come from. I don't know how, or even if, you'll ever find your way home again."

Bizarre though her situation was, oddly enough, Moira found herself adjusting to it far more quickly than she would have thought possible. It was almost like being in a dream where you just accept things as they come along, except she knew this wasn't a dream— just as she knew that she was getting the brush off.

"Listen," she said. "I appreciate your help a moment ago, but don't worry about me. I'll get by."

"What I do know, however," Jack went on as though she hadn't spoken, "is that this is a place for those who have no other place to go."

"What're you saying? That's it's some kind of a dead end place?"

The way her life was going, it sounded like it had been made for her.

"It's a forgotten place."

"Forgotten by who?"

"By the world in which it exists," Jack said.

"How can a place this weird be forgotten?" she asked.

Moira looked around at the bridges as she spoke. They were everywhere, of every size and shape and persuasion. One that looked like it belonged in a Japanese tea garden stood side by side with part of what had to be an interstate overpass, but somehow the latter didn't overshadow the former, although both their proportions were precise. She saw rope bridges, wooden bridges and old stone bridges like the Kelly Street Bridge that crossed the Kickaha River in that part of Newford called the Rosses.

She wondered if she'd ever see Newford again.

"The same way people forget their dreams," Jack replied. He touched her elbow, withdrawing his hand before she could take offense. "Come walk with me if you like. I've a previous appointment, but I can show you around a bit on the way."

Moira hesitated for a long moment, then fell into step beside him. They crossed a metal bridge, the heels of their boots ringing. Of course, she thought, they couldn't go anywhere without crossing a bridge. Bridges were the only kind of roads that existed in this place.

"Do you live here?" she asked.

Jack shook his head. "But I'm here a lot. I deal in possibilities and that's what bridges are in a way—not so much the ones that already exist to take you from one side of something to another, but the kind we build for ourselves."

"What are you talking about?"

"Say you want to be an artist—a painter, perhaps. The bridge you build between when you don't know which end of the brush to hold to when you're doing respected work can include studying under another artist, experimenting on your own, whatever. You build the bridge and it either takes you where you want it to, or it doesn't."

"And if it doesn't?"

His teeth flashed in the moonlight. "Then you build another one and maybe another one until one of them does."

Moira nodded as though she understood, all the while asking herself, what am I *doing* here?

"But this," he added, "is a place of failed dreams. Where bridges that go nowhere find their end."

Wonderful, Moira thought. A forgotten place. A dead end.

They started across an ornate bridge, its upper chords were all filigreed metal, its roadway cobblestone. Two thirds of the way across, what she took to be a pile of rags shifted and sat up. It was a beggar with a tattered cloak wrapped around him or her—Moira couldn't tell the sex of the poor creature. It seemed to press closer against the railing as they came abreast of it.

"Cancer victim," Jack said, as they passed the figure. "Nothing left to live for, so she came here."

Moira shivered. "Can't you—can't we do anything for her?"

"Nothing to be done for her," Jack replied.

The dusty tones of his voice made it impossible for her to decide if that was true, or if he just didn't care.

"But—"

"She wouldn't be here if there was," he said.

Wood underfoot now—a primitive bridge of rough timbers. The way Jack led her was a twisting path that seemed to take them back the way they'd come as much as forward. As they crossed an arched stone walkway, Moira heard a whimper. She paused and saw a child huddled up against a doorway below.

Jack stopped, waiting for her to catch up.

"There's a child," she began.

"You'll have to understand," Jack said, "that there's nothing you can do for anyone here. They've long since given up Hope. They belong to Despair now."

"Surely—"

"It's an abused child," Jack said. He glanced at his wrist watch. "I've time. Go help it."

"God, you're a cold fish."

Jack tapped his watch. "Time's slipping away."

Moira was trapped between just wanting to tell him to shove off and her fear of being stuck in this place by herself. Jack wasn't much, but at least he seemed to know his way around.

"I'll be right back," she said.

She hurried back down the arched path and crossed a rickety wooden bridge to the doorway of the building. The child looked up at her approach, his whimpers muting as he pushed his face against his shoulder.

"There, there," Moira said. "You're going to be okay."

She moved forward, pausing when the child leapt to his feet, back against the wall. He held his hands out before him, warding her away.

"No one's going to hurt you."

She took another step, and he started to scream.

"Don't cry!" she said, continuing to move forward. "I'm here to help you."

The child bolted before she could reach him. He slipped under her arm and was off and away, leaving a wailing cry in his wake. Moira stared after him.

"You'll never catch him now," Jack called down from above. She looked up at him. He was sitting on the edge of the arched walkway, legs dangling, heels tapping against the stonework.

"I wasn't going to hurt him," she said.

"He doesn't know that. I told you, the people here have long since given up hope. You can't help them—nobody can. They can't even help themselves anymore."

"What are they doing here?"

Jack shrugged. "They've got to go somewhere, don't they?"

Moira made her back to where he was waiting for her, anger clouding her features.

"Don't you even *care*?" she demanded.

His only reply was to start walking again. She hesitated for a long moment, then hurried to catch up. She walked with her arms wrapped around herself, but the chill she felt came from inside and it wouldn't go away.

They crossed bridges beyond her ability to count as they made their way into the central part of the city. From time to time they passed the odd streetlight, its dim glow making a feeble attempt to push back the shadows; in other places, the ghosts of flickering neon signs crackled and hissed more than they gave off light. In some ways the lighting made things worse for it revealed the city's general state of decay—cracked walls, rubbled streets, refuse wherever one turned.

Under one lamp post, she got a better look at her companion. His features were strong rather than handsome; none of the callousness she sensed in his voice was reflected in them. He caught her gaze and gave her a thin smile, but the humor in his eyes was more mocking than companionable.

They continued to pass by dejected and lost figures that hunched in the shadows, huddled against buildings, or bolted at their approach. Jack listed their despairs for her—AIDS victim, rape victim, abused wife, paraplegic—until Moira begged him to stop.

"I can't take anymore," she said.

"I'm sorry. I thought you wanted to know."

They went the rest of the way in silence, the bridges taking them higher and higher until they finally stood on the top of an enormous building that appeared to be the largest and most centrally placed of the city's structures. From its heights, the city was spread out around them on all sides.

It made for an eerie sight. Moira stepped back from the edge of the roof, away from the pull of vertigo that came creeping up the small of her back to whisper in her ear. She had only to step out, into the night sky, it told her. Step out and all her troubles would be forever eased.

At the sound of a footstep, she turned gratefully away from the disturbing view. A woman was walking towards them, pausing when she was a few paces away. Unlike the other inhabitants of the city, she gave the impression of being self-assured, of being in control of her destiny.

She had pale skin, and short spiky red hair. A half dozen silver earrings hung from one ear; the other had a small silver stud in the shape of a star. Like Jack, she was dressed casually: black jeans, black boots, white tank-top, a black leather jacket draped over one shoulder. And like Jack, her eyes, too, seemed like a reservoir for the moonlight.

"You're not alone," she said to Jack.

"I never am," Jack replied. "You know that. My sister, Diane," he added to Moira, then introduced her to Diane.

The woman remained silent, studying Moira with her moon-bright eyes until Moira couldn't help but fidget. The dreamlike quality of her situation was beginning to filter away. Once again a panicked feeling was making itself felt in the pit of her stomach.

"Why are you here?" Diane asked her finally.

Her voice had a different quality from her brother's. It was a warm, rounded sound that carried in it a sweet scent like that of cherry blossoms or rose buds. It took away Moira's panic, returning her once more to that sense of it all just being a dream.

"I . . . I don't know," she said. "I was just crossing a bridge on my way home and the next thing I knew I was . . . here. Wherever here is. I—look. I just want to go home. I don't want any of this to be real."

"It's very real," Diane said.

"Wonderful."

"She wants to help the unhappy," Jack offered, "but they just run away from her."

Moira shot him a dirty look.

"Do be still," Diane told him, frowning as she spoke. She returned her attention to Moira. "Why don't you go home?"

"I—I don't know *how* to. The bridge that brought me here . . . when I went to go back across it, its roadway was gone."

Diane nodded. "What has my brother told you?"

Nothing that made sense, Moira wanted to say, but she related what she remembered of her conversations with Jack.

"And do you despair?" Diane asked.

"I . . ."

Moira hesitated. She thought of the hopeless, dejected people she'd passed on the way to this rooftop.

"Not really, I guess. I mean, I'm not happy or anything, but . . ."

"You have hope? That things will get better for you?"

A flicker of faces passed through her mind. Ghosts from the distant and recent past. Boys from high school. Eddie. She heard Eddie's voice.

Either you come across, or you walk. . . .

She just wanted a normal life. She wanted to find something to enjoy in it. She wanted to find somebody she could have a good relationship with, she wanted to enjoy making love with him without worrying about people thinking she was a tramp. She wanted him to be there the next morning. She wanted there to be more to what they had than just a roll in the hay.

Right now, none of that seemed very possible.

"I don't know," she said finally. "I want it to. I'm not going to give up, but . . ."

Again, faces paraded before her—this time they belonged to those lost souls of the city. The despairing.

"I know there are people a lot worse off than I am," she said. "I'm not sick, I've got the use of my body and my mind. But I'm missing something, too. I don't know how it is for other people—maybe they feel the same and just handle it better—but I feel like there's a hole inside me that I just can't fill. I get so lonely . . ."

"You see," Jack said then. "She's mine."

Moira turned to him. "What are you talking about?"

It was Diane who answered. "He's laying claim to your unhappiness," she said.

Moira looked from one to the other. There was something going on here, some undercurrent, that she wasn't picking up on.

"What are you *talking* about?" she asked.

"This city is ours," Diane said. "My brother's and mine. We are two sides to the same coin. In most people, that coin lies with my face up, for you are an optimistic race. But optimism only carries some so far. When my brother's face lies looking skyward, all hope is gone."

Moira centered on the words, "you are an optimistic race," realizing from the way Diane spoke it was as though she and her brother weren't human. She looked away, across the cityscape of bridges and tilting buildings. It was a dreamscape—not exactly a nightmare, but not at all pleasant either. And she was trapped in it; trapped in a dream.

"Who are you people?" she asked. "I don't buy this 'Jack and Diane' bit—that's like out of that John Mellencamp song. Who are you *really?* What is this place?"

"I've already told you," Jack said.

"But you only gave her half the answer," Diane added. She turned to Moira. "We are Hope and Despair," she said. She touched a hand to her breast. "Because of your need for us, we are no longer mere allegory, but have shape and form. This is our city."

Moira shook her head. "Despair I can understand—this place reeks of it. But not Hope."

"Hope is what allows the strong to rise above their despair," Diane said. "It's what makes them strong. Not blind faith, not the certain knowledge that someone will step in and help them, but the understanding that through their own force of will they cannot merely survive, but succeed. Hope is what tempers that will and gives it the strength to carry on, no matter what the odds are ranked against them."

"Don't forget to tell her how too much hope will turn her into a lazy cow," her brother said.

Diane sighed, but didn't ignore him. "It's true," she said. "Too much hope can also be harmful. Remember this: Neither hope nor despair have power of their own; they can only provide the fuel that you will use to prevail or be defeated."

"Pop psychology," Moira muttered.

Diane smiled. "Yet, like old wives' tales, it has within it a kernel of truth, or why would it linger?"

"So what am I doing here?" Moira asked. "I never gave up. I'm still trying."

Diane looked at her brother. He shrugged his shoulders.

"I admit defeat," he said. "She is yours."

Diane shook her head. "No. She is her own. Let her go."

Jack turned to Moira, the look of a petulant child marring his strong features before they started to become hazy.

"You'll be back," he said. That dry voice was like a desert wind, its fine sand filling her heart with an aching forlornness. "Hope is sweet, I'll admit that readily, but once Despair has touched you, you can never be wholly free of its influence."

A hot flush ran through Moira. She reeled, dizzy, vision blurring, only half hearing what was being said. Her head was thick with a heavy buzz of pain.

But Hope is stronger.

Moira wasn't sure if she'd actually heard that, the sweet scent of blossoms clearing her heart of Despair's dust, or if it came from within herself—something she wanted—*had* to believe. But it overrode Despair's dry voice. She no longer fought the vertigo, but just let it take her away.

Moira was suddenly aware that she was on her hands and knees, with dirty wood under her. Where . . . ?

Then she remembered: Walking across the covered bridge. The city. Hope and Despair.

She sat back on her haunches and looked around herself. She was back in her own world. Back—if she'd ever even gone anywhere in the first place.

A sudden roaring filled her head. Lights blinded her as a car came rushing up on the far side of the bridge. She remembered Eddie, her fear of some redneck hillbillies, but there was nowhere to run to. The car screeched to a halt on the wood, a door opened. A man stepped out onto the roadway of the bridge and came towards her.

Backlit by the car's headbeams, he seemed huge—a monstrous shape. She wanted to bolt. She wanted to scream. She couldn't seem to move, not even enough to reach into her purse for her switchblade.

"Jesus!" the stranger said. "Are you okay?"

He was bent down beside her now, features pulled tight with concern.

She nodded slowly. "I just . . . felt dizzy, I guess."

"Here. Let me help you up."

She allowed him to do that. She let him walk her to his car. He opened up the passenger's door and she sank gratefully onto the seat. The man looked down to the end of the bridge by which she'd entered it what seemed like a lifetime ago.

"Did you have some car trouble?" the man asked.

"You could say that," she said. "The guy I was with dumped me from his car a few miles back."

"Are you hurt?"

She shook her head. "Just my feelings."

"Jesus. What a crappy thing to do."

"Yeah. Thanks for stopping."

"No problem. Can I give you a lift somewhere?"

Moira shook her head. "I'm going back to Newford. I think that's a little far out of your way."

"Well, I'm not just going to leave you here by yourself."

Before she could protest, he closed the door and went back around to the driver's side.

"Don't worry," he said as he got behind the wheel. "After what you've been through, a guy'd have to be a real heel to—well, you know."

Moira had to smile. He actually seemed embarrassed.

"We'll just drive to the other side of the bridge and turn around and then—"

Moira touched his arm. She remembered what had happened the last time she'd tried to go through this bridge.

"Do me a favor, would you?" she asked. "Could you just back out instead?"

Her benefactor gave her a funny look, then shrugged. Putting the car into reverse, he started backing up. Moira held her breath until they were back out on the road again. There were pines and cedars pushing up against the verge, stars overhead. No weird city. No bridges.

She let out her breath.

"What's your name?" she asked as he maneuvered the car back and forth on the narrow road until he had its nose pointed towards Newford.

"John—John Fraser."

"My name's Moira."

"My grandmother's name was Moira," John said.

"Really?"

He nodded.

He seemed like a nice guy, Moira thought. Not the kind who'd try to pull anything funny.

The sweet scent of blossoms came to her for just a moment, then it was gone.

John's showing up so fortuitously as he had—that had to be Hope's doing, she decided. Maybe it was a freebie of good luck to make up for her brother's bad manners. Or maybe it was true: if you had a positive attitude, you had a better chance that things would work out.

"Thanks," she said. She wasn't sure if Hope could hear her, but she wanted to say it all the same.

"You're welcome," John said from beside her.

Moira glanced at him, then smiled.

"Yeah," she said. "You, too."

His puzzled look made her smile widen.

"What's so funny?" he asked.

She just shrugged and settled back into her seat. "It's a long weird story and you wouldn't believe me anyway."

"Try me."

"Maybe some other time," she said.

"I might just hold you to that," he said.

Moira surprised herself with the hope that maybe he would.

⊰ OUR LADY OF THE ⊱ HARBOUR

PEOPLE DON'T BEHAVE THE WAY THEY SHOULD; THEY BEHAVE THE WAY THEY DO.
—JIM BEAUBIEN AND KAREN CAESAR

She sat on her rock, looking out over the lake, her back to the city that reared up behind her in a bewildering array of towers and lights. A half mile of water separated her island from Newford, but on a night such as this, with the moon high and the water still as glass, the city might as well have been on the other side of the planet.

Tonight, an essence of *Marchen* prevailed in the darkened groves and on the moonlit lawns of the island.

For uncounted years before Diederick van Yoors first settled the area in the early part of the nineteenth century, the native Kickaha called the island Myeengun. By the turn of the century, it had become the playground of Newford's wealthy, its bright facade first beginning to lose its luster with the Great Depression when wealthy landowners could no longer keep up their summer homes; by the end of the Second World War it was an eyesore. It wasn't turned into a park until the late 1950s. Today most people knew it only by the anglicized translation of its Kickaha name: Wolf Island.

Matt Casey always thought of it as *her* island.

The cast bronze statue he regarded had originally stood in the garden of an expatriate Danish businessman's summer home, a faithful reproduction of the well-known figure that haunted the waterfront of the Dane's native Copenhagen. When the city expropriated the man's land for the park, he was generous enough to donate the statue, and so she sat now on the island, as she had for fifty years, looking out over the lake, motionless, always looking, the moonlight gleaming on her bronze features and slender form.

The sharp blast of a warning horn signaling the last ferry back to the city cut through the night's contemplative mood. Matt turned to look to the far side of the island where the ferry was docked. As he watched, the lights on the park's winding paths winked out, followed by those in the island's restaurant and the other buildings near the dock. The horn gave one last blast. Five minutes later, the ferry lurched away from the dock and began the final journey of the day back to Newford's harbour.

Now, except for a pair of security guards who, Matt knew, would spend the night watching TV and sleeping in the park's offices above the souvenir store, he had the island to himself. He turned back to look at the statue. It was still silent, still motionless, still watching the unfathomable waters of the lake.

He'd been here one afternoon and watched a bag lady feeding gulls with bits of bread that she probably should have kept for herself. The gulls here were all overfed. When the bread was all gone, she'd walked up to the statue.

"Our Lady of the Harbour," she'd said. "Bless me."

Then she'd made the sign of the cross, as though she was a Catholic stepping forward into the nave of her church. From one of her bulging shopping bags, she took out a small plastic flower and laid it on the stone by the statue's feet, then turned and walked away.

The flower was long gone, plucked by one of the cleaning crews no doubt, but the memory remained.

Matt moved closer to the statue, so close that he could have laid his palm against the cool metal of her flesh.

"Lady," he began, but he couldn't go on.

Matt Casey wasn't an easy man to like. He lived for one thing, and that was his music. About the only social intercourse he had was with the members of the various bands he had played in over the years, and even that was spotty. Nobody he ever played with seemed willing to just concentrate on the music; they always wanted to hang out together as though they were all friends, as though they were in some kind of social club.

Music took the place of people in his life. It was his friend and his lover, his confidant and his voice, his gossip and his comfort.

It was almost always so.

From his earliest years he suffered from an acute sense of xenophobia: everyone was a stranger to him. All were foreigners to the observer captured in the flesh, blood and bone of his body. It was not something he understood, in the sense that one might be aware of a problem one had; it was just the way he was. He could trust no one—perhaps because he had never learned to trust himself.

His fellow musicians thought of him as cold, aloof, cynical—descriptions that were completely at odds with the sensitivity of his singing and the warmth that lay at the heart of his music. The men he played with sometimes thought that all he needed was a friend, but his rebuffs to even the most casual overtures of friendship always cured such notions. The women he played with sometimes thought that all he needed was a lover, but though he slept with a few, the distance he maintained eventually cooled the ardor of even the most persistent.

Always, in the end, there was only the music. To all else, he was an outsider.

He grew up in the suburbs north of the city's center, part of a caring family. He had an older brother and two younger sisters, each of them outgoing and popular in their own way. Standing out in such contrast to them, even at an early age, his parents had sent him to a seemingly endless series of child specialists and psychologists, but no one could get through except for his music teachers—first in the school orchestra, then the private tutors that his parents were only too happy to provide for him.

They saw a future in music for him, but not the one he chose. They saw him studying music at a university, taken under the wing of some master whenever he finally settled on a chosen instrument, eventually playing concert halls, touring the world with famous orchestras. Instead he left home at sixteen. He turned his back on formal studies, but not on learning, and played in the streets. He traveled all over North America, then to Europe and the Middle East, finally returning home to busk on Newford's streets and play in her clubs.

Still the outsider; more so, perhaps, rather than less.

It wasn't that he was unfriendly; he simply remained uninvolved, animated only in the presence of other musicians and then only to discuss the esoterics of obscure lyrics and tunes and instruments, or to play. He never thought of himself as lonely, just as alone; never considered himself to be a social misfit or an outcast from the company of his fellow men, just an observer of the social dance to which most men and women knew the steps rather than one who would join them on the dance floor.

An outsider.

A gifted genius, undoubtedly, as any who heard him play would affirm, but an outsider all the same.

It was almost always so.

In the late seventies, the current band was Marrowbones and they had a weekend gig at a folk club in Lower Crowsea called Feeney's Kitchen—a popular hangout for those Butler University students who shunned disco and punk as well as the New Wave. The line-up was Matt on his usual bouzouki and guitar and handling the vocals, Nicky Doyle on fiddle, Johnny Ryan on tenor banjo, doubling on his classic Gibson mando-cello for song accompaniments, and Matt's long-time musical associate Amy Scallan on Uillean pipes and whistles.

They'd been playing together for a year and a half now and the band had developed a big, tight sound that had recently brought in offers for them to tour the college and festival circuits right across the country.

But it'd never happen, Amy thought as she buckled on her pipes in preparation for the selection of reels with which they were going to end the first set of the evening.

The same thing was going to happen that always happened. It was already starting. She'd had to listen to Nicky and Johnny going on about Matt earlier this afternoon when the three of them had gotten together to jam with a couple of other friends at The Harp. They couldn't deal with the dichotomy of Matt offstage and on. Fronting the band, Matt projected the charming image of a friendly and outgoing man that you couldn't help but want to get to know; offstage, he was taciturn and withdrawn, uninterested in anything that didn't deal with the music.

But that was Matt, she'd tried to explain. You couldn't find a better singer or musician to play with and he had a knack for giving even the simplest piece a knockout arrangement. Nobody said you had to like him.

But Nicky had only shaken his head, brown curls bobbing. "Your man's taking all the *craic* from playing in a band."

Johnny nodded in agreement. "It's just not fun anymore. He'll barely pass the time of day with you, but on stage he's all bloody smiles and jokes. I don't know how you put up with him."

Amy hadn't been able to come up with an explanation then and looking across the stage now to where Matt was raising his eyebrows to ask if she was ready, then winking when she nodded back that she was, she couldn't explain it any better. She'd just learned over the years that what they shared was the music—and the music was very good; if she wanted more, she had to look for it elsewhere.

She'd come to terms with it where most people wouldn't, or couldn't, but then there was very little in the world that ever fazed her.

Matt started a G-drone on his bouzouki. He leaned close to the mike, just a touch of a welcoming smile tugging the corner of his mouth as a handful of dancers, anticipating what was to come, stepped onto the tiny wooden dance floor in front of the stage. Amy gave him a handful of bars to lock in the tempo, then launched into the first high popping notes of "The Road West," the opening salvo in this set of reels.

She and Matt played the tune through twice on their own and room on the dance floor grew to such a premium that the dancers could do little more than jig in one spot. Their elbows and knees could barely jostle against one another.

It wasn't quite a sea of bobbing heads, Amy thought, looking down from the stage. More like a small lake, or even a puddle.

The analogy made her smile. She kicked in her pipe drones as the fiddle and tenor banjo joined in on "The Glen Allen." It was halfway through that second tune that she became aware of the young woman dancing directly in front of Matt's microphone.

She was small and slender, with hair that seemed to be made of spun gold and eyes such a deep blue that they glittered like sapphires in the light spilling from the stage. Her features reminded Amy of a fox—pointed and tight like a Rackham sprite, but no less attractive for all that.

The other dancers gave way like reeds before a wind, drawing back to allow her the room to swirl the skirt of her unbelted flowered dress, her tiny feet scissoring intricate steps in their black Chinese slippers. Her movements were at once sensual and innocent. Amy's first impression was that the young woman was a professional dancer, but as she watched more closely, she realized that the girl's fluidity and grace were more an inherent talent than a studied skill.

The dancer's gaze caught and held on Matt, no matter how her steps turned her about, her attention fixed and steady as though he had bewitched her, while Matt, to Amy's surprise, seemed just as entranced. When they kicked into "Sheehan's Reel," the third and final tune of the set, she almost thought Matt was going to leave the stage to dance with the girl.

"Again!" Matt cried out as they neared the usual end of the tune. Amy didn't mind. She pumped the bellows of her pipes, long fingers dancing on the chanter, more than happy to play the piece all night if the dancer could keep up. But the tune unwound to its end, they ended with a flourish, and suddenly it was all over. The dance floor cleared, the girl was swallowed by the crowd.

When the applause died down, an odd sort of hush fell over the club. Amy unbuckled her pipes and looked over to see that Matt had already left the stage. She hadn't even seen him go. She tugged her chanter mike up to mouth level.

"We're, uh, going to take a short break, folks," she said into the mike. Her voice seemed to boom in the quiet. "Then," she added, "we'll be right back with some more music, so don't go away."

The patter bookending the tunes and songs was Matt's usual job. Since Amy didn't feel she had his natural stage charm, she just kept it simple.

There was an another smatter of applause that she acknowledged with a smile. The house system came on, playing a Jackson Browne tune, and she turned to Nicky, who was putting his fiddle in its case.

"Where'd Matt go?" she asked.

He gave her a "who cares?" shrug. "Probably chasing that bird who was shaking her tush at him all through the last piece."

"I don't envy her," Johnny added.

Amy knew exactly what he meant. Over the past few months they'd all seen the fallout of casualties who gathered like moths around the bright flame of Matt's stage presence only to have their wings burnt with his indifference. He'd charm them in a club, sometimes sleep with them, but in the end, the only lover he kept was the music.

Amy knew all too well. There was a time . . .

She pushed the past away with a shake of her head. Putting a hand above her eyes to shade them from the lights, she scanned the crowd as the other two went to get themselves a beer but she couldn't spot either Matt or the girl. Her gaze settled on a black-haired Chinese woman sitting alone at at small table near the door and she smiled as the woman raised her hand in a wave. She'd forgotten that Lucia had arrived halfway through their first set—fashionably late, as always—and now that she thought about it, hadn't she seen the dancer come in about the same time? They might even have come in together.

Lucia Han was a performance artist based in Upper Foxville and an old friend of Amy's. When they'd first met, Amy had been told by too many people to be careful because Lucia was gay and would probably make a pass at her. Amy just ignored them. She had nothing against gays to begin with and she soon learned that the gossips' reasoning for their false assumption was just that Lucia only liked to work with other women. But as Lucia had explained to Amy once, "There's just not enough women involved in the arts and I want to support those who do make the plunge—at least if they're any good."

Amy understood perfectly. She often wished there were more women players in traditional music. She was sick to death of going to a music session where she wasn't known. All too often she'd be the only woman in a gathering of men and have to play rings around them on her pipes just to prove that she was as good as them. Irish men weren't exactly noted for their liberated standards.

Which didn't mean that either she or Lucia weren't fond of the right sort of man. *"Au contraire,"* as Lucia would say in the phony Parisian accent she liked to affect, "I am liking them too much."

Amy made her way to the bar, where she ordered a beer on her tab, then took the brimming draught glass through the crowd to Lucia's table, trying to slosh as little of the foam as she could on her new jeans.

"Bet you thought I wouldn't come," Lucia said as Amy sat down with her stein relatively full. The only spillage had joined the stickiness of other people's spills that lay underfoot.

Lucia was older than Amy by at least six or seven years, putting

her in her mid-thirties. She had her hair in a wild spiky do tonight—
to match the torn white T-shirt and leather jeans, no doubt. The
punk movement had barely begun to trickle across the Atlantic as
yet, but it was obvious that Lucia was already an eager proponent.
A strand of safety pins dangled from one earlobe; others held the
tears of her T-shirt closed in strategic places.

"I don't even remember telling you about the gig," Amy said.

Lucia waved a negligent hand towards the small poster on the wall
behind her that advertised the band's appearance at Feeney's Kitchen
this weekend.

"But you are famous now, *ma cherie*", she said. "How could I *not*
know?" She dropped the accent to add, "You guys sound great."

"Thanks."

Amy looked at the tabletop. She set her stein down beside a glass
of white wine, Lucia's cigarettes and matches and a half-filled ashtray. There was also an empty teacup with a small bright steel teapot
on one side of it and a used tea bag on the lip of its saucer.

"Did you come alone?" she asked.

Lucia shook her head. "I brought a foundling—fresh from who
really knows where. You probably noticed her and Matt making
goo-goo eyes at each other all through the last piece you did." She
brought a hand to her lips as soon as she'd made the last comment.
"Sorry. I forgot about the thing you used to have going with him."

"Old history," Amy said. "I've long since dealt with it. I don't
know that Matt ever even knew anything existed between us, but
I'm cool now."

"It's for the better."

"Definitely," Amy agreed.

"I should probably warn my little friend about him," Lucia said,
"but you know what they're like at that age—it'd just egg her on."

"Who *is* your little friend? She moves like all she was born to do
was dance."

"She's something, isn't she? I met her on Wolf Island about a
week ago, just before the last ferry—all wet and bedraggled like
she'd fallen off a boat and been washed to shore. She wasn't wearing
a stitch of clothing and I thought the worst, you know? Some
asshole brought her out for a quick wham, bam, and then just
dumped her."

Lucia paused to light a cigarette.

"And?" Amy asked.

Lucia shrugged, blowing out a wreath of blue-grey smoke. "Seems she fell off a boat and took off her clothes so that they wouldn't drag her down while she swam to shore. Course, I got that from her later."

Just then the door to the club opened behind Lucia and a gust of cool air caught the smoke from Lucia's cigarette, giving it a slow dervishing whirl. On the heels of the wind, Amy saw Matt and the girl walk in. The seemed to be in the middle of an animated discussion—or at least Matt was, so they had to be talking about music.

Amy felt the same slight twinge of jealousy watching him with the dancer as she did in the first few moments of every one of the short relationships that came about from some girl basically flinging herself at him halfway through a gig. Though perhaps "relationship" was too strong a word, since any sense of responsibility to a partner was inevitably one-sided.

The girl laughed at what he was saying—but it was a silent laugh. Her mouth was open, her eyes sparkled with a humored appreciation, but there was no sound. She began to move her hands in an intricate pattern that, Amy realized, was the American Sign Language used by deaf-mutes.

"Her problem right then," Lucia was saying, "was finding something to wear so that she could get into town. Luckily I was wearing my duster—you know, from when I was into my Sergio Leone phase—so she could cover herself up."

"She took off everything while she was in the water?" Amy asked, her gaze returning to her friend. "Even her underwear?"

"I guess. Unless she wasn't wearing any in the first place."

"Weird."

"I don't see you wearing a bra."

"You know what I meant," Amy said with a laugh.

Lucia nodded. "So anyway, she came on the ferry with me—I paid her fare—and then I brought her back to my place because it turned out she didn't have anywhere else to go. Doesn't know a soul in town. To be honest, I wasn't even sure she spoke English at first."

Amy looked over Lucia's shoulder to where Matt was answering whatever it was that the girl's hands had told him. Where had he learned sign language? she wondered. He'd never said anything about it before, but then she realized that for all the years she'd known him, she really didn't *know* much about him at all except that he was a brilliant musician and good in bed, related actions, perhaps, since she didn't doubt that they both were something he'd regard as a performance.

Meow, she thought.

"She's deaf-mute, isn't she?" she added aloud.

Lucia looked surprised. "Mute, but not deaf. How you'd know?"

"I'm watching her talk to Matt with her hands right now."

"She couldn't even do that when I first met her," Lucia said.

Amy returned her attention to Lucia once more. "What do you mean?"

"Well, I know sign language—I learned it when I worked at the Institute for the Deaf up on Gracie Street when I first got out of college—so when I realized she was mute, it was the first thing I tried. But she's not deaf—she just can't talk. She didn't even try to communicate at first. I thought she was in shock. She just sat beside me, looking out over the water, her eyes getting bigger and bigger as we approached the docks.

"When we caught a bus back to my place, it was like she'd never been in a city before. She just sat beside me all wide-eyed and then took my hand—not like she was scared, it was more like she just wanted to share the wonder of it all with me. It wasn't until we got back to my place that she asked for pen and paper." Lucia mimed the action as she spoke.

"It's all kind of mysterious, isn't it?" Amy said.

"I'll say. Anyway, her name's Katrina Ludvigsen and she's from one of those little towns on the Islands further down the lake—the ones just past the mouth of the Dulfer River, you know?"

Amy nodded.

"Her family came over from Norway originally," Lucia went on. "They were Lapps—as in Lapland—except she doesn't like to be called that. Her people call themselves Sami."

"I've heard about that," Amy said. "Referring to them as Lapps is a kind of insult."

"Exactly." Lucia took a final drag from her cigarette and butted it out in the ashtray. "Once she introduced herself, she asked me to teach her sign language. Would you believe she picked it up in *two* days?"

"I don't know," Amy said. "Is that fast?"

"Try *fantastique, ma cherie.*"

"So what's she doing here?"

Lucia shrugged. "She told me she was looking for a man—like, aren't we all, ha ha—only she didn't know his name, just that he lived in Newford. She just about had a fit when she spotted the picture of Matt in the poster for this gig."

"So she knows him from before."

"You tell me," Lucia said.

Amy shook her head. "Only Matt knows whatever it is that Matt knows."

"Katrina says she's twenty-two," Lucia went on, "but if you ask me, I think she's a lot younger. I'll bet she ran away from home—maybe even stowed away on some tourist's powerboat and jumped ship just outside the harbor because they were about to catch her and maybe take her back home."

"So what are you going to do about it?"

"Not a damn thing. She's a nice kid and besides," she added as Katrina and Matt walked by their table, heading for the bar, "I've got the feeling she's not even going to be my responsibility for much longer."

"Don't count on it," Amy said. "She'll be lucky if she lasts the night."

Although maybe not. Katrina *was* pretty, and she certainly could dance, so there was the musical connection, just as there had been with her.

Amy sighed. She didn't know why she got to feeling the way she did at times like this. She wouldn't even *want* to make a go at it with Matt again.

Lucia reached across the table and put her hand on Amy's, giving it a squeeze. "How're you handling this, Amy? I remember you were pretty messed up about him at one point."

"I can deal with it."

"Well—what's that line of yours? More power to your elbow then if you can, though I still can't figure out how you got past it enough to still be able to play with him."

Amy looked over to the bar where Matt was getting the girl a cup of tea. She wished the twinge of not so much jealousy, as hurt, would go away.

Patience, she told herself. She'd seen Matt with who knew how many women over the years, all of them crazy over him. The twinge only lasted for a little while—a reminder of a bad time, not the bad time itself. She was past that now.

Well, mostly.

"You just change your way of thinking about a person," she said after a few moments, trying to convince herself as much as Lucia. "You change what you need from them, your expectations. That's all."

"You make it sound easy."

Amy turned back to her friend. "It's not," she said in a quiet voice.

Lucia gave her hand a squeeze.

The girl was drunk on Matt, Amy realized. There was no other explanation for the way she was carrying on.

For the rest of the night, Amy could see Katrina sitting with Lucia at the back of the club, chin cupped in her hands as she listened to Matt sing. No, not just listening. She drank in the songs, swallowed them whole. And with every dance set they played, she was up on her feet at the front of the stage, the sinuous grace of her movement, the swirl and the lift and the rapid fire steps of her small feet capturing each tune to perfection.

Matt was obviously complimented by her attention—or at least whatever it was that he'd feel that would be close to flattered—and why not? Next to Lucia, she was the best looking woman in the club, and Lucia wasn't exactly sending out "available" signals, not dressed the way she was.

Matt and the girl talked between each set, filling up the twenty minutes or so of canned music and patron conversation with a forest of words, his spoken, hers signed, each of them oblivious to their surroundings, to everything except for each other.

Maybe Katrina will be the one, Amy thought.

Once she got past her own feelings, that was what she usually found herself hoping. Although Matt could be insensitive once he stepped off the stage, she still believed that all he really needed was someone to care about to turn him around. Nobody who put such heart into his music, could be completely empty inside. She was sure that he just needed someone—the right someone. It hadn't been her, fine. But somewhere there had to be a woman for him—a catalyst to take down the walls though which only his music dared forth to touch the world.

The way he'd been so attentive towards Katrina all night, Amy was sure he was going to take her home with him, but all he did was ask her out tomorrow.

Okay, she thought standing beside Lucia while Matt and Katrina "talked." That's a start and maybe a good one.

Katrina's hands moved in response to Matt's question.

"What's she saying?" Amy asked, leaning close to whisper to Lucia.

"Yes," Lucia translated. "Now she's asking him if they can ride the ferry."

"The one to Wolf Island?" Amy said. "That's where you found her."

"Whisht," Lucia told her.

"We'll do whatever you want," Matt was saying.

And then Katrina was gone, trailing after Lucia with a last lingering wave before the world outside the club swallowed her and the door closed behind the pair of them.

Matt and Amy returned to the stage to pack up their instruments.

"I was thinking of heading up to The Harp to see if there's a session on," Matt said. He looked around at the other three. "Anyone feel like coming?"

If there were enough musicians up for the music, Joe Breen, the proprietor of The Harp, would lock the doors to the public after closing hours and just let the music flow until the last musician packed it in, acting no different on this side of the Atlantic than he had with the pub he'd run back home in Ireland.

Johnny shook his head. "I'm beat. It's straight to bed for me tonight."

"It's been a long night," Nicky agreed.

Nicky looked a little sullen, but Amy doubted that Matt even noticed. He just shrugged, then looked to her.

Well, and why not? she thought.

"I'll give it a go," she told him.

Saying their goodbyes to the other two outside the club, she and Matt walked north to the Rosses where The Harp stood in the shadow of the Kelly Street Bridge.

"Katrina seemed nice," Amy said after a few blocks.

"I suppose," he said. "A little intense, maybe."

"I think she's a little taken with you."

Matt nodded unselfconsciously. "Maybe too much. But she sure can dance, can't she?"

"Like an angel," Amy agreed.

Conversation fell flat then, just as it always did.

"I got a new tune from Geordie this afternoon," Amy said finally. "He doesn't remember where he picked it up, but it fits onto the end of 'The Kilavel Jig' like it was born to it."

Matt's eyes brightened with interest. "What's it called?"

"He didn't know. It had some Gaelic title that he'd forgotten, but it's a lovely piece. In G-major, but the first part has a kind of a modal flavor so that it almost feels as though it's being played out of C. It'd be just lovely on the bouzouki."

The talk stayed on tunes the rest of the way to The Harp—safe ground. At one point Amy found herself remembering a gig they'd played a few months ago and the story that Matt had used to introduce a song called "Sure, All He Did Was Go" that they'd played that night.

"He couldn't help himself," Matt had said, speaking of the fiddler in the song who gave up everything he had to follow a tune. "Music can be a severe mistress, demanding and jealous, and don't you doubt it. Do her bidding and isn't it just like royalty that she'll be treating you, but turn your back on her and she can take back her gift as easily as it was given. Your man could find himself holding only the tattered ribbons of a tune and song ashes and that's the God's own truth. I've seen it happen."

And then he'd laughed, as though he'd been having the audience on, and they'd launched into the song, but Amy had seen more than laughter in Matt's eyes as he started to sing. She wondered then, as she wondered now, if he didn't half believe that little bit of superstition, picked up somewhere on his travels, God knew where.

Maybe that was the answer to the riddle that was Matt Casey: he thought he'd lose his gift of music if he gave his heart to another. Maybe he'd even written that song himself, for she'd surely never heard it before. Picked it up in Morocco, he'd told her once, from one of the Wild Geese, the many Irish-in-exile, but she wasn't so sure.

Did you write it? She was ready to ask him right now, but then they were at The Harp and there was old Joe Breen flinging open the door to welcome them in and the opportunity was gone.

Lucia put on a pot of tea when she and Katrina returned to the apartment. While they waited for it to steep, they sat on the legless sofa pushed up against one wall of the long open loft that took up the majority of the apartment's floor space.

There was a small bedroom and a smaller bathroom off this main room. The kitchen area was in one corner—a battered fridge, its paint peeling, a sink and a counter with a hot plate on it and storage cupboards underneath and a small wooden kitchen table with five mismatching chairs set around it.

A low coffee table made of a plank of wood set on two apple crates crouched before the couch, laden with magazines and ashtrays. Along a far wall, three tall old mirrors had been fastened to the wall with a twelve-foot long support bar set out in front of them. The other walls were adorned with posters of the various shows in which Lucia had performed. In two she had headlined—one a traditional ballet, while the other had been a very outre multimedia event written and choreographed by a friend of hers.

When the tea was ready, Lucia brought the pot and two cups over to the sofa and set them on a stack of magazines. She poured Katrina a cup, then another for herself.

"So you found him," Lucia said as she returned to her seat on the sofa.

Katrina nodded happily.

He's just the way I remember him, she signed.

"Where did you meet him?" Lucia asked.

Katrina gave a shy smile in response, then added, *Near my home. He was playing music.*

The bright blue fire of her eyes grew unfocused as she looked across the room, seeing not plaster walls and the dance posters upon them, but the rough rocky shore of a coastline that lay east of the city by the mouth of the Dulfer River. She went into the past, and the past was like a dream.

She'd been underlake when the sound of his voice drew her up from the cold and the dark, neither of which she felt except as a kind of malaise in her spirit; up into the moonlight, bobbing in the white-capped waves; listening, *swallowing* that golden sound of strings and voice, and he so handsome and all alone on the shore. And sad. She could hear it in his song, feel the timbre of his loneliness in his voice.

Always intrigued with the strange folk who moved on the shore with their odd stumpy legs, this time she was utterly smitten. She swam closer and laid her arms on a stone by the shore, her head on her arms, to watch and listen.

It was his music that initially won her, for music had been her first love. Each of her four sisters was prettier than the next, and each had a voice that could charm moonlight from a stone, milk from a virgin, a ghost from the cold dark depths below, but her voice was better still, as golden as her hair and as rich and pure as the first larksong at dawn.

But if it was his music that first enchanted her, then he himself completed the spell. She longed to join her voice to his, to hold him and be held, but she never moved from her hiding place. One look at her, and he would be driven away, for he'd see only that which was scaled, and she had no soul, not as did those who walked ashore.

No soul, no soul. A heart that broke for want of him, but no immortal soul. That was the curse of the lake-born.

When he finally put away his instrument and walked further inland, up under the pines where she couldn't follow, she let the waves close over her head and returned to her home underlake.

For three nights she returned to the shore and for two of them he was there, his voice like honey against the beat of the waves that the wind pushed shoreward and she only loved him more. But on the fourth night, he didn't come, nor the on the fifth night, nor the sixth, and she despaired, knowing he was gone, away in the wide world, lost to her forever.

Her family couldn't help her; there was no one to help her. She yearned to be rid of scales, to walk on shore, no matter the cost, just so that she could be with him, but as well ask the sun not rise, or the wind to cease its endless motion.

"No matter the cost," she whispered. Tears trailed down her cheek, a sorrowful tide that would not ebb.

"Maraghreen," the lake replied as the wind lifted one of its waves to break upon the land.

She lifted her head, looked over the white caps, to where the lake grew darker still as it crept under the cliffs into the hidden cave where the lake witch lived.

She was afraid, but she went. To Maraghreen. Who took her scales and gave her legs with a bitter potion that tasted of witch blood; satisfied her impossible need, but took Katrina's voice in payment.

"A week and a day," the lake witch told her before she took Katrina's voice. "You have only so long to win him and your immortal soul, or to foam you will return."

"But without my voice . . ." It was through song, she'd thought to win him, voices joined in a harmony so pure how could he help but love her? "Without it . . ."

"He must speak of his love first, or your soul will be forfeit."

"But without my voice . . ."

"You will have your body; that will need be enough."

So she drank the blood, bitter on her tongue; gained legs, and each step she took was fiery pain and would be so until she'd gained a soul; went in search of he who held her love, for whose love she had paid such a dear price. Surely he would speak the words to her before the seven days were past and gone?

"Penny for your thoughts," Lucia said.

Katrina only smiled and shook her head. She could tell no one. The words must come unbidden from him or all would be undone.

Matt was late picking Katrina up on Sunday. It was partly his own fault—he'd gotten caught up with a new song that he was learning from a tape a friend had sent him from Co. Cork and lost track of the time—and partly from trying to follow the Byzantine directions that Lucia had used to describe the route to her Upper Foxville apartment.

Katrina didn't seem to mind at all; she was just happy to see him, her hands said, moving as graceful in speech as the whole of her did when she danced.

You didn't bring your guitar, she signed.

"I've been playing it all day. I thought I'd leave it at home."

Your voice . . . your music. They are a gift.

"Yeah, well . . ."

He looked around the loft, recognizing a couple of the posters from having seen them around town before, pasted on subway walls or stuck in amongst the clutter of dozens of other ads in the front of restaurants and record stores. He'd never gone to any of the shows. Dance wasn't his thing, especially not modern dance or the performance art that Lucia was into. He'd seen a show of hers once. She'd spent fifteen minutes rolling back and forth across the stage, wrapped head to toe in old brown paper shopping bags to a sound-track that consisted of water dripping for its rhythm, the hypnotic drone only occasionally broken by the sound of footsteps walking through broken glass.

Definitely not his thing.

Lucia was not his idea of what being creative was all about. In his head, he filed her type of artist under the general heading of lunatic fringe. Happily, she was out for the day.

"So," he said, "do you want to head out to the island?"

Katrina nodded. *But not just yet,* her hands added.

She smiled at him, long hair clouding down her back. She was wearing clothes borrowed from Lucia—cotton pants a touch too big and tied closed with a scarf through the belt loops, a T-shirt advertising a band that he'd never heard of and the same black Chinese slippers she'd been wearing last night.

"So what do you want—" he began.

Katrina took his hands before he could finish and placed them on her breasts. They were small and firm against his palms, her heartbeat echoing through the thin fabric, fluttering against his skin. Her own hands dropped to his groin, one gently cupping him through his jeans, the other pulling down the zipper.

She was gentle and loving, each motion innocent of artifice and certainly welcome, but she'd caught Matt off-guard.

"Look," he said, "are you sure you . . . ?"

She raised a hand, laying a finger against his lips. No words. Just touch. He grew hard, his penis uncomfortably bent in the confines of his jeans until she popped the top button and pulled it out. She put her small hand around it, fingers tight, hand moving slowly up and down. Speaking without words, her emotions laid bare before him.

Matt took his hands from her breasts and lifted the T-shirt over her head. He let it drop behind her as he enfolded her in an embrace. She was like liquid against him, a shimmer of movement and soft touches.

No words, he thought.

She was right. There was no need for words.

He let her lead him into Lucia's bedroom.

Afterwards, he felt so still inside it was though the world had stopped moving, time stalled, no one left but the two of them, wrapped up together, here in the dusky shadows that licked across the bed. He raised himself up on one elbow and looked down at her.

She seemed to be made of light. An unearthly radiance lay upon her pale skin like an angelic nimbus, except he doubted that any angel in heaven knew how to give and accept pleasure as she did. Not unless heaven was a very different place from the one he'd heard about in Sunday school.

There was a look in her eyes that promised him everything—not just bodily pleasures, but heart and soul—and for a moment he wanted to open up to her, to give to her what he gave his music, but then he felt something close up thick inside him. He found himself remembering a parting conversation he'd had with another woman. Darlene Flatt, born Darlene Johnston. Belying her stage name, she was an extraordinarily well-endowed singer in one of the local country bands. Partial to slow-dancing on sawdusted floors, bolo ties, fringed jackets and, for the longest time, to him.

"You're just a hollow man," she told him finally. "A sham. The only place you're alive is on stage, but let me tell you something, Matt, the whole world's a stage if you'd just open your eyes and see."

Maybe in Shakespeare's day, he thought, but not now, not here, not in this world. Here you only get hurt.

"If you gave a fraction of your commitment to music to another person, you'd be . . ."

He didn't know what Darlene thought he'd be because he tuned her out. Stepped behind the wall and followed the intricate turns of a song he was working on at the time until she finally got up and left his apartment.

Got up and left.

He swung his feet to the floor and looked for his clothes. Katrina caught his arm.

What's wrong? she signed. *What have I done?*

"Nothing," he said. "It's not you. It's not anything. It's just . . . I've just got to go, okay?"

Please, she signed. *Just tell me . . .*

But he turned away so that he couldn't see her words. Got dressed. Paused in the doorway of the bedroom, choking on words that tried to slip through the wall. Turned finally, and left. The room. The apartment. Her, crying.

Lucia found Katrina when she came home later, red-eyed and sitting on the sofa in just a T-shirt, staring out the window, unable or unwilling to explain what was wrong. So Lucia thought the worst.

"That sonuvabitch," she started. "He never even showed up, did he? I should have warned you about what a prick he can be."

But Katrina's hands said, *No. It wasn't his fault. I want too much.*

"He was here?" Lucia asked.

She nodded.

"And you had a fight?"

The shrug that came in response said, sort of, and then Katrina began to cry again. Lucia enfolded her in her arms. It was small, cold comfort, she knew, for she'd had her own time in that lonely place in which Katrina now found herself, but it was all Lucia had to offer.

Matt found himself on the ferry, crossing from the city over to Wolf Island, as though, by doing so, he was completing some unfinished ritual to which neither he nor Katrina had quite set the parameters. He stood at the rail on the upper deck with the wind in his face and let the words to long-dead ballads run through his mind so that he wouldn't have to think about people, about relationships, about complications, about Katrina.

But in the dusking sky and in the wake that trailed behind the ferry, and later on the island, in the shadows that crept across the lawn and in the tangle that branches made against the sky, he could see only her face. Not all the words to all the songs he knew could free him from the burden of guilt that clung to him like burrs gathered on a sweater while crossing an autumn field.

He stopped at the statue of the little mermaid, and of course even she had Katrina's face.

"I didn't ask to start anything," he told the statue, saying now what he should have said in Lucia's bedroom. "So why the hell do I have to feel so guilty?"

It was the old story, he realized. Everything, everybody wanted to lay claim to a piece of your soul. And if they couldn't have it, they made you pay for it in guilt.

"I'm not a hollow man," he told the statue, saying what he should have said to Darlene. "I just don't have what you want me to give."

The statue just looked out across the lake. The dusk stretched for long impossible moments, then the sun dropped completely behind the horizon and the lamps lit up along the island's pathways. Matt turned and walked back to where the ferry waited to return him to Newford.

He didn't see Katrina again for two days.

I'm sorry, was the first thing she said to him, her hands moving quickly before he could speak.

He stood in the hallway leading into Lucia's apartment, late on a Wednesday afternoon, not even sure what he was doing here. Apologizing. Explaining. Maybe just trying to understand.

"It wasn't your fault," he said. "It's just . . . everything happened too fast."

She nodded. *Do you want to come in?*

Matt regarded her. She was barefoot, framed by the doorway. The light behind her turned the flowered dress she was wearing into gossamer, highlighting the shape of her body under it. Her hair was the colour of soft gold. He remembered her lying on the bed, radiant in the afterglow of their lovemaking.

"Could we go out instead?" he said. "Just for a walk or something?"

Let me get my shoes.

He took her to the lakefront and they walked the length of the boardwalk and the Pier, and then, when the jostle of the crowds became too much, they made their way down to the sand and sat near the shoreline. For the most part, his voice, her hands, were still. When they did talk, it was to make up stories about the more colorful characters with whom they shared the beach, both using their hands to speak so that they wouldn't be overheard, laughing as each tried to outdo the other with an outrageous background for one person or another.

Where did you learn sign language? she asked him at one point.

My cousin's deaf, he replied, his hands growing more deft, remembering old patterns, the longer they spoke. *Our parents were pretty close and we all saw a lot of each other, so everybody in the family learned.*

They had dinner at Kathryn's Cafe. Afterwards, they went to the Owlnight, another of Newford's folk clubs, but this one was on the Butler University campus itself, in the Student Center. Garve MacCauley was doing a solo act, just guitar and gravely voice, mostly his own material.

You're much better, Katrina signed to Matt after the first few songs.

"Just different," he said.

Katrina only smiled and shook her head.

After the last set, he took her back to Upper Foxville and left her at Lucia's door with a chaste kiss.

Thursday evening they took in a play at the Standish, a small concert hall that divided its evenings between repertory theatre and music concerts. Katrina was entranced. She'd never seen live actors before, but then there was so much she didn't know about this new world in which she found herself and still more that she hadn't experienced in his company.

It was just past eleven by the time they got back to the apartment. Lucia had gone out, so they could have the place to themselves but when Katrina invited Matt in, he begged off. His confused mumble of an explanation made little sense. All Katrina knew was that the days were slipping away. Saturday night, the lake witch's deadline, was blurring all too close, all too fast.

When he bent to kiss her on the forehead as he had the night before, she lifted her head so that their lips met. The kiss lasted a long time, a tangle of tongues. She pressed in close to him, hands stroking his back, but he pulled away with a confused panic fluttering in his eyes.

Why do I frighten you? she wanted to ask, but she had already guessed that it wasn't just her. It was any close relationship. Responsibility frightened him and perhaps more to the point, he just didn't love her. Maybe he would, given time, but by then it would be too late. Days went by quickly; hours were simply a rush, one tumbling into the other.

She gave him a sad smile and let him go, listened to his footsteps in the stairwell, then slowly went into the apartment and closed the door behind her. Each step she took, as it always did since she stepped onto the land, was like small knives cutting through her feet. She remembered the freedom of the waves, of movement without pain, but she had turned her back on scales and water. For better or worse, she belonged on the land now.

But that night her dreams were of foam. It gathered against the craggy shore near her home as the wind drove the lake water onto the rocks. Her sisters swam nearby, weeping.

Late Friday afternoon, Amy and Lucia were sitting on a bench in Fitzhenry Park, watching the traffic go by on Palm Street. They'd been to the Y to swim laps and they each nursed a coffee now, bought from one of the vendors in the little parade of carts that set up along the sidewalk first thing every morning. The sky was overcast, with the scent of rain in the air, but for all the weather report's warnings, it had held off all day.

"So how's Katrina doing?" Amy asked.

An expression that was more puzzlement than a frown touched Lucia's features. She took a sip of her coffee then set it down on the bench between them and took out her cigarettes.

"Well, they started off rocky on Sunday," she said. "He left her crying."

"God, so soon?"

"It's not as bad as it sounds," Lucia said.

She got her cigarette lit and blew out a wreath of smoke. Amy coughed.

"Sorry," Lucia said. She moved the cigarette away.

"It's not the smoke," Amy told her, lifting a hand to rub her throat. "I've had a tickle in my throat all day. I just hope I'm not coming down with something." She took a sip of her coffee and wished she had a throat lozenge. "So what did happen?" she asked.

"He didn't show up for a couple of days, didn't call—well, I guess he wouldn't want to speak to me, would he?—but then he's been real nice ever since he did show up on Wednesday. Took her to see your friend MacCauley over at the Owlnight, the next night they went to that production of Lizzie's play that's running at the Standish and earlier today they were out just mooching around town, I guess."

"He really needs someone," Amy said.

"I suppose. But knowing your history with him, I don't know if I wish him on Katrina."

"But at least they're doing things. He's *talking* to her."

"Yeah, but then he told her today that he's going to be away this weekend."

"That's right. He canceled Saturday morning band practice because he's got a gig at that little bar in Hartnett's Point. What's the problem with that? That's his job. She must know that."

Lucia shrugged. "I just think he should've taken her with him when he left this afternoon."

Amy sighed in sympathy. "Matt's not big on bringing his current belle to a gig. I remember how it used to really piss me off when we were going together."

"Well, she's heartbroken that he didn't ask her to come along. I told her she should just go anyway—show up and meet him there; I even offered to lend her the money for the bus—but she thinks he'd get mad."

"I don't know. He seemed to like her dancing when we played at Feeney's last weekend." Amy paused. "Of course he'll just be doing songs on his own. There won't be anything for her to dance to."

"She likes his songs, too," Lucia said.

Amy thought of the intensity with which Katrina had listened to Matt's singing that night at Feeney's and she knew exactly why Matt hadn't asked Katrina along to the gig.

"Maybe she likes them too much," she said. "Matt puts a lot into his music, and you know how bloody brilliant he is, but he's pretty humble about it all at the same time. He probably thinks it'd freak him too much having her sitting there just kind of—" her shoulders lifted and fell "—I don't know, swallowing the songs."

"Well, I wish he'd given it a try all the same. I've got to help Sharon with some set decorations, so Katrina's going to be on her own all night, just moping about the apartment. I asked her to come along, but she didn't want to go out."

"I could drop by your place," Amy said.

Lucia grinned. "I thought you'd never offer."

Amy punched her lightly on the arm. "You set me up!"

"Has she still got it or what?" Lucia asked, blowing on her fingernails.

Amy laughed and they went through a quick little flurry of slapping at each other's hands until they were too giddy to continue. They both leaned back on the park bench.

"I bet I'll have a better time," Amy said after a moment. "I've helped Sharon before. If she's got anything organized at all, it'll only be because someone else did it."

Lucia nodded glumly. "Don't I know it."

Amy went home to change and have a bite to eat before she took the subway north to Upper Foxville. Looking in the mirror as she put on her makeup, she saw that she was looking awfully pale. Thinking about feeling sick made her throat tickle again and she coughed. She stopped for some lozenges at a drug store that was on her way. They helped her throat, but she felt a little light-headed now.

She should just go home, she thought, but she'd promised Lucia and she couldn't help but be sympathetic towards Katrina. She'd just stay a little while, that was all.

It was just going on nightfall when she reached Lucia's street. She paused at the corner, as she saw a small familiar figure step from the stoop of Lucia's building and head off the other way down the street.

She almost called Katrina by name, but something stopped her. Curiosity got the better of her and she kept still, following along behind instead.

It was easy to keep track of her—Katrina's cloud of gold hair caught the light of every streetlamp she passed under and seemed to reflect a burnished glow up into the night. She led Amy down to MacNeil Street, turning west once she reached it. Her stride was both purposeful and wearied, but always graceful.

Poor kid, Amy thought.

More than once she started to hurry to catch up with Katrina, but then her curiosity would rise to the fore and she'd tell herself to be patient just a little longer. Since Katrina didn't know anyone in Newford—according to Lucia she didn't even know the city—Amy couldn't figure out where Katrina might be going.

Where MacNeil ended at Lee Street, Katrina crossed over and went down to the bank of the Kickaha River. She followed the riverbank southward, pausing only when she came near the Gracie Street Bridge. There the fenced-off ruins of the old L & B sawmill reared up in the darkness, ill-lit, drowning the riverbank with its shadow. It took up enough room that a person walking along the river by its chain-link fence would be almost invisible from any of the more peopled areas roundabout. Even across the river there were only empty warehouses.

Amy started to hurry again, struck by the sudden fear that Katrina meant to do herself harm. The river ran quicker here, rapiding over a descending shelf of broken stone slabs from where an old railway bridge had collapsed a few years ago. The city had cleared a channel through the debris, but that just made the river run more quickly through the narrower course. More than one person had drowned on this stretch of water—and not always by accident.

Matt's not worth it, she wanted to tell Katrina. Nobody's worth it.

Before she could reach Katrina, she came to an abrupt halt again. She stifled a cough that reared up in her throat and leaned against a fence post, suddenly dizzy. But it wasn't the escalating onset of a flu bug that had made her stop. Rather it was what she had spied, bobbing in the swift-moving water.

The light was bad, just a diffused glow from the streets a block or so over, but it was enough for her to make out four white shapes in the dark water. They each seemed as slender and graceful as Katrina, with the same spun gold hair, except theirs was cut short to their skulls, highlighting the fox-like shape of their features. They probably had, Amy thought, the same blue eyes, too.

What were they *doing* there?

Another wave of dizziness came over her. She slid down the side of the fence pole until she was crouched on the ground. She remembered thinking that this way she wouldn't have as far to fall if she fainted. Clutching the pole for support, she looked back to the river.

Katrina had moved closer to the shore and was holding her arms out to the women. As their shapes moved closer, Amy's heartbeat drummed into overtime for she realized that they had no legs. They were propelling themselves through the water with scaled fish tails. There was no mistaking the shape of them as the long tail fins broke the surface of the water.

Mermaids, Amy thought, no longer able to breathe. They were mermaids.

It wasn't possible. *How* could it be possible?

And what did it make Katrina?

The sight of them blurred. For a moment she was looking through a veil, then it was like looking through a double-paned window at an angle, images all duplicated and laid over each other.

She blinked hard. She started to lift her hand to rub at her eyes, but she was suddenly so weak it was all she could do to just crouch beside the pole and not tumble over into the weeds.

The women in the river drew closer as Katrina stepped to the very edge of the water. Katrina lifted her hair, then let it drop in a clouding fall. She pointed at the women.

"Cut away and gone," one of the women said.

"All gone."

"We gave it to Maraghreen."

"For you, sister."

"We traded, gold for silver."

Amy pressed her face against the pole as the mermaids spoke. Through her dizziness, their voices seemed preternaturally enhanced. They chorused, one beginning where another ended, words molten, bell-like, sweet as honey, and so very, very pure.

"She gave us this."

The foremost of the women in the river reached up out of the water. Something glimmered silver and bright in her hand. A knife.

"Pierce his heart."

"Bathe in his blood."

"Your legs will grow together once more."

"You'll come back to us."

"Oh, sister."

Katrina went down on her knees at the water's edge. She took the knife from the mermaid's hand and laid it gingerly on her lap.

"He doesn't love you."

"He will never love you."

The women all drew close. They reached out of the water, stroking Katrina's arms and her face with gentling hands.

"You must do it—before the first dawn light follows tomorrow night."

"Or foam you'll be."

"Sister, please."

"Return to those who love you."

Katrina bowed her head, making no response. One by one the women dove into the river deeps and were gone. From her hiding place, Amy tried to rise—she knew Katrina would be coming back soon, coming back this way, and she didn't want to be caught—but she couldn't manage it, even with the help of the pole beside her. Then Katrina stepped away from the river and walked towards her, the knife held gingerly in one hand.

As their gazes met, another wave of dizziness rose in Amy, this one a tsunami, and in its wake she felt the ground tremble underfoot, but it was only herself, tumbling into the dirt and weeds. She closed her eyes and let the darkness take her away.

It was late afternoon when Amy awoke on the sofa in Lucia's loft. Her surroundings and the wrong angle of the afternoon light left her disoriented and confused, but no longer feeling sick. It must have been one of those 24-hour viruses, she thought as she swung her legs to the floor, then leaned back against the sofa's cushions.

Lucia looked up from the magazine she was reading at the kitchen table. Laying it down she walked over and joined Amy on the sofa.

"I was *très* surprised to find you sleeping here when I got in last night," she said. "Katrina said you got sick, so she put you to bed on the sofa and slept on the floor herself. How're you feeling now, *ma cherie?*"

Amy worked through what Lucia had just said. None of it quite jibed with her own muddled memory of the previous evening.

"Okay . . . I guess," she said finally. She looked around the loft. "Where's Katrina?"

"She borrowed the bus money from me and went to Hartnett's Point after all. True love wins over all, *n'est-ce pas?*"

Amy thought of mermaids swimming in the Kickaha River, of Katrina kneeling by the water, of the silver knife.

"Oh, shit," she said.

"What's the matter?"

"I . . ."

Amy didn't know what to say. What she'd seen hadn't made any sense. She'd been sick, dizzy, probably delirious. But it had seemed so real.

Pierce his heart . . . bathe in his blood. . . .

She shook her head. None of it could have happened. There were no such things as mermaids. But what if there were? What if Katrina was carrying that silver knife as she made her way to Matt's gig? What if she did just what those . . . mermaids had told her . . .

You must do it—before the first dawn light that follows tomorrow night. . . .

What if—

Or foam you'll be . . .

—it was real?

She bent down and looked for her shoes, found them pressed up against one of the coffee table's crate supports. She put them on and rose from the sofa.

"I've got to go," she told Lucia.

"Go where? What's going on?"

"I don't know. I don't have time to explain. I'll tell you later."

Lucia followed her across the loft to the door. "Amy, you're acting really weird."

"I'm fine," Amy said. "Honest."

Though she still didn't feel quite normal. She was weak and didn't want to look in a mirror for fear of seeing the white ghost of her own

face looking back at her. But she didn't feel that she had any choice.
If what she'd seen last night *had* been real . . .

Lucia shook her head uncertainly. "Are you sure you're—"

Amy paused long enough to give her friend a quick peck on the
cheek, then she was out the door.

Borrowing a car was easy. Her brother Pete had two and was used
to her sudden requests for transportational needs, relieved that he
wasn't required to provide a chauffeur service along with it. She was
on the road by seven, tooling west along the old lakeside highway
in a gas-guzzling Chev, stopping for a meal at a truck stop that
marked the halfway point and arriving at Harnett's Point just as Matt
would be starting his first set.

She pulled in beside his VW van—a positive antique by now, she
liked to tease him—and parked. The building that housed Murphy's
Bar where Matt had his gig was a ramshackle affair, log walls here
in back, plaster on cement walls in front. The bar sat on the edge of
the point from which the village got its name, with a long pier out
behind the building, running into the lake. The water around the
pier was thick with moored boats.

She went around front to where the neon sign spelling the name
of the bar crackled and spat an orange glow and stepped inside to the
familiar sound of Matt singing Leon Rosselson's "World Turned
Upside Down." The audience, surprisingly enough for a backwoods
establishment such as this, was actually paying attention to the music.
Amy thought that only a third of them were probably even aware
of the socialist message the song espoused.

The patrons were evenly divided between the back-to-the-earth
hippies who tended organic farms west of the village, all jeans and
unbleached cotton, long hair and flower-print dresses; the locals
who'd grown up in the area and would probably die here, heavier
drinkers, also in jeans, but tending towards flannel shirts and baseball
caps, T-shirts and workboots; and then those cottagers who hadn't
yet closed their places up for the year, a hodgepodge of golf shirts
and cotton blends, short skirts and, yes, even one dark blue captain's
cap, complete with braided rope trim.

She shaded her eyes and looked for Katrina, but didn't spot her.
After a few moments, she got herself a beer from the bar and found

a corner table to sit at that she shared with a pair of earth-mothers and a tall skinny man with drooping eyes and hair longer than that of either of his companions, pulled back into a ponytail that fell to his waist. They made introductions all around, then settled back into their chairs to listen to the music.

As Matt's set wound on, Amy began to wonder just exactly what it was that she was doing here. Even closing her eyes and concentrating, she could barely call up last night's fantastic images with any sort of clarity. What if the whole thing *had* just been a delirium? What if she'd made her way to Lucia's apartment only to pass out on the sofa and have dreamt it all?

Matt stopped by the table when he ended his set.

"What brings you up here, Scallan?" he asked.

She shrugged. "Just thought I'd check out how you do without the rest of us to keep you honest."

A touch of humor crinkled around his eyes. "So what's the verdict?"

"You're doing good." She introduced him to her companions, then asked, "Do you want to get a little air?"

He nodded and let her lead the way outside. They leaned against the back of somebody's Bronco up and looked down the length of one of the village's two streets. This one cut north and south, from the bush down to the lake. The other was merely the highway as it cut through the village.

"So have you seen Katrina?" Amy asked.

Matt nodded. "Yeah, we walked around the Market for awhile yesterday afternoon."

"You mean, she's not up here?"

"Not so's I know."

Amy sighed. So much for her worries. But if Katrina hadn't borrowed the money from Lucia to come up here, then where *had* she gone?

"Why are you so concerned about Katrina?" Matt asked.

Amy started to make up some excuse, but then thought, screw it. One of them might as well be up front.

"I'm just worried about her."

Matt nodded. He kicked at the gravel underfoot, but didn't say anything.

"I know it's none of my business," Amy said.

"You're right. It's not." There was no rancor in Matt's voice. Just a kind of weariness.

"It's just that—"

"Look," he said, turning to Amy, "she seems nice, that's all. I think maybe we started out on the wrong foot, but I'm trying to fix that. For now, I just want to be her friend. If something else comes up later, okay. But I want to take it as it comes. Slowly. Is that so wrong?"

Amy shook her head. And then it struck her. For the first time that they weren't on stage together, or working out an arrangement, Matt actually seemed to focus on her. To listen to what she was saying, and answer honestly. Protective walls maybe not completely down, but there *was* a little breach in them.

"I think she loves you," Amy said.

Matt sighed. "It's kind of early for that—don't you think? I think it's more a kind of infatuation. She'll probably grow out of it just as fast as she fell into it."

"I don't know about that. Seems to me that if you're going to be at all fair, you'd be just a little bit more—"

"Don't talk to me about responsibility," Matt said, breaking in. "Just because someone falls in love with you, it doesn't mean you owe them anything. I've got no control over how other people feel about me—"

That's where you're wrong, Amy thought. If you'd just act more human, more like this . . .

"—and I'm sure not going to run my life by their feelings and schedules. I'm not trying to sound self-centered, I'm just trying to . . . I don't know. Protect my privacy."

"But if you don't give a little, how will you ever know what you might be missing?"

"Giving too much, too fast—that just leaves you open to being hurt."

"But—"

"Oh, shit," Matt said, glancing at his watch. "I've got another set to do." He pushed away from the Bronco. "Look, I'm sorry if I don't measure up to how people want me to be, but this is just the way I am."

Why didn't you open yourself up even this much while we were going out together? Amy wanted to ask. But all she did was nod and say, "I know."

"Are you coming in?"

She shook her head. "Not right away."

"Well, I've got—"

"I know." She waved him off. "Break a leg or whatever."

She moved away from the Bronco once he'd gone inside and crossed the parking lot, gravel crunching underfoot until she reached the grass verge. She followed it around to the lawn by the side of the building and down to the lakefront. There she stood, listening to the vague sound of Matt's voice and guitar as it carried through an open window. She looked at all the boats clustered around the pier. A splash drew her attention to the far end of the wooden walkway where a figure sat with its back to the shore having just thrown something into the lake.

Amy had one of those moments of utter clarity. She knew immediately that it was Katrina sitting there, feet dangling in the water, long hair clouding down her back, knew as well that it was the silver knife she'd thrown into the lake. Amy could almost see it, turning end on slow end as it sank in the water.

She hesitated for the space of a few long breaths, gaze tracking the surface of the lake for Katrina's sisters, then she slowly made her way down to the pier. Katrina turned at the sound of Amy's shoes on the wooden slats of the walkway. She nodded once, then looked back out over the lake.

Amy sat beside her. She hesitated again, then put her arm comfortingly around Katrina's small shoulders. They sat like that for a long time. The water lapped against the pilings below them. An owl called out from the woods to their left, a long mournful sound. A truck pulled into the bar's parking lot. Car doors slammed, voices rose in laughter, then disappeared into the bar.

Katrina stirred beside Amy. She began to move her hands, but Amy shook her head.

"I'm sorry," she said. "I can't understand what you're saying."

Katrina mimed steering, both hands raised up in front of her, fingers closed around an invisible steering wheel.

Amy nodded. "I drove up in my brother's car."

Katrina pointed to herself then to Amy and again mimed turning a steering wheel.

"You want me to drive you somewhere?"

Katrina nodded.

Amy looked back towards the bar. "What about Matt?"

Katrina shook her head. She put her hands together, eyes eloquent where her voice was silent. Please.

Amy looked at her for a long moment, then she slowly nodded. "Sure. I can give you a lift. Is there someplace specific you want to go?"

Katrina merely rose to her feet and started back down the pier towards shore. Once they were in the Chev, she pointed to the glove department.

"Go ahead," Amy said.

As she started the car, Katrina pulled out a handful of roadmaps. She sorted through them until she came to one that showed the whole north shore of the lake. She unfolded it and laid it on the dashboard between them and pointed to a spot west of Newford. Amy looked more closely. The place where Katrina had her finger was where the Dulfer River emptied into the lake. The tip of her small finger was placed directly on the lakeside campgrounds of the State Park there.

"Jesus," Amy said. "It'll take us all night to get there. We'll be lucky to make it before dawn."

As Katrina shrugged, Amy remembered what Katrina's sisters had said last night.

Before the first dawn light follows tomorrow night.

That was tonight. *This* morning.

Or foam you'll be.

She shivered and looked at Katrina.

"Tell me what's going on," she said. "Please, Katrina. Maybe I can help you."

Katrina just shook her head sadly. She mimed driving, hands around the invisible steering wheel again.

Amy sighed. She put the car in gear and pulled out of the parking lot. Katrina reached towards the radio, eyebrows raised quizzically. When Amy nodded, she turned it on and slowly wound through the stations until she got Newford's WKPN–FM. It was too early for

Zoe B.'s "Nightnoise" show, so they listened to Mariah Carey, the Vaughan Brothers and the like as they followed the highway east.

Neither of them spoke as they drove; Katrina couldn't and Amy was just too depressed. She didn't know what was going on. She just felt as though she'd become trapped in a Greek tragedy. The story-line was already written, everything was predestined to a certain outcome and there was nothing she could do about it. Only Matt could have, if he'd loved Katrina, but she couldn't even blame him. You couldn't force a person to love somebody.

She didn't agree with his need to protect his privacy. Maybe it stopped him from being hurt, but it also stopped him from being alive. But he was right about one thing: he couldn't be held responsible for who chose to love him.

They crossed over the Dulfer River just as dawn was starting to pink the eastern horizon. When Amy pulled into the campgrounds, Katrina directed her down a narrow dirt road that led to the park's boat launch.

They had the place to themselves. Amy pulled up by the water and killed the engine. The pines stood silent around them when they got out of the car. There was birdsong, but it seemed strangely muted. Distant. As though heard through gauze.

Katrina lifted a hand and touched Amy's cheek, then walked towards the water. She headed to the left of the launching area where a series of broad flat rocks staircased down into the water. After a moment's hesitation, Amy followed after. She sat down beside Katrina, who was right by the edge of the water, arms wrapped around her knees.

"Katrina," she began. "Please tell me what's going on. I—"

She fussed in her purse, looking for pen and paper. She found the former, and pulled out her checkbook to use the back of a check as a writing surface.

"I want to help," she said, holding the pen and checkbook out to her companion.

Katrina regarded her for a long moment, a helpless look in her eyes, but finally she took the proffered items. She began to write on the back of one of the checks, but before she could hand it back to

Amy, a wind rose up. The pine trees shivered, needles whispering against each other.

An electric tingle sparked across every inch of Amy's skin. The hairs at the nape of her neck prickled and goosebumps traveled up her arms. It was like that moment before a storm broke, when the air is so charged with ions that it seems anything might happen.

"What . . . ?" she began.

Her voice died in her throat as the air around them thickened. Shapes formed in the air, pale diffused airy shapes, slender and transparent. Their voices were like the sound of the wind in the pines.

"Come with us," they said, beckoning to Katrina.

"Be one with us."

"We can give you what you lack."

Katrina stared at the misty apparitions for the longest time. Then she let pen and checkbook fall to the rock and stood up, stretching her arms towards the airy figures. Her own body began to lose its definition. She was a spiderweb in the shape of a woman, gossamer, smoke and mist. Her clothing fell from her transparent form to fall into a tangle beside Amy.

And then she was gone. The wind died. The whisper stilled in the pines.

Amy stared open-mouthed at where Katrina had disappeared. All that lay on the rock were Katrina's clothes, the pen and the checkbook. Amy reached out towards the clothes. They were damp to the touch.

Or foam you'll be.

Amy looked up into the lightning sky. But Katrina hadn't just turned to foam, had she? Something had come and taken her away before that happened. If any of this had even been real at all. If she hadn't just lost it completely.

She heard weeping and lowered her gaze to the surface of the lake. There were four women's heads there, bobbing in the unruly water. Their hair was short, cropped close to their heads, untidily, as though cut with garden shears or a knife. Their eyes were red with tears. Each could have been Katrina's twin.

Seeing her gaze upon them, they sank beneath the waves, one by one, and then Amy was alone again. She swallowed thickly, then picked up her checkbook to read what Katrina had written before what could only have been angels came to take her away:

"Is this what having a soul means, to know such bittersweet pain? But still, I cherish the time I had. Those who live forever, who have no stake in the dance of death's inevitable approach, can never understand the sanctity of life."

It sounded stiff, like a quote, but then Amy realized she'd never heard how Katrina would speak, not the cadence of her voice, nor its timbre, nor her diction.

And now she never would.

The next day, Matt found Amy where her brother Pete said she was going. She was by the statue of the little mermaid on Wolf Island, just sitting on a bench and staring out at the lake. She looked haggard from a lack of sleep.

"What happened to you last night?" he asked.

She shrugged. "I decided to go for a drive."

Matt nodded as though he understood, though he didn't pretend to have a clue. The complexities that made up people's personalities were forever a mystery to him.

He sat down beside her.

"Have you seen Katrina?" he asked. "I went by Lucia's place looking for her, but she was acting all weird—" not unusual for Lucia, he added to himself "—and told me I should ask you."

"She's gone," Amy said. "Maybe back into the lake, maybe into the sky. I'm not really sure."

Matt just looked at her. "Come again?" he said finally.

So Amy told him about it all, of what she'd seen two nights ago by the old L & N sawmill, of what had happened last night.

"It's like in that legend about the little mermaid," she said as she finished up. She glanced at the statue beside them. "The real legend—not what you'd find in some kid's picturebook."

Matt shook his head. " 'The Little Mermaid' isn't a legend," he said. "It's just a story, made up by Hans Christian Andersen, like 'The Emperor's New Clothes' and 'The Ugly Duckling.' They sure as hell aren't real."

"I'm just telling you what I saw."

"Jesus, Amy. Will you listen to yourself?"

When she turned to face him, he saw real anguish in her features.

"I can't help it," she said. "It really happened."

Matt started to argue, but then he shook his head. He didn't know what had gotten into Amy to go on like this. He expected this kind of thing from Geordie's brother who made his living gussying up fantastical stories from nothing, but Amy?

"It looks like her, doesn't it?" Amy said.

Matt followed her gaze to the statue. He remembered the last time he'd been on the island, the night when he'd walked out on Katrina, when everything had looked like her. He got up from the bench and stepped closer. The statue's bronze features gleamed in the sunlight.

"Yeah," he said. "I guess it does."

Then he walked away.

He was pissed off with Amy for going on the way she had and brooded about her stupid story all the way back to the city. He had a copy of the Andersen Fairy Tales at home. When he got back to his apartment, he took it down from the shelf and read the story again.

"Aw, shit," he said as he closed the book.

It was just a story. Katrina would turn up. They'd all share a laugh at how Amy was having him on.

But Katrina didn't turn up. Not that day, nor the next, nor by the end of the week. She'd vanished from his life as mysteriously as she'd come into it.

That's why I don't want to get involved with people, he wanted to tell Amy. Because they just walk out of your life if you don't do what they want you to do.

No way it had happened as Amy had said it did. But he found himself wondering about what it would be like to be without a soul, wondering if he even had one.

Friday of that week, he found himself back on the island, standing by the statue once again. There were a couple of tattered silk flowers on the stone at its base. He stared at the mermaid's features for a long time, then he went home and started to phone the members of Marrowbones.

★ ★ ★

"Well, I kind of thought this was coming," Amy said when he called to tell her that he was breaking up the band, "except I thought it'd be Johnny or Nicky quitting."

She was sitting in the windowseat of her apartment's bay window, back against one side, feet propped up against the other. She was feeling better than she had when she'd seen him on Sunday, but there was still a strangeness inside her. A lost feeling, a sense of the world having shifted underfoot and the rules being all changed.

"So what're you going to do?" she added when he didn't respond.

"Hit the road for awhile."

"Gigging, or just traveling?"

"Little of both, I guess."

There was another long pause and Amy wondered if he was waiting for her to ask if she could come. But she was really over him now. Had been for a long time. She wasn't looking to be anybody's psychiatrist, or mother. Or matchmaker.

"Well, see you then," he said.

"Bon voyage," Amy said.

She cradled the phone. She thought of how he had talked with her the other night up at Hartnett's Point, opening up, actually *relating* to her. And now . . . She realized that the whole business with Katrina had just wound him up tighter than ever before.

Well, somebody else was going to have to work on those walls and she knew who it had to be. A guy named Matt Casey.

She looked out the window again.

"Good luck," she said.

Matt was gone for a year. When he came back, the first place he went to was Wolf Island. He stood out by the statue for a long time, not saying anything, just trying to sort out why he was here. He didn't have much luck, not that year, nor each subsequent year that he came. Finally, almost a decade after Katrina was gone—walked out of his life, turned into a puddle of lake water, went sailing through the air with angels, whatever—he decided to stay overnight, as though being alone in the dark would reveal something that was hidden from the day.

"Lady," he said, standing in front of the statue, drowned in the thick silence of the night.

He hadn't brought an offering for the statue—Our Lady of the Harbour, as the baglady had called her. He was just here, looking for something that remained forever out of reach. He wasn't trying to understand Katrina or the story that Amy had told of her. Not anymore.

"Why am I so empty inside?" he asked.

"I can't believe you're going to play with him again," Lucia said when Amy told her about her new band, Johnny Jump Up.

Amy shrugged. "It'll just be the three of us—Geordie's going to be playing fiddle."

"But he hasn't changed at all. He's still so—cold."

"Not on stage."

"I suppose not," Lucia said. "I guess all he's got going for him is his music."

Amy nodded sadly.

"I know," she said.

≋ PAPERJACK ≋

Churches aren't havens of spiritual enlightenment; they enclose the spirit. The way Jilly explains it, organizing Mystery tends to undermine its essence. I'm not so sure I agree, but then I don't really know enough about it. When it comes to things that can't be logically explained, I take a step back and leave them to Jilly or my brother Christy—they thrive on that kind of thing. If I had to describe myself as belonging to any church or mystical order, it'd be one devoted to secular humanism. My concerns are for real people and the here and now; the possible existence of God, faeries, or some metaphysical Otherworld just doesn't fit into my worldview.

Except . . .

You knew there'd be an "except," didn't you, or else why would I be writing this down?

It's not like I don't have anything to say. I'm all for creative expression, but my medium's music. I'm not an artist like Jilly, or a writer like Christy. But the kinds of things that have been happening to me can't really be expressed in a fiddle tune—no, that's not entirely true. I can express them, but the medium is such I can't be assured that, when I'm playing, listeners hear what I mean them to hear.

That's how it works with instrumental music, and it's probably why the best of it is so enduring: the listener takes away whatever he or she wants from it. Say the composer was trying to tell us about the aftermath of some great battle. When we hear it, the music might speak to us of a parent we've lost, a friend's struggle with some debilitating disease, a doe standing at the edge of a forest at twilight, or any of a thousand other unrelated things.

Realistic art like Jilly does—or at least it's realistically rendered; her subject matter's right out of some urban update of those Andrew Lang color-coded fairy tale books that most of us read when we were kids—and the collections of urban legends and stories that my brother writes don't have that same leeway. What goes down on the canvas or on paper, no matter how skillfully drawn or written, doesn't allow for much in the way of an alternate interpretation. So that's why I'm writing this down: to lay it all out in black and white where maybe I can understand it myself.

For the past week, every afternoon after busking up by the Williamson Street Mall for the lunchtime crowds, I've packed up my fiddle case and headed across town to come here to St. Paul's Cathedral. Once I get here, I sit on the steps about halfway up, take out this notebook, and try to write. The trouble is, I haven't been able to figure out where to start.

I like it out here on the steps. I've played inside the cathedral—just once, for a friend's wedding. The wedding was okay, but I remember coming in on my own to test the acoustics an hour or so before the rehearsal; ever since then I've been a little unsure about how Jilly views this kind of place. My fiddling didn't feel enclosed. Instead the walls seemed to open the music right up; the cathedral gave the reel I was playing a stately grace—a spiritual grace—that it had never held for me before. I suppose it had more to do with the architect's design than the presence of God, still I could've played there all night only—

But I'm rambling again. I've filled a couple of pages now, which is more than I've done all week, except after just rereading what I've written so far, I don't know if any of it's relevant.

Maybe I should just tell you about Paperjack. I don't know that it starts with him exactly, but it's probably as good a place as any to begin.

It was a glorious day, made all the more precious because the weather had been so weird that spring. One day I'd be bundled up in a jacket and scarf, cloth cap on my head, with fingerless gloves to keep the cold from my finger joints while I was out busking, the next I'd be in a T-shirt, breaking into a sweat just thinking about standing out on some street corner to play tunes.

There wasn't a cloud in the sky, the sun was halfway home from noon to the western horizon, and Jilly and I were just soaking up the rays on the steps of St. Paul's. I was slouched on the steps, leaning on one elbow, my fiddlecase propped up beside me, wishing I had worn shorts because my jeans felt like leaden weights on my legs. Sitting beside me, perched like a cat about to pounce on something terribly interesting that only it could see, Jilly was her usual scruffy self. There were flecks of paint on her loose cotton pants and her short-sleeved blouse, more under her fingernails, and still more half-lost in the tangles of her hair. She turned to look at me, her face miraculously untouched by her morning's work, and gave me one of her patented smiles.

"Did you ever wonder where he's from?" Jilly asked.

That was one of her favorite phrases: "Did you ever wonder . . . ?" It could take you from considering if and when fish slept, or why people look up when they're thinking, to more arcane questions about ghosts, little people living behind wallboards, and the like. And she loved guessing about people's origins. Sometimes when I was busking she'd tag along and sit by the wall at my back, sketching the people who were listening to me play. Invariably, she'd come up behind me and whisper in my ear—usually when I was in the middle of a complicated tune that needed all my attention—something along the lines of, "The guy in the polyester suit? Ten to one he rides a big chopper on the weekends, complete with a jean vest."

So I was used to it.

Today she wasn't picking out some nameless stranger from a crowd. Instead her attention was on Paperjack, sitting on the steps far enough below us that he couldn't hear what we were saying.

Paperjack had the darkest skin I'd ever seen on a man—an amazing ebony that seemed to swallow light. He was in his mid-sixties, I'd guess, short corkscrew hair all gone grey. The dark suits he wore were threadbare and out of fashion, but always clean. Under his suit jacket he usually wore a white T-shirt that flashed so brightly in the sun it almost hurt your eyes—just like his teeth did when he gave you that lopsided grin of his.

Nobody knew his real name and he never talked. I don't know if he was mute, or if he just didn't have anything to say, but the only sounds I ever heard him make were a chuckle or a laugh. People started calling him Paperjack because he worked an origami gig on the streets.

He was a master at folding paper into shapes. He kept a bag of different colored paper by his knee; people would pick their color and then tell him what they wanted, and he'd make it—no cuts, just folding. And he could make anything. From simple flower and animal shapes to things so complex it didn't seem possible for him to capture their essence in a piece of folded paper. So far as I know, he'd never disappointed a single customer.

I'd seen some of the old men come down from Little Japan to sit and watch him work. They called him *sensei,* a term of respect that they didn't exactly bandy around.

But origami was only the most visible side of his gig. He also told fortunes. He had one of those little folded paper Chinese fortune-telling devices that we all played around with when we were kids. You know the kind: you fold the corners in to the center, turn it over, then fold them in again. When you're done you can stick your index fingers and thumbs inside the little flaps of the folds and open it up so that it looks like a flower. You move your fingers back and forth, and it looks like the flower's talking to you.

Paperjack's fortune-teller was just like that. It had the names of four colors on the outside and eight different numbers inside. First you picked a color—say, red. The fortune-teller would seem to talk soundlessly as his fingers moved back and forth to spell the word, R-E-D, opening and closing until there'd be a choice from four of the numbers. Then you picked a number, and he counted it out until the fortune-teller was open with another or the same set of numbers revealed. Under the number you choose at that point was your fortune.

Paperjack didn't read it out—he just showed it to the person, then stowed the fortune-teller back into the inside pocket of his jacket from which he'd taken it earlier. I'd never had my fortune read by him, but Jilly'd had it done for her a whole bunch of times.

"The fortunes are always different," she told me once. "I sat behind him while he was doing one for a customer, and I read the fortune over her shoulder. When she'd paid him, I got mine done. I picked the same number she did, but when he opened it, there was a different fortune there."

"He's just got more than one of those paper fortune-tellers in his pocket," I said, but she shook her head.

"He never put it away," she said. "It was the same fortune-teller, the same number, but some time between the woman's reading and mine, it changed."

I knew there could be any number of logical explanations for how that could have happened, starting with plain sleight of hand, but I'd long ago given up continuing arguments with Jilly when it comes to that kind of thing.

Was Paperjack magic? Not in my book, at least not the way Jilly thought he was. But there was a magic about him, the magic that always hangs like an aura about someone who's as good an artist as Paperjack was. He also made me feel good. Around him, an overcast day didn't seem half so gloomy, and when the sun shone, it always seemed brighter. He just exuded a glad feeling that you couldn't help but pick up on. So in that sense, he was magic.

I'd also wondered where he'd come from, how he'd ended up on the street. Street people seemed pretty well evenly divided between those who had no choice but to be there, and those who chose to live there like I do. But even then there's a difference. I had a little apartment not far from Jilly's. I could get a job when I wanted one, usually in the winter when the busking was bad and club gigs were slow.

Not many street people have that choice, but I thought that Paperjack might be one of them.

"He's such an interesting guy," Jilly was saying.

I nodded.

"But I'm worried about him," she went on.

"How so?"

Jilly's brow wrinkled with a frown. "He seems to be getting thinner, and he doesn't get around as easily as he once did. You weren't here when he showed up today—he walked as though gravity had suddenly doubled its pull on him."

"Well, he's an old guy, Jilly."

"That's exactly it. Where does he live? Does he have someone to look out for him?"

That was Jilly for you. She had a heart as big as the city, with room in it for everyone and everything. She was forever taking in strays, be they dogs, cats, or people.

I'd been one of her strays once, but that was a long time ago.

"Maybe we should ask him," I said.

"He can't talk," she reminded me.

"Maybe he just doesn't *want* to talk."

Jilly shook her head. "I've tried a zillion times. He hears what I'm saying, and somehow he manages to answer with a smile or a raised eyebrow or whatever, but he doesn't talk." The wrinkles in her brow deepened until I wanted to reach over and smooth them out. "These days," she added, "he seems haunted to me."

If someone else had said that, I'd know that they meant Paperjack had something troubling him. With Jilly though, you often had to take that kind of a statement literally.

"Are we talking ghosts now?" I asked.

I tried to keep the skepticism out of my voice, but from the flash of disappointment that touched Jilly's eyes, I knew I hadn't done a very good job.

"Oh, Geordie," she said. "Why can't you just *believe* what happened to us?"

Here's one version of what happened that night, some three years ago now, to which Jilly was referring:

We saw a ghost. He stepped out of the past on a rainy night and stole away the woman I loved. At least that's the way I remember it. Except for Jilly, no one else does.

Her name was Samantha Rey. She worked at Gypsy Records and had an apartment on Stanton Street, except after that night, when the past came up to steal her away, no one at Gypsy Records remembered her anymore, and the landlady of her Stanton Street apartment had never heard of her. The ghost hadn't just stolen her, he'd stolen all memory of her existence.

All I had left of her was an old photograph that Jilly and I found in Moore's Antiques a little while later. It had a photographer's date on the back: 1912. It was Sam in the picture, Sam with a group of strangers standing on the front porch of some old house.

I remembered her, but she'd never existed. That's what I had to believe. Because nothing else made sense. I had all these feelings and memories of her, but they had to be what my brother called *jamais vu.* That's like *déjà vu,* except instead of having felt you'd been somewhere before, you remembered something that had never happened. I'd never heard the expression before—he got it from a

David Morrell thriller that he'd been reading—but it had an authentic ring about it.

Jamais vu.

But Jilly remembered Sam, too.

Thinking about Sam always brought a tightness to my chest; it made my head hurt trying to figure it out. I felt as if I were betraying Sam by trying to convince myself she'd never existed, but I had to convince myself of that, because believing that it really *had* happened was even scarier. How do you live in a world where anything can happen?

"You'll get used to it," Jilly told me. "There's a whole invisible world out there, lying side by side with our own. Once you get a peek into it, the window doesn't close. You're always going to be *aware* of it."

"I don't want to be," I said.

She just shook her head. "You don't really get a lot of choice in this kind of thing," she said.

You always have a choice—that's what I believe. And I chose to not get caught up in some invisible world of ghosts and spirits and who knew what. But I still dreamed of Sam, as if she'd been real. I still kept her photo in my fiddlecase.

I could feel its presence right now, glimmering through the leather, whispering to me.

Remember me . . .

I couldn't forget. *Jamais vu.* But I wanted to.

Jilly scooted a little closer to me on the step and laid a hand on my knee.

"Denying it just makes things worse," she said, continuing an old ongoing argument that I don't think we'll ever resolve. "Until you accept that it really happened, the memory's always going to haunt you, undermining everything that makes you who you are."

"Haunted like Paperjack?" I asked, trying to turn the subject back onto more comfortable ground, or at least focus the attention onto someone other than myself. "Is that what you think's happened to him?"

Jilly sighed. "Memories can be just like ghosts," she said.

Didn't I know it.

I looked down the steps to where Paperjack had been sitting, but he was gone, and now a couple of pigeons were waddling across the steps. The wind blew a candy bar wrapper up against a riser. I laid my hand on Jilly's and gave it a squeeze, then picked up my fiddle-case and stood up.

"I've got to go," I told her.

"I didn't mean to upset you . . ."

"I know. I've just got to walk for a bit and think."

She didn't offer to accompany me and for that I was glad. Jilly was my best friend, but right then I had to be alone.

I went rambling; just let my feet just take me wherever they felt like going, south from St. Paul's and down Battersfield Road, all the way to the Pier, my fiddlecase banging against my thigh as I walked. When I got to the waterfront, I leaned up against the fieldstone wall where the Pier met the beach. I stood and watched the fishermen work their lines farther out over the lake. Fat gulls wheeled above, crying like they hadn't been fed in months. Down on the sand, a couple was having an animated discussion, but they were too far away for me to make out what they were arguing about. They looked like figures in some old silent movie; caricatures, their move-ments larger than life, rather than real people.

I don't know what I was thinking about; I was trying *not* to think, I suppose, but I wasn't having much luck. The arguing couple depressed me.

Hang on to what you've got, I wanted to tell them, but it wasn't any of my business. I thought about heading across town to Fitz-henry Park—there was a part of it called the Silenus Gardens filled with stone benches and statuary where I always felt better—when I spied a familiar figure sitting down by the river west of the Pier: Paperjack.

The Kickaha River was named after that branch of the Algonquin language family that originally lived in this area before the white men came and took it all away from them. All the tribe had left now was a reservation north of the city and this river named after them. The Kickaha had its source north of the reserve and cut through the city on its way to the lake. In this part of town it separated the business section and commercial waterfront from the Beaches where the money lives.

There are houses in the Beaches that make the old stately homes in Lower Crowsea look like tenements, but you can't see them from here. Looking west, all you see is green—first the City Commission's manicured lawns on either side of the river, then the treed hills that hide the homes of the wealthy from the rest of us plebes. On the waterfront itself are a couple of country clubs and the private beaches of the *really* wealthy whose estates back right onto the water.

Paperjack was sitting on this side of the river, doing I don't know what. From where I stood, I couldn't tell. He seemed to be just sitting there on the riverbank, watching the slow water move past. I watched him for awhile, then hoisted my fiddlecase from where I'd leaned it against the wall and hopped down to the sand. When I got to where he was sitting, he looked up and gave me an easy, welcoming grin, as if he'd been expecting me to show up.

Running into him like this was fate, Jilly would say. I'll stick to calling it coincidence. It's a big city, but it isn't that big.

Paperjack made a motion with his hand, indicating I should pull up a bit of lawn beside him. I hesitated for a moment—right up until then, I realized later, everything could have worked out differently. But I made the choice and sat beside him.

There was a low wall, right down by the water, with rushes and lilies growing up against it. Among the lilies was a family of ducks— mother and a paddling of ducklings—and that was what Paperjack had been watching. He had an empty plastic bag in his hand, and the breadcrumbs that remained in the bottom told me he'd been feeding the ducks until his bread ran out.

He made another motion with his hand, touching the bag, then pointing to the ducks.

I shook my head. "I wasn't planning on coming down," I said, "so I didn't bring anything to feed them."

He nodded, understanding.

We sat quietly awhile longer. The ducks finally gave up on us and paddled farther up the river, looking for better pickings. Once they were gone, Paperjack turned to me again. He laid his hand against his heart, then raised his eyebrows questioningly.

Looking at that slim black hand with its long narrow fingers lying against his dark suit, I marveled again at the sheer depth of his ebony coloring. Even with the bit of a tan I'd picked up busking the last few weeks, I felt absolutely pallid beside him. Then I lifted my gaze to his eyes. If his skin swallowed light, I knew where it went: into his eyes. They were dark, so dark you could barely tell the difference between pupil and cornea, but inside their darkness was a kind of glow—a shine that resonated inside me like the deep hum that comes from my fiddle's bass strings whenever I play one of those wild Shetland reels in A minor.

I suppose it's odd, describing something visual in terms of sound, but right then, right at that moment, I *heard* the shine of his eyes, singing inside me. And I understood immediately what he'd meant by his gesture.

"Yeah," I said. "I'm feeling a little low."

He touched his chest again, but it was a different, lighter gesture this time. I knew what that meant as well.

"There's not much anybody can do about it," I said.

Except Sam. She could come back. Or maybe if I just knew she'd been *real* . . . But that opened a whole other line of thinking that I wasn't sure I wanted to get into again. I wanted her to have been real, I wanted her to come back, but if I accepted that, I also had to accept that ghosts were real and that the past could sneak up and steal someone from the present, taking them back into a time that had already been and gone.

Paperjack took his fortune-telling device out of the breast pocket of his jacket and gave me a questioning look. I started to shake my head, but before I could think about what I was doing, I just said, "What the hell," and let him do his stuff.

I chose blue from the colors, because that was the closest to how I was feeling; he didn't have any colors like confused or lost or foolish. I watched his fingers move the paper to spell out the color, then chose four from the numbers, because that's how many strings my fiddle has. When his fingers stopped moving the second time, I picked seven for no particular reason at all.

He folded back the paper flap so I could read my fortune. All it said was: "Swallow the past."

I didn't get it. I thought it'd say something like that Bobby McFerrin song, "Don't Worry, Be Happy." What it did say didn't make any sense at all.

"I don't understand," I told Paperjack. "What's it supposed to mean?"

He just shrugged. Folding up the fortune-teller, he put it back in his pocket.

Swallow the past. Did that mean I was supposed to forget about it? Or . . . well, swallow could also mean believe or accept. Was that what he was trying to tell me? Was he echoing Jilly's argument?

I thought about that photo in my fiddlecase, and then an idea came to me. I don't know why I'd never thought of it before. I grabbed my fiddlecase and stood up.

"I . . ." I wanted to thank him, but somehow the words just escaped me. All that came out was, "I've gotta run."

But I could tell he understood my gratitude. I wasn't exactly sure what he'd done, except that that little message on his fortune-teller had put together a connection for me that I'd never seen before.

Fate, I could hear Jilly saying.

Paperjack smiled and waved me off.

I followed coincidence away from Paperjack and the riverbank and back up Battersfield Road to the Newford Public Library in Lower Crowsea.

Time does more than erode a riverbank or wear mountains down into tired hills. It takes the edge from our memories as well, overlaying everything with a soft focus so that it all blurs together. What really happened gets all jumbled up with the hopes and dreams we once had and what we wish had really happened. Did you ever run into someone you went to school with—someone you never really hung around with, but just passed in the halls, or had a class with— and they act like you were the best of buddies, because that's how they remember it? For that matter, maybe you *were* buddies, and it's you that's remembering it wrong. . . .

Starting some solid detective work on what happened to Sam took the blur from my memories and brought her back into focus for me. The concepts of ghosts or people disappearing into the past just got pushed to one side, and all I thought about was Sam and tracking her down; if not the Sam I had known, then the woman she'd become in the past.

My friend Amy Scallan works at the library. She's a tall, angular woman with russet hair and long fingers that would have stood her in good stead at a piano keyboard. Instead she took up the Uillean pipes, and we play together in an on-again, off-again band called Johnny Jump Up. Matt Casey, our third member, is the reason we're not that regular a band.

Matt's a brilliant bouzouki and guitar player and a fabulous singer, but he's not got much in the way of social skills, and he's way too cynical for my liking. Since he and I don't really get along well, it makes rehearsals kind of tense at times. On the other hand, I love playing with Amy. She's the kind of musician who has such a good time playing that you can't help but enjoy yourself as well. Whenever I think of Amy, the first image that always comes to mind is of her rangy frame folded around her pipes, right elbow moving back and forth on the bellows to fill the bag under her left arm, those long fingers just dancing on the chanter, foot tapping, head bobbing, a grin on her face.

She always makes sure that the gig goes well, and we have a lot of fun, so it balances out I guess.

I showed her the picture I had of Sam. There was a street number on the porch's support pillar to the right of the steps and enough of the house in the picture that I'd be able to match it up to the real thing. If I could find out what street it was on. If the house still existed.

"This could take forever," Amy said as she laid the photo down on the desk.

"I've got the time."

Amy laughed. "I suppose you do. I don't know how you do it, Geordie. Everyone else in the world has to bust their buns to make a living, but you just cruise on through."

"The trick's having a low overhead," I said.

Amy just rolled her eyes. She'd been to my apartment, and there wasn't much to see: a spare fiddle hanging on the wall with a couple of Jilly's paintings; some tune books with tattered covers and some changes of clothing; one of those old-fashioned record players that had the turntable and speakers all in one unit and a few albums leaning against the side of the apple crate it sat on; a couple of bows that desperately needed rehairing; the handful of used paperbacks I'd picked up for the week's reading from Duffy's Used Books over on Walker Street; and a little beat-up old cassette machine with a handful of tapes.

And that was it. I got by.

I waited at the desk while Amy got the books we needed. She came back with an armload. Most had Newford in the title, but a few also covered that period of time when the city was still called Yoors, after the Dutchman Diederick van Yoors, who first settled the area in the early 1800s. It got changed to Newford back around the turn of the century, so all that's left now to remind the city of its original founding father is a street name.

Setting the books down before me on the desk, Amy went off into the stacks to look for some more obscure titles. I didn't wait for her to get back, but went ahead and started flipping through the first book on the pile, looking carefully at the pictures.

I started off having a good time. There's a certain magic in old photos, especially when they're of the place where you grew up. They cast a spell over you. Dirt roads where now there was pavement, sided by office complexes. The old Brewster Theatre in its heyday—I remembered it as the place where I first saw Phil Ochs and Bob Dylan, and later all-night movie festivals, but the Williamson Street Mall stood there now. Boating parties on the river. Old City Hall—it was a youth hostel these days.

But my enthusiasm waned with the afternoon. By the time the library closed, I was no closer to getting a street name for the house in Sam's photo than I had been when I came in. Amy gave me a sympathetic "I told you so" look when we separated on the front steps of the library. I just told her I'd see her tomorrow.

I had something to eat at Kathryn's Cafe. I'd gone there hoping to see Jilly, only I'd forgotten it was her night off. I tried calling her when I'd finished eating, but she was out. So I took my fiddle over to the theatre district and worked the crowds waiting in line there for an a hour or so before I headed off for home, my pockets heavy with change.

That night, just before I fell asleep, I felt like a hole sort of opened in the air above my bed. Lying there, I found myself touring Newford—just floating through its streets. Though the time was the present, there was no color. Everything appeared in the same sepia tones as in my photo of Sam.

I don't remember when I finally did fall asleep.

The next morning I was at the library right when it opened, carrying two cups of take-out coffee in a paper bag, one of which I offered to Amy when I got to her desk. Amy muttered something like, "when owls prowl the day, they shouldn't look so bloody cheerful about it," but she accepted the coffee and cleared a corner of her desk so that I could get back to the books.

In the photo I had of Sam there was just the edge of a bay window visible beside the porch, with fairly unique rounded gingerbread trim running off from either side of its keystone. I'd thought it would be the clue to tracking down the place. It looked almost familiar, but I was no longer sure if that was because I'd actually seen the house at some time, or it was just from looking at the photo so much.

Unfortunately, those details weren't helping at all.

"You know, there's no guarantee you're going to find a picture of the house you're looking for in those books," Amy said around mid-morning when she was taking her coffee break. "They didn't exactly go around taking pictures of everything."

I was at the last page of *Walks Through Old Crowsea*. Closing the book, I set it on the finished pile beside my chair and then leaned back, lacing my fingers behind my head. My shoulders were stiff from sitting hunched over a desk all morning.

"I know. I'm going to give Jack a call when I'm done here to see if I can borrow his bike this afternoon."

"You're going to pedal all around town looking for this house?"

"What else can I do?"

"There's always the archives at the main library."

I nodded, feeling depressed. It had seemed like such a good idea yesterday. It was still a good idea. I just hadn't realized how long it would take.

"Or you could go someplace like the Market and show the photo around to some of the older folks. Maybe one of them will remember the place."

"I suppose."

I picked up the next book, *The Architectural Heritage of Old Yoors,* and went back to work.

And there it was, on page thirty-eight. The house. There were three buildings in a row in the photo; the one I'd been looking for was the middle one. I checked the caption: "Grasso Street, circa 1920."

"I don't believe it," Amy said. I must have made some kind of a noise, because she was looking up at me from her own work. "You found it, didn't you?" she added.

"I think so. Have you got a magnifying glass?"

She passed it over, and I checked out the street number of the middle house. One-forty-two. The same as in my photo.

Amy took over then. She phoned a friend who worked in the land registry office. He called back a half hour later and gave us the name of the owner in 1912, when my photo had been taken: Edward Dickenson. The house had changed hands a number of times since the Dickensons had sold it in the forties.

We checked the phone book, but there were over a hundred Dickensons listed, twelve with just an initial "E" and one Ed. None of the addresses were on Grasso Street.

"Which makes sense," Amy said, "since they sold the place fifty years ago."

I wanted to run by that block on Grasso where the house was— I'd passed it I don't know how many times, and never paid much attention to it or any of its neighbors—but I needed more background on the Dickensons first. Amy showed me how to run the microfiche, and soon I was going through back issues of *The Newford Star* and *The Daily Journal,* concentrating on the local news sections and the gossip columns.

The first photo of Edward Dickenson that came up was in *The Daily Journal,* the June 21st, 1913, issue. He was standing with the Dean of Butler University at some opening ceremony. I compared him to the people with Sam in my photo and found him standing behind her to her left.

Now that I was on the right track, I began to work in a kind of frenzy. I whipped through the microfiche, making notes of every mention of the Dickensons. Edward turned out to have been a stockbroker, one of the few who didn't lose his shirt in subsequent market crashes. Back then the money lived in Lower Crowsea, mostly on McKennitt, Grasso, and Stanton Streets. Edward made the papers about once a month—business deals, society galas, fund-raising events, political dinners, and the like. It wasn't until I hit the October 29, 1915, issue of *The Newford Star* that I had the wind knocked out of my sails.

It was the picture that got to me: Sam and a man who was no stranger. I'd seen him before. He was the ghost that had stepped out of the past and stolen her away. Under the photo was a caption announcing the engagement of Thomas Edward Dickenson, son of the well-known local businessman, to Samantha Rey.

In the picture of Sam that I had, Dickenson wasn't there with the rest of the people—he'd probably taken it. But here he was. Real. With Sam. I couldn't ignore it.

Back then they didn't have the technology to make a photograph lie.

There was a weird buzzing in my ears as that picture burned its imprint onto my retinas. It was hard to breathe, and my T-shirt suddenly seemed too tight.

I don't know what I'd been expecting, but I knew it wasn't this. I suppose I thought I'd track down the people in the picture and find out that the woman who looked like Sam was actually named Gertrude something-or-other, and she'd lived her whole life with that family. I didn't expect to find Sam. I didn't expect the ghost to have been real.

I was in a daze as I put away the microfiche and shut down the machine.

"Geordie?" Amy asked as I walked by her desk. "Are you okay?"

I remember nodding and muttering something about needing a break. I picked up my fiddle and headed for the front door. The next thing I remember is standing in front of the address on Grasso Street and looking at the Dickensons' house.

I had no idea who owned it now; I hadn't been paying much attention to Amy after she told me that the Dickensons had sold it. Someone had renovated it fairly recently, so it didn't look at all the same as in the photos, but under its trendy additions, I could see the lines of the old house.

I sat down on the curb with my fiddlecase across my knees and just stared at the building. The buzzing was back in my head. My shirt still felt too tight.

I didn't know what to do anymore, so I just sat there, trying to make sense out of what couldn't be reasoned away. I no longer had any doubt that Sam had been real, or that a ghost had stolen her away. The feeling of loss came back all over again, as if it had happened just now, not three years ago. And what scared me was, if she and the ghost were real, then what else might be?

I closed my eyes, and headlines of supermarket tabloids flashed across my eyes, a strobing flicker of bizarre images and words. That was the world Jilly lived in—one in which anything was possible. I didn't know if I could handle living in that kind of world. I needed rules and boundaries. Patterns.

It was a long time before I got up and headed for Kathryn's Cafe.

The first thing Jilly asked when I got in the door was, "Have you seen Paperjack?"

It took me a few moments to push back the clamor of my own thoughts to register what she'd asked. Finally I just shook my head.

"He wasn't at St. Paul's today," Jilly went on, "and he's always there, rain or shine, winter or summer. I didn't think he was looking well yesterday, and now . . ."

I tuned her out and took a seat at an empty table before I could fall down. That feeling of dislocation that had started up in me when I first saw Sam's photo in the microfiche kept coming and going in waves. It was cresting right now, and I found it hard to just sit in the chair, let alone listen to what Jilly was saying. I tuned her back in when the spaciness finally started to recede.

". . . heart attack, who would he call? He can't *speak*."

"I saw him yesterday," I said, surprised that my voice sounded so calm. "Around mid-afternoon. He seemed fine."

"He did?"

I nodded. "He was down by the Pier, sitting on the riverbank, feeding the ducks. He read my fortune."

"He *did*?"

"You're beginning to sound like a broken record, Jilly."

For some reason, I was starting to feel better. That sense of being on the verge of a panic attack faded and then disappeared completely. Jilly pulled up a chair and leaned across the table, elbows propped up, chin cupped in her hands.

"So tell me," she said. "What made you do it? What was your fortune?"

I told her everything that had happened since I had seen Paperjack. That sense of dislocation came and went again a few times while I talked, but mostly I was holding firm.

"Holy shit!" Jilly said when I was done.

She put her hand to her mouth and looked quickly around, but none of the customers seemed to have noticed. She reached a hand across the table and caught one of mine.

"So now you believe?" she asked.

"I don't have a whole lot of choice, do I?"

"What are you going to do?"

I shrugged. "What's to do? I found out what I needed to know—now I've got to learn to live with it and all the other baggage that comes with it."

Jilly didn't say anything for a long moment. She just held my hand and exuded comfort as only Jilly can.

"You could find her," she said finally.

"Who? Sam?"

"Who else?"

"She's probably—" I stumbled over the word dead and settled for "—not even alive anymore."

"Maybe not," Jilly said. "She'd definitely be old. But don't you think you should find out?"

"I . . ."

I wasn't sure I wanted to know. And if she were alive, I wasn't sure I wanted to meet her. What could we say to each other?

"Think about it, anyway," Jilly said.

That was Jilly; she never took no for an answer.

"I'm off at eight," she said. "Do you want to meet me then?"

"What's up?" I asked, halfheartedly.

"I thought maybe you'd help me find Paperjack."

I might as well, I thought. I was becoming a bit of an expert in tracking people down by this point. Maybe I should get a card printed: Geordie Riddell, Private Investigations and Fiddle Tunes.

"Sure," I told her.

"Great," Jilly said.

She bounced up from her seat as a couple of new customers came into the cafe. I ordered a coffee from her after she'd gotten them seated, then stared out the window at the traffic going by on Battersfield. I tried not to think of Sam—trapped in the past, making a new life for herself there—but I might as well have tried to jump to the moon.

By the time Jilly came off shift I was feeling almost myself again, but instead of being relieved, I had this great load of guilt hanging over me. It all centered around Sam and the ghost. I'd denied her once. Now I felt as though I was betraying her all over again. Knowing what I knew—the photo accompanying the engagement notice in that old issue of *The Newford Star* flashed across my mind—the way I was feeling at the moment didn't seem right. I felt too normal; and so the guilt.

"I don't get it," I said to Jilly as we walked down Battersfield towards the Pier. "This afternoon I was falling to pieces, but now I just feel . . ."

"Calm?"

"Yeah."

"That's because you've finally stopped fighting yourself and accepted that what you saw—what you remember—really happened. It was denial that was screwing you up."

She didn't add, "I told you so," but she didn't have to. It echoed in my head anyway, joining the rest of the guilt I was carrying around with me. If I'd only listened to her with an open mind, then . . . what?

I wouldn't be going through this all over again?

We crossed Lakeside Drive and made our way through the closed concession and souvenir stands to the beach. When we reached the Pier, I led her westward to where I'd last seen Paperjack, but he wasn't sitting by the river anymore. A lone duck regarded us hopefully, but neither of us had thought to bring any bread.

"So I track down Sam," I said, still more caught up in my personal quest than in looking for Paperjack. "If she's not dead, she'll be an old lady. If I find her—then what?"

"You'll complete the circle," Jilly said. She looked away from the river and faced me, her pixie features serious. "It's like the Kickaha say: everything is on a wheel. You stepped off the one that represents your relationship with Sam before it came full circle. Until you complete your turn on it, you'll never have peace of mind."

"When do you know you've come full circle?" I asked.

"You'll know."

She turned away before I could go on and started back towards the Pier. By day the place was crowded and full of noise, alive with tourists and people out relaxing, just looking to have a good time; by night, its occupancy was turned over to gangs of kids, fooling around on skateboards or simply hanging out, and the homeless: winos, bag ladies, hoboes, and the like.

Jilly worked the crowd, asking after Paperjack, while I followed in her wake. Everybody knew him, or had seen him in the past week, but no one knew where he was now, or where he lived. We were about to give up and head over to Fitzhenry Park to start over again with the people hanging out there, when we heard the sound of a harmonica. It was playing the blues, a soft, mournful sound that drifted up from the beach.

We made for the nearest stairs and then walked back across the sand to find the Bossman sitting under the boardwalk, hands cupped around his instrument, head bowed down, eyes closed. There was no one listening to him except us. The people with money to throw in his old cloth cap were having dinner now in the fancy restaurants across Lakeside Drive or over in the theatre district. He was just playing for himself.

When he was busking, he stuck to popular pieces—whatever was playing on the radio mixed with old show tunes, jazz favorites, and that kind of thing. The music that came from his harmonica now was pure magic. It transformed him, making him larger than life. The blues he played held all the world's sorrows in its long sliding notes and didn't so much change it, as make it bearable.

My fingers itched to pull out my fiddle and join him, but we hadn't come to jam. So we waited until he was done. The last note hung in the air for far longer than seemed possible, then he brought his hands away from his mouth and cradled the harmonica on his lap. He looked up at us from under drooping eyelids, the magic disappearing now that he'd stopped playing. He was just an old, homeless black man now, with the faint trace of a smile touching his lips.

"Hey, Jill—Geordie," he said. "What's doin'?"

"We're looking for Paperjack," Jilly told him.

The Bossman nodded. "Jack's the man for paperwork, all right."

"I've been worried about him," Jilly said. "About his health."

"You a doctor now, Jill?"

She shook her head.

"Anybody got a smoke?"

This time we both shook our heads.

From his pocket he pulled a half-smoked butt that he must have picked up off the boardwalk earlier, then lit it with a wooden match that he struck on the zipper of his jeans. He took a long drag and let it out so that the blue-grey smoke wreathed his head, studying us all the while.

"You care too much, you just get hurt," he said finally.

Jilly nodded. "I know. But I can't help it. Do you know where we can find him?

"Well now. Come winter, he lives with a Mex family down in the Barrio."

"And in the summer?"

The Bossman shrugged. "I heard once he's got himself a camp up behind the Beaches."

"Thanks," Jilly said.

"He might not take to uninvited guests," the Bossman added. "Body gets himself an out-of-the-way squat like that, I'd think he be lookin' for privacy."

"I don't want to intrude," Jilly assured him. "I just want to make sure he's okay."

The Bossman nodded. "You're a stand-up kind of lady, Jill. I'll trust you to do what's right. I've been thinkin' old Jack's lookin' a little peaked myself. It's somethin' in his eyes—like just makin' do is gettin' to be a chore. But you take care, goin' back up in there. Some of the 'boes, they're not real accommodatin' to havin' strangers on their turf."

"We'll be careful," Jilly said.

The Bossman gave us both another long, thoughtful look, then lifted his harmonica and started to play again. Its mournful sound followed us back up to the boardwalk and seemed to trail us all the way to Lakeside Drive where we walked across the bridge to get to the other side of the Kickaha.

I don't know what Jilly was thinking about, but I was going over what she'd told me earlier. I kept thinking about wheels and how they turned.

Once past the City Commission's lawns on the far side of the river, the land starts to climb. It's just a lot of rough scrub on this side of the hills that make up the Beaches and every summer some of the hoboes and other homeless people camp out in it. The cops roust them from time to time, but mostly they're left alone, and they keep to themselves.

Going in there I was more nervous than Jilly; I don't think she's scared of anything. The sun had gone down behind the hills, and while it was twilight in the city, here it was already dark. I know a lot of the street people and get along with them better than most—everyone likes a good fiddle tune—but some of them could look pretty rough, and I kept anticipating that we'd run into some big wild-eyed hillbilly who'd take exception to our being there.

Well, we did run into one, but—like ninety percent of the street people in Newford—he was somebody that Jilly knew. He seemed pleased, if a little surprised to find her here, grinning at us in the fading light. He was a tall, big-shouldered man, dressed in dirty jeans and a flannel shirt, with big hobnailed boots on his feet and a shock of red hair that fell to his neck and stood up on top of his head in matted tangles. His name, appropriately enough, was Red. The smell that emanated from him made me want to shift position until I was standing upwind.

He not only knew where Paperjack's camp was, but took us there, only Paperjack wasn't home.

The place had Paperjack stamped all over it. There was a neatly rolled bedroll pushed up against a knapsack which probably held his changes of clothing. We didn't check it out, because we weren't there to go through his stuff. Behind the pack was a food cooler with a Coleman stove sitting on top of it, and everywhere you could see small origami stars that hung from the tree branches. There must have been over a hundred of them. I felt as if I were standing in the middle of space with stars all around me.

Jilly left a note for Paperjack, then we followed Red back out to Lakeside Drive. He didn't wait for our thanks. He just drifted away as soon as we reached the mown lawns that bordered the bush.

We split up then. Jilly had work to do—some art for Newford's entertainment weekly, *In the City*—and I didn't feel like tagging along to watch her work at her studio. She took the subway, but I decided to walk. I was bone-tired by then, but the night was one of those perfect ones when the city seems to be smiling. You can't see the dirt or the grime for the sparkle over everything. After all I'd been through today, I didn't want to be cooped up inside anywhere. I just wanted to enjoy the night.

I remember thinking about how Sam would've loved to be out walking with me on a night like this—the old Sam I'd lost, not necessarily the one she'd become. I didn't know that Sam at all, and I still wasn't sure I wanted to, even if I could track her down.

When I reached St. Paul's, I paused by the steps. Even though it was a perfect night to be out walking, something drew me inside. I tried the door, and it opened soundlessly at my touch. I paused just inside the door, one hand resting on the back pew, when I heard a cough.

I froze, ready to take flight. I wasn't sure how churches worked. Maybe my creeping around here at this time of night was . . . I don't know, sacrilegious or something.

I looked up to the front and saw that someone was sitting in the foremost pew. The cough was repeated, and I started down the aisle.

Intuitively, I guess I knew I'd find him here. Why else had I come inside?

Paperjack nodded to me as I sat down beside him on the pew. I laid my fiddlecase by my feet and leaned back. I wanted to ask after his health, to tell him how worried Jill was about him, but my day caught up with me in a rush. Before I knew it, I was nodding off.

I knew I was dreaming when I heard the voice. I had to be dreaming, because there was only Paperjack and I sitting on the pew, and Paperjack was mute. But the voice had the sound that I'd always imagined Paperjack's would have if he could speak. It was like the movement of his fingers when he was folding origami—quick, but measured and certain. Resonant, like his finished paper sculptures that always seemed to have more substance to them than just their folds and shapes.

"No one in this world views it the same," the voice said. "I believe that is what amazes me the most about it. Each person has his or her own vision of the world, and whatever lies outside that worldview becomes invisible. The rich ignore the poor. The happy can't see those who are hurting."

"Paperjack . . . ?" I asked.

There was only silence in reply.

"I . . . I thought you couldn't talk."

"So a man who has nothing he wishes to articulate is considered mute," the voice went on as though I hadn't interrupted. "It makes me weary."

"Who . . . who are you?" I asked.

"A mirror into which no one will look. A fortune that remains forever unread. My time here is done."

The voice fell silent again.

"Paperjack?"

Still silence.

It was just a dream, I told myself. I tried to wake myself from it. I told myself that the pew was made of hard, unyielding wood, and far too uncomfortable to sleep on. And Paperjack needed help. I remembered the cough and Jilly's worries.

But I couldn't wake up.

"The giving itself is the gift," the voice said suddenly. It sounded as though it came from the back of the church, or even farther away. "The longer I remain here, the more I forget."

Then the voice went away for good. I lost it in a dreamless sleep.

I woke early, and all my muscles were stiff. My watch said it was ten to six. I had a moment's disorientation—where the hell *was* I?—and then I remembered. Paperjack. And the dream.

I sat up straighter in the pew, and something fell from my lap to the floor. A piece of folded paper. I bent stiffly to retrieve it, turning it over and over in my hands, holding it up to the dim grey light that was creeping in through the windows. It was one of Paperjack's Chinese fortune-tellers.

After awhile I fit my fingers into the folds of the paper and looked down at the colors. I chose blue, same as I had the last time, and spelled it out, my fingers moving the paper back and forth so that it looked like a flower speaking soundlessly to me. I picked numbers at random, then unfolded the flap to read what it had to say.

"The question is more important than the answer," it said.

I frowned, puzzling over it, then looked at what I would have gotten if I'd picked another number, but all the other folds were blank when I turned them over. I stared at it, then folded the whole thing back up and stuck it in my pocket. I was starting to get a serious case of the creeps.

Picking up my fiddlecase, I left St. Paul's and wandered over to Chinatown. I had breakfast in an all-night diner, sharing the place with a bunch of blue-collar workers who were all talking about some baseball game they'd watched the night before. I thought of calling Jilly, but knew that if she'd been working all night on that *In the City* assignment, she'd be crashed out now and wouldn't appreciate a phone call.

I dawdled over breakfast, then slowly made my way up to that part of Foxville that's called the Rosses. That's where the Irish immigrants all lived in the forties and fifties. The place started changing in the sixties when a lot of hippies who couldn't afford the rents in Crowsea moved in, and it changed again with a new wave of immigrants from Vietnam and the Caribbean in the following decades. But the area, for all its changes, was still called the Rosses. My apartment was in the heart of it, right where Kelly Street meets Lee and crosses the Kickaha River. It's two doors down from The Harp, the only real Irish pub in town, which makes it convenient for me to get to the Irish music sessions on Sunday afternoons.

My phone was ringing when I got home. I was half-expecting it to be Jilly, even though it was only going on eight, but found myself talking to a reporter from *The Daily Journal* instead. His name was Ian Begley, and it turned out he was a friend of Jilly's. She'd asked him to run down what information he could on the Dickensons in the paper's morgue.

"Old man Dickenson was the last real businessman of the family," Begley told me. "Their fortunes started to decline when his son Tom took over—he's the one who married the woman that Jilly said you were interested in tracking down. He died in 1976. I don't have an obit on his widow, but that doesn't necessarily mean she's still alive. If she moved out of town, the paper wouldn't have an obit for her unless the family put one in."

He told me a lot of other stuff, but I was only half listening. The business with Paperjack last night and the fortune-telling device this morning were still eating away at me. I did take down the address of Sam's granddaughter when it came up. Begley ran out of steam after another five minutes or so.

"You got enough there?" he asked.

I nodded, then realized he couldn't see me. "Yeah. Thanks a lot."

"Say hello to Jilly for me and tell her she owes me one."

After I hung up, I looked out the window for a long time. I managed to shift gears from Paperjack to thinking about what Begley had told me, about wheels, about Sam. Finally I got up and took a shower and shaved. I put on my cleanest jeans and shirt and shrugged on a sports jacket that had seen better days before I bought it in a retro fashion shop. I thought about leaving my fiddle behind, but knew I'd feel naked without it—I couldn't remember the last time I'd gone somewhere without it. The leather handle felt comforting in my hand as I hefted the case and went out the door.

All the way over to the address Begley had given me I tried to think of what I was going to say when I met Sam's granddaughter. The truth would make me sound like I was crazy, but I couldn't seem to concoct a story that would make sense.

I remember wondering—where was my brother when I needed him? Christy was never at a loss for words, no matter what the situation.

It wasn't until I was standing on the sidewalk in front of the house that I decided to stick as close to the truth as I could—I was an old friend of her grandmother's, could she put me in touch with her?— and take it from there. But even my vague plans went out the door when I rang the bell and stood face-to-face with Sam's granddaughter.

Maybe you saw this coming, but it was the last thing I'd expected. The woman had Sam's hair, Sam's eyes, Sam's face . . . to all intents and purposes it *was* Sam standing there, looking at me with that vaguely uncertain expression that most of us wear when we open the door to a stranger standing on our steps.

My chest grew so tight I could barely breathe, and suddenly I could hear the sound of rain in my memory—it was always raining when Sam saw the ghost; it was raining the night he stole her away into the past.

Ghosts. *I* was looking at a ghost.

The woman's expression was starting to change, the uncertainty turning into nervousness. There was no recognition in her eyes. As she began to step back—in a moment she'd close the door in my face, probably call the cops—I found my voice. I knew what I was going to say—I was going to ask about her grandmother—but all that came out was her name: "Sam."

"Yes?" she said. She looked at me a little more carefully. "Do I know you?"

Jesus, even the name was the same.

A hundred thoughts were going through my head, but they all spiraled down into one mad hope: this was Sam. We could be together again. Then a child appeared behind the woman. She was a little girl no more than five, blonde-haired, blue-eyed, just like her mother—just like her *mother's* grandmother. Reality came crashing down around me.

This Sam wasn't the woman I knew. She was married, she had children, she had a life.

"I . . . I knew your grandmother," I said. "We were . . . we used to be friends."

It sounded so inane to my ears, almost crazy. What would her grandmother—a woman maybe three times my age if she was still alive—have to do with a guy like me?

The woman's gaze traveled down to my fiddlecase. "Is your name Geordie? Geordie Riddell?"

I blinked in surprise, then nodded slowly.

The woman smiled a little sadly, mostly with her eyes.

"Granny said you'd come by," she said. "She didn't know when, but she said you'd come by one day." She stepped away from the door, shooing her daughter down the hall. "Would you like to come in?"

"I . . . uh, sure."

She led me into a living room that was furnished in mismatched antiques that, taken all together, shouldn't have worked, but did.

The little girl perched in a Morris chair and watched me curiously as I sat down and set my fiddlecase down by my feet. Her mother pushed back a stray lock with a mannerism so like Sam's that my chest tightened up even more.

"Would you like some coffee or tea?" she asked.

I shook my head. "I don't want to intrude. I . . ." Words escaped me again.

"You're not intruding," she said. She sat down on the couch in front of me, that sad look back in her eyes. "My grandmother died a few years ago—she'd moved to New England in the late seventies, and she died there in her sleep. Because she loved it so much, we buried her there in a small graveyard overlooking the sea."

I could see it in my mind as she spoke. I could hear the sound of the waves breaking on the shore below, the spray falling on the rocks like rain.

"She and I were very close, a lot closer than I ever felt to my mother." She gave me a rueful look. "You know how it is."

She didn't seem to be expecting a response, but I nodded anyway.

"When her estate was settled, most of her personal effects came to me. I . . ." She paused, then stood up. "Excuse me for a moment, would you?"

I nodded again. She'd looked sad, talking about Sam. I hoped that bringing it all up hadn't made her cry.

The little girl and I sat in silence, looking at each other until her mother returned. She was such a serious kid, her big eyes taking everything in; she sat quietly, not running around or acting up like most kids do when there's someone new in the house that they can show off to. I didn't think she was shy; she was just . . . well, serious.

Her mother had a package wrapped in brown paper and twine in her hands when she came back. She sat down across from me again and laid the package on the table between us.

"Granny told me a story once," she said, "about her first and only real true love. It was an odd story, a kind of ghost story, about how she'd once lived in the future until granddad's love stole her away from her own time and brought her to his." She gave me an apologetic smile. "I knew it was just a story because, when I was growing up I'd met people she'd gone to school with, friends from her past before she met granddad. Besides, it was too much like some science fiction story.

"But it was true, wasn't it?"

I could only nod. I didn't understand how Sam and everything about her except my memories of her could vanish into the past, how she could have a whole new set of memories when she got back there, but I knew it was true.

I accepted it now, just as Jilly had been trying to get me to do for years. When I looked at Sam's granddaughter, I saw that she accepted it as well.

"When her effects were sent to me," she went on, "I found this package in them. It's addressed to you."

I had seen my name on it, written in a familiar hand. My own hand trembled as I reached over to pick it up.

"You don't have to open it now," she said.

I was grateful for that.

"I . . . I'd better go," I said and stood up. "Thank you for taking the time to see me."

That sad smile was back as she saw me to the door.

"I'm glad I got the chance to meet you," she said when I stepped out onto the porch.

I wasn't sure I could say the same. She looked so much like Sam, *sounded* so much like Sam, that it hurt.

"I don't think we'll be seeing each other again," she added.

No. She had her husband, her family. I had my ghosts.

"Thanks," I said again and started off down the walk, fiddlecase in one hand, the brown paper package in the other.

I didn't open the package until I was sitting in the Silenus Gardens in Fitzhenry Park, a place that always made me feel good; I figured I was going to need all the help I could get. Inside there was a book with a short letter. The book I recognized. It was the small J. M. Dent & Sons edition of Shakespeare's *A Midsummer Night's Dream* that I'd given Sam because I'd known it was one of her favorite stories.

There was nothing special about the edition, other than its size— it was small enough for her to carry around in her purse, which she did. The inscription I'd written to her was inside, but the book was

far more worn than it had been when I'd first given it to her. I didn't
have to open the book to remember that famous quotation from
Puck's final lines:

> *If we shadows have offended,*
> *Think but this, and all is mended,*
> *That you have but slumber'd here,*
> *While these visions did appear.*
> *And this weak and idle theme,*
> *No more yielding but a dream . . .*

But it hadn't been a dream—not for me, and not for Sam. I set the
book down beside me on the stone bench and unfolded the letter.

"Dear Geordie," it said. "I know you'll read this one day, and
I hope you can forgive me for not seeing you in person, but I wanted
you to remember me as I was, not as I've become. I've had a full and
mostly happy life; you know my only regret. I can look back on our
time together with the wisdom of an old woman now and truly
know that all things have their time. Ours was short—too short, my
heart—but we did have it.

"Who was it that said, 'better to have loved and lost, than never
to have loved at all'? We loved and lost each other, but I would
rather cherish the memory than rail against the unfairness. I hope
you will do the same."

I sat there and cried. I didn't care about the looks I was getting
from people walking by, I just let it all out. Some of my tears were
for what I'd lost, some were for Sam and her bravery, and some were
for my own stupidity at denying her memory for so long.

I don't know how long I sat there like that, holding her letter, but
the tears finally dried on my cheeks. I heard the scuff of feet on the
path and wasn't surprised to look up and find Jilly standing in front
of me.

"Oh Geordie, me lad," she said.

She sat down at my side and leaned against me. I can't tell you
how comforting it was to have her there. I handed her the letter and
book and sat quietly while she read the first and looked at the latter.
Slowly she folded up the letter and slipped it inside the book.

"How do you feel now?" she asked finally. "Better or worse?"

"Both."

She raised her eyebrows in a silent question.

"Well, it's like what they say funerals are for," I tried to explain. "It gives you the chance to say goodbye, to settle things, like taking a—" I looked at her and managed to find a small smile "—final turn on a wheel. But I feel depressed about Sam. I know what we had was real, and I know how it felt for me, losing her. But I only had to deal with it for a few years. She carried it for a lifetime."

"Still, she carried on."

I nodded. "Thank god for that."

Neither of us spoke for awhile, but then I remembered Paperjack. I told her what I thought had happened last night, then showed her the fortune-telling device that he'd left with me in St. Paul's. She read my fortune with pursed lips and the start of a wrinkle on her forehead, but didn't seem particularly surprised by it.

"What do you think?" I asked her.

She shrugged. "Everybody makes the same mistake. Fortune-telling doesn't reveal the future; it mirrors the present. It resonates against what your subconscious already knows and hauls it up out of the darkness so that you can get a good look at it."

"I meant about Paperjack."

"I think he's gone—back to wherever it was that he came from."

She was beginning to exasperate me in that way that only she could.

"But who was he?" I asked. "No, better yet, *what* was he?"

"I don't know," Jilly said. "I just know it's like your fortune said. It's the questions we ask, the journey we take to get where we're going that's more important than the actual answer. It's good to have mysteries. It reminds us that there's more to the world than just making do and having a bit of fun."

I sighed, knowing I wasn't going to get much more sense out of her than that.

It wasn't until the next day that I made my way alone to Paperjack's camp in back of the Beaches. All his gear was gone, but the paper stars still hung from the trees. I wondered again about who he was. Some oracular spirit, a kind of guardian angel, drifting around, trying to help people see themselves? Or an old homeless black man with a gift for folding paper? I understood then that my fortune made a certain kind of sense, but I didn't entirely agree with it.

Still, in Sam's case, knowing the answer had brought me peace.

I took Paperjack's fortune-teller from my pocket and strung it with a piece of string I'd brought along for that purpose. Then I hung it on the branch of a tree so that it could swing there, in among all those paper stars, and I walked away.

⨯ TALLULAH ⨯

NOTHING IS TOO WONDERFUL
TO BE TRUE.
—MICHAEL FARADAY

For the longest time, I thought she was a ghost, but I know what she is now. She's come to mean everything to me; like a lifeline, she keeps me connected to reality, to this place and this time, by her very capriciousness.

I wish I'd never met her.

That's a lie, of course, but it comes easily to the tongue. It's a way to pretend that the ache she left behind in my heart doesn't hurt.

She calls herself Tallulah, but I know who she really is. A name can't begin to encompass the sum of all her parts. But that's the magic of names, isn't it? That the complex, contradictory individuals we are can be called up complete and whole in another mind through the simple sorcery of a name. And connected to the complete person we call up in our mind with the alchemy of their name comes all the baggage of memory: times you were together, the music you listened to this morning or that night, conversation and jokes and private moments—all the good and bad times you've shared.

Tally's name conjures up more than just that for me. When the *gris-gris* of the memories that hold her stir in my mind, she guides me through the city's night like a totem does a shaman through Dreamtime. Everything familiar is changed; what she shows me goes under the skin, right to the marrow of the bone. I see a building and I know not only its shape and form, but its history. I can hear its breathing, I can almost read its thoughts.

It's the same for a street or a park, an abandoned car or some secret garden hidden behind a wall, a late night cafe or an empty lot. Each one has its story, its secret history, and Tally taught me how to read each one of them. Where once I guessed at those stories, chasing rumors of them like they were errant fireflies, now I know.

I'm not as good with people. Neither of us are. Tally, at least, has an excuse. But me . . .

I wish I'd never met her.

My brother Geordie is a busker—a street musician. He plays his fiddle on street corners or along the queues in the theatre district and makes a kind of magic with his music that words just can't describe. Listening to him play is like stepping into an old Irish or Scottish fairy tale. The slow airs call up haunted moors and lonely coastlines; the jigs and reels wake a fire in the soul that burns with the awesome wonder of bright stars on a cold night, or the familiar warmth of red coals glimmering in a friendly hearth.

The funny thing is, he's one of the most pragmatic people I know. For all the enchantment he can call up out of that old Czech fiddle of his, I'm the one with the fey streak in our family.

As far as I'm concerned, the only difference between fact and what most people call fiction is about fifteen pages in the dictionary. I've got such an open mind that Geordie says I've got a hole in it, but I've been that way for as long as I can remember. It's not so much that I'm gullible—though I've been called that and less charitable things in my time; it's more that I'm willing to just suspend my disbelief until whatever I'm considering has been thoroughly debunked to my satisfaction.

I first started collecting oddities and curiosities as I heard about them when I was in my teens, filling page after page of spiral-bound notebooks with little notes and jottings—neat inky scratches on the paper, each entry opening worlds of possibility for me whenever I reread them. I liked things to do with the city the best because that seemed the last place in the world where the delicate wonders that are magic should exist.

Truth to tell, a lot of what showed up in those notebooks leaned towards a darker side of the coin, but even that darkness had a light in it for me because it still stretched the realms of what was into a thousand variable what-might-be's. That was the real magic for me: the possibility that we only have to draw aside a veil to find the world a far more strange and wondrous place than its mundaneness allowed it could be.

It was my girlfriend back then—Katie Deren—who first convinced me to use my notebooks as the basis for stories. Katie was about as odd a bird as I was in those days. We'd sit around with the music of obscure groups like the Incredible String Band or Dr. Strangely Strange playing on the turntable and literally talk away whole nights about anything and everything. She had the strangest way of looking at things; everything had a soul for her, be it the majestic old oak tree that stood in her parents' back yard, or the old black iron kettle that she kept filled with dried weeds on the sill of her bedroom window.

We drifted apart, the way it happens with a lot of relationships at that age, but I kept the gift she'd woken in me: the stories.

I never expected to become a writer, but then I had no real expectations whatsoever as to what I was going to be when I "grew up." Sometimes I think I never did—grow up that is.

But I did get older. And I found I could make a living with my stories. I called them urban legends—independently of Jan Harold Brunvand, who also makes a living collecting them. But he approaches them as a folklorist, cataloguing and comparing them, while I retell them in stories that I sell to magazines and then recycle into book collections.

I don't feel we're in any kind of competition with each other, but then I feel that way about all writers. There are as many stories to be told as there are people to tell them about; only the mean-spirited would consider there to be a competition at all. And Brunvand does such a wonderful job. The first time I read his *The Vanishing Hitchhiker,* I was completely smitten with his work and, like the hundreds of other correspondents Brunvand has, made a point of sending him items I thought he could use for his future books.

But I never wrote to him about Tally.

I do my writing at night—the later the better. I don't work in a study or an office and I don't use a typewriter or computer, at least not for my first drafts. What I like to do is go out into the night and just set up shop wherever it feels right: a park bench, the counter of some all-night diner, the stoop of St. Paul's Cathedral, the doorway of a closed junk shop on Grasso Street.

I still keep notebooks, but they're hardcover ones now. I write my stories in them as well. And though the stories owe their existence to the urban legends that give them their quirky spin, what they're really about is people: what makes them happy or sad. My themes are simple. They're about love and loss, honor and the responsibilities of friendship. And wonder . . . always wonder. As complex as people are individually, their drives are universal.

I've been told—so often I almost believe it myself—that I've got a real understanding of people. However strange the situations my characters find themselves in, the characters themselves seem very real to my readers. That makes me feel good, naturally enough, but I don't understand it because I don't feel that I know people very well at all.

I'm just not good with them.

I think it comes from being that odd bird when I was growing up. I was distanced from the concerns of my peers, I just couldn't get into so many of the things that they felt was important. The fault was partly the other kids—if you're different, you're fair game. You know how it can be. There are three kinds of kids: the ones that are the odd birds, the ones that pissed on them, and the ones that watched it happen.

It was partly my fault, too, because I ostracized them as much as they did me. I was always out of step; I didn't really care about belonging to this gang or that clique. A few years earlier and I'd have been a beatnik, a few years later, a hippie. I got into drugs before they were cool; found out they were messing up my head and got out of them when everybody else starting dropping acid and MDA and who knows what all.

What it boiled down to was that I had a lot of acquaintances, but very few friends. And even with the friends I did have, I always felt one step removed from the relationship, as though I was observing what was going on, taking notes, rather than just being there.

That hasn't changed much as I've grown older.

How that—let's call it aloofness, for lack of a better word— translated into this so-called gift for characterization in my fiction, I can't tell you. Maybe I put so much into the stories, I had nothing left over for real life. Maybe it's because each one of us, no matter how many or how close our connections to other people, remains in the end, irrevocably on his or her own, solitary islands separated by expanses of the world's sea, and I'm just more aware of it than others. Maybe I'm just missing the necessary circuit in my brain.

Tally changed all of that.

I wouldn't have thought it, the first time I saw her.

There's a section of the Market in Lower Crowsea, where it backs onto the Kickaha River, that's got a kind of Old World magic about it. The roads are too narrow for normal vehicular traffic, so most people go through on bicycles or by foot. The buildings lean close to each other over the cobblestoned streets that twist and wind in a confusion that not even the city's mapmakers have been able to unravel to anyone's satisfaction.

There are old shops back in there and some of them still have signage in Dutch dating back a hundred years. There are buildings tenanted by generations of the same families, little courtyards, secret gardens, any number of sly-eyed cats, old men playing dominoes and checkers and their gossiping wives, small gales of shrieking children by day, mysterious eddies of silence by night. It's a wonderful place, completely untouched by the yuppie renovation projects that took over the rest of the Market.

Right down by the river there's a public courtyard surrounded on all sides by three-story brick and stone town houses with mansard roofs and dormer windows. Late at night, the only manmade sound comes from the odd bit of traffic on the McKennitt Street Bridge a block or so south, the only light comes from the single streetlamp under which stands a bench made of cast iron and wooden slats. Not a light shines from the windows of the buildings that enclose it. When you sit on that bench, the river murmurs at your back and the streetlamp encloses you in a comforting embrace of warm yellow light.

It's one of my favorite places to write. I'll sit there with my notebook propped up on my lap and scribble away for hours, my only companion, more often than not, a tattered-eared tom sleeping on the bench beside me. I think he lives in one of the houses, though he could be a stray. He's there most times I come—not waiting for me. I'll sit down and start to work and after a half-hour or so he'll come sauntering out of the shadows, stopping a half-dozen times to lick this shoulder, that hind leg, before finally settling down beside me like he's been there all night.

He doesn't much care to be patted, but I'm usually too busy to pay that much attention to him anyway. Still, I enjoy his company. I'd miss him if he stopped coming.

I've wonder about his name sometimes. You know that old story where they talk about a cat having three names? There's the one we give them, the one they use among themselves and then the secret one that only they know.

I just call him Ben; I don't know what he calls himself. He could be the King of the Cats, for all I know.

He was sleeping on the bench beside me the night she showed up. He saw her first. Or maybe he heard her.

It was early autumn, a brisk night that followed one of those perfect crisp autumn days—clear skies, the sunshine bright on the turning leaves, a smell in the air of a change coming, the wheel of the seasons turning. I was bundled up in a flannel jacket and wore half-gloves to keep my hands from getting too cold as I wrote.

I looked up when Ben stirred beside me, fur bristling, slit-eyed gaze focused on the narrow mouth of an alleyway that cut like a tunnel through the town houses on the north side of the courtyard. I followed his gaze in time to see her step from the shadows.

She reminded me of Geordie's friend Jilly, the artist. She had the same slender frame and tangled hair, the same pixie face and wardrobe that made her look like she did all her clothes buying at a thrift shop. But she had a harder look than Jilly, a toughness that was reflected in the sharp lines that modified her features and in her gear: battered leather jacket, jeans stuffed into low-heeled black cowboy boots, hands in her pockets, a kind of leather carryall hanging by its strap from her shoulder.

She had a loose, confident gait as she crossed the courtyard, boot heels clicking on the cobblestones. The warm light from the street-lamp softened her features a little.

Beside me, Ben turned around a couple of times, a slow chase of his tail that had no enthusiasm to it, and settled back into sleep. She sat down on the bench, the cat between us, and dropped her carryall at her feet. Then she leaned back against the bench, legs stretched out in front of her, hands back in the pockets of her jeans, head turned to look at me.

"Some night, isn't it?" she said.

I was still trying to figure her out. I couldn't place her age. One moment she looked young enough to be a runaway and I waited for the inevitable request for spare change or a place to crash, the next she seemed around my age—late twenties, early thirties—and I didn't know what she might want. One thing people didn't do in the city, even in this part of it, was befriend strangers. Not at night. Especially not if you were young and as pretty as she was.

My lack of a response didn't seem to faze her in the least.

"What's your name?" she asked.

"Christy Riddell," I said. I hesitated for a moment, then reconciled myself to a conversation. "What's yours?" I added as I closed my notebook, leaving my pen inside it to keep my place.

"Tallulah."

Just that, the one name. Spoken with the brassy confidence of a Cher or a Madonna.

"You're kidding," I said.

Tallulah sounded like it should belong to a '20s flapper, not some punky street kid.

She gave me a smile that lit up her face, banishing the last trace of the harshness I'd seen in her features as she was walking up to the bench.

"No, really," she said. "But you can call me Tally."

The melody of the ridiculous refrain from that song by—was it Harry Belafonte?—came to mind, something about tallying bananas.

"What're you doing?" she asked.

"Writing."

"I can *see* that. I meant, what kind of writing?"

"I write stories," I told her.

I waited then for the inevitable questions: Have you ever been published? What name do you write under? Where do you get your ideas? Instead she turned away and looked up at the sky.

"I knew a poet once," she said. "He wanted to capture his soul on a piece of paper—really capture it." She looked back at me. "But of course, you can't do that, can you? You can try, you can bleed honesty into your art until it feels like you've wrung your soul dry, but in the end, all you've created is a possible link between minds. An attempt at communication. If a soul can't be measured, then how can it be captured?"

I revised my opinion of her age. She might look young, but she spoke with too much experience couched in her words.

"What happened to him?" I found myself asking. "Did he give up?"

She shrugged. "I don't know. He moved away." Her gaze left mine and turned skyward once more. "When they move away, they leave my life because I can't follow them."

She mesmerized me—right from that first night. I sensed a portent in her casual appearance into my life, though a portent of what, I couldn't say.

"Did you ever want to?" I asked her.

"Want to what?"

"Follow them." I remember, even then, how the plurality bothered me. I was jealous and I didn't even know of what.

She shook her head. "No. All I ever have is what they leave behind."

Her voice seemed to diminish as she spoke. I wanted to reach out and touch her shoulder with my hand, to offer what comfort I could to ease the sudden malaise that appeared to have gripped her, but her moods, I came to learn, were mercurial. She sat up suddenly and stroked Ben until the motor of his purring filled the air with its resonance.

"Do you always write in places like this?" she asked.

I nodded. "I like the night; I like the city at night. It doesn't seem to belong to anyone then. On a good night, it almost seems as if the stories write themselves. It's almost as though coming out here plugs me directly into the dark heart of the city night and all of its secrets come spilling from my pen."

I stopped, suddenly embarrassed by what I'd said. It seemed too personal a disclosure for such short acquaintance. But she just gave me a low-watt version of her earlier smile.

"Doesn't that bother you?" she asked.

"Does what bother me?"

"That perhaps what you're putting down on paper doesn't belong to you."

"Does it ever?" I replied. "Isn't the very act of creation made up of setting a piece of yourself free?"

"What happens when there's no more pieces left?"

"That's what makes it special—I don't think you ever run out of the creative spark. Just doing it, replenishes the well. The more I work, the more ideas come to me. Whether they come from my subconscious or some outside source, isn't really relevant. What is relevant is what I put into it."

"Even when it seems to write itself?"

"Maybe especially so."

I was struck—not then, but later, remembering—by the odd intensity of the conversation. It wasn't a normal dialogue between strangers. We must have talked for three hours, never about ourselves, our histories, our pasts, but rather about what we were now, creating an intimacy that seemed surreal when I thought back on it the next day. Occasionally, there were lulls in the conversation, but they, too, seemed to add to the sense of bonding, like the comfortable silences that are only possible between good friends.

I could've kept right on talking, straight through the night until dawn, but she rose during one of those lulls.

"I have to go," she said, swinging the strap of her carryall onto her shoulder.

I knew a moment's panic. I didn't know her address or her phone number. All I had was her first name.

"When can I see you again?" I asked.

"Have you ever been down to those old stone steps under the Kelly Street Bridge?"

I nodded. They dated back from when the river was used to haul goods from upland, down to the lake. The steps under the bridge were all that was left of an old dock that had serviced the Irish-owned inn called The Harp. The dock was long abandoned, but The Harp still stood. It was one of the oldest buildings in the city. Only the solid stone structures of the city's Dutch founding fathers, like the ones that encircled us, were older.

"I'll meet you there tomorrow night," she said. She took a few steps, then paused, adding, "Why don't you bring along one of your books?"

The smile she gave me, before she turned away again, was intoxicating. I watched her walk back across the courtyard, disappearing into the narrow mouth of the alleyway from which she'd first come. Her footsteps lingered on, an echoing tap-tap on the cobblestones, but then that too faded.

I think it was at that moment that I decided she was a ghost.

I didn't get much writing done over the next few weeks. She wouldn't—she said she couldn't—see me during the day, but she wouldn't say why. I've got such a head filled with fictions that I honestly thought it was because she was a ghost, or maybe a succubus or a vampire. The sexual attraction was certainly there. If she'd sprouted fangs one night, I'd probably just have bared my neck and let her feed. But she didn't, of course. Given a multiple-choice quiz, in the end I realized the correct answer was none of the above.

I was also sure that she was at least my own age, if not older. She was widely read and, like myself, had eclectic tastes that ranged from genre fiction to the classics. We talked for hours every night, progressed to walking hand in hand through our favorite parts of the benighted city and finally made love one night in a large, cozy sleeping bag in Fitzhenry Park.

She took me there on one of what we called our rambles and didn't say a word, just stripped down in the moonlight and then drew me down into the sweet harbor of her arms. Above us, I heard geese heading south as, later, I drifted into sleep. I remember thinking it was odd to hear them so late at night, but then what wasn't in the hours I spent with Tally?

I woke alone in the morning, the subject of some curiosity by a couple of old winos who casually watched me get dressed inside the bag as though they saw this kind of thing every morning.

Our times together blur in my mind now. It's hard for me to remember one night from another. But I have little fetish bundles of memory that stay whole and complete in my mind, the *gris-gris* that collected around her name in my mind, like my nervousness that second night under the Kelly Street Bridge, worried that she wouldn't show, and three nights later when, after not saying a word about the book of my stories I'd given her when we parted on the old stone steps under the bridge, she told me how much she'd liked them.

"These are my stories," she said as she handed the book back to me that night.

I'd run into possessive readers before, fans who laid claim to my work as their own private domain, who treated the characters in the stories as real people, or thought that I carried all sorts of hidden and secret knowledge in my head, just because of the magic and mystery that appeared in the tales I told. But I'd never had a reaction like Tally's before.

"They're about me," she said. "They're your stories, I can taste your presence in every word, but each of them's a piece of me, too."

I told her she could keep the book and the next night, I brought her copies of my other three collections, plus photocopies of the stories that had only appeared in magazines to date. I won't say it's because she liked the stories so much, that I came to love her; that would have happened anyway. But her pleasure in them certainly didn't make me think any the less of her.

Another night she took a photograph out of her carryall and showed it to me. It was a picture of her, but she looked different, softer, not so much younger as not so tough. She wore her hair differently and had a flower print dress on; she was standing in sunlight.

"When . . . when was this taken?" I asked.

"In happier times."

Call me small-minded that my disappointment should show so plain, but it hurt that what were the happiest nights of my life, weren't the same for her.

She noticed my reaction—she was always quick with things like that—and laid a warm hand on mine.

"It's not you," she said. "I love our time together. It's the rest of my life that's not so happy."

Then be with me all the time, I wanted to tell her, but I already knew from experience that there was no talking about where she went when she left me, what she did, who she was. I was still thinking of ghosts, you see. I was afraid that some taboo lay upon her telling me, that if she spoke about it, if she told me where she was during the day, the spell would break and her spirit would be banished forever like in some hokey B-movie.

I wanted more than just the nights, I'll admit freely to that, but not enough to risk losing what I had. I was like the wife in "Blue-beard," except I refused to allow my curiosity to turn the key in the forbidden door. I could have followed her, but I didn't. And not just because I was afraid of her vanishing on me. It was because she trusted me not to.

We made love three times, all told, every time in that old sleeping bag of hers, each time in a different place, each morning I woke alone. I'd bring back her sleeping bag when we met that night and she'd smile to see its bulk rolled under my arm.

The morning after the first time, I realized that I was changing; that she was changing me. It wasn't by anything she said or did, or rather it wasn't that she was making me change, but that our relationship was stealing away that sense of distancing I had carried with me through my life.

And she was changing, too. She still wore her jeans and leather jacket most of the time, but sometimes she appeared wearing a short dress under the jacket, warm leggings, small trim shoes instead of her boots. Her face kept its character, but the tension wasn't so noticeable anymore, the toughness had softened.

I'd been open with her from the very first night, more open than I'd ever been with friends I'd known for years. And that remained. But now it was starting to spill over to my other relationships. I found my brother and my friends were more comfortable with me, and I with them. None of them knew about Tally; so far as they knew I was still prowling the nocturnal streets of the city in search of inspiration. They didn't know that I wasn't writing, though Professor Dapple guessed.

I suppose it was because he always read my manuscripts before I sent them off. We had the same interests in the odd and the curious—it was what had drawn us together long before Jilly became his student, before he retired from the university. Everybody still thought of him as the Professor; it was hard not to.

He was a tiny wizened man with a shock of frizzy white hair and glasses who delighted in long conversations conducted over tea, or if the hour was appropriate, a good Irish whisky. At least once every couple of weeks the two of us would sit in his cozy study, he reading one of my stories while I read his latest article before it was sent off to some journal or other. When the third visit went by in which I didn't have a manuscript in hand, he finally broached the subject.

"You seem happy these days, Christy."

"I am."

He'd smiled. "So is it true what they say—an artist must suffer to produce good work?"

I hadn't quite caught on yet to what he was about.

"Neither of us believe that," I said.

"Then you must be in love."

"I . . ."

I didn't know what to say. An awful sinking feeling had settled in my stomach at his words. Lord knew, he was right, but for some reason, just as I knew I shouldn't follow Tally when she left me after our midnight trysts, I had this superstitious dread that if the world discovered our secret, she would no longer be a part of my life.

"There's nothing wrong with being in love," he said, mistaking my hesitation for embarrassment.

"It's not that," I began, knowing I had nowhere to go except a lie and I couldn't lie to the Professor.

"Never fear," he said. "You're allowed your privacy—and welcome to it, I might add. At my age, any relating of your escapades would simply make me jealous. But I worry about your writing."

"I haven't stopped," I told him. And then I had it. "I've been thinking of writing a novel."

That wasn't a lie. I was always thinking of writing a novel; I just doubted that I ever would. My creative process could easily work within the perimeters of short fiction, even a connected series of stories such as *The Red Crow* had turned out to be, but a novel was too massive an undertaking for me to understand, little say attempt. I had to have the whole of it in my head and to do so with anything much longer than a short novella was far too daunting a process for me to begin. I had discovered, to my disappointment because I did actually *want* to make the attempt, that the longer a piece of mine was, the less . . . substance it came to have. It was as though the sheer volume of a novel's wordage would somehow dissipate the strengths my work had to date.

My friends who did write novels told me I was just being a chickenshit; but then they had trouble with short fiction and avoided it like the plague. It was my firm belief that one should stick with what worked, though maybe that was just a way of rationalizing a failure.

"What sort of a novel?" the Professor asked, intrigued since he knew my feelings on the subject.

I gave what I hoped was a casual shrug.

"That's what I'm still trying to decide," I said, and then turned the conversation to other concerns.

But I was nervous leaving the Professor's house, as though the little I had said was enough to turn the key in the door that led into the hidden room I shouldn't enter. I sensed a weakening of the dam that kept the mystery of our trysts deep and safe. I feared for the floodgate opening and the rush of reality that would tear my ghostly lover away from me.

But as I've already said, she wasn't a ghost. No, something far stranger hid behind her facade of pixie face and tousled hair.

I've wondered before, and still do, how much of what happens to us we bring upon ourselves. Did my odd superstition concerning Tally drive her away, or was she already leaving before I ever said as much as I did to the Professor? Or was it mere coincidence that she said goodbye that same night?

I think of the carryall she'd had on her shoulder the first time we met and have wondered since if she wasn't already on her way then. Perhaps I had only interrupted a journey already begun.

"You know, don't you?" she said when I saw her that night.

Did synchronicity reach so far that we would part that night in that same courtyard by the river where we had first met?

"You know I have to go," she added when I said nothing.

I nodded. I did. What I didn't know was—

"Why?" I asked.

Her features seemed harder again—like they had been that first night. The softness that had grown as our relationship had was more memory than fact, her features seemed to be cut to the bone once more. Only her eyes still held a touch of warmth, as did her smile. A tough veneer masked the rest of her.

"It's because of how the city is used," she said. "It's because of hatred and spite and bigotry; it's because of homelessness and drugs and crime; it's because the green quiet places are so few while the dark terrors multiply; it's because what's old and comfortable and rounded must make way for what's new and sharp and brittle; it's because a mean spirit grips its streets and that meanness cuts inside me like a knife.

"It's changing me, Christy, and I don't want you to see what I will become. You wouldn't recognize me and I wouldn't want you to.

"That's why I have to go."

When she said go, I knew she meant she was leaving me, not the city.

"But—"

"You've helped me keep it all at bay, truly you have, but it's not enough. Neither of us have enough strength to hold that mean spirit at bay forever. What we have was stolen from the darkness. But it won't let us steal any more."

I started to speak, but she just laid her fingers across my lips. I saw that her sleeping bag was stuffed under the bench. She pulled it out and unrolled it on the cobblestones. I thought of the dark windows of the town houses looking into the courtyard. There could be a hundred gazes watching as she gently pulled me down onto the sleeping bag, but I didn't care.

I tried to stay awake. I lay beside her, propped up on an elbow and stroked her shoulder, her hair. I marveled at the softness of her skin, the silkiness of her hair. In repose, the harsh lines were gone from her face again. I wished that there was some way I could just keep all her unhappiness at bay, that I could stay awake and protect her forever, but sleep snuck up on me all the same and took me away.

Just as I went under, I thought I heard her say, "You'll know other lovers."

But not like her. Never like her.

When I woke the next morning, I was alone on the sleeping bag, except for Ben who lay purring on the bag where she had lain.

It was early, too early for anyone to be awake in any of the houses, but I wouldn't have cared. I stood naked in the frosty air and slowly got dressed. Ben protested when I shooed him off the sleeping bag and rolled it up.

The walk home, with the sleeping bag rolled up under my arm, was never so long.

No, Tally wasn't a ghost, though she haunts the city's streets at night—just as she haunts my mind.

I know her now. She's like a rose bush grown old, gone wild; untrimmed, neglected for years, the thorns become sharper, more bitter; her foliage spreading, grown out of control, reaching high and wide, while the center chokes and dies. The blossoms that remain are just small now, hidden in the wild growth, memories of what they once were.

I know her now. She's the spirit that connects the notes of a tune—the silences in between the sounds; the resonance that lies under the lines I put down on a page. Not a ghost, but a spirit all the same: the city's heart and soul.

I don't wonder about her origin. I don't wonder whether she was here first, and the city grew around her, or if the city created her. She just is.

Tallulah. Tally. A reckoning of accounts.

I think of the old traveling hawkers who called at private houses in the old days and sold their wares on the tally system—part payment on account, the other part due when they called again. Tallymen.

The payments owed her were long overdue, but we no longer have the necessary coin to settle our accounts with her. So she changes; just as we change. I can remember a time when the city was a safer place, how when I was young, we never locked our doors and we knew every neighbor on our block. Kids growing up today wouldn't even know what I'm talking about; the people my own age have forgotten. The old folks remember, but who listens to them? Most of us wish that they didn't exist; that they'd just take care of themselves so that we can get on with our own lives.

Not all change is for the good.

I still go out on my rambles, most every night. I hope for a secret tryst, but all I do is write stories again. As the new work fills my notebooks, I've come to realize that the characters in my stories were so real because I really did want to get close to people, I really did want to know them. It was just easier to do it on paper, one step removed.

I'm trying to change that now.

I look for her on my rambles. She's all around me, of course, in every brick of every building, in every whisper of wind as it scurries down an empty street. She's a cab's lights at 3:00 A.M., a siren near dawn, a shuffling bag lady pushing a squeaky grocery cart, a dark-eyed cat sitting on a shadowed stoop.

She's all around me, but I can't find her. I'm sure I'd recognize her—

I don't want you to see what I will become.

—but I can't be sure. The city can be so many things. It's a place where the familiar can become strange with just the blink of an eye. And if I saw her—

You wouldn't recognize me and I wouldn't want you to.

—what would I do? If she could, she'd come to me, but that mean spirit still grips the streets. I see it in people's faces; I feel it in the coldness that's settled in their hearts. I don't think I would recognize her; I don't think I'd want to. I have the *gris-gris* of her memory in my mind; I have an old sleeping bag rolled up in a corner of my hall closet; I'm here if she needs me.

I have this fantasy that it's still not too late; that we can still drive that mean spirit away and keep it at bay. The city would be a better place to live in if we could and I think we owe it to her. I'm doing my part. I write about her—

They're about me. They're your stories, I can taste your presence in every word, but each of them's a piece of me, too.

—about her strange wonder and her magic and all. I write about how she changed me, how she taught me that getting close can hurt, but not getting close is an even lonelier hurt. I don't preach; I just tell the stories.

But I wish the ache would go away. Not the memories, not the *gris-gris* that keeps her real inside me, but the hurt. I could live without that hurt.

Sometimes I wish I'd never met her.

Maybe one day I'll believe that lie, but I hope not.